MW0435756

Reviews for Blizzard!! The Great White Hurricane

This account of the Blizzard of '88 was truly one of the most captivating, must-read accounts of a truly historic weather event I have ever read. Your mix of what was happening weatherwise and a very believable account of how the people reacted to a lone voice warning of a major life-threatening event reminded me of what happened in the Galveston Hurricane of 1900 and the hurricane of '38. Your description of how your meteorological savant, William Augustus Roebling, saw the pieces coming together and like the farmers and sailors of old, observed the big picture weather and locally the sky and wind to see signs of threats was something I can relate to in my youth in NYC. In the days before the models and the internet, I too attached the high-level cirrus clouds and the direction of the surface wind as indications in winter whether a snowstorm would occur near the coast. I remember the great blizzards of the 1960s and 1970s and did my Master's thesis on Explosive Development in East Coast storms, of which the Blizzard of '88 was clearly one. This is a remarkable read and I highly recommend it for weather and history buffs.

Joe D'Aleo, CCM
Chief Forecaster, WeatherBELL Analytics

Absolutely LOVE the book. Adds a new layer and more of an emotional component to all the weather data I've studied about this event. Would add this as a must-read companion to weather history.

Steven DiMartino
Owner/Partner/Meteorologist
Weather Concierge
NY NJ PA Weather

ISBN: 978-1-54398-748-5 (print)
ISBN: 978-1-54398-749-2 (ebook)

BLIZZARD!!

The Great White Hurricane

Timothy R. Minnich

With Siri I. Shaw

TIMOTHY R. MINNICH

BLIZZARD!!
THE GREAT WHITE HURRICANE

Tim Minnich is a meteorologist and atmospheric scientist. As far back as he can remember, which is somewhere between the ages of two and three, the weather always held a great fascination for him. Born in Mt. Vernon, New York, he and his sweetheart Siri (who also happens to be his wife) currently reside in New Jersey, where he runs a successful air quality consulting firm. *Blizzard!! The Great White Hurricane* is his first novel.

FACTS, FICTION,
AND ACKNOWLEDGMENTS

From Monday, March 11, through Wednesday, March 13, 1888, a savage blizzard pummeled the northeastern United States, the likes of which New York City and the surrounding region had never before experienced – and has yet to again, in all the years since. Were the Great Blizzard of '88 to occur today, it would certainly cause far less suffering and fewer deaths, despite the population of the New York metropolitan area having nearly quadrupled over this time. The primary reason for this, of course, would be the early warning forecasting tools now available in the form of satellites and computer models.

No advance notice of the impending storm was given, as the government's weather forecasting agency, headquartered in the nation's capital, Washington City, located in the newly formed District of Columbia, had no way of knowing what was about to transpire. The United States Signal Service, predecessor of the current National Weather Service, had access only to the most primitive technology compared to today's modern standards. While the Signal Service was able to track storms as they moved across the country, generally from west to east, it was incapable of predicting their formation. As a result, virtually everyone in the Blizzard's path was caught completely off-guard.

Like so many other meteorologists and weather hobbyists, for as long as I can remember I've had a recurring fantasy that before I die, I would one day have the opportunity to experience a snowstorm with the awesome, majestic furor of that unbridled beast. To this day, it remains the Northeast winter storm against which all others are measured.

So when the calling first came in the summer of 2012 to write a novel about the Blizzard of '88 (coined, some years hence, "the Great White Hurricane"), the idea was too delicious to ignore. I knew in an instant its central character would be a meteorological "superhero" of sorts with forecasting skills decades ahead of his time, giving him special and disturbing insight in the days leading up to this "super-storm." I also knew that the story would remain factually true (to the maximum degree possible) as far as all of the events surrounding the Blizzard. This required an accurate time line based on fastidious attention to the historical details described in myriad references. Finally, I was intent on creating an exciting storyline, one which would be woven like a seamless tapestry into an otherwise authentic land-scape of this historic event. As a result, the reader could gain knowl-edge of both the Great Blizzard of '88 and life in New York City in the late Nineteenth Century – in addition to, hopefully, being entertained and engaged. As a bonus, anyone with an avocational interest in mete-orology will find plenty of passages to augment their understanding of the field.

At this point, I think it appropriate to acknowledge that while every attempt has been made to ensure the historical integrity of this account, the responsibility for any inaccuracies is mine alone.

In the vein of factual accuracy, considerable effort was expended to research and employ language conforming to common usage in the late 1880's. This includes late-Nineteenth Century slang and idiomatic expressions in dialogue, as well as punctuation such as conventions governing hyphenation and spelling. The purpose, of course, is not to distract the reader, but rather to help create, as authentically as possible, the setting of the period.

While the majority of characters in the body of the novel are fictitious, some are historical. These historical characters, and many relevant others, are introduced here and in the Prologue, where the only fictitious characters are our protagonist Will Roebling and his parents. All of the men credited with the amazing advances in weather forecasting of the last century and a half are real and their accounts accurate (with only a modicum of poetic license).

The name of our meteorological savant, William Augustus Roebling, might have a familiar ring to it. It was created as a tribute to the famous German-born civil engineer John Augustus Roebling, who designed and oversaw the initial construction of the great Brooklyn Bridge – long an object of supreme fascination for young Will, as you shall see.

I am deeply indebted to four dedicated authors who, in their painstaking efforts to compile accurate accounts of this legendary storm, spent countless hours reviewing and consolidating thousands of first-hand accounts reported in hundreds of east-coast newspapers, magazines, historical societies, and library records from Connecticut to Virginia. I refer to these individuals as the "pre-internet trailblazers;" the fruits of their arduous labor have made my endeavor incalculably easier.

They are: Mary Cable, "The Blizzard of '88" (1988); Judd Caplovich, "Blizzard! The Great Storm of '88" (1988); Jim Murphy, "Blizzard!" (2000); and Tracee de Hahn, "The Blizzard of 1888" (2001). I recommend all of them highly.

As for the actual (synoptic) meteorology spanning the days immediately preceding and during the storm, I borrowed liberally from the classic analysis published in 1983 in the American Meteorological Society's bulletin, "An Analysis of the Blizzard of '88," by Paul J. Kocin. The Kocin analysis contains an Appendix providing excerpts from the log of the New York pilot boat, the Charles H. Marshall, from which I also borrowed extensively.

Another fine source of information upon which I drew heavily, accessible from the greatest lazy man's research tool, is a history of the National Weather Service, including fascinating accounts from key individuals during this era.

To construct a credible narrative of Mr. Roebling's experience in the Signal Service, I synthesized the personal views of many of the Agency's early pioneers such as Professor Cleveland Abbe, Henry J. Cox, John P. Finley, H.C. Frankenfield, Glynn Gardner, John S. Hazen, and Wilford M. Wilson, to name a few. Special thanks to Mr. Wilson, who described in great detail the laborious procedure he developed for compiling monthly meteorological records for Professor Abbe. As this was the perfect project with which to begin the stellar career of our young Superhero, I therefore (shamelessly) stole it.

A wealth of information on General Albert Myer, General William Hazen, and Major General Adolphus Greely – each of whom served as Chief Signal Officer during the Signal Service's early years – was provided by Wikipedia and its references. The same is true for Professor Elias Loomis, Will's mentor at Yale University (then Yale College). Information on the extraordinary history of Sergeant Francis Long, Will Roebling's boss in the New York Field Office, can be found online with a minimum of effort.

Of course, it was necessary to take a certain degree of license in order to flesh out Will's relationships with his historical cohorts – most notably Professor Abbe, Glynn Gardner, Professor Loomis, and Sergeant Long.

My apologies to Chief Elias B. Dunn, Sergeant Long's boss in the New York Office. The storyline evolved more organically without him, so he ended up "on the cutting room floor."

A most useful internet source for this novel was the New York Transit Museum website, which chronicles public transportation in New York City. Informative histories of the New York City subways, especially the elevated trains (els), can easily be found online, as well.

Much of the information presented on the great American scientist Joseph Henry was derived from "Joseph Henry and the National Academy of Sciences," Proceedings of the National Academy of Sciences, Volume 58, Number 1, July 15, 1967 – a speech by Leonard Carmichael presented at the Academy's annual dinner. It's content was based largely on published books.

The fictitious character of Will Roebling's love-interest, Kira Smith, is an aspiring dancer and actress. Musicals 101.com, the Cyber Encyclopedia of Musical Theatre, Film & Television, is a wonderful site which describes in great detail the Broadway theatre scene of the time.

Albert Washington and all the other employees of the Grand Hotel are fictitious, as are Wilma Duncan, Blanche and Charley Potts, Frank and Alex Gorman, Pat McCormack, Jon and Mabel O'Malley, and Nancy Petersen. May Morrow, however, a remarkable young woman decades ahead of her time, was an actual employee of Mr. Garrigues when the Great Blizzard struck (although considerable license has been taken with the rest of her history).

I am deeply grateful to Joyce Snyder for her invaluable suggestions and corrections to the manuscript.

Last, but certainly not least, words are inadequate to express the debt of gratitude I owe to Siri Shaw (who doubles as my sweetheart and wife) for the many hundreds of hours she generously, and laboriously, spent in rewriting, editing, and adding to the text, as well as for our continual back-and-forth interaction – all of which has added considerable life to the characters and events. She transformed each sentence and paragraph from my originally crude composition into the eminently readable rendering which I hope you'll agree this finished product is. It is for these reasons that her name appears on the cover.

As for my first novel, if you derive half as much pleasure in its reading as I did in its writing, that will be my metric for its success.

Tim Minnich
October 2019

PROLOGUE

PROLOGUE

The Early Years

WILLIAM AUGUSTUS ROEBLING WAS BORN APRIL 9, 1864 ON A farm in Wisconsin, to hard-working German immigrant parents. A tumultuous time in the life of this great country, Will's birth was one year to the day before General Robert E. Lee surrendered to Lieutenant General Ulysses S. Grant at Appomattox Court House, Virginia, ending the American Civil War.

From a very early age, Will, an only child, demonstrated a keen intellect and an unusual degree of inquisitiveness. Probably his most notable characteristic though was the special connection he had with nature, weather in particular, which his parents would have best described as verging on the supernatural – on the order of a sixth sense. He had an uncanny ability to know when it was going to rain, even if there were no clouds in evidence. He could also sense from the behaviour of the farm animals – the chickens, cows, and especially the horses – when dramatic changes in the weather were coming.

Once, one early autumn day when he was about six or seven, Will looked up at the sky and, marveling at the streams of southward-migrating birds, proclaimed, matter-of-factly, that it was going to be an unusually early and harsh winter. By that point his parents no longer had any doubts about his prognosticative gift, and were simply grateful for the ample time they now had to lay in a double supply of wood, hay, and other provisions.

As he progressed through grade-school, Will's generalized interest in nature gradually became more and more focused on the weather. Interestingly enough, he also developed a particular fascination with bridges, especially those of the suspension-type, reading as many books as he could on the subject. By the age of ten, he could recite an enormous volume of facts concerning all the suspension bridges in the world.

Will gained quite a reputation for his scientific acumen among his fellow school-mates when, in the fourth grade, his imaginative and brilliant demonstration of how lightning occurs won first prize in a prestigious science fair – quite a feat, as the fair was intended primarily for high-school students. His project was based largely on the work of Joseph Henry, America's most widely recognized scientist of the time, and Will's personal hero.

Will spent countless hours reading about Joseph Henry and his extraordinary accomplishments. Unfortunately, Will was just fourteen when Henry died, so he never got the opportunity to meet his childhood idol. But in his wildest dreams, the budding young scientist could never have imagined how profoundly his later life and career would be impacted by the many scientific advancements and inventions of the prolific Joseph Henry.

Even before he had completed his primary schooling, there was never a question that Will would be college-bound to further his education, despite his family's modest circumstances. He only hoped his professors there would prove themselves more challenging than his Wisconsin teachers. Intellectually, he had surpassed the majority of them somewhere around the sixth grade. Receiving a full academic scholarship, not common in those days, Will enrolled at Yale College in the fall of 1882.

Much to his surprise and chagrin, Will initially found himself struggling in his new academic environment. In fact, during his first few weeks, he was overwhelmed, as it seemed his professors introduced concept upon concept with which he wasn't even remotely familiar. Recalling his concern that they might not have more to offer than his teachers in Wisconsin, Will had a good laugh at himself, acknowledging he'd certainly been "brought down a peg or two."

He had to admit having some resentment about having led such a sheltered life. Growing up on a farm, it was obvious to him that he had missed out on the learning opportunities which had been afforded his class-mates, most of whom came from large cities. For all of his smarts, at this point in his life Will lacked the maturity to understand that without his unique childhood experiences, he could never have cultivated his extraordinary connection with nature – a connection which, over the next few years, would serve him remarkably well.

Fortunately, after this early period of adjustment, Will settled in rather nicely as the semester wore on. With a mind like a sponge, he absorbed, processed, and quickly excelled in all of his course-work, especially engineering, mechanics, mathematics, and, of course, meteorology.

He also made time to run for the track team. During the long practice sessions he could mentally compose his assignments without distraction and, in the evening, put them down on paper with as much accuracy and detail as if he had conceived them only minutes earlier. He was able to do this because of a nearly eidetic memory, another of his talents which would prove to serve him well, although he was reluctant to call attention to it among his peers. Even in grade-school, Will had seen how the other students struggled with studies which had always come easily to him. He'd learned early on that he would be more readily accepted by his class-mates if he pretended he had to work hard, even though most of the time it was all he could do to conceal his boredom. After his initial floundering, things were no different at Yale, so Will wisely chose to downplay his exceptional talent there as well.

Will earned his engineering degree in only three years. Had a baccalaureate in meteorology been available, he would have jumped at the chance, but that opportunity would be several years in the offing. Even as late as his final semester, he remained unsure about what he wanted to do after graduation. More than one of his professors had encouraged him to stay on at Yale and teach. Basically, they had said the road to professorship would be a smooth one for him and that he'd easily be able to attract funding for any number of research areas he might wish to pursue.

Will had little interest in teaching. Of one thing he was sure: his career would be in the field of meteorology, either in applied research or, more likely, in his prevailing interest since childhood – forecasting the weather.

Joint Congressional Resolution of 1870

The United States Department of War's Army Signal Service Corps was created in 1860. Its mission was to "provide an independent, trained professional military signal service for employment of aerial telegraphy as a means of visual communication."

In 1870, a Joint Congressional Resolution was established to add meteorological observations to the Signal Service's province. Under this Resolution, the Secretary of War was required to "provide for taking meteorological observations at the military stations in the interior of the continent and at other points in the States and Territories . . . and for giving notice on the northern (Great) lakes and on the seacoast by magnetic telegraph and marine signals, of the approach and force of storms."

The Joint Resolution, which served to create this fledgling predecessor of the agency later known as the National Weather Service, was introduced in early February by General Halbert E. Paine, Congressman from Milwaukee, and within seven days was signed into law by the newly elected commander-in-chief, President Ulysses S. Grant. A strong supporter of the Resolution was Brevet Brigadier

General Albert James Myer, a former Army doctor who happened to be Chief of the Signal Service since its inception.

It was General Myer himself who coined the formal name of this new meteorological group: *the U.S. Army Signal Service's Division of Telegrams and Reports for the Benefit of Congress*. General Myer would remain in charge of the Signal Service till his death on August 24, 1880, at which time President Rutherford Birchard Hayes appointed General William Babcock Hazen Chief Signal Officer of the U.S. Army – a post he too held till his death.

Integral to the fulfillment of all the Signal Service's responsibilities (meteorological and otherwise) was the electric telegraph, development of which went back more than three decades. In 1835, Samuel Morse, then Professor of Arts and Design at New York University, had used pulses of current to deflect an electromagnet which, in turn, moved a marker to produce written codes on a strip of paper – the invention of the Morse code. One year later, the device was modified to emboss the paper with dots and dashes, and in 1843 Congress funded Morse the princely sum of thirty-thousand dollars to construct an experimental telegraph line from Washington to Baltimore, a distance of forty miles. The electric telegraph became operational in 1845, and the idea of an early warning system to notify the affected public of advancing storms, simply by telegraphing ahead, would soon be accepted as an eventual reality.

The telegraph was the sole means of rapid long-distance communication during this era, as it would be thirty years before Alexander Graham Bell's famous conversation with his assistant Thomas Watson would demonstrate the efficacy of the telephone, and at least ten more after that before full commercialization of the device would begin. Dispatching trains by telegraph started in 1851, the same year that Western Union began business operations. Western Union built its first transcontinental telegraph line in 1861, mainly along railroad rights-of-way. By the time the Signal Service was established, a trained Morse operator could transmit forty- to fifty-words-per-minute.

Professor Henry and the Smithsonian

Joseph Henry, a great pioneer of American science selflessly dedicated to its advancement and research, played an integral role in both the development of the telegraph and the genesis of the Joint Congressional Resolution of 1870.

Born in 1797 in Albany, New York, Joseph Henry was the first-generation American son of parents who'd emigrated from Scotland in the turbulent year 1775. Henry was to enroll in the Albany Academy which, at the time, provided the equivalent of a college education. Initially too poor to pay the tuition, he was unable to matriculate till the rather late age of twenty-one, despite having been accepted for admission several years earlier. Even before graduating from the Academy, Henry was working there as both a chemical assistant and a lecture preparer. When a position opened up in 1826, Will Roebling's childhood idol became the school's Professor of Mathematics and Natural Philosophy. It was then that he began his scientific research on electromagnetism and his developmental work on the telegraph.

By this time, Joseph Henry had already made some important scientific contributions, including the invention of a powerful electromagnet and the first electromagnetic machine – a device in which electricity produced mechanical movement. He also developed an electromagnetic telegraph, where signals were transmitted by exciting an electromagnet located a considerable distance from the battery. This device allowed bells to be struck and, thus, became the basis for the invention of the doorbell.

Others had developed many practical offshoots of Henry's discoveries in the field of electromagnetism. Undoubtedly, many of these applications would not have been brought to market till many years later were it not for Henry's altruistic determination to never patent a single one of his inventions or profit financially, in any way, from his widely applied scientific achievements. By 1832, Joseph Henry's work drew the attention of Princeton University, then known as the College of New Jersey. In that year, Henry accepted an appointment as Princeton's Professor of Natural Philosophy where he would continue his work on electromagnetism and electricity, as well as on phenomena such as phosphorescence, sunspots, lightning, and the aurora. America's most famous scientist was best known for his work on the electromagnetic relay, the basis of Morse's electric telegraph. In 1837, Henry's tour of the European scientific centers expanded his reputation to an international arena.

By all accounts, Professor Henry found happiness and fulfillment in his lucrative position at Princeton; he might well have spent the rest of his career there were it not for the creation of the Smithsonian Institution in 1846. An "establishment for the increase and diffusion of knowledge," the Smithsonian, founded on English scientist James Smithson's five-hundred-and-fifty-thousand-dollar bequest – a large fortune at the time – was in need of a Secretary, i.e., a Chief Executive Officer.

Henry's achievements and reputation as both an educator and a scientist made him an excellent candidate for this position and, on December 3, 1846, after receiving seven out of twelve votes from the Board of Regents, he took the reins as the Smithsonian Institution's first Secretary. Of necessity, Henry had to transition quickly from the role of scientific investigator to one of research administrator and promoter of young scientists. He established laboratories and secured the nucleus of a well-balanced staff in physics, chemistry, and related sciences – all of which would serve the Institute admirably for many years to come.

One of Henry's closest friends was the Great Emancipator himself, Abraham Lincoln. A trusted science advisor to the beleaguered

President during the Civil War, as well as an enthusiastic supporter of his politics, Joseph Henry did all he could to assist northern military development and operations. He visited the Union Army in the field, more than once driving his own buggy to the combat zone. Lincoln reciprocated and valued his friendship, often walking to the Smithsonian for long conversations on a variety of topics with "The Professor," as Lincoln fondly referred to him. Henry's knowledge and influence made possible the use of manned hydrogen balloons by the Union Army, for battlefield reconnaissance. At his suggestion, the balloon operators were in constant contact with the ground via an electric telegraph wire. Thus it can be said that Joseph Henry inaugurated air-to-ground communication.

Like his adoring acolyte Will Roebling, Joseph Henry always had a keen interest in meteorology. In 1845, well before the advent of the electric telegraph, Henry visualized a communications system for advance storm warnings and the tremendous benefit people would realize by having this information early enough to make appropriate preparations. So it was no surprise that, as Secretary of the newly established Smithsonian, one of the first things Joseph Henry did was propose creation of "a system of observation which shall extend as far as possible over the North American continent... The Citizens of the United States are now scattered over every part of the southern and western portions of North America, and the extended lines of the telegraph will furnish a ready means of warning the more northern and eastern observers to be on the watch from the first appearance of an advancing storm." His fascination with meteorology had taught him that weather systems generally tended to move across the country in an easterly, or northeasterly, direction.

The Professor had grown accustomed to having his visions realized. Within three short years, he had amassed a network of one-hundred-and-fifty volunteers regularly reporting weather observations to the Smithsonian. By 1860, some five-hundred of Henry's stations were furnishing daily telegraphic weather observations to the Evening Star, Washington's newspaper of record since its founding in 1852. He designed the first system of graphically depicting the nation's weather on a large map which he posted each morning in the Smithsonian entry-way.

Henry's volunteer system would continue for ten more years, essentially unchanged. Over that time it became apparent that a more formal and systematic approach to observing the weather would be necessary if the leap were to be made from simply reporting the existing weather to providing useful, accurate weather "forecasts." Henry knew that this transformation would require the structure and organization of a government agency, with paid employees coordinating meteorological observations across the country.

And so, Joseph Henry single-handedly established the infrastructure of the newly chartered meteorological division of the Signal Service. Under the disciplined, precise leadership of Brevet Brigadier General Albert James Myer, the number of field offices collecting systemized and synchronous reports from trained observers grew rapidly – from a mere twenty-four in 1870 to two-hundred-and-eighty-four by 1878.

Fort Myer and the School of Instruction

General Hazen, the Chief Signal Officer in 1885, was a long-time friend of Professor Elias Loomis, young Mr. Roebling's mentor for his meteorology studies. Loomis had achieved a level of fame in his own right, authoring the first-ever treatise on tornadoes. One day, after a long meeting with Roebling to discuss his plans for life after Yale, Loomis wrote a letter to Hazen saying that he had a most remarkable and gifted student nearing graduation who, if hired by the Signal Service, would surely prove to be a huge asset to the nation's elite forecasting team.

The very next afternoon, after receiving a circular which had been distributed to all colleges, Loomis was convinced: this was, most certainly, nothing short of divine Providence. That missive, sent out by General Hazen himself, set forth the many benefits that the U.S. Signal Service could offer to qualified students who would enlist – not least of which was the starting salary of a whopping seventy-six-dollars-per-month.

As it turned out, some forty aspiring young men hailing from a variety of colleges around the country were eventually accepted into the Signal Service as a result of that circular. But with that eerily timely, glowing endorsement from his renowned professor, a compelling application essay, and stellar grades (a 3.88 grade-point average out of a possible 4.0), William Roebling was far and away the highest-ranked collegiate applicant recruited that year. So it was that Will began his career with the U.S. Army Signal Service in July 1885.

Will's induction came five years before the Signal Service made its transition from a military to a civilian agency. On October 1, 1890, Congress would grant President Benjamin Harrison's request to transfer the meteorological responsibilities of the Signal Service to the newly created Weather Bureau within the U.S. Department of Agriculture. There they would remain till 1940, when they would again be transferred, this time to the newly established Environmental Science Services Administration (ESSA) within the U.S. Department of Commerce. In 1970, the nation's meteorological responsibilities would be transferred one last time when ESSA would become the National Oceanic and Atmospheric Administration (NOAA), and the Weather Bureau the National Weather Service.

Like all enlistees, Will was assigned to the Signal Service School of Instruction at Fort Myer, Virginia, where he immediately began a rigorous training program designed to help master the skills and discipline which would be demanded of him by the U.S. Army. At the Fort, there were two classes, or sections: the Meteorological Section, of which Will was a member, and the more popular and established Military

Signal Corps Section. Named after the first Chief Signal Officer, Fort Myer was situated high atop the banks of the Potomac River, just three miles from the Signal Service Headquarters in Washington City. While the rigid routine certainly took some getting used to by all of the men, it was especially challenging for the collegiate recruits who had, by and large, been living a far less strenuous existence than their less-fortunate cohorts. Days were long, beginning with reveille at five-thirty a.m. and ending with taps at nine-thirty at night.

There was much to learn every day and little tolerance for incompetence or under-achievement. In the words of H.C. Frankenfield, who'd graduated from the School of Instruction three years before Will Roebling, "It was not eight hours of work, eight hours for play, and eight hours for sleep . . ." Instead it was "eight hours of work, six more hours of work, two hours for recreation, and eight hours for sleep, the latter not guaranteed."

John P. Finley, a Fort Myer graduate who preceded Frankenfield by five years, was a meticulous researcher and prolific writer, destined to become well-known for the many contributions he made to the field of severe-weather forecasting. Finley went into more detail about life at the School of Instruction: "Military signaling at Fort Myer embraced both day and night work at the School, and at distances varying from one to forty miles or more. The drill in telegraph line building and cable work was carried on at the School. Lines of a mile or more had to be constructed with lance poles and suspending insulators, a message or more put through, after which the entire construction was dismantled, wire reeled up, poles lowered, and the whole equipment placed on the accompanying trucks, horse drawn, and returned to the storehouses at the School. The men were marched back to quarters and barracks."

In the fifteen years prior to Will's November 1885 graduation from the School, more than three-hundred men had completed their training and embarked on careers with the Signal Service, ranging from installation and repair of cables, to telegraph signaling, to weather observation and forecasting.

With the territory to be covered by the Signal Service continuing to expand to the west and south into rural, unexplored regions, assignments often took these men to places where they would encounter significant danger. Even so, with the relative scarcity of jobs during this period, they generally followed orders with little complaint. The omnipresent threat of rattlesnakes and Indian attacks, the great Chicago fire of 1871, the suppression of the labor riots in 1873, and the yellow fever epidemics in the Southeast during the late 1870's all served as proof that the country was not an altogether safe place for these young men.

Training for the Signal Service had always been conducted at Fort Myer, although it had been known as Fort Whipple up till General Myer's death in 1880. During the Meteorology Section's first decade, most training was practically oriented and not too dissimilar from the training afforded the Military Signal Corps Section personnel. However, in 1881, a sophisticated theoretical course of meteorological instruction was initiated when four Signal Service lieutenants introduced Deschanel's Physics. That began a period during which the curriculum was rapidly upgraded. By the time Will arrived, it already included an extensive array of lectures and instructions, supplemented by monthly examinations, on subjects such as instrument theory, chartography, general meteorology, and thermodynamics of the atmosphere. Of course, Will excelled in every aspect of his training.

All of these new courses were taught by the famous Professor Cleveland Abbe. A graduate of the New York Free Academy, later known as the City College of New York, Abbe was an older brother of Robert Abbe, famous in his own right as a physician and pioneer in the introduction of radiation therapy for the treatment of cancer. Cleveland Abbe was a civilian meteorologist, widely considered the nation's leading expert on forecasting when he joined the Signal Service in 1871 as Special Assistant to General Myer. Courses taught by other notables of the time included theoretical meteorology, practical meteorology and weather predictions, topographic surveying and drawing, and electricity. Certainly, none could deny that the Signal Service was in its heyday.

Once again, circumstances proved fortuitous for young Mr. Roebling. In early 1886, only months after Will's graduation from the School of Instruction, the Meteorology Section was closed after Congress failed to appropriate the funds necessary for its maintenance. The instructors were assigned to various Field Offices around the country.

Headquarters, Professor Abbe, and Will's Research

It was one week before Thanksgiving 1885, when Will received word he had been assigned to the Chief Office in Washington City for a one-year detail under the direct supervision of Professor Abbe, still lead-forecaster for the Signal Service, now headed-up by General Hazen. Will was thrilled! Everyone knew these details were rare, reserved for the top echelon of students, and that only the luckiest ones sometimes received offers to stay on with Headquarters. Will immediately rented himself a one-bedroom apartment, two short blocks away.

While at the School, Will had taken it upon himself to learn as much as he could about Abbe's view of science, and found that it resonated deeply with him. In fact, he subconsciously began the process of slowly and methodically refining his own views of the scientific world so they might be more consistent with Abbe's. On his fourth day at 1719 G Street N.W., he heard Professor Abbe tell his staff, "True science is never speculative; it employs hypotheses as suggesting points for inquiry, but it never adopts the hypotheses as though they were demonstrated propositions. There should be no mystery in our use of the word science; it means knowledge, not theory nor speculation; nor hypothesis, but hard facts, and the framework of laws to which they belong; the observed phenomena of meteorology and the well-established laws of physics are the two extremes of the science of meteorology between which we trace the connection of cause and effect; insofar as we can do this successfully, meteorology becomes an exact deductive science."

That was the moment Will declared, if only to himself, that he would one day become the country's greatest forecaster.

Abbe's responsibilities as lead-forecaster for the nation continued to grow with the expansion of the network of Field Offices. It would not be till 1888 that responsibility for the nation's weather forecasts would be delegated to select Regional Offices. In the meantime, in addition to his forecasting obligations, Abbe managed several research initiatives as well as a number of special projects, the most important of which was the compilation of monthly meteorology records from all the reporting stations in the world. This records compilation, known as the scientific journal "Monthly Weather Review," was founded by Abbe in July 1872 and has been published – uninterrupted – ever since.

Professor Cleveland Abbe knew that only a special type of individual, one with certain particularly developed skills, could be trusted to assist him in his vital records-compilation project. That person needed to be: highly motivated; a fast worker, yet meticulous in attention to detail; patient enough to withstand the tedium of the required tasks; and intelligent enough to reasonably interpolate missing or illegible data. Months before Will Roebling graduated from the Fort, the consensus among his superior officers was that he would be the ideal man for the job. Abbe could not have been more pleased.

The process Will followed to compile the meteorological records began initially with his being given twelve catalogues or "books," each one uniquely identified: January 1883, February 1883, and so on, through December 1883 (December 1882 having been the most recently completed book). Each book, fastened at the top, had a single page for each day; the day of the month was listed in the upper right-hand corner. Each page had nine columns and more than a hundred rows and measured nearly thirty inches from top to bottom. The columns were headed, from left to right: Station, Latitude, Longitude, Time of Observation, Barometer, Temperature, Wind Direction, Force of Wind (essentially wind speed), and State of Weather. Pre-filled in the column headed "Station" on every page were the names of the reporting stations in alphabetical order; all other columns were blank. Even though most stations reported these data three-times-per-day, for convention's sake only the morning data were compiled for each catalogue.

Will began with the Alpena, Michigan station, entering all the data from January 1883 in the first row, one-day-per-page. He then entered the data from the second station, Amarillo, Texas in the second row on all thirty-one pages, and so on, till he had entered the entire month's data for all of the nearly two-hundred reporting stations, thus completing the book for January 1883. He was able to complete the first twelve books in about three-and-a-half months. By November 1886, much to Abbe's delight, Will had brought the records-compilation project completely up-to-date.

During his assignment at Headquarters, Will barely had time for anything beyond this project, often working many overtime hours, including the occasional Sunday. There was a reason for this insane work ethic, excessive even for him. He had devised a system which allowed him to identify and examine in detail a wealth of information on fourteen significant full-latitude extratropical (i.e., non-tropical) storms which had impacted the east coast, particularly the Northeast, during the nearly four-year period covered by the books. Each evening, when he got home, he would record the data, largely from memory. He knew that analyzing this information would be important in improving his forecasting skills. Knowing that storms generally moved across the country from west to east, or southwest to northeast, he was able to correlate the occurrence of significant

Northeast storms – and this was key – with certain conditions at the more westerly stations, two or three days prior. Till now, common knowledge had not moved beyond a simple understanding of the movement of weather systems. Access to the gold-mine of data his project provided, coupled with his fierce determination, superior intellect, and youthful confidence, set Will firmly on the path to a remarkable future, one in which he would vastly improve upon the ability to predict east-coast storms. Even had he not been being paid to do so, he would gladly have worked on this project for Abbe.

On Sunday, his one day off each week, Will pored over these data and plotted his own surface depictions, more informative than even the official Signal Service maps based on the prototype developed by Joseph Henry. He used his maps to identify spatial correlations and relationships, particularly wind direction and pressure changes – forecasting tools which would prove indispensable over the next several decades.[1]

Even though Will never let on about his off-hours research, Professor Abbe could see, without a doubt, that this was a brilliant young man who would one day make an excellent forecaster. Abbe made no secret of the fact that he very much wanted Will to stay on in Washington City, where he could be groomed to take over the important and esteemed position of lead-forecaster after his retirement. While Will seemed reasonably content in his current position, Abbe had often heard him speak in glowing terms about the excitement and adventure to be found in New York City. Still, since Will knew that all forecasts for the nation were made from Headquarters, and he'd already accepted an extension on his one-year detail, Abbe felt

---

1 It would not be till Carl-Gustaf Arvid Rossby's 1939 discovery of large-scale atmospheric waves coupled with information gleaned from the experience of World War II fighter pilots about fast-flowing ribbons of air currents miles above the earth's surface, jet streams, that the efficacy of Will's empirical predictive techniques would be fully understood.

reasonably confident the exceptional young man would choose to remain there at least for the foreseeable future.

Unfortunately for Abbe, he had seriously underestimated just how captivated Will was by the allure of the great, bustling metropolis to the north. He was quite upset when he learned that Will had indeed put in a request to transfer to the New York Field Office, even though there were no current openings there. More puzzling still to Abbe was the fact that should the transfer go through, Will would end up having to take a sizable cut in pay.

Neither Abbe nor Roebling could have foreseen the unfolding of yet another set of improbable circumstances which were to have a defining impact upon Will's nascent career. General William Babcock Hazen died on January 16, 1887 after a long bout with Bright's disease – a painful kidney affliction, later to be more commonly known as nephritis. Hazen's replacement as the Signal Service's Chief Officer was General Adolphus Greely. Serendipitous for Will was the fact that Greely felt he literally owed his life to one Sergeant Francis Long, who just happened to be in charge of the New York City Signal Service Field Office.

Born in 1852 and a naturalized immigrant from Germany, Francis Long enlisted in the U.S. Army in the late 1860's and survived more than a decade of Indian fighting, even claiming to have been the one who found the body of General Custer in 1876, the day after the infamous Battle of Little Bighorn. It was in 1881 that the Sergeant volunteered as cook for an Arctic expedition under General Greely's command. Through a series of unfortunate events, the expedition became lost. By the time rescue arrived three very long years later, the six surviving members, including Greely and Long, were just days from their own death by starvation. Greely credited Long with having saved his life during this ordeal.

When General Greely was told by his superiors in confidence that New York was to be among the Signal Service Field Offices which would be taking on responsibility for their own regional forecasts beginning sometime in the early months of 1888, he simply could not resist appropriating the young forecasting phenomenon as a "gift" for his trusted comrade-in-arms, Sergeant Long – Professor Abbe's vehement objection not-withstanding.

So it was that on Monday, April 4, 1887, Will Roebling assumed his new position of Meteorological Specialist, reporting directly to Sergeant Long of the New York Field Office, in the tower which sat atop the seventh floor of the Equitable Life Assurance Building at 120 Broadway, in the Financial District of lower Manhattan.

PART I

The Calm

The 1880s had brought astonishing new inventions and discoveries that were already benefitting the rich and promising to ease and brighten life for everyone. The great eastern cities now had telephones, steam-heated buildings (a few hundred of each), and electric lights (on main streets and in wealthy households). In New York City, anyone with five cents could ride on the elevated railroads, which, by 1888, had been in service for about nine years; and all but the very poor were blessed with indoor plumbing. The decade had brought major medical breakthroughs, such as antiseptic surgery, local anesthesia, and antirabies vaccine, to say nothing of such pleasing amenities as flatirons, fountain pens, and adding machines. Improvements to earlier technology kept coming as well: the modern bicycle (1884), the alternating-current transformer (1885), the Kodak camera (1888), and the electric trolley (not quite ready in 1888 but on its way).

On the national scene, there seemed nothing much to worry about. The deep wounds left by the Civil War were slowly healing, and no other wars appeared imminent. In the West, the last defiant Apaches had been removed to detention camps in Florida, and the frontier was now secure for settlers. By and large, the nation looked safe, sober, and promising, at least to its ruling middle class, a group that tended to be daring in technological advance and high-flying in business, yet conservative politically and glad to have a conservative president, Grover Cleveland. All in all, most Americans in 1888 felt tranquil and hopeful. Their world looked fine and likely to get better. And, in the face of recent medical miracles, even death seemed to have moved back a little.

People who lived in the eastern states were apt to be more smug and self-satisfied than westerners, whom they often looked down upon as rough innocents. Most arrogant of all were the New Yorkers, who saw themselves as living at the forefront of civilization. If there had been

T-shirts a hundred years ago, they might have read as some do today: "When you leave New York, you ain't goin' nowhere."

Then, suddenly, into that city of technological marvels came the Blizzard of '88 and turned it upside down. Not that other parts of the northeast did not suffer acutely; but in smaller places and in the country, people were still living a simpler life and had time-honored ways of dealing with storms. They stayed home and turned to supplies laid in during the previous autumn; they didn't miss electricity, or running water, or telephones because they weren't used to them; nor did they look to anyone but themselves and their neighbors to plow the roads. If no help appeared for days, they could wait. They were on an ancient time schedule, while New York had already anticipated the twentieth century.

And so the tale of the blizzard keeps leading back to New York City, chiefly because of the striking contrast between its seeming strength and its real fragility. "Society cannot bear anarchy," Barbara Tuchman wrote in A Distant Mirror. *The Blizzard of '88 swept down on a self-satisfied society and showed it what anarchy might look like.*

-"The Blizzard of '88," by Mary Cable (1988)

CHAPTER 1

SUNDAY, SEPTEMBER 11, 1887

Will almost laughed aloud when he caught his reflection in the hallway mirror. Just the mere thought of that fabulous face and figure was enough to transform his normally even features into a goofy, lop-sided school-boy grin. Maybe that's why he was in such a wonderful mood this cool, pleasant Sunday afternoon in September, his one day off this week, as he prepared to begin the leisurely trip which would take him to her doorstep. As he was pulling the front door closed behind him, he heard the kindly voice of his landlady calling down the stairs, "Good-bye, dear! You have fun with Kira to-night!" He hollered back up his farewell and thanks, assuring her that he would.

Wilma Duncan was mighty fond of young Will, as she frequently referred to him. She often thought she'd never met such a fine gentlemen. She had told him several times since he'd answered her room-for-rent ad in early April that she considered him a special gift from God, never having been blessed with children of her own.

Next month would be fifteen years since her beloved's fatal heart attack, bless his dear departed soul. The day Mrs. Duncan buried her Walter was the same day she knew she would have to find a way to supplement the modest income she received from the life insurance policy he'd had the foresight to purchase, so very fortunately, only weeks before his death.

Wilma remembered, with considerable chagrin, all the poor choices she had made in selecting her previous tenants. She sometimes wondered how this great country would be able to survive till the twentieth century if her experience of man's abject lack of morality and responsibility were only half-way representative of to-day's generation. Of course, she'd thought on more than one occasion that living in such close proximity to the Navy Yard might have something to do with it.

All of which left her with a weighty conundrum. Part of her hoped, for Will's sake, that in Kira he'd met the love of his life, even though she had yet to meet the young lady. And in the natural course of events, they would marry and move into a home of their own. At the same time, another purely self-interested part of her prayed that Will would remain her tenant forever. Truth be told, she could even see herself one day bequeathing him the two-story Victorian home on the corner of Sands and Pearl. Her health was certainly good now, but at the age of fifty-nine she knew how quickly things could change.

Will's journey to and from work took him across his beloved bridge six days-a-week. Even before his transfer to the U.S. Army Signal Service Field Office in Manhattan, he'd decided he would rent a room in nearby Brooklyn so he'd be able to walk the Bridge daily, in the company of thousands of fellow pedestrian commuters. Will had such a long-standing fascination with suspension bridges, he often tried to imagine just how incredibly challenging it must have been to build this one – his favorite, and by far the longest in the world.

Will had been thrilled to learn, during his second year at Yale College, that the Bridge was finally officially open on May 24, 1883. He'd been following the progress of the Bridge's construction since a little more than year after they first broke ground in January 1870.

During the thirteen long years of this monumental undertaking, Will had read whatever articles he could find in order to keep abreast of the builders' progress.

To this day, he simply could not fathom how it was possible that people could organize themselves to build such a majestic structure, yet never come to any agreement on what to call it. The names *New York and Brooklyn Bridge, East River Bridge,* and *Great Bridge* were just as commonly used as was the *Brooklyn Bridge.* But because Mrs. D, as he fondly referred to his sweet landlady, always called it the latter, the Brooklyn Bridge moniker was just fine with him.[2]

As Will neared the Manhattan-end of the main, or center, span, he was once again struck by the sheer volume of traffic which crossed the East River every single day. Running along the outer edges of the eighty-five-foot-wide structure were the lanes reserved for horse-drawn vehicles, which included both private carts and wagons, and the larger commercial vehicles.[3]

Down the middle of the Bridge, on its south side, lay a single track for the elevated trains, or els, as they were commonly called. There were several railways which operated throughout Brooklyn and Manhattan, but the New York & Brooklyn Bridge Railway provided the only option for intercity el commuters: a cable-hauled shuttle line spanning the length of the Bridge, connecting the Park Row Terminal in Manhattan with the Sands Street Terminal in Brooklyn.

On the north side, sandwiched between the els and the horse-drawn vehicles, was a single lane for pedestrians, many of them commuters who twice-daily walked the full length of this modern

---

2 It would not be till the year 1915 that the designation "Brooklyn Bridge" would become official.

3 These included omnibuses, essentially glorified stage coaches, and horsecars – streetcars pulled along raised iron or steel tracks by a team of two horses, designed to carry more people and offer a smoother ride than the omnibuses.

marvel – a fair distance measuring slightly more than one-and-one-eighth miles.

Will often found himself thinking that Manhattan was so much more civilized and modern compared to Washington City, and Washington likewise to New Haven. And, of course, New Haven to his tiny home-town farming community in Wisconsin. Yes, there was no doubt, Will Roebling was *very* happy to be living and working in the great metropolis of New York City.

At the moment, he was also happy the oppressive heat had broken the day before. He now felt confident that the worst of a long, hot summer was finally over. As he passed the many hard-working horses along the way, he was able to sense their relief, as well.

In addition to the mile or so he had already walked, it would be another two-and-a-half to get to Kira's: one more to reach Broadway, then another one-and-a-half to get up-town. To-night would be his fourth outing with Kira, and only the third time he'd ventured that far north in the City.

An aspiring actress and dancer, Kira Smith stood out from the crowd, not only because of her unusual height – five-feet-seven-inches – but also for her lovely face, beautiful shining chestnut hair, alluring green eyes, and lithe and voluptuous figure.

In June, Kira had graduated from a two-year program at the American Academy of Dramatic Arts. With the exception of a minor role she'd landed as a replacement dancer in some obscure musical, at an even more obscure theatre near Madison Square, she had nothing to show for the past three months but a handful of bitter disappointments. To be sure, she was a very good dancer and an even better actress, at least according to her instructors at the Academy. Unfortunately, the competition was fierce for the few roles which were available. She often wondered how it was even possible for a girl to make it in this damned cut-throat industry without having some type of inside track. Perhaps, as she'd often heard whispered, some girls accomplished this by compromising their virtue with the producer or director – clearly an impossibility for someone with her upbringing.

To-day was Kira's twenty-second birthday. To surprise her, Will had sprung for third-row orchestra seats for the operetta *Gasparone* at the Standard Theatre, on the corner of 33rd and Sixth. Although the tickets had set him back a pretty penny, Kira was certainly worth it. Had she not mentioned the popularity of the show during their prior get-together, Will would never have heard of *Gasparone,* as he really didn't have that much interest in the theatre.

Like most red-blooded American males, however, he certainly knew all about the actress playing the lead role of Carlotta: the beautiful Lillian Russell. After Kira had spoiled his intended surprise with her relentless wheedling, eventually coaxing him into revealing his plan for her birthday, Will found her excitement contagious. He was now actually looking forward to the evening. *I guess that's what love will do,* he thought, chuckling to himself.

Will arrived at the Standard at six-fifteen. As he and Kira were scheduled to meet at the main door at six-forty, he decided he'd pass the time in Greeley Square, directly across the street from the theatre. Sitting on the bench, he lost himself for a few minutes in reminiscing about their first meeting. Hard to believe it was just six short weeks ago; in some ways he felt as if he'd known her forever.

Kira's best friend, Alexandra, who six months earlier had married Will's colleague, Frank Gorman, had introduced them on an arranged outing at a respectable restaurant. Prior to Will's arrival at the New York Field Office, Frank had been a Senior Technician there for three years. And even though, as the new Meteorological Specialist Will was Frank's superior, Frank was happy to take on the role of showing him the ropes around the Office. The two soon became fast friends.

Over the past several months, Will had twice been Frank and Alex's dinner guest. He'd been grateful for the invitations, as he hadn't really had the time to develop much of a social life since moving to New York. For all intents and purposes, Will had been romantically unavailable for the past few years – unwilling even to entertain the possibility of a meaningful relationship with a member of the fairer sex. During the nearly year-and-a-half he'd been at Headquarters, he'd spent all his time immersed in Professor Abbe's research project, using all of his off-hours to develop a system to forecast the weather. And up till now in the New York Field Office, he'd felt such a strong need to prove himself to his Superior Officer, Sergeant Long, that it had been easy to justify avoiding such a relationship, with all its attendant distractions. Although development of his forecasting system still placed an inordinate demand on his time and attention, Will felt he might finally, at long last, have room in his schedule to begin to explore other interests.

It's not that Will wasn't considered a "good catch;" apparently, at least according to Mrs. D and Alex, it was quite the contrary. Physically, they'd said, he was more than handsome enough, with his six-foot, lean muscular frame and rugged outdoors appearance. But it was his other characteristics which really made him outstanding husband material – his strength, intelligence, wry sense of humor, ambition, drive, and, most important of all, his kindness. Of course, knowing of their deep affection for him, Will took these accolades with a healthy grain of salt and was even a bit embarrassed by them. At the same time, he reckoned there was enough truth in there somewhere that he had at least a reasonable chance of success, once he decided to put himself "on the market."

Will recalled the day in early August when Frank had first mentioned Alex's idea to set up a meeting between him and Kira. According to Frank, Alex had acknowledged that the two of them had very different personalities and interests. Even so, given they were both such lovely people, and that often opposites *do* attract, she'd felt it likely they'd make a splendid couple.

Frank had confessed to Will that he had his doubts about Alex's assessment, and he'd told her so at the time. It was his opinion, Frank had gone on, that on top of them having virtually nothing in common, a match would be highly unlikely, as Will had always given him the impression that he had little interest in courting.

Will recalled clearly what he'd said to Frank in response: "Well, you're certainly right about that, Frank, there's no denying it. But let's examine this logically, shall we? What harm could there be in just one meeting? Please tell Alex I'd be delighted to take her up on the offer."

Will could still see the look of surprise on Frank's face. But then again, when it came right down to it, did he really have anything to lose? He liked Frank very much, and adored Alex. And after all, he had figured, he would have to explore the possibility of a relationship with a woman at some point, would he not?

Kira and Alex were very close, bonded by their mutual love of the theatre and a passionate determination to make it big on the Broadway stage. Each had been a year or two older than most of the other Academy students, but by markedly different circumstances. It had taken that long for Kira to convince her well-to-do father she was mature enough to live on her own in Manhattan, and ambitious enough not to waste the money he'd be paying for her tuition and living expenses. It saddened Kira that Alex, on the other hand, had had to work two full-time jobs, scrimping and saving every penny to pay her own tuition, with barely enough left over for an austere existence in a tiny flat.

After meeting sometime early in their first year of training, the two young women had become inseparable – so much so that Kira had insisted Alex move into her palatial third-floor suite on West 34th Street, near Seventh. It did not take them long to discover they made fabulous room-mates, and things between them could not have been better. All that changed, however, about mid-way through their last semester. It was then that Alex met Frank, and Kira could only look on as the two promptly fell head-over-heels in love. Immediately after graduation, they were married.

Although she would never say anything against Frank, Kira believed that falling in love with him had caused Alex to "lose her edge." While certainly happy for her friend's joy in her new-found love, Kira was disappointed that Alex had lost, and would probably never regain, the passion and dedication which were absolute necessities if one hoped to become a star on Broadway. She reasoned that Frank, by providing Alex with the life she now enjoyed, had enabled her to become too comfortable, without even factoring in the many distractions inherent in any marriage.

If she were really being honest with herself, Kira knew that, on some level, she resented Alex for having someone in her life who meant more to her than she did. And on the deepest level, Kira struggled with the fear that maybe Alex, in finding true love, had found a happiness she never would or could.

Ironically, Alex thought that Kira was the one who, left to her own devices, lacked the drive required to become a star. For that reason, she felt Will would be a great influence on her, providing precisely the kind of stability and focus she needed. Not that Kira was wild, or anything like that. Alex just sensed that perhaps she was a bit spoiled. Alex really loved Kira, and felt strongly that Will's sweet nature and clear-headed determination would be just perfect for her.

Alex had been raised by loving, but dirt-poor, parents who had moved to New York from Appalachia when she was seven, seeking a better life for their children. Her childhood recollections of going long stretches without enough food and warm clothing would forever be etched in her memory. As would the shame she'd felt in grade-school, having to wear, over and over, the same few hand-me-down outfits. Her embarrassment growing up had been so acute, it never even registered that most of her class-mates came from families just as poor as hers.

She knew that, by stark contrast, Kira's family had always been quite well-off. Kira had gone into great detail about how her father, a mechanical engineer, had been recruited as an assistant manager by the Singer Sewing Machine Company when it was established in 1871. Working hard to climb the corporate ladder, by 1878 Thomas Smith was a Vice President of the six-thousand-employee factory on Newark Bay in Elizabeth, New Jersey. Life had indeed been good for the Smith family.

"Good Heavens! Kira, you look positively stunning!," Will exclaimed, recovering from being startled after she'd snuck up behind him and given him a goose. "How did you know I was over here?" He glanced at his watch, which showed nearly six-forty-five. "My goodness, I'm so sorry, I guess I lost track of the time."

"Oh, yes, I clean up quite nicely," she preened, ignoring his apology. The self-satisfied grin on her face evidenced how much she enjoyed his compliment. After a pause she added, "I'm thinking that maybe you'll be wanting to take me out somewhere, perhaps for a libation, after the show."

Will was working the early shift this week and was fully aware of the ridiculous hour he would have to get up to-morrow in order to make it to the Office on time; he could ill-afford to be staying out so late. Somehow, though, in this particular moment, that didn't seem to make the least bit of difference.

"Why, that sounds wonderful! As a matter of fact, now that you happen to mention it, I do remember taking notice of a charming little place I passed by, on my way up here."

"Well...," Kira teased coyly, twirling several loose strands of hair around her finger and giving him a saucy wink, "we're in *my* neck of the woods now, and I have just the place in mind."

Will found her behaviour a bit odd, yet at the same time very exciting. Kira had always been perfectly lady-like on their three previous outings, and now she was being outright flirtatious. Not that he minded, not even a bit – it was just completely confounding, is all. Always one ruled by logic, he struggled to make sense of her demeanor. The best explanation he could come up with was that perhaps she was expressing a desire for more intimacy in their relationship. He happily chose to embrace that thought.

They proceeded to the theatre, and Will handed their tickets to the attendant. Kira, who'd expected to be ushered to seats somewhere in the back of the balcony, let out a shriek when they were led, instead, to the third row of the Orchestra section.

"Oh, my God! You got *orchestra* seats? I thought you said balcony!"

"Well..." Now it was his turn to toy with her. "Surely you didn't expect me not to keep *some* of this evening a surprise? So maybe I did mislead you...just a wee bit." In child-like and gleeful response, she threw her arms around his neck and planted a big kiss on his cheek. Will reddened a bit, shocked by the forwardness of her gesture, yet pleased that his little surprise had made her so happy.

While they both were waiting for the show to begin, Kira took the opportunity to fill him in on some background information about *Gasparone*. "The whole story takes place in Sicily, on the Mediterranean Sea," she said hurriedly. "What is really clever about the story is that the title character, Gasparone, never even appears on stage. Baboleno, the Mayor, uses him as a scapegoat in a complicated and hilarious scheme he contrives to have his son, Sindulfo, marry Carlotta, the rich Countess, so he, Baboleno, can convince her to pay off some of his debts."

Will couldn't tell if Kira were rushing because of her excitement, or if she were simply trying to relate as much as possible before the show began. She started to say something else about a wealthy innkeeper who owed Baboleno back-mortgage payments and a kidnaping scheme involving Sindulfo, when the audience suddenly erupted in a loud cheer. The curtain had gone up, leaving Will to learn the rest for himself. Kira reached across and took his hand gently into hers.

Gasparone certainly lived up to its advance billing. Will and Kira each had a wonderful time, enjoying it thoroughly. Afterward, she steered him towards a delightful, intimate little pub nearby, with a warm old-European ambience – perfectly suited for the pleasant mood they were in following the show.

Exhibiting her familiarity with contemporary mores, Kira ordered a Tom Collins brandy. Will, not really much of a drinker, opted for the bartender's recommendation of the best beer available on tap.

They talked all about the show, Kira providing lots of interesting "insider" insights about the singing, dancing, and overall production values. She identified several scenes in which there had been miscues, but Will had to settle for taking her word on it; to his mind, the performances had been flawless. After exhausting the subject of *Gasparone*, Will ordered himself another beer (Kira was still fine with her Collins), and the conversation logically segued into Kira's career.

Of all the time they sat talking together, Will thought the best part was listening to Kira fantasize about what it would be like for her to play the lead in the show, instead of Lillian Russell. For the first time he really felt he understood her passion for the theatre, which made him feel that much closer to her.

They could have stayed and talked a great deal longer, probably far into the night. But when Kira mentioned that she didn't have any plans for to-morrow and felt very fortunate she could stay abed for most of the morning, a harsh reality suddenly set in for Will. It was already nearly eleven o'clock, and by the time he saw her to her door and completed the long walk home, he figured it would be at least twelve-thirty. Three-and-a-quarter very short hours after that, he would have to be getting up for work.

Fifteen minutes later he was placing a chaste good-night kiss on Kira's cheek as they bade each other farewell in front of her suite. Energy abounding even at this late hour, he set off on a fast pace for home, reflecting upon the evening. While there was no denying he'd had a marvelous time overall, something had happened at the very end of their conversation which had unsettled him a bit. Somehow, he'd gotten the impression that it didn't seem to matter very much to her that he had to get up so early the next morning.

Or maybe that was just his over-active imagination, getting all worked up over something of no consequence. Not wishing to put a damper on what was, after all, a remarkably pleasant evening, Will decided to file these thoughts away for further consideration at some later time.

CHAPTER 2

MONDAY, SEPTEMBER 12, 1887

F̲our a.m. came much too quickly, as he'd known it would. And, even at that, it was fifteen minutes later than he usually awoke whenever he worked the early shift.

Fortuitously, Will had taken full advantage of the opportunity to have a lie-in for several hours yesterday morning, or he might well have contemplated calling in late to-day. Not only would that have been a first for him, to his disciplined mind it would have been a small failure of sorts. He had to admit, though, if only to himself, that the wonderful time he and Kira had shared celebrating her birthday last night was well worth the fatigue he knew he would be feeling the rest of the day.

He quickly completed his morning ablutions, quietly made himself some eggs, toast, and coffee – most importantly the coffee, extra-strong – and at four-twenty tiptoed softly out the door. As usual, he took great pains to avoid making any noise which might disturb the slumbering Mrs. D.

As tired as he was, he'd made sure he was wearing his special issue Signal Service Corps uniform, a tradition Sergeant Long demanded of all Office personnel every Monday, no exceptions. No one knew precisely why Long insisted on this bit of protocol, but neither did anyone have the courage to ask, so no one had ever shown up dressed in anything else. Without really giving it too much thought, Will had come to the realization that donning this distinctive outfit, once-a-week, actually gave him a certain sense of pride and belonging, so he always wore it willingly, if not eagerly.

The insignia on his khaki uniform shirt, starting just below the shoulder on each sleeve, was two crossed signal flags: the right, or dexter, being white with a red center, and the left, or sinister, red with a white center. The staffs were gold, bisected vertically by a flaming torch, also gold. The crossed flags had been a part of the Signal Service's insignia since 1868, with the burning torch added in 1884. As Will had learned at Fort Myer, the flags and torch, fittingly, were symbolic of signaling or communication.

In spite of his exhaustion, Will refused to consider taking the el across the Bridge. And though he could have easily afforded the fare, a horse-car was also entirely out of the question. Before he'd even signed his lease, Will had made the firm commitment to himself to briskly walk the three miles each way, to and from the Office, rain or shine. In this fashion, he figured he would be able to maintain at least a minimally acceptable degree of physical fitness without having to focus any extra time or attention on such a critical component of a balanced life. As a bonus, he was frequently able to make excellent use of his commute time in contemplation, mulling over any unresolved issues he might have, work-related or otherwise. To-day he would just have to quicken his pace a bit, maybe even break into a slow run, at least for part of the way, to avoid being late.

After leaving Mrs. D's, Will walked the three blocks west to the Brooklyn Bridge entrance. He quickly traversed the modestly populated pedestrian path-way (traffic would increase dramatically over the course of the next few hours), then headed south on Park Row to pick up Broadway at Vesey Street, as he had done six-days-a-week for the past five months. From there, it was only five short blocks south on Broadway to the Equitable Life Assurance Building, also known as the Equitable Life Building, or simply the Equitable Building, as it was most often called.

The New York Field Office of the U.S. Army Signal Service Corps occupied the tower of the seven-and-a-half-story structure located at the corner of Broadway and Cedar Street, directly across from the Trinity Church cemetery. The Equitable Building was home to the Equitable Life Assurance Society of the United States, a leader in the rapidly growing life insurance business. New York City's tallest building at the time, with a height of one-hundred-and-thirty feet, the Equitable Building was considered by some to be a "sky-scraper," the world's first. The ground floor housed a fancy restaurant, one which Will knew was well above his pay grade. He'd gone in once to peruse the menu but, unfortunately, found it written in French, a language with which he had not even a nodding acquaintance. Undaunted, he'd told himself that someday he would definitely have to try a meal there, even if it were just a bowl of soup, or maybe a light lunch.

Will knew that the Equitable Building's greatest claim to fame, however, was being the first office-building in the world to feature passenger elevators, based on a design patented in 1861 by Elisha Otis. Up till now, these modern conveniences were to be found only in the fanciest hotels and a single department store in New York City – AT Stewart's, on Broadway's east side. Henry Baldwin Hyde, Equitable's president, was the first to entice the more successful business firms into renting the upper floors; formerly, they had been considered undesirable because of the many flights of stairs which had to be negotiated at least twice-daily. Hyde was able to turn on a five-cent piece the entrenched mind-set whereby highly paid lawyers and prominent businessmen would consider occupying only ground-floor spaces.

The tower suite, with its unobstructed views in all directions, was certainly the ideal location for the Signal Service. Fortunately for them, they had signed a long-term lease many years earlier, well before the upper floors began renting at a premium.

Will's office faced slightly north of due-east, giving him a bird's-eye view of much of Manhattan's lower east side. From that vantage point, he could easily take in the many shops, hotels, office-buildings, and docks, as well as the myriad streets in constant motion with horsecars, cabs, carriages, wagons, and, of course, the never-ending multitude of pedestrians. When Will was in a reflective mood, his eyes would invariably be drawn to his favorite structure in all of Manhattan, and one at which he never tired of gazing – the ever-magnificent Brooklyn Bridge.

Will got to the Office at three minutes past five. Whenever he worked the early shift, it was practically unheard of for him not to be the first one in, let alone the last to arrive, as was the case to-day. Frank Gorman, who'd also drawn the short stick for this week, took full advantage of the opportunity to welcome him in with just a bit of good-natured ribbing.

"So, Will, you must've had yourself a pretty darned-good time, last night. With Kira, I mean, of course. Hell's bells, man – I actually got here this morning before you did. Now that's a first, pal."

"Ha, ha, ha – aren't you just the in-house comedian," Will replied, sardonically, glancing around quickly to make sure they were alone. "Seriously, though, Frank, listen here. We did have a really great time together at the show, then went out for a couple of drinks afterward. I knew I'd be paying the price to-day, but, believe me, it was worth it. Let me tell you, she was really flirtatious the whole night; it was like some sort of switch got activated, or something. I know I don't have a lot of experience with women, but you can trust me when I tell you that this was really something out of the ordinary."

"Gosh, Will – that sounds pretty great to me. I have to say I'm happy for you."

"Gee, thanks for that, partner."

"You know, now that we're on the subject, the truth is I've really got to hand it to Alex on this one. She was the one who thought the two of you could make quite a good couple. I have to admit – I didn't see it at first. I mean, you must agree, you and Kira really do have mighty different personalities."

"Well, that's certainly true enough..." Will wondered where Frank was going with this conversation. Didn't he remember they'd had essentially the same discussion just last month?

"No, I'm just saying – Alex is a whole lot more perceptive than I am when it comes to relationships and all those other 'female-centric' things."

Will turned to leave. "Well, I guess that makes sense, since she's the female. I'll see you later, Frank – I'd better get to my desk and start in on the day."

Walking away, Will realized he'd neglected to mention Kira's apparent lack of empathy about his having to get up so early. He thought it would be interesting to hear Frank's opinion on the matter, and made a mental note to discuss it with him later.

As smart as Will was in many arenas, he was well aware that when it came to understanding women, he was still a babe in the woods.

CHAPTER 3

WEDNESDAY, OCTOBER 5, 1887

At one-thirty in the afternoon, Kira gave her telephone handcrank a few turns, then asked the operator to connect her to Will's Office; she knew he was working the late shift this week. In previous discussions, he'd made it clear that he didn't want her to get into the habit of disturbing him at work, and she generally honored his wish. To-day, though, she was feeling so down in the dumps she just really needed to hear his voice.

"Will?" she said into the transmitter when she heard his "hello" coming through the earpiece. "Oh, Will, I do hope you'll forgive the interruption, but it's just that I'm feeling so badly," she sighed, her voice trembling as she tried her best to hold back the tears. "I got another rejection notice to-day. Remember the audition I had on Monday, for the play I told you about? Well, to-day I got word that they picked someone else for my part – the one I was so terribly excited about."

"Oh, goodness, no, Kira, that's just awful – I know you were feeling really confident about this one." She could tell he was keeping his voice low and his hand cupped around the mouthpiece, to avoid being overheard by any of his Office-mates.

"Yes, you're right, this time I truly was, more's the pity." She sighed again, briefly, then paused for a moment before continuing. "Will, I don't wish to keep you, but there is something I wanted to ask. I know this is rather short notice, so you must feel free to decline, but is there any chance that I could see you to-night, after you get off work?"

"Of course, Kira, of course. I can be at your place about nine-forty-five, ten the latest."

"That's wonderful, Will. And I know that'll be kind of on the late side, but ... I just need to see you, is all."

"Absolutely Kira, I understand completely. Don't you worry, I'll be there."

"I'm so happy to hear you say that. And don't concern yourself about dinner; I'm sure I can whip us up something fairly appetizing in no time at all."

She smiled as she placed the receiver back on its hook, already feeling the dark cloud beginning to lift just a bit.

Will wasted no time in summoning the operator to place a call to his neighbor, Mrs. Potts, and was gratified when the connection went through immediately. After a polite exchange inquiring after her and her husband's well-being, he asked if she wouldn't mind letting Mrs. D know that he would not be home for dinner, as he would be going to Kira's, instead. Mrs. Potts was Mrs. D's dearest friend, so Will knew she would be happy to convey the message. Wednesday night was pasta night at Mrs. D's, and Will had a standing invitation to join her for dinner, an event that he missed only rarely. He was touched that it never seemed to bother her in the least, having to hold dinner for so long whenever he worked the late shift.

Even though Alexander Graham Bell had received the patent on his world-changing invention more than a decade earlier, it would still be several years before the telephone would become affordable for the general population. At the moment, only some government agencies, some businesses and businessmen, and the more well-to-do had the means to pay for this luxury. It went without saying that Kira, a single woman living alone in Manhattan, would be far safer if she had her own telephone. Will was glad that she'd been able to convince her caring and generous father to embrace this reality.

The New York Field Office had had its own telephone subscription for several months now, along with the entire Signal Service Corps. This one single development created a dramatic improvement in Interoffice communication, revolutionizing the speed and quality of the weather indications which were issued by Headquarters.

"Gee, Kira, that really is too bad about the part," Will said, still trying to remember the name of the play. For once, his eidetic memory failed him; he supposed he must have had his mind on something else when she told him.

"Thank-you again for that, Will. I guess it's hitting me so hard this time because I'd been thinking that this was the perfect role for me. At the audition, I got to sing, dance, and even read a few lines. I know I simply could not have done it any better, not even a bit. And they really seemed to like me, they really did."

"I'm sure they did. How could they not?" He gave her a broad smile, then reached out to take her hand in his, patting it gently as he looked at her with great sympathy. "I can't begin to imagine how hard this must be for you. I'm so sorry you have to go through this, time and time again; it really hurts me to see you suffering like this. But there will be other auditions, you know that. I have this feeling, don't ask me why, that a really great part is out there waiting for you, and that it's just around the corner. And once the public gets a good look at you and what you can do, my dearest, trust me – you'll be well on your way to stardom."

"Oh, Will, do you really think so?" She looked up at him, eyes brimming.

He reached out to embrace her, holding her close for a long moment. "Of course I do, sweetheart."

Kira let out a long sigh. "You know something? I think I'm beginning to feel a whole lot better already." She favored him with a sweet smile.

"That's wonderful, Kira, I'm very glad to hear it."

"Well then, I guess it's about time we started in on dinner, don't you think? I made us spaghetti with meatballs, and a salad. How does that sound to you?"

"It sounds just perfect. Oh, and I bet we could put this bottle of wine to some good use, not to mention this bouquet of flowers," he said coyly, promptly producing the gifts from the clever hiding place he'd found for them on his way into her suite.

"Oh, Will, thank-you ever so much. You know, you really didn't have to, but I'm *so* glad you did." This time her smile lit up the room.

This was the second opportunity he'd had to see Kira since her birthday celebration. As he hadn't experienced any recurrence of what he'd thought might be a lack of empathy on her part, he was beginning to think that maybe it had been just his imagination after all.

They enjoyed a nice dinner, and Will left to go home shortly before midnight.

CHAPTER 4

THURSDAY, NOVEMBER 10, 1887

Will found himself in the unenviable position of having to decline the invitation Mrs. D had extended to him and Kira to join her at home for an intimate Thanksgiving Dinner. He realized he'd probably made something of a mess of things, letting her get her hopes up in the first place. In all fairness to Kira, by the time he'd asked her, she and her parents had already discussed making the special day even more so by bringing him home with her for the first time. So while he wasn't feeling too upset for himself, he did feel badly about disappointing Mrs. D, and took pains to tell her so.

"Oh, fiddlesticks, that's sheer nonsense, Will, don't you give it a second thought. Of course I understand completely. It will be much more exciting for Kira to be introducing you to her parents, and on Thanksgiving to boot. That really is quite a big deal, you know."

"Well, I guess I can't argue with that. But I was really looking forward to her meeting you."

"You know that makes two of us, Will. I mean, really, that's a meeting that's long overdue, when you stop and think about it." Will nodded his agreement as she paused here for a moment, face working as if she were puzzling out an intricate piece of business. Suddenly her eyes flew open and her jaw dropped. "Wait a minute, hold your horses. I think I might've just come up with a smashing idea. I'm a little hesitant to share it, because it's, well, maybe a wee bit on the sneaky side, but..."

"Come on, out with it, Mrs. D! What's this great new idea of yours?"

"Well," she began slyly, a wicked gleam in her eye, "Kira will naturally be thinking that I'm going to be one sad, sorry, lonely little old lady – now that you two won't be able to make it for dinner on Thanksgiving, that is. Am I right?"

"Now you hang on there, just a minute, Mrs. D. What in the world are you getting up to?"

"Who, me? Why, whatever do you mean?" Mrs. D placed her right palm on her chest and raised both eyebrows high in dramatically feigned innocence. A moment later she chucked him on the arm and let out a giggle.

"Alright, alright then, my good man, listen up. All you need to do is lay on the guilt, a little thick. Shrug your shoulders with a sigh and roll your eyes Heaven-ward as you tell her there must be *some* way the two of you can make it up to poor lonesome me. If you play your cards just right, I promise you she will be the one to suggest that you offer me a rain-check – and then you can steer her towards the following Sunday. But the main point of it all is that she thinks it was her idea, which will guarantee that she'll be excited about coming. And the three of us will have ourselves a rollicking good time, not to mention a great dinner!"

"Brilliant, Mrs. D! Slightly devious, admittedly, but brilliant." He gave her an appraising look accompanied by a wry, knowing grin. "I guess it's fair to say that Mr. D never stood a chance, did he – not once you put your mind to something, that is."

His crafty compatriot accepted the compliment by nodding slowly in response, all the while smiling warmly at him, eyes twinkling merrily.

> ✷

"Would you care for some more wine?" Alex asked Kira, as she returned to the kitchen with a fresh bottle in tow.

"Thank-you, no, Alex. By now I'm sure I've had quite enough."

"Well, you can suit yourself, of course," she said, as she poured herself another glass. She took a sip, then gave Kira a bright smile before asking, casually, "So, do your plans for Thanksgiving this year include Will?"

"It's interesting that you should ask. As a matter of fact, they do. It turns out he'll be coming with me to my parents' home, in New Jersey."

"Oh, that's right, Will hasn't met your folks yet, has he?"

"No, actually, this will be their first meeting."

"So I'm curious – why do you say that it's 'interesting' that I should ask?"

"Oh, it's just that he told me we'd been invited to dinner at his 'Mrs. D's.' And even though he seemed happy enough to be coming with me to my parents, I could tell he was still somewhat disappointed we won't be going there."

"You really don't like her very much, do you." Kira heard Alex's communication as far more a statement than a question.

"How could I possibly say? I haven't even met the woman yet. Of course, all he does is go on and on about her, 'Mrs. D' this and 'Mrs. D' that."

"Well, what in the world is wrong with that? Obviously she's very special to him."

"Yes, obviously, and I didn't say that there's anything wrong with it, exactly, it's just that – oh, I don't know, never mind . . . Let's talk about something else, shall we? Didn't you say Frank would be getting home soon?"

"Yes, I think he should be here in about an hour. Why do you ask?"

"Oh, no particular reason, really. I'm just curious, I guess. I'll be leaving soon, anyway. I have to get back home, eat dinner, and get to bed early. I really need my beauty sleep to-night; I've got another audition early in the morning."

"Kira, that's wonderful!" Alex's face lit up. "You hadn't told me anything about it before now. Is it a big part? Does Will know?"

"No, and no. It's not a big part, not even an exciting one, really, and I don't think I'll get it, anyway. But I can't be in the business of turning down parts now, can I? I have to go out there and audition." Kira paused here for a moment and gave a small sigh, then continued, a little less bitterly, "And as far as mentioning anything to Will, I actually hadn't been planning to. Unless, of course, they call me back for a second reading, that is."

"Gee, Kira, I don't know . . ."

"And just exactly what is it that you 'don't know,' Alex?" Although, truth be told, Kira was well aware that Alex thought she was making a big mistake in her relationship with Will by not sharing more of herself with him. The other night Alex had gone so far as to say she was very much afraid he'd eventually lose interest if Kira continued on with what Alex described as her pattern of "keeping him at arm's length."

"You know precisely what it is I'm talking about, Kira, and don't pretend you don't. I'm talking about you not letting Will in. He is so much in love with you, and I know you know it. Why, then, do you insist on doing things which undermine your relationship with him?"

"I am not doing a single thing to 'undermine' anything, Alex. And you know what else? I don't wish to discuss this with you. Not now, not ever. Besides, since you brought up the subject of not letting people in, what about you?"

Alex gave a startled laugh. "Me? What *about* me?"

"Well, it's become pretty obvious to me, even though you've never actually said a word about it, that you've all but given up on pursuing an acting career. Now, all of a sudden, being at home and a house-wife seems to be enough for you. Whatever happened to all your ambition, your dreams? Those same dreams we've shared since the day we met?"

Alex got quiet for a long moment, apparently deliberating about what she should say next. "Well, Kira," she began, deliberately, "I was going to wait awhile before mentioning anything about this, and I can see it's certainly not the best time, but . . ."

"But? But *what?*"

"Well, it's just that Frank and I . . . we . . . we have decided that it's time we got down to the business of starting a family. We're going to try to, well, you know, have me 'in a family way,' along about February."

Kira was silent. "Well, I must say, Alex," she finally offered, coolly, "this really is quite a surprise. I surely didn't see that coming."

Alex smiled thinly, as Kira continued to stare at her for a long moment.

"Well, then," Kira finally said, "I guess I'll be on my way now." She didn't have it in her to offer up any sort of congratulation or best wishes for the future, and was just relieved when the door closed behind her, putting an end to their uncomfortable and unfortunate interaction.

For some time now, Frank had been after Alex to invite Will and Kira over for dinner. He had pointed out that pairing them up had been her idea in the first place. Now that they were a couple, the logical convention would seem to dictate that she engineer some type of social engagement. He found it a bit odd that Will, his friend, not to mention boss, had been to dinner twice now while Kira, her best friend and former room-mate, had never even been to their house for a meal. As far as Frank was concerned, on the face of it, Alex was long overdue in extending an invitation to the two of them.

Alex was well aware that she resisted having Kira over as a dinner guest, with or without Will. The precise reason, though, hadn't been so easy to put her finger on. About one thing, however, she was crystal clear: the heated words she and Kira had exchanged to-day served only to further her reluctance.

She realized that some part of it, at least with respect to inviting them over as a couple, centered about the fact that Will was Frank's boss. Even though she was the one who'd originally played matchmaker, she certainly did not want to be held responsible, in any way, should things between Kira and Will begin to deteriorate; there was simply no way of knowing if any negative repercussions might fall on Frank as a result. Alex was determined to avoid doing anything that might "rock the boat," all the more so now, having set in motion their plan to start a family. They were both keenly aware of just how fortunate they were that he had such a good job in the first place. So many these days were struggling to find gainful employment, or working under intolerable conditions for pitiable wages.

But it was all a bit more complicated than that, as it so often is when dealing with human relationships. It was only after hearing Kira's angry, accusatory words earlier to-day that Alex was finally able to discern the true reason she'd been resisting proffering an invitation: her fear of what Frank would be likely to learn about the woman he'd married.

Some of what Kira had said about her really hit home, especially the part about losing her ambition and letting go of her dreams. And even though it was a fact that she had given up any realistic hope of achieving the career she'd worked so hard to prepare for, Alex now saw that she had yet to come to terms, fully, with the reality and the finality of it. A part of her, the part she struggled to keep hidden from Frank, really missed the excitement of performing. Quite simply, it made her feel good; it gave her purpose, an opportunity to express herself creatively. She'd known that Kira would likely open that Pandora's Box of a conversation over dinner, and she'd wanted to avoid discussing that side of herself. And if Will were there as well, that could only further complicate matters.

Somehow, though, all of that had changed the day she'd decided she was ready to start a family. Having a child was now the most important thing in her life, giving it a whole new purpose. All those intoxicating visions of stardom she'd once held so dear seemed to gently evaporate in the wake of something so profoundly life-altering.

When she told Kira about their decision to have a baby, she'd omitted large parts of what had actually been transpiring the past few months between her and Frank. For one thing, she'd neglected to mention that their relationship had been somewhat strained, of late. Frank had been thinking for some while now that it was time they'd started a family, but she hadn't felt quite ready. Her mind and heart held no doubt that she loved Frank dearly and wanted a family with him, someday. Till very recently, though, the time just had not felt right to her.

Alex was also a bit afraid of bringing a child into this world. She remembered how difficult it had been for her parents, raising her and her two sisters. Intellectually, she understood that her situation was far better than her parents' had ever been, as Frank had a steady job with a good paycheck. But somehow, that knowledge alone had not been enough to erase the emotional scars left over from her childhood deprivations.

Sometime in the past few weeks, oddly enough, Alex had suddenly experienced a change of heart; she wasn't exactly sure why. Perhaps it was because Frank had seemed to ease up a bit about the whole issue, or maybe she'd just reached that level of maturity which comes with turning twenty-two. Another possibility could be related to Will. With an immediate superior of Will's stature, not to mention admirable character, Frank's position now seemed more secure – especially given the warmth of their friendship. She didn't know. All she knew was that, finally, she was in agreement with her husband: the time was right to start trying for a baby.

Frank, of course, was elated.

Ironically, before their rather heated disagreement earlier to-day, Alex had also been feeling the time was right to extend that dinner invitation to Kira and Will. Now, though, she decided it would be better to give Kira a wide berth, at least for the immediate future. Besides, there was plenty enough for her to concentrate on at home, what with the exciting new path to which she and Frank were now committed.

CHAPTER 5

SUNDAY, NOVEMBER 27, 1887

Will could not help but feel sorry for Kira when he glanced over at her reddened face. Though she did her best to hide it, he could still hear how labored her breathing was as she struggled to keep up with him. He'd already slackened his pace twice, but it hadn't seemed to help all that much.

He would be willing to wager a week's salary that the poor girl was now fervently wishing she'd taken him up on his suggestion they travel by horsecar. He would have insisted, but not only did he know how hard she worked to keep her dancer's body in superb physical condition, she'd also gone out of her way to convince him that she'd be "just fine" on their long walk to Brooklyn.

He hoped that, at the very least, she was able to enjoy the spectacular view surrounding them on all sides as they made their way across his beloved Bridge. As always, he drew inspiration from just being on it, and came up with the idea to distract his beleaguered companion with a little cheerful conversation.

"Well, I must say again, having Thanksgiving Dinner with your folks definitely turned out to be a terrific idea," he began brightly. I really am glad I finally got the chance to meet them; they surely are nice people."

"Yes, they are, and they were thrilled to meet you, too. My father, especially, seemed quite taken by your description of your early days at the Signal Service, and I know he was most impressed with your position as a 'Meteorological Specialist.' I even think he was secretly wishing that he, himself, had had the opportunity to pursue a career in that direction."

"Oh, I don't know about all that, Kira. I think he was just being polite."

"No, really, I mean it; believe me, I know my father, and I'm quite certain he was being serious."

"Well, either way, it was wonderful to have had the opportunity to spend some time with them. And I have to tell you again what a great idea you had about coming over to Mrs. D's to-day, for a good old-fashioned Sunday dinner. She told me again, just this morning, how excited she was to finally be meeting you. She's going to absolutely love you, I just know it. And you're going to love her too, trust me. And on top of all that, as far as our meal goes, you're in for a real treat, I can promise you that. She's an utterly amazing cook."

"Yes, Will, as I recall, that's what you've been telling me." Will looked over at her face, but her pleasant smile belied the slight edge he thought he'd detected in her voice.

"Well, there you go," he responded, laughing lightly.

A few moments passed in companionable silence. Kira then began, brightly, "My goodness, but you were right on the money when you described how amazing the view from the Bridge is. I've been on it before, of course, but always in some form of conveyance, never on foot. I realize now that before this moment, I'd never really looked, I mean truly looked, at the view of the water below and how beautifully the light reflects off all the different buildings along the banks."

Will was gratified to hear Kira express her appreciation. "Yes, it's quite spectacular, isn't it. The marvelous weather this afternoon doesn't hurt, either. I do some of my best thinking on my commute each day, truth be told. It's strange, I know, but just being on the Bridge can have such an effect on me that I sometimes feel I've been transported back to another time." Kira smiled politely, but offered nothing in response.

The afternoon was pleasantly mild, unusually so for this late in November. Will noticed that high, wispy clouds were invading the skies from the southwest, promising to make for a gorgeous sunset in about an hour. He pointed out a number of interesting landmarks along the Brooklyn side of the East River, all the while marveling silently at the filtering hues of the sun setting behind them. These colors, combined with the exceptionally clean dry air, created a dazzling display of the sometimes drab-looking buildings.

As they neared the center span, the highest point above the water, Will, feeling calm and carefree, asked, "Did you know that this Thanksgiving marked four-and-a-half years, to the day, since the Bridge first opened? May 24, 1883."

"No, Will, I did not know that."

"Well, it did," he replied, warming to his subject with child-like enthusiasm. "And that it's the longest suspension bridge in the world, and it took more than thirteen years to build?"

"I must confess that I didn't know any of that, either."

"Then it's probably a safe bet that you also don't know the name of the man who designed it."

"You know what, Will, you're right – I can't imagine a safer bet than that." Will couldn't be sure, but he thought he detected a trace of sarcasm, or condescension, in her tone.

"Well," he continued, putting that thought out of his mind, "the great Brooklyn Bridge was designed by none other than the famous civil engineer, John Augustus Roebling."

That certainly got her attention. "Did you say Roebling? As in *Will Augustus Roebling?*"

"Yes, Kira, one and the same."

"Oh, my goodness! Are you any relation?"

"Actually, no, not as far as I can tell, anyway, and I have done some research on it. He is a direct German immigrant, as are my parents. Apparently, though, the Roebling surname in Germany is a fairly common one."

"Well, who knows? Maybe you *are* related." Her face lit up. "And you know what? If you are, maybe that partially explains your deep fascination with bridges. Especially this one."

"Hmm...I guess anything's possible. I do remember I was about seven when I first learned of the Bridge and John Roebling, and from then on I could not get enough of it. So who's to say whether there isn't some type of...hereditary connection, or if the name is merely a coincidence."

It was clear that Kira was very interested now. "What about Augustus? Why did your parents give you that one? Now there's a name that doesn't strike me as being very common."

Will smiled at her, sheepishly. "Well, Kira, believe it or not, I never asked them."

"Never asked them?" She looked at him quizzically. "Are you serious? That's so hard to believe – it just doesn't make any sense."

"You know, now that you mention it, I think you're absolutely right. I really can't explain it but, somehow or other, the subject just never came up, as odd as that seems at this point."

A few moments later he added, "Looking back now, I guess as a child I was always intrigued by how things worked. And for whatever reason, the engineering aspect of building a suspension bridge was, oh, I don't know...irresistible to me."

Will could sense from her silence that Kira was losing interest in the conversation, so he brought it back around to the Roebling name, which she seemed to find so fascinating.

"And I suppose that since the similarity in our names never registered when I was a kid, I just never gave it much thought as I got older. I admit now, though, it does seem a bit strange that I didn't wonder more about the whole thing, especially in light of all the research I did. I'll definitely ask my folks about it the next time I write or visit. I'm thinking of making a trip back home to see them, maybe sometime in the spring." He glanced over quickly, giving her a shy grin and a little wink. "And, who knows? By then you might be interested in asking them yourself."

"My goodness, wouldn't it just be something if you *are* related? Imagine me being able to tell everyone that my beau is a relative of someone so famous and important!"

Will chuckled. "Oh, well, now . . . I wouldn't go getting my hopes up, not just yet."

As they continued on across the Bridge, Will became reflective, wondering if it were even possible that she was really being serious. Could something like that really mean so much, and make such a difference to her?

It also did not escape his notice that she'd completely stepped over his inference that she might wish to accompany him to see his parents. He decided he'd chalk that up to the overall excitement of the day.

"What a charming little house," Kira remarked as they made their way up the front walk and onto the porch.

Will, opening the front door, called out, "Mrs. D, hello! We've arrived."

"Oh, welcome, welcome, I'm so glad that you're here!" she called back. "Come on out into the kitchen, won't you – I'm just now season-ing the pork chops."

Will helped Kira off with her wrap and hung it up on the wooden tree near the door.

Turning to greet them, Mrs. D exclaimed, "Land sakes, Kira! You are even lovelier than I imagined, and I imagined pretty lovely."

"Why, thank-you so much, Mrs. Duncan," she said, her face light-ing up as a slight blush came into her cheeks.

"Oh, we don't stand on formality so much around this house. Why don't you go ahead and call me Mrs. D, like young Will here does."

"'Young Will,' is it? How interesting . . . ," she teased, arching an eyebrow in his direction. Now it was Will's turn to blush a bit.

"Here, come on over and sit down at the table, the two of you. Let me get you each a glass of wine to enjoy while I finish up this seasoning. Then we can all go into the sitting room and relax a bit. Would you prefer red or white?"

"I'll have white, please."

"Yes, white will be fine for me too," Will agreed.

Mrs. D finished up at the stove while Kira and Will sipped their wine. A minute later the three of them were sitting comfortably in the parlour, Kira and Will on the loveseat and Mrs. D in the easy chair by the fireplace. The room was warm without being stifling. The combination of overstuffed chintz sofas and chairs and gleaming wooden furniture created a cozy, inviting atmosphere which always made Will feel right at home.

"So, Kira, I would love to know, from an 'insider's' perspective . . . what is it really like being a dancer and aspiring actress? Will has been telling me how competitive it is for you out there."

Kira seemed happy that the conversation had turned to her and her career. "Oh, yes, and sometimes I get so discouraged," she began eagerly. "When I graduated from the Academy last June, I fully expected that it would take awhile to work my way up to some really good parts. I knew I'd have to start out in something small, maybe as a dancer or in a non-speaking or non-singing part, before getting the chance to act, which is really my goal. But I audition and audition and audition, and, with one small exception, have yet to get any part at all, which has been *so* frustrating. Not to mention disappointing. And to tell you the truth, Mrs. D, the more I see, the more I don't want to see."

"Oh?"

"What I mean is, it just seems as if the deck is really stacked against someone like me. So many of the girls I meet, really nice girls, otherwise, are, umm, well, how do I say this – willing to trade certain 'favors' to get ahead." Here, she paused and shook her head, frowning. "Besides being so ugly, it's just so darned unfair."

"Well, whatever you do, my dear, do not compromise your morals or your integrity. Don't give in. You're young, there's plenty of time. And with your natural assets, if you continue to work hard at your craft and do things the right way, I'm sure you'll have a long, successful, and satisfying career ahead of you."

"Well, thank-you, I really appreciate you saying that, and I couldn't agree with you more about not compromising. Incidentally, Will says the same thing." She smiled as she glanced over at him. "I'm certainly not about to try and get to the top that way, don't worry, Will. But, Mrs. D, you should know, as far as the industry is concerned, at twenty-two I am not considered so young anymore. We girls have a shelf-life as they say and, unfortunately, it's not a very long one at that. If you don't make it in this business by the time you're twenty-four or -five, word gets out that there must be something wrong with you. You'd be amazed by just how much corruption there really is – physical favors, payoffs, political favors, who knows what else. Believe it or not, the majority of the girls out there, vying for the same roles I audition for, are younger than I am, by at least a year or two."

Apparently at a loss for anything helpful to offer in response to this, Mrs. D simply nodded, smiling sympathetically. After a moment, she changed the subject.

"So, Kira, did you two enjoy your walk here to-day?"

"Actually, yes, quite a bit. It was certainly long and, therefore, a little tiring but, overall, most pleasant."

"That's good. Then am I correct in assuming the two of you have worked up something of an appetite?"

"Oh, yes, indeed," she answered brightly. Will responded with a big smile and an affirmative nod.

They moved to the dining room table, which had been laid out in Wilma's best linens and china.

"Well, Mrs. D, I must say – you're certainly putting on the dog to-day," Will kidded gently. Out of the corner of his eye, he caught the appraising glance Kira cast over the two of them. He was gratified to see her smiling warmly at their obvious camaraderie.

"Oh, Will," Mrs. D clucked, tapping him lightly on the arm as she reddened a bit. "You know this is the first real dinner party I've given since you moved in. You certainly didn't expect me to serve a guest as special as Kira on our everyday ware, did you?"

And with that, the three of them dug in. Will and Kira spent the next hour oohing and aahing over a succession of delightful dishes. When Mrs. D brought out the last course, an enticing home-baked pumpkin pie topped with whipped cream, Kira sat back after one bite, shaking her head and smiling.

"Well Will, you certainly did not exaggerate. Mrs. D, allow me to reiterate – you certainly are an amazing cook." Mrs. D ducked her head in modest acceptance of the compliment, grinning sweetly.

Chatting easily, they remained seated comfortably around the table with their coffee for some time, talking mostly about Kira's life and interests. At around nine-thirty, she signalled to Will that she was ready to go.

→ ✳ ←

It was nearly midnight by the time Will made it back home. Fortunately, he'd been assigned the late shift this week, and could, therefore, afford to sleep in. Mrs. D was still up waiting for him, and seemed very happy they'd have the chance for a nice chat and a good gossip.

"Well, Will, I think she's very nice," she began, once he'd settled in, obviously anticipating his question and jumping in without much in the way of preliminaries. "And it's easy to see that she's had a fine upbringing."

Will took a sip from the glass of water she had brought him, eyeing her carefully. "Well, yes, you're right . . . as always, I might add. But I think by now I know you better than that, Mrs. D," he said, eyebrows arched.

"Whatever are you talking about, Will?" She put down her own glass and stared frankly at him.

"I'm talking about you holding back, giving me your polite assessment . . . not telling me what you really think."

"Now, you hold on there just a minute," she said, waggling her finger at him. "I do indeed think she's very nice and well-brought-up."

Will held up his right palm. "Oh, to be sure, I'm not arguing with that assessment at all." He laced his fingers, lightly tapping the tips of his forefingers together. "What I *am* saying is that there's something else you're *not* saying."

Mrs. D laid both palms on the table and sat for a long moment regarding him intently before giving a small sigh and continuing. "Oh, alright then, since you insist. I suppose I'd have to say I found her, well . . . I don't know . . . kind of guarded. Also, maybe a little bit spoiled, and just a tad self-centered."

Her words really hit home for Will, and with quite a wallop. Suddenly, all those niggling little thoughts he'd been suppressing for months came clamoring to the surface, and his confusion and disappointment were written all over his face.

"Oh, Will, dear, please don't take on so. I surely never meant to upset you, and I do regret my bluntness. Sometimes, when one just blurts out the truth like that, it can sound a bit harsher than was intended. Kira really is a very nice girl, not to mention an incredibly lovely one and, truth be told, aren't we all a little bit self-centered, when it comes right down to it?"

"You know, I think you're right, there, Mrs. D. And again, as always." The small smile he gave her lightened his face, at least a little, and she smiled back warmly as she reached over to give his hand a pat.

A few moments passed before he continued. "It's just that . . . I don't know . . . you put into words, and rather easily at that, something I've been sensing for some time now, but hadn't quite been able to articulate. And I guess it was hard for me to hear."

A tear had formed in Will's eye. If Mrs. D saw it, though, she discreetly chose not to comment, hurrying instead to reassure him.

"But Will, don't you see? Even with all that, there's nothing to be overly concerned about. I mean, she's young, she's just finding her way. Which is only that much harder for her to do *because* she's been so sheltered and spoiled. And there's still plenty of time for her to grow out of that – especially with your fine influence. Didn't you tell me that was one of the reasons Alex thought the two of you would be good together?"

"Actually it was, come to think of it, now that you mention it." He paused reflectively. "But I did want to ask you, when you said you found her 'kind of guarded,' what did you mean by that, exactly?"

"Ah, yes, that," she said, giving a quick nod. "Alright then, how's this for an idea: what say you and I sit for a spell and have ourselves a little nightcap – some brandy, perhaps? – and we'll see where the conversation takes us."

"I say that sounds like a fantastic idea, Mrs. D." He smiled at her gratefully. "But I'm thinking maybe you should make mine a double," he added, with a look of mischief.

When they'd each warmed themselves up with a few sips of brandy, Mrs. D began by telling Will she thought he might have missed several clues in some of what Kira had said, or more precisely not said, about her relationship with her father, especially when it came to her life before entering the Academy. Will agreed. He'd been so busy reveling in the fact that his two favorite ladies were having a conversation at all, and getting on so well in the process, that pretty much everything else went right over his head.

Mrs. D nodded in understanding. She then continued by saying that she could tell Kira's father, while a good man, had probably been quite demanding as she was growing up. In her experience, when a young girl had to work so hard to gain her father's approval, she often grew up somewhat unsure of herself, sometimes remaining that way even into adulthood. The bottom-line, in Mrs. D's opinion, was that Kira, though appearing poised and confident on the outside, deep-down lacked a basic, healthy, strong image of herself. Therefore, to guard against life's fear and confusion, in other words to protect herself, she is sometimes cautious and reserved with people, where she might otherwise be open and free.

Mrs. D told Will the most important thing for him to glean from all this was that he should not take any of it personally. "In all probability, Will, Kira puts up these walls with everyone she knows, even Alex. It's just an automatic way of being, something she really can't control."

Will gazed at her with deep admiration, head shaking ever-so-slightly, side-to-side. "At this point, Mrs. D, I simply must ask the obvious question: has anyone ever told you that you missed your true calling? You sound far more like a Manhattan psychiatrist than a Brooklyn landlady to me," he kidded her gently.

She laughed, throwing back her shaking head. "Oh, my dear young Will. Well, when you've lived as long as I have, I suppose you do tend to gain a few morsels of wisdom along the way. In the 'final analysis,' if you'll pardon the pun, I guess it's just life's experience talking," she finished, with a wink. Will rewarded her clever play on words with an exaggerated eye roll and appreciative chuckle.

Once they'd settled back down, Mrs. D went on to explain that, rather than meaning that he and Kira should go their separate ways, or anything of the sort, Will could instead use this new-found insight to improve the quality of their relationship. They were both still so young and inexperienced; if they truly loved each other, working through these difficult and uncomfortable areas now could only pay great dividends later.

At the close of their "session," Will was made to understand that he was the only person to whom Mrs. D would confide such sensitive information. He knew she trusted him well enough to be assured that he'd receive it solely in the positive manner in which it was intended.

"I want to thank you so much, Mrs. D," Will said warmly, reaching over to give her hand a squeeze. They rose from the table. "This has really been an enormous help to me. Not only that, you've given me plenty to think about and grow with." He started to turn away from her, then reversed course and waved his right hand expansively as he said, "Oh, and by all means, please feel free to add your 'fee' to this month's rent."

"Oh, pshaw," she retorted, slapping him playfully on the arm as they both laughed. Finally, he gave her a big hug, and wished her a pleasant good-night.

"A very good-night to you too, Will, dear. And sweet dreams, my boy," she called out softly as he headed for the stairs.

CHAPTER 6

MONDAY, DECEMBER 5, 1887

Will eased his head to the side to glance at the bedside clock, wearily noting that it was still only ten-thirty. Plenty of time to get himself going if he wanted to make it into the Office for the start of his shift. He had awoken sometime earlier with congestion, chills, and a fever of nearly one-hundred-and-three. Instead of feeling better than he had yesterday, as he'd been hoping, he actually felt much worse.

He heard the squeak of his bedroom-door hinges, followed by the sound of Mrs. D tiptoeing over to the bed. When she saw that he was awake, she smiled warmly at him as she reached over to feel his forehead and cheek.

"Alright then, Will, that does it. You are *not* going in to the Office to-day, and I won't hear another word about it. You may work on your research here at home if you like, but you are not going out in this wet, stormy weather, sick as you are, and that's that. Sergeant Long can certainly get along well enough without you for one measly day." Mrs. D folded both arms across her chest and gave her head a quick snap for emphasis, which Will knew meant she'd brook no disagreement.

"You're right," Will managed weakly, forced to agree, "I do believe that he can. But I'll need to get word to him somehow that I won't be able to make it in to-day."

"Well, that's no problem at all. I already have the telephone exchange for your Office, so I'll just take myself over to Mrs. Potts' and call him from there. I'll simply explain that you're sick as a dog and cannot leave the house in your condition, and that's all there is to it. And then I'll rush right back here and make you some of my famous chicken soup. It's from a special recipe that's been handed down through the generations in my family, going back at least as far as my great-great-grandmother, and contains a secret mixture of herbs and spices. You'll see. A few bowls of that beneficial broth will have you on the mend in no time at all."

"Mrs. D, you are an angel sent straight from Heaven, about that there can be no doubt. Oddly enough, though, I can't seem to recall anything in our lease agreement about the kindly landlady devoting herself to the care of the sick tenant."

"Now, don't you start getting all mushy with me, young man," she responded, giving his shoulder a playful shove. "I tell you what – why don't you go take yourself a nice hot bath while I head on over to the Potts' house to make that call."

Blanche Potts and her husband Charley had moved into the house next door on Sands just a few short weeks after Walter's untimely passing. For the first few months after that, it seemed to Wilma that Blanche was constantly at her side, yet without ever being intrusive. She was always ready with a hug, a good hot cup of tea, a warm casserole, or just a shoulder to cry on. From the depths of her grief, Wilma felt a profound gratitude for her new friend's unfailing kindness and generosity.

As the years passed, their initial fondness grew into something closer and deeper, till they were like loving sisters who were also best friends. Blanche often expressed how grateful she was for their closeness, as her two children were already grown and living on their own. Often-times, Wilma wished that her Walter had gotten the chance to know Charley, as well; she knew they would have been great friends. Of course, thoughts like that got her to day-dreaming, wistfully, about how wonderful life with Walter would have been, had they been blessed with the opportunity to reach their golden years together.

Charley Potts had worked on sea-faring vessels for more than four decades now. He'd started out when he was just a gangly teenager, swabbing decks as an Ordinary Seaman, and worked his way steadily up through the ranks. For the past fifteen years, he'd worked as a harbor pilot. A harbor pilot had the job of shepherding large ships – usually transatlantic liners – safely into port. While American ships were given the choice to accept or decline a pilot's assistance, the service was mandatory for all foreign ships. Fees were earned on a sliding scale, depending on the size of the ship piloted.

Earning a harbor-pilot license was a grueling, nine-year process, and the business was highly competitive. One might logically assume the occupation would be lucrative but, strangely enough, such was not the case. Pilots almost universally chose this unusual vocation first, because of their enduring love for the sea, and second, because they seldom had to be away from home for more than two days at a time.

Harbor pilots relied on small sail boats, called pilot boats, to transport them out to the incoming ships. Each boat usually carried several pilots, at least two or three, and sometimes as many as five or six – especially on Saturdays, the busiest day for arriving foreign vessels.

The pilot boats would gather off Sandy Hook, New Jersey, waiting for that first glimpse of faint smoke on the horizon, the unmistakable indicator of an incoming ocean liner. Then, in a wild frenzy, they would race to be the first to get to the ship. As it was not unusual for a half-dozen pilot boats to be competing for a single vessel, collisions and loss of life were the inevitable, if only occasional, outcome. There was no denying that it was a brutal and dangerous profession.

Almost as if to add insult to injury, on any given day a pilot had no guarantee he'd earn a nickel in fees. To begin with, his boat had to be the first to arrive and, even then, he might be fourth or fifth in line behind his fellow pilots. Often, there weren't enough vessels to go around, and the boats would return with more than one unlucky pilot still aboard. And now-a-days, to make matters even worse, the exorbitant fee for the telephone subscription, without which a pilot would only lose out on more opportunities, had to be paid regularly – whether he was or not.

Despite the danger and the daily grind, Charley Potts had never even considered looking for an alternate way to earn a living. He knew he would not be able to pilot forever. Fortunately, however, he felt he still had a few good years left in him.

After he'd had his bath and soup, Will did begin to notice an improvement in the way he felt. His congestion had eased somewhat and the chills were nearly gone. In fact, he felt good enough to sit up at his desk for awhile and get some work done on his forecasting system. He'd left the Office Saturday armed with the transcribed copies of the weather observations from the past several days, telegraphed into Headquarters from across the country and Canada. He'd also brought a fresh supply of the large, blank base maps on which he would plot the obs, as well as the detailed notes he'd made over the previous two days on the movement of the high, wispy cirrus clouds.

Will knew that before he unveiled his forecasting system to Sergeant Long, he would need to fine-tune and verify it using a number of winter-type storms. He'd been able to use one such storm to date, and was hopeful that to-day's rainstorm would be the second. After spending so much of the past day-and-a-half sick in bed, he felt heartened at the thought that he'd now be able to get some work done at last.

After only about an hour, though, having gotten scarcely halfway through creating his surface-map depictions, he suddenly experienced a wave of lethargy so strong it sent him straight back to bed.

In that semi-conscious, semi-dream state often experienced just before falling off to sleep, Will imagined himself engaged in a conversation with his childhood hero, Joseph Henry. He was so grateful that he finally had the chance to express his profound gratitude for the enormous contribution the renowned scientist had made to the field of meteorology.

Will was convinced that were it not for Henry, the system for communicating meteorological observations across the country would still be in its primitive stages. He believed that without Henry's selfless dedication and tireless effort, to-day's technologically advanced system would still be five, or even ten, years away. What imagination and insight this genius of a man had possessed! Not only did he have the clear vision and wherewithal to set up the observation reporting network around the country, he'd been instrumental in developing the electromagnetic relay – the very basis of the telegraph.

And, after all, without the telegraph, where in the world would we be? The Stone Age is where!

I know one thing for sure, Will thought as he drifted off, *I know that if it hadn't been for Joseph Henry, I never would have had the opportunity to develop my own forecasting system. I can't thank him enough for that, and will always be deeply indebted to him.*

Mrs. D watched with interest as Will shuffled slowly into the kitchen, where she was busily preparing dinner. "Welcome, dear boy. By my calculation, you slept for at least five hours – I peeked through your door a little after one and saw that you were fast asleep."

"I know, that's amazing. I guess my body really did need the rest to aid in its recuperation. I can't seem to recall having slept so soundly in a very long time. And you know what else? I think I'm feeling quite a bit better now ... it must have been the soup ... could it really have been the soup?" He peered out the window. "Is it still raining out there?"

"No, the rain ended just before it got dark. The wind has shifted, and I think the storm is over." Mrs. D was proud of the forecasting acumen she'd gained over the past eight months, just from being around Will and paying attention. "And as far as your feeling better goes, you'd best believe the soup played a big part in it, of that I'm sure."

Mrs. D turned back to the stove, dinner plate in hand. "I made something special to-night, Will, in the hopes that you'd be able to take in some solid food, at last. What do you say to a meal of pot roast and mashed potatoes?"

"I say, 'Hallelujah, bring it on' – and, as ever, Mrs. D surely knows best." He gave her an exaggerated wink and the two of them shared a laugh as they sat down to enjoy their dinner.

→ ✳ ←

More than three weeks had now passed since Kira's last visit to Alex, when she had blown up at her. Finally realizing that an apology to her best friend was long overdue, and with no other demands on her time or attention this afternoon, Kira made her way over to Alex's apartment.

"Alex, my dearest friend, I do hope that you can forgive me. I never meant to say those things to you, at least not in the way that I said them. And I know now that what you said about me needing to be more open with Will was only your loving way of trying to support me in having a better relationship with him. And you were absolutely right, I *had* been keeping him at arm's length, at least to some degree. But I want you to know that I took what you said to heart. I've really been working on letting him in more, just as you encouraged me to."

"Oh, Kira, I'm so very glad to hear you say that. For goodness sake, we've never, never, gone three weeks without speaking to each other!

Let's not let that happen again, ever, no matter what the circumstances are. And I want you to know that I'm awfully sorry, too. I've come to see, with the clarity of vision that only comes with hindsight, of course, that I might have been a bit harsh in the things I said to you, as well."

Kira smiled, nodding her acceptance of Alex's apology, then suddenly brightened as she reached out to grasp both of Alex's hands. "Oh, and I simply cannot believe it's taken me this long to say, but better late than never, I suppose. I want to congratulate you and Frank on your decision to start a family, and offer you both my heart-felt best wishes. That really is something!"

"Gee, thanks, Kira, I really do appreciate it. Of course, we'll have to see how things go, but fertility certainly runs in both our families, so we are reasonably optimistic."

Kira's mind had already wandered on to the next subject: Will.

"You know, this seems like an appropriate time to fill you in on some very interesting thinking I've been doing lately, myself. About Will, that is," Kira said, smiling broadly, eyes sparkling. She paused here briefly for dramatic effect – a technique they both had learned from their training at the Academy. "I guess what it all comes down to is this," she went on, finally. "He really is 'the one,' Alex, I just know it. I think, maybe, I'm actually getting to the point where I'll soon be ready to settle down and get married, too."

"Kira, you don't say!" Alex's eyes grew wide. "Have the two of you had any discussion about that?"

"Well, no, not exactly; not even in so many words, really. But I can tell you this, things have certainly been getting more and more serious between the two of us."

"Well, that's just wonderful to hear, and I'm very happy for both of you. And I'll be sure to keep my fingers crossed."

Not at all convinced Kira had accurately assessed her relationship with Will, Alex wisely decided to "let sleeping dogs lie." For some reason, though, she couldn't shake the oddest feeling that, from Will's perspective, things might look somewhat different. Maybe even more than somewhat.

Still . . . maybe the time finally has come for us to extend that dinner invitation to them.

CHAPTER 7

WEDNESDAY, DECEMBER 14, 1887

Will had come up with the idea of sending the telegram while he'd been laid up at home with the flu. Or whatever the heck that bothersome illness had been. Last week's rainstorm had let him resume the verification process for his forecasting system which, for some reason, made him think about reaching out to his former mentor at Yale, Professor Elias Loomis. After all, it was Professor Loomis who had first suggested that it might be possible to use physics and mathematics to actually predict the weather. Thus, in a very real sense, it could be said that Loomis' inquiry had been the genesis of Will's system.

When Will answered the Office telephone, just after three in the afternoon, he could barely contain his excitement when he heard the caller say, "Hello. This is Elias Loomis calling. May I speak with Will Roebling, please?"

"Professor! Professor Loomis! This is he . . . it's me . . . this is Will!" His heart was fairly racing.

"By George, Will, so it is. I'm so glad I reached you.

"Me too, Professor, me too. Thank-you so much for calling."

"While you're certainly welcome, Will, it is really I who should be thanking you, for having sent me that telegram in the first place. Let me start by saying that I'm interested in hearing how you've been and, of course, all about this forecasting system you made mention of. I want you to know that I think about you often, and wonder how life with the Signal Service is treating you. I was quite pleased to hear that you are now in the New York Field Office, so I would say congratulations are in order."

"Why, thank-you, sir!"

"Oh, and by the way, I'm sorry it's taken me so long to get back to you. I was out of town all of last week, and returned only yesterday to find your telegram waiting for me. As I recall, though, you indicated there might be some issue with confidentiality, and that you might not be able to speak freely?"

"Well, we're in luck, Professor. I happen to be the only one in the Office at the moment, and will be for the next hour or so, so that won't be a problem at all."

"Wonderful, Will, that's just wonderful. And, please, I think it's time you started calling me Elias."

Will started by giving the Professor a thumb-nail sketch of his home-life in Brooklyn and work-life in Manhattan. Then, for the next twenty minutes, he dove into a detailed discussion of his forecasting system and how he'd developed it. He began by recounting his assignment at the U.S. Army Signal Service Headquarters, specifically his work on Professor Cleveland Abbe's massive, ongoing research project to catalogue years of weather observations across North America. He described the painstaking process of compiling the observations from the United States and Canada and, more importantly, how, during that process, the creative spark for his forecasting system was born. The precise phrase he used to describe this burst of imagination was "the catalyst for the coalescence of all the otherwise extraneous knowledge amassed over a lifetime of immersion in empirical and theoretical study of the weather."

Loomis' silence was one Will couldn't seem to read. Was he listening intently? Perhaps he was wondering if Will were altogether in his right mind. Either way, Will chose to press forward.

He described the innovative process he'd developed to improve upon the standard surface map.[4] Basically, it involved adding the degree to which the pressure, temperature, and wind direction had changed at each station since the prior observation. He introduced this new feature by drawing isopleths for these three new parameters. The resultant map elegantly portrayed the primary elements he needed to predict future storms.

He then brought the discussion current, explaining that by studying the observations from across the country which had preceded recent, local storms, he'd been afforded the opportunity to fine-tune and verify his system. He told Loomis he'd need only a few more large-scale storms to complete this verification process, after which he would be ready for the "big reveal:" showing his system to Sergeant Long.

Will had saved the best for last. He was excited to share with the Professor what he considered the *pièce de résistance,* of which he was particularly proud: the ingenious method he'd devised to track the movement of cirrus clouds. He traced the deductive reasoning which had led to his understanding of the crucial role that wind speed at the height of those clouds (about eighteen-thousand feet) played in storm development, or cyclogenesis, and how his system took this critical factor into account. Will knew that with the possible exception of Cleveland Abbe, Elias Loomis was almost certainly the only man alive who would be able to fully understand what he was talking about.

"Well, Will," Loomis began, when it was obvious the dissertation had come to a close, "I must say that certainly sounds most impressive." The Professor spoke in a deliberate, even tone, seeming to choose his words carefully. "Please do be sure to keep me informed as to how

---

4 The standard surface map showed the observed barometric pressure, temperature, and wind (speed and direction) at each station, all recorded at a common time. It also included an array of *isopleths* – the technical term for those curvy lines on a map connecting points of equal value for a specific entity or physical quality. The standard map depicted two types of isopleths: *isobars,* delineating areas of equal pressure (high or low); and *isotherms,* delineating areas of equal temperature.

things progress. Should this system of yours work as well as you project, my young friend, I'd say it's very likely that you are destined for fame and fortune. But I'm afraid you'll really have to excuse me just now, or I'll run the risk of being late for the next class I'm to teach this afternoon."

Will took down the Professor's telephone number, and they exchanged pleasant good-byes. Just after hanging up the receiver, though, the strangest feeling came over him. He was experiencing that same odd sensation he'd had several times before with Kira – a vague presentiment that Loomis, although appearing completely sincere outwardly, was perhaps, underneath it all, actually being a trifle condescending.

Then again, a man with the enormous stature of an Elias Loomis might find it incumbent upon himself to maintain a certain reserve when discussing his field of expertise. Especially when the ideas being discussed had the potential to cause a revolution in that field – ideas put forth by a relative novice, no less.

Will snorted aloud at such hubris. *Me? A revolutionary?* He made his way back to his desk, shaking his head and having a good laugh at himself.

CHAPTER 8

It was shortly before one o'clock on Will's first day back in the Office following a much-needed respite. Even though Christmas had fallen on a Sunday this year, the holiday was observed on Monday, the twenty-sixth, and only a skeleton crew was required that day in the Signal Service Field Offices. By using only one of his precious-few vacation days on Saturday, Will had been able to stretch his holiday into a three-day break.

Two weeks earlier, when he had seen the assignment list giving him Monday off, Will's first thought was that he must have somehow earned some type of seniority. But he quickly realized that couldn't be the case; nobody had transferred into New York or been hired on since his arrival from Headquarters nearly nine months ago. In actuality then, as he clearly had the least seniority, there had to be some other explanation for his good fortune. Thinking he'd be much better off not looking a gift horse in the mouth, Will chose to keep his counsel, at least for the moment, and see how things transpired.

It didn't take him long to discover the real reason he'd been so "lucky."

"Will," Sergeant Long called out to him, punching the time clock as he arrived, "you're just the man I'm looking for. I hope you enjoyed a good three-day holiday. Did you?"

"Why, yes sir, I did, and thank-you for asking. I spent Christmas Eve with Kira's family in New Jersey, and Sunday at home in Brooklyn with Mrs. Duncan – Mrs. D, as I like to call her. I'm happy to report that we all had a very good time."

"That's nice, that's nice," Long responded, obviously not really caring all that much about the answer to what seemed a perfunctory inquiry. "Please come into my office, will you, just as soon as you get settled in. There's something important I need to discuss with you."

"Yes sir, of course. I'll be there in just a minute."

Will wondered what the Sergeant could possibly want to talk to him about. After hanging up his coat he got himself another cup of coffee. He had gotten into the habit of doing that lately: one cup before he left home, and another just as soon as he arrived at the Office, regardless of which shift he was working. Mug in hand, he knocked on Long's door.

"Come on in, Will. Here, have a seat, make yourself comfortable." Long removed some papers from one of the visitor's chairs, then took his own seat behind the desk and cleared his throat before beginning.

"You might or might not be aware of this, Will, but once-a-year, during the week between Christmas and New Year's Eve, we open our Office to the public for tours each day, from noon till five o'clock. The people will come in droves, many of them simply wanting to see the view of the City from the tower here. Others will be more interested in learning about the instruments and observing the staff as they go about performing their various functions. And we are under strict orders from Headquarters to be at all times polite, cooperative, welcoming, and gracious. And to show them anything and everything they might wish to see." Here Long paused for a moment, giving him the oddest little smile. "And, Will," he continued, "I bet you'll never guess what."

Will couldn't begin to imagine what the Sergeant had up his sleeve. "What would that be, sir?" he asked, guardedly.

"Well, my boy, this year I've decided that I'm going to put you in charge of the visitor detail. Isn't that exciting?"

As Will had no idea whether his boss was being serious or joking, he decided he'd better play it safe and go along. "Why, yes, of course it is."

"I want you to be the 'point man' as far as our interactions with the public go – and that's for the entire week, Will."

Oh, my good God – he's actually serious!

"You can explain all about the instruments, what we do here, our connection to Washington City and all the other Offices nationwide, et cetera, et cetera. Really play it up as to how we are all here to 'serve the public.' Headquarters maintains that this is a very important function of this Office, being that it is New York you know, and we certainly don't want to disappoint the boys down there. It was once explained to me that what happens in this City can have a huge impact on Congressional funding – logically so, as far as I'm concerned. And I'm sure I don't have to tell you about the politics of Congressional funding."

"No, boss, I understand completely. And I'm on board, of course." Will forced a broad smile to cover his deep chagrin. "I'll be happy to take care of it. You can count on me."

"That's great to hear, Will. Oh, and I hope this won't be a problem for you, but even though you're officially on the late shift this week, I'd really like you to be here before noon every day."

Will had been in the Army long enough to recognize an order when he heard one, even if it were couched as a request. "Absolutely, sir, that won't be any problem at all for me."

Long gave Will a satisfied smile. "Well, I'm certainly glad that that's all settled now. Oh, and Downstairs tells me that your first group of about twenty-five has been patiently awaiting your arrival . . . so good luck – and 'break a leg,' as the theatre folks say."

It was widely known among the New York Field Office veteran staff that Francis Long had, in years past, not only excelled in creating a very positive public image for the Signal Service during these holiday tours, but also fairly reveled in doing so. A physically imposing, burly man with a full head of striking red hair, Sergeant Long's larger-than-life demeanor and unique story-telling ability more often than not captivated his audiences, making him something of a modern-day legend around the Service.

Adding to the popularity of Long's tours was both the exquisite view from atop the Equitable Building, the tallest structure in Manhattan, and the considerable novel appeal of riding in one of the world's first passenger elevators. All things considered, then, the staff was quite surprised to hear that this year Long had chosen to replace himself with Will as Tour Guide for the week. The delegation of such a plum and coveted assignment, especially to a relative newcomer like Will, was certainly a testament to the Sergeant's faith in the young man's talent and ability.

Much to his own surprise, Will did not disappoint. In fact, after the first two or three tours, he warmed to the task, developing his own unique style of presentation which was very well-received by the public. He entertained his audiences by interjecting hilarious anecdotes of life at the Signal Service School of Instruction at Fort Myer, where the young recruits were first sent to master the skills and discipline the U.S. Army would demand of them. And his broad, deep knowledge of meteorology served him extremely well when it came to answering technical questions, even the occasional sophisticated one, posed by a generally curious populace.

Ironically, as the week drew to a close, Will discovered that he was actually feeling a bit let down at the thought that he was giving his final few tours.

CHAPTER 9

Will was nervously making a final check of the notes and other materials he'd prepared for the Office's inaugural seminar as Sergeant Long and the rest of the senior staff settled into their chairs. Long had announced last week that a series of eight, two-hour seminars would be held each Saturday morning at nine o'clock. A presentation on Will's system for forecasting severe, extratropical east-coast storms was to be the first. Each subsequent seminar would feature a presentation from a renowned expert, invited from a select group of distinguished universities across the country, on some relevant meteorological topic. The Sergeant had made it abundantly clear that attendance at all eight seminars was mandatory.

It all began about six weeks ago, after Long had received the confirmation from Headquarters which ended months of speculation and rumors:

"Beginning Monday, April 2, 1888, Washington City will no longer be making indications for the entire country. Instead, this responsibility will be shared by Headquarters and six newly appointed Regional Offices."

The New York Field Office was one of them.

It took three weeks for Headquarters to approve Long's new organizational plan. He and the heads of the five other designated Field Offices had been asked to submit evidence that they could continue to perform their observational duties while taking on this massive new responsibility. As soon as he'd received the approval, Sergeant Long announced to his people both the name change – the New York Field

Office would henceforth be called the New York Regional Office – and the enormity of their new mission.

Will had been elated the moment he'd heard about this latest turn of events. He knew immediately that this would be the perfect time to arrange a sit-down with Long to give him an overview of his forecasting system, even though he was still in the process of completing some fine-tuning.

After having listened to Will's initial fifteen-minute synopsis of his forecasting system, Long had retained only three things. First, Will had conceived it while on assignment under Abbe at Headquarters. Second, he had developed it based on the compilation of years of meteorological observations from across North America. And third, it involved the ability to predict advancing storms along the east coast by extrapolating conditions from upwind (western) stations.

While all that was well and good, Long basically had no idea how Will's system actually worked. At the same time, though, he could sense that it probably would work – making it enormously applicable to the exciting new mission of his recently anointed Regional Office.

Long was thunderstruck. It was a remarkable coincidence – almost eerie, really – that his Office had received the assignment to begin forecasting at practically the precise moment Will was completing the development of a ground-breaking system designed exactly for that purpose. He was eager to learn as much about it as he possibly could, and was thus inspired to create the weekly seminar training series – with Will as the first guest speaker.

As everyone waited for Will to begin, Long took the opportunity to reflect on how grateful he was that his close friend, and the Signal Service's Chief Officer, General Adolphus Greely, had given him the great gift of approving Will's transfer to the New York Field Office, nine months earlier. He looked up at Will and smiled, eagerly anticipating learning more about this prognosticative product so cleverly created by the Signal Services' resident meteorological savant, as by now he'd taken to thinking of the bright young man.

Sergeant Long could not have known just how extraordinarily sophisticated Will's system was, or the many hundreds of hours it had taken him to develop and refine it, or the endless trial-and-error verification process that he had so painstakingly implemented to fine-tune it. But he and select members of his staff were about to get their first glimpse.

Looking out on Long and all the other senior staffers gathered in the large conference room, patiently waiting for him to begin, Will flashed back for an instant to his halcyon days at Yale College and the encouragement he'd received from a number of his professors to choose teaching as a career. The thought ran through his mind that this is what it would have been like had he gone down that path. Feeling as nervous as he did right now, he was grateful he didn't have to do this every day.

"So ...," he began haltingly, measuring his words carefully, trying hard to overcome his jitters, "Sergeant Long has asked me to give you an overview of the forecasting system I've developed, and continue to refine, since the beginning of my assignment at Headquarters, just over two years ago now. As some of you might know, after graduating the Fort I was lucky enough to be singled out to assist the great Cleveland Abbe in his ongoing research project, which afforded me this extraordinary opportunity."

His nerves starting to calm a bit, Will took a few relaxing breaths, then began to describe the project he'd worked on for Abbe, in which he'd compiled the meteorological records from all the reporting stations in the world between January 1883 and November 1886. He told how he had made notes of the observations for the several days preceding each of fourteen major storms which had impacted the Northeast during this period. And, for those days leading up to each storm, he discussed how he had plotted detailed weather maps for the nation, three-times-per-day, based on the notes he'd made. He spent at least fifteen minutes detailing why changes in surface pressure, temperature, and wind direction were so important in understanding cyclogenesis, and how he used this information as a key predictive tool in his forecasting system.

At about the fifty-minute mark of his talk, which included the presentation of complex charts, tables, and graphs, Will opened the floor for questions, expecting a deluge. He was, therefore, at a complete loss when not a single hand was raised. Surely *someone* must have a question, he thought.

Will shifted his weight uneasily as he stood at the podium. It simply had never occurred to him that his audience felt intimidated by this overload of information, too much in awe to do anything but stare helplessly, glassy-eyed. After a few moments of this strained and bewildering silence, he did the only thing he could think of: he soldiered on.

"Right. Now, I've saved the best for last. The truth of the matter is, I could never get the accuracy of my system to a point where I was quite satisfied. Which, I suppose, was one of the main reasons I had been keeping it to myself."

He put up another table. "I applied all types of statistical tests, but no matter how I parameterized the measured variables, I could never get a satisfactory correlation or, in statistical jargon, coefficient of determination. I knew this meant there must be a key variable missing from my calculations, some relevant information which wasn't being recorded during the observations. After months of fruitless specula-tion, suddenly, one day, right before my transfer here last April, it hit me like a ton of bricks."

He was so excited at this point that he had to take a moment to compose himself. "It turned out to be something so obvious, I feel a bit embarrassed now about how long it took me to see it."

He did not notice his audience's sideward, questioning glances at one another.

"How can any system of forecasting be worth its weight in salt if it ignores what happens in the atmosphere above? I mean, it's intuitive that the weather which occurs here at ground-level is . . . well, dictated, for lack of a better word, by what goes on up there." He pointed and gazed upward at the ceiling. Comically, his mesmerized listeners looked up in unison, as well.

"And, of course, despite all our great technological advances of the past decade, we still have no way of actually measuring what is happening aloft."[5]

"I don't pretend to fully understand it," he went on, "but based on observation and incorporation into my predictive system, it would seem a virtual certainty that the air flow at heights well above the earth's surface plays an integral role in the weather here on the ground." He noticed one or two heads slowly moving up and down in apparent agreement. He took that to be a good sign.

Will paused at this point calling for a brief bathroom break, then proceeded to exit the conference room. Amazingly, not another soul stirred. There was a lot of quiet chatter, but each person remained riveted in his seat, apparently having no desire to risk being responsible for delaying continuation of the presentation.

Five minutes later, Will returned to the podium to resume his lecture. "So, let's take a moment to review what I've covered up till this point. During my time at Headquarters, working with years of collected observations and created surface maps, I was unable to nail down a satisfactory correlation between my predictive system and the occurrence of significant storms. Compounding matters was the fact that I was forced to deduce, days in advance, key forecasting information about these cyclones and the weather conditions. Remember, I was

---

5 In 1909, free-rising balloons would be employed for the first time to measure atmospheric conditions high above the earth's surface.

constrained by having to work with only recorded observations. I needed the wealth of information that can only be provided by observing actual 'live' storms, so I could monitor the key features or characteristics I wanted my system to simulate. For example, when the storm would begin and end, when the cold front would pass, how strong the winds would be, or how much rain or snow would fall – things which simply could not be determined from the sparse observations that had been recorded only once-every-eight-hours. I needed to have these real storms so I could carefully monitor and record all the key aspects that I wanted my system to account for. Are you with me?"

This time he noted a few friendly heads nodding definitively in the affirmative.

"Okay, good, that's good." Will smiled out at his captivated audience, giving them a few quick nods in return.

"So, as I was saying, the final piece to my system was developed just nine months ago, right before my transfer up here to New York. It involved incorporating the upper-air data. Keep in mind, of course, that no upper-air information of any kind is recorded in the observations. Therefore, if I wanted to improve my system enough to make it worth using, I had no choice but to apply it to real-life storms, where I would be able to rely on my own first-hand, all-encompassing observations.

"And I felt I was ready."

Now he noticed a few smiles gracing the attentive faces of his listeners. That was definitely a good response.

"I could observe the storms myself, and then go back to verify, or validate, the system by incorporating all the information, including the upper-air wind data, using the laborious, but time-tested, trial-and-error approach to determine which combination provided the best results. I tested at least thirty unique combinations for each storm, to see which resulted in the most accurate prediction, or forecast. I did this for a total of nine storms – seven I classified as minor and two as major." His audience now remained perfectly still, clearly having grasped enough of the information presented to see at least a glimpse of the system's awesome potential.

"You will recall," he continued, now really catching his stride, "that cirrus clouds generally occur at heights somewhere around eighteen- or twenty-thousand feet. From our meteorology courses, you will also recall that the mid-point of the atmosphere – and by that I mean that height above sea-level at which equal amounts of air lie above and below – this mid-point is, on average, somewhere around eighteen-thousand-plus feet.

"I speculated, and recent advances in theoretical meteorology confirm, that this represents a very important level of the atmosphere. And, if there were a way for me to estimate the wind velocity at this height – that's wind speed *and* direction – and factor it into my system, well, I might be able to dramatically improve its predictive skills. Are you still with me?"

Will was heartened to note that at least half the assembly of eight was now clearly acknowledging that they were.

"So what I had to do was come up with a reliable way of estimating how the velocity of the cirrus clouds changes over time as the storm approaches. Incidentally," he added, "cirrus clouds almost always appear between two and three days before a significant storm." He wisely decided not to delve into a discussion on why this was so; first, because he was already nearing the end of the seminar's time allotment, and second, to avoid what he felt was the real possibility of overloading his colleagues with too much information. For these same reasons, he also chose not to elaborate on how he estimated the change in cloud velocity. He figured it would be easy enough to do at some later time, should anyone ask.

"Well . . . ," he continued, displaying yet another set of graphs, "as you can clearly see from these statistical test results, the wind velocity at the level of the cirrus clouds was indeed the key – the essential ingredient that had been missing from the recipe. True, it's only based on nine storms, but you can see that this improvement enabled a full *eighty-five percent* of the variability to be accounted for by this parameterization scheme."

Will couldn't help but smile. His audience now appeared genuinely impressed, even though this final statistical presentation was probably one of the few things that they had actually been able to completely understand.

"Well, that's about all I have for to-day. So now, please, I'd be happy to take any of your questions." He looked at each of his fellow staffers in turn, an eager smile on his face. "Any questions at all that you might have." The only response was a round of brief, somewhat uncertain applause.

After it became clear that, once again, no questions would be forthcoming, Sergeant Long stood up. Everyone in the room immediately focused their attention on the boss. "Mr. Roebling," he began very deliberately, akin to an attorney making closing arguments to a jury, "do you know what this system you've created, if it performs anywhere near as well as you say – and mind you, I'm not at all saying it won't – do you know what it will mean to this Office, come April, when we begin to make our own indications, or forecasts?"

Will started to formulate an appropriate answer, but realized just in the nick of time that the question was a purely rhetorical one.

"It means, dear Sir," the Sergeant continued in his best elocutionary manner, "that we will absolutely *wipe the floor* with Headquarters, not to mention the other Regional Offices, when it comes to the success rate of our predicted forecasts. And, it means that you, my young friend, will one day be famous."

A wide-eyed Will felt as if he could have been knocked over by a feather in that moment. He was not only astonished by the Sergeant's words, but also could not recall ever having seen him so animated and passionate, about anything. "Uh, yes, well, of course, I still need to continue with further trial runs," he managed to mumble, suddenly sounding rather sheepish.

"Well, my good man, you've got about a week shy of three months – before the second of April, that is – to do just that. All you have to do is let me know what you need, and I'll see to it that you get it. Between now and then, I want you spending all your time on this."

Long turned his attention back to the group. "Oh, and one more very important thing – and this communication is for all of you." After looking each man in the eye, he lowered his voice and, speaking deliberately, said, "I do not want a single word about Will's system breathed outside of this room – not to your wives, not to your friends, not to your parents, and not even amongst yourselves or to your subordinates. Not one single word."

Will watched in silence as the Sergeant paused here for several moments, moving his gaze across each man's face, letting his stern admonition really sink in. "What we are looking at here is an amazing opportunity," he finally went on, "a *huge* one, really – and I need some time to figure out how to make it work in the best interest of this Office. So, till further notice from me, on this topic your lips are to remain sealed. I trust I have made myself eminently clear."

Well, it's easy to see that there are no politics in play here, was the irreverent thought that ran through Will's mind, as he noticed every other head in the room nodding vigorously in acknowledgment of Long's directive.

Judging by the Sergeant's authoritative nod in response, Will could see that Long was confident his subordinates understood just how the government game was played. All of which would keep his marvelous new secret, for the time being at least, safely under wraps.

CHAPTER 10

WEDNESDAY, JANUARY 11, 1888

Sergeant Long was still ecstatic. It was late in the afternoon, four days after Will's presentation, and a relative sense of normalcy had only now begun to return to the senior staff. Putting both feet up on his desk, he leaned back in his chair as he took a sip from the two fingers of scotch whisky he'd poured from a small bottle he kept hidden in the bottom drawer. Strictly for special occasions, of course.

I can hardly wait till Headquarters, and especially that foul little bastard Abbe, gets a load of New York's indication accuracy statistics, come April. Clearly, there was no love lost between Francis Long and Cleveland Abbe.

Long had already decided he'd wait till the end of April, or perhaps even early May, to disclose the existence of Roebling's system to General Greely. It wouldn't make much sense to reveal it before then, anyway. Will had said he needed some time to "fine-tune" it, whatever that entailed, which presumably would only serve to improve its accuracy. And this improved accuracy would happily translate into more money in Long's paycheck. Prediction verification was to be closely monitored for the six Regional Offices, with the remuneration of each Region's Chief Officer to be based, in part, upon the accuracy of their Office's indications – a fact he'd prudently chosen not to disclose to his staff.

Of course, the Sergeant would always be beholden to his good friend Adolphus, first and foremost for his career with the Signal Service and, more recently, for approving Roebling's transfer. Still, he saw no compelling reason to unveil his surprise before his Office began making its own indications. Should Congress find out about Will's forecasting system before then, it was entirely possible that it could even work against him. He'd certainly seen stranger things happen in the Army – even the Signal Service – than the rescission of a transfer order. Including one that had been granted a full nine-months earlier.

It is entirely possible that the Sergeant might have come to a different conclusion about sharing Will's forecasting system had it not been for the intense animosity he'd long been harboring towards Abbe. Still painfully fresh in Long's mind was the ugly comment of Abbe's he'd inadvertently overheard during a routine quarterly meeting at Headquarters, just two weeks after Will's transfer to New York. Long had been in earshot when Abbe had remarked to another Headquarters staff member something to the effect, "It's really too bad Roebling got his transfer because, honestly, I doubt that Long guy is even smart enough to know what a tremendous talent he is. I give him six months at the outside before he gets disillusioned and leaves the Service altogether."

Long had been stunned hearing this blatant attack on his professional competence. Of course, it was certainly possible – maybe even likely – that Abbe's offhand, malicious remark had far less to do with his real feelings about Long than it did his deep anger towards Greely, for having approved Will's transfer in the first place. Even taking all that into consideration, Long still found Abbe's remark inexcusable and unforgivable. The Sergeant, a much larger man than Abbe, had wanted to beat the tar out of him right then and there, but wisely refrained. He knew there would be hell to pay if he did, regardless of Greely's friendship. So he'd swallowed his pride and opted for patience, biding his time. *Besides,* he'd thought in that moment, *they do say that revenge is a dish best served cold. I'm sure I'll get my chance yet.*

He took another sip of his whisky before placing the glass on his desk and leaning back even further, both hands laced behind his head, staring up at the ceiling with a smug, self-satisfied grin on his face.

"So, Will," said Mrs. D, as they sat down at the table to enjoy their customary Wednesday night pasta dinner, "how was work to-day? Any new developments concerning 'you-know-what?'"

"You-know-what" was their not-so-subtly coded designation for Will's forecasting system. Although Long had been adamant about his employees keeping it all completely under wraps, Will of course had long ago shared everything about it with Mrs. D, at least as much as she was able to comprehend. So even though he was technically under the same non-disclosure order as the rest of the staff, he figured that Long's edict couldn't very well be applied to Mrs. D retroactively. Not only that, but last Saturday night Mrs. D had confided to Will that she had already gone over most of the information with Blanche and Charley, well before hearing of the Sergeant's mandate of secrecy. The only thing that Will could do now was request that the three of them keep quiet about what they'd heard, from here on out. Mrs. D had assured him that his secret would be safe with them. Besides, she'd said, really, who would they tell?

"No, nothing new to report there. Things have finally started to quiet down and get back to normal after all the excitement generated by my seminar. Now I'm just waiting to hear what Sergeant Long intends to do about the whole issue of sharing my system with Headquarters. Say, would you mind passing me the grated cheese, please? Thanks."

CHAPTER 11

MONDAY, JANUARY 16, 1888

Sergeant Long caught up with Will in the hallway, just outside the break-room. It was six o'clock in the morning; Long had assigned himself and Will to the early shift this week. Thus far, he had received no indication that any word of Will's system had made its way back to Headquarters. Then again, it had only been a little over a week since the presentation. Still, he was pleased.

"So, Will," the Sergeant began, casually, "how are things going with the fine-tuning of that forecasting system of yours?"

"Good, sir. Very good, actually. I've been tinkering with it since the seminar, and have managed to resolve a few minor problems, but I'm hoping we'll get one or two really good nor'easters that I can work with, before April rolls around. There's a further improvement I still want to make, and I need at least one more storm to do it. But even if we don't – get another storm by April, that is – I think my baby is pretty reliable as it is."

The Sergeant cocked his head and gave Will the oddest look, but only for a moment. *Your "baby," eh? Now isn't that an interesting choice of nomenclature.* In the next moment, he was once again all smiles.

"Well, Will, I have been giving this a lot of thought, as I told you I would. If possible, I'd like to go on keeping your system a secret, at least till April second, that is. Then, once we score the coup on the very next big storm, we can unveil it to Headquarters – in all its glory." Long raised both palms towards the ceiling, arms spread wide. His face was beaming.

Will responded to the effusive compliment with a shrug and a small chuckle. "Sergeant, I'm happy to say that it makes absolutely no difference to me. Truth be told, I'm just grateful for all the time you're giving me, letting me work on it during regular Office hours. It really is very generous of you."

"Think nothing of it, my boy – it's my pleasure, I assure you," Long replied heartily, clapping Will on the shoulder. "After all, I'm sure we'll all be reaping the rewards of your labors for some time to come."

As both men turned to walk back to their respective offices, the Sergeant couldn't help but notice the satisfied smile on Will's face; it matched his own.

Will sat back in his chair, appreciative of the chance to finally relax for a few moments. He had been immersed for hours in his preparations for the improvement he planned to make to his forecasting system, and had just reached what felt like an appropriate point to take a short break. Sergeant Long had left the Office around noon for an appointment which would keep him out the remainder of the day, so Will knew he'd be able to work uninterrupted for the rest of his shift. But first, he felt the urge to sit and talk with Frank for a bit, as a way of taking a breather. Before he'd even raised himself half-way out of his chair, though, he was surprised to hear a quick treble knock on the door, followed by the sight of Frank's head poking into his office.

"Frank! How serendipitous – I was just this very minute coming to see you," he said cheerily, as he regained his seat. "Please, do come in and sit down, make yourself comfortable. It seems to me that you and I have had very few chances to really talk lately, what with the changing shifts and all. And I know just where to start – you can tell me how things are faring in the world of our two fair and favorite ladies, these days!" Will gave his good friend an impish grin.

Frank returned his smile. "You know, you're absolutely right – it has been awhile ... and as a matter of fact, much has happened. But first, lest I forget, the reason I popped in here in the first place. Alex has asked me to extend an invitation to you and Kira, for the two of you to come to dinner at our house."

"Well, that's mighty generous of her. And it sure sounds like it'll be a lot of fun, too."

"How does the Saturday after this next one look for you? I believe that's the twenty-eighth."

"Let's see. I know that I don't have any conflicts on that date, so that'll work just fine for me. And if it's all the same to you, I'll ask Kira; I think I'd prefer to be the one who extends the invitation." Frank nodded his agreement. "Good. Alright then, I'll try to reach her by telephone, before I leave the Office to-day. Now that that's settled, please do fill me in on the latest events you alluded to. As the saying goes, I'm all ears."

"Well, I don't think I ever mentioned anything to you about the big fight they had a couple of weeks before Thanksgiving, did I? Although maybe I shouldn't really call it a 'big fight;' I guess you could say it was more like an intense argument."

"No, you did not, and I am sorry to hear they had such a heated disagreement. Kira didn't say anything to me about it either, and that was, what, two months ago?

"Yes, well ..." Frank, fidgeting uncomfortably in his chair, seemed to be finding it difficult to know exactly how to proceed. Will gave him a nudge which he hoped would move the conversation forward.

"Perhaps you could tell me what the argument was about?"

"You see, that's just it – I suppose one could say it was about you, mostly."

"Me?" Will was surprised.

"Yes. Alex told me she was trying to get Kira to open up more. And especially when it came to you – so there it is." Frank looked off to the right for a moment, then back at Will, his forehead creased in a slight frown. "Listen, Will, I wouldn't even be telling you all this now. Besides sounding dangerously close to 'women's talk,' it's really none of my business, you know? I guess I only really brought it up at all because Alex made it a point to mention to me that she'd been noticing quite a change in Kira over the past few weeks. Almost as if she'd been doing some real soul-searching, since their not-so-little tiff. Alex said she thinks it might have had something to do with Kira's coming to terms with our plans to start a family. She thinks –"

"Whoa!" Will moved so far forward in his chair, he nearly fell. "Hold your horses right there, Frank. *What* did I just hear you say?"

"What – about planning to start a family, you mean?" Frank responded, a puzzled look on his face.

"Yes, I mean about 'planning to start a family.' This is how I hear news of such tremendous import?" Will couldn't help feeling slighted that he'd been kept in the dark till now.

Frank sat all the way back in his chair, looking somewhat deflated. "Gee, I'm so sorry, good buddy. I guess I just sort of assumed that Kira would have said something to you about it, long before now."

"As a matter of fact, no, she never mentioned it. Hmm . . . I suppose that's just the kind of thing Alex was referring to, when she talked about her not being all that open with me." Will's attention wandered briefly, but he quickly brought his focus back to Frank. "Be that as it may, that's wonderful news about you and Alex. I give you my heartiest congratulations, and wish you both the very best of luck. I know the two of you will make wonderful parents."

"Thank-you, Will. That's very kind of you to say. And I'll be sure to pass along your felicitations to my better half, you can count on it. Anyway, Alex says she's really gotten the impression that Kira has turned over some kind of a new leaf." Frank paused here for a moment, fingers drumming on the desk-top. Then he leveled what appeared to be a momentous look at his friend. "Apparently, she even mentioned something about having come to the realization that you are 'the one,' as they say in the vernacular."

"Kira said that?" Will's eyes went wide.

Frank grinned at him. "Yessiree Bob. According to Alex, those were the precise words she used."

Will shook his head slowly, side-to-side. "That's pretty amazing to hear, Frank. You know, come to think of it, I *have* noticed a difference in her lately, and quite a positive one at that." He sat back in his chair, his face wreathed in a contented smile.

"Well, I'd have to say that sounds very encouraging, Will," Frank said, as he rose to go. "And I'm sure Alex will be pleased to hear about it, too. Plus, I think it bodes well for our get-together on the twenty-eighth; the four of us should have quite the time at dinner."

CHAPTER 12

For some inexplicable reason, Kira had the feeling that Will was going to propose to her to-night, after their dinner at Alex and Frank's house. There was nothing specific she could point to which gave her this distinct impression. It was more her general sense of the way things were. She hummed a little tune and smiled to herself as she danced her way into her dressing-room to pick out a special ensemble for the evening.

"What to wear, what to wear," she mused aloud, thumbing methodically through the dresses hanging in her over-sized wardrobe. She grabbed her emerald-green silk taffeta evening dress, the one with the velvet and lace-fitted bodice. "Hmm, this looks good. And with my eyes, it looks great on me, too. Not too formal, just a bit tantalizing, and I know Will hasn't seen it yet."

She found herself looking forward to her wedding day. Years earlier, her father had assured her that when she met the right man, he'd see to it they'd have an absolutely splendid wedding followed by a lavish celebration. The only condition he'd imposed in return for this generosity was that the marriage ceremony itself be performed at the Trinity Episcopal Church – the Smith family's house of worship from the time Kira was a small child.

The Trinity was the only church that Kira had ever attended. Her childhood memories there were all pleasant ones, so she had no problem at all agreeing with her father's reasonable request, especially knowing of his deep affection for the landmark edifice.

The Trinity Episcopal Church was designed by Richard Upjohn, an English-born architect noted for his Gothic Revival style. It was located in down-town Elizabeth, only a couple of miles from the Singer Sewing Machine Company. Thomas Smith's allegiance to the Trinity was largely due to his avid interest in architecture – in particular, the designs that Upjohn created for his churches. While still a young man, Smith had been duly impressed after reading *Rural Architecture,* Upjohn's influential book on church design, penned in 1852. When he joined the staff of Singer in 1871, Smith was quite pleased to discover how close his new company was to the Trinity. Fortuitously, the church had been completed that very same year, and the Smith family was soon settled into its new, and ultimately permanent, spiritual home.

Will was just finishing up his shift. He'd been working all day on his forecasting system, ever since the conclusion, earlier that morning, of the fourth in Sergeant Long's seminar series: a presentation on – what else? – forecasting, by some big-shot professor from the Polytechnic Institute of New York University. All in all, he'd found it to be a pretty mediocre offering, but he was much too kind to say so to anyone.

His plan now was to go home, take a leisurely bath and shave, then head back into Manhattan to meet up with Kira at Frank's for dinner. He had plenty of time, as he'd already cleared it with Long to leave a little early to-day, at four o'clock instead of five, his usual departure time on Saturdays.

Frank and Alex Gorman lived about twenty blocks closer to Mrs. D than Kira did, in a lovely brownstone apartment just off Sixth Avenue on West 13th Street. Will looked forward to the walk home and then on to Frank's, as the weather was uncustomarily temperate for late January. In particular, he appreciated the opportunity to get in some extra exercise. He seldom had the time these days to go running, his preferred method of staying in good physical condition. Fortunately, he knew that brisk walking was almost as beneficial.

Will had a strong feeling, almost a knowing, really – reminiscent of certain prognosticative episodes from his childhood – that the proverbial piper would have to be paid, and soon, for this recent stretch of unusually mild winter weather. He decided not to dwell on that, for the moment. Instead, he stopped by the telephone on his way out of the Office and rang for the operator, asking to be connected to Kira's exchange. When she came on the line he said a quick hello, then confirmed he'd be leaving momentarily and arriving at Frank's by seven, as planned.

It was precisely seven o'clock. "Welcome, good buddy!" Frank, smiling broadly, pulled the front door open wide, even before Will had had a chance to knock.

"Hello, Frank, and thank-you. It's good to be here. Has Kira arrived yet?"

"She got here just a little while ago. Come on in; she's out in the kitchen, helping Alex with some last-minute preparations of something or other." Frank took the two bottles of wine that Will proffered.

"As I didn't know what the lady of the house would be preparing, I figured I could play it safe by getting one red and one white."

"You know, you didn't have to do that." Frank gave his friend a quick grin. "But I must confess, I'm awfully glad you did."

"Hi, honey," Kira said sweetly, greeting Will with a warm hug and a chaste kiss when he got to the kitchen doorway. "I thought I heard you out there, talking with Frank."

"Hello, sweetheart." Will attempted to emulate her tone, and returned her embrace. After a few moments she released him, and he continued into the kitchen. "Let me say hello to Alex.

"Ah, here's our lovely hostess." Will planted a peck on Alex's cheek. "My goodness, Alex, but the aroma in here is absolutely heavenly!"

"Why, thank-you, Will," she responded, giving him a merry grin. "Now, let's just hope the finished product lives up to its 'olfactory advertising!'" He gave her a big smile in return.

"Alright, then, Will, please make yourself at home, won't you? Dinner will be ready in about fifteen minutes." Alex smiled warmly at her guests before turning her attention back to her preparations. "I can't tell you how glad I am that the two of you are here.

"Kira, dear, would you mind giving me a hand with this salad? We're having one of your favorites, Will." Alex craned her neck over her shoulder, directing her communication to him. "Pot roast, mashed potatoes, green beans, and a garden salad. Plus, a special surprise for dessert."

"Yum, yum . . . you've certainly set my mouth to watering," Will replied, rubbing his palms together in the universal symbol of anticipation. "I can hardly wait!"

Happily leaving the ladies to their domestic ministrations, Will sauntered into the parlour and took a seat in what, by now, was considered "his" armchair. But before he had a chance to stretch out and relax, Frank hurried in and took the seat next to his, saying he wanted to discuss a particular "technical issue" he'd been thinking about.

It was Will's considered opinion that Frank had the makings of a good meteorologist, even though he was currently just a Senior Technician. True, he'd only had a year or two of university training, but he was definitely intelligent. And a quick study, to boot.

Despite Sergeant Long's edict disallowing any discussion of Will's forecasting system, even internally, Will and Frank had rationalized that no harm would come of them bending the rule, just a smidgeon. In their occasional spare time at the Office, whenever their schedules coincided and privacy allowed, Will had been giving Frank brief tutorials on select aspects of his system, and felt that he was probably the one with the most comprehensive understanding of it, at least at this point. He thought that Frank had a natural aptitude for meteorology, and knew he was eager to learn. As his best friend, Will was happy to make himself available to mentor him.

"I've been thinking about what you said during 'you-know-when,'" Frank began, with a wink. "About cirrus clouds being an indication of the wind, high in the atmosphere. Tell me more about that, if you would. Also, why is what's happening at, what, eighteen-thousand feet so important to the weather on the ground?"

"That's a really good question, Frank. I'll try my best to answer it, but I'm sure we'll only get to scratch the surface – if you will pardon the pun – before Alex has dinner ready for us."

"That's a good one, Will. And I know you're probably right, but let's at least start, anyway; we can always pick up the conversation again, later on or another time."

"Well, that's certainly true. It's not like we don't run into each other often enough." Will grinned at his friend and chucked him on the knee. "Okay, here goes. It starts with what are called the 'Equations of Motion,' which describe the behaviour of a physical system in terms of its motion as a function of time. That is, as a set of mathematical functions in terms of dynamic variables –"

"Whoa, there. Hold on for just a minute, good buddy. That's some mouthful-and-a-half you just said and, frankly, I don't have a clue as to what any of it means. Do me a favor and see if there isn't some way you can bring it down a little closer to my level of understanding."

"I'm sorry, Frank. Please forgive me. Alright, let me start over. Suffice to say that what happens at that level of the atmosphere, which by the way is referred to as the level of non-divergence, is –"

"The level of non-what?"

"The level of non-divergence. That's the height in the atmosphere throughout which the horizontal velocity divergence is zero. And that height, about eighteen-thousand feet, corresponds to a pressure of about five-hundred or five-hundred-and-fifty millibars – and is the level, give or take, at which cirrus clouds exist. It marks the separation of the horizontal divergence and convergence associated with the vertical structure of mid-latitude extratropical cyclones." Will couldn't help but be a bit put off by the blank look on Frank's face. For a moment, he even thought he could see his eyes beginning to glaze over.

"What does 'horizontal velocity divergence' mean?"

"Well . . . divergence means the spreading out of a vector field, and –"

"Oh! I remember vector fields from what you told me the other day," Frank interrupted again, his face brightening considerably. It was obvious that he was trying his best to comprehend something, anything, that Will was saying. "Velocity is a vector."

"Well, yes, that's right." Now Will was flummoxed. It was clear to him that Frank was not following this conversation at all, which left him at a loss as to how to proceed. He certainly did not want to cause his friend any embarrassment, especially right before sitting down to dinner with the ladies.

Fortunately, just at that moment, Alex popped her head into the parlour. "I'm sorry to have to interrupt such a serious conversation," she said, smiling broadly, "but, I am very pleased to announce that dinner is served."

Will rose from the armchair. *Saved by the bell; thank goodness. I guess maybe I need to re-evaluate my estimation of my good friend Frank's level of understanding – not to mention my prowess as a teacher!*

Will realized, in that moment, that it would likely be an up-hill climb to explain his system in detail, to Long or anyone else in the Office. They'd barely grasped the cursory treatment he'd given it in his presentation, and, unlike Frank, had not been privy to any follow-up instruction. Not wanting to bring this unsettling thought with him to the dinner table, he filed it away for contemplation at a later time.

"So, Will," Alex began casually, as she was passing him the pota-toes, "Frank tells me you're quite the celebrity around the Office, these days."

"Well now, Alex, I don't think I'd go as far as all that."

"Really? That's not what I hear. Frank says you've developed some pretty remarkable and sophisticated forecasting tools, and the Sergeant seems quite taken by them. Apparently he feels that they have the potential to be quite revolutionary."

"A-hem!" Frank interrupted, suddenly looking alarmed and nearly choking on his mouthful of pot roast. He quickly reached for his wine glass and took a healthy swig. "I think perhaps it might be better if we changed the subject, dear."

"Oh, my goodness!" Alex's hands flew up to her face. In an instant, her complexion had coloured to become the perfect complement for the green beans, had it been Christmas-time. "I'm so sorry! What was I thinking? I guess I must have had a little too much of that good wine you brought."

She looked at Will beseechingly, seeming to hope that her feeble excuse would somehow be acceptable. In all likelihood, she knew just how weak it truly was.

"It's okay, really," Will said, directing his assurance to both Frank and Alex.

Feeling confused and adrift, Kira was unable to follow the strange turn the conversation had just taken. She couldn't help but be disturbed, what with being relegated to spectator status as her close friends suddenly began to take on so. Determined to get to the bottom of this mystery, and quickly, she interjected herself into the conversation, consciously keeping her tone of voice as even as she could.

"What is okay? What on earth is going on here, may I ask?" Kira's head swivelled from Will to Alex to Frank and back to Will again. "What in the world are you all talking about? And why are you being so deadly serious, all of a sudden?"

After an uncomfortable pause, a forlorn-looking Frank turned to Kira and said, "I'm afraid I've made rather a mess of things." He glanced sheepishly at Will before continuing.

"You see, Kira, as Alex mentioned, Will has indeed developed some rather exciting forecasting tools. But once they'd been brought to Sergeant Long's attention, he made it patently clear that they were not to be discussed under any circumstances, whatsoever – in or out of the Office. I guess it's pretty obvious that I violated his edict, by sharing some of the information with Alex."

Pausing, he turned back to Will, then added, "Will, I am so sorry."

Kira's eyes grew large as she sat silently, stock-still, her dinner fork poised just above her plate. Her training as an actress came rushing to the fore; though outwardly calm and serene, inside she was seething.

"Don't be too hard on yourself," Will said to his subordinate and friend, without a trace of anger. "I mean, what harm has been done, really? Let's all just move on to a different topic and forget the whole thing, shall we?

"But first let me promise you, Alex, dear – it really *is* okay. Even though, as Frank said, Long did forbid us to talk about it at all, under any circumstances, his main objective was to make sure that Headquarters didn't find out, at least for now. So, unless you're planning to be in touch with the good folks at the Washington City Office anytime soon," he joked, trying to lighten the mood, "it's okay. Really, I mean it – it is."

Will gave them both a warm and reassuring smile as he returned to his dinner. He retained a hope that Frank had not mentioned anything to Alex about the Office beginning to make its own forecasts starting in April, but he was not optimistic.

Oh well, he thought to himself, shrugging mentally, *as the saying goes – what's done is done.*

Will found Mrs. D reading at the kitchen table when he arrived home. She looked up at him, eyebrows raised high.

"My goodness, Will, but you're back early. Heavens, it's not even eleven o'clock yet."

"Yes, I know, Mrs. D. Let's just say that things didn't go quite as well as planned," Will replied, dejectedly. "Kira and I . . . well, we, we . . . kind of had our first fight, I guess, as I was walking her back to her place after dinner."

"Oh, well, that's not really so bad now, is it? I mean, after all, your first fight had to happen sometime, didn't it? Come to think of it, a case could easily be made that, by now, yours and Kira's was getting to be just a bit overdue. And my dear, although it might be hard for you to hear, right at the moment, so forgive me, but this I know for sure – there will be many more to come."

She reached over to give his arm a few consoling pats. "Believe it or not, Will, that's not at all what's important. No, not at all. Since it's pretty much inevitable that a couple will fight, from time to time, the only really important thing is how they fight."

That last comment really caught Will's attention. "What an interesting thing to say. What, exactly, do you mean by that?"

Mrs. D cocked her head at him for just a moment, as if considering. In spite of his low spirits, Will almost laughed aloud – gazing at the expression on her face, he could almost see the "wheels turning."

"I tell you what, dear," she said, with a quick nod and a smile, "why don't you and I discuss this over a nice glass of sherry?"

Will sat back and relaxed, giving out a small sigh and looking at her with a pleased grin. "That sounds just wonderful to me. I sure feel like I could use some of your marvelous advice, right about now, I can tell you that." He sat quietly for a moment or two, drumming his fingers idly on the tabletop. Then suddenly he sat upright, a concerned look on his face. "But, then again, I wouldn't want to be keeping you up too late, Mrs. D."

"Oh, poppycock! Now is as good a time as any, if the conversation's important enough – and this one surely is." Will knew that Mrs. D was always happy to be a contribution to him, any time, any place. It probably ranked at the very top of the long list of things about their relationship for which he was grateful.

In no time at all, she had the glasses and bottle on the table. "Well," he began, taking a sip of his sherry, "believe it or not, it all had to do with a conversation about work, during dinner with Frank and Alex. Specifically, the seminar I gave at the Office a few weeks ago. Do you remember me telling you about that?"

"Of course I do, Will. That was a pretty big deal for you, being asked to introduce your forecasting system to the senior staff. You told me all about what you said in that seminar, how you explained to your colleagues that it had all started with the research you did during your detail at Headquarters. You were working on some kind of special project for that professor – Appey or Abbey or some such thing, as I remember – right up till your transfer to New York."

"Yes, exactly – your recall is quite impressive. Anyway, you probably also remember that Sergeant Long swore us all to secrecy concerning the whole thing, at least for the time being. We were to say nothing to anyone, and that included family and friends, explicitly."

"That's right, Will, I remember all that, too. Of course, when it came to me, Blanche, and Charley, the horse was already long out of the barn on that one." She gave him a rueful smile.

"Yes, well, some things just can't be helped now, can they. I mean, after all, there isn't a man alive – or dead, for that matter – who's ever figured out how to un-ring a bell." He smiled wryly in return. "Anyway, I had barely even mentioned the seminar to Kira. I just figured that when the time came, and there was no longer any need to keep my system a secret, well, I'd simply tell her all about it then. Frankly, I'd given the matter almost no thought at all, probably because in all the time we'd been together, she had never shown much of a real interest in my work. And please don't hear that as any sort of complaint, because it isn't, truly. I'd always thought that was perfectly fine. All the more so as I'd never had much interest in the theatre, either."

"Alright..."

"Well, Frank was one of the staff members at that seminar. Therefore, he got the same exact order I did from the boss: no discussing this with anyone, not even his wife, till Long gave the all-clear." Will took another sip of sherry.

"The problem arose when Alex, probably just a bit in her cups by then, and therefore somewhat lacking in her customary inhibition, brought the subject up over dinner. In an effort to pay me a compliment, she said something about Frank having told her that my 'revolutionary' new forecasting system was making me some sort of Office 'celebrity.' When Frank heard that, he went into a bit of a panic, immediately suggesting that the subject be changed. She realized instantly that she shouldn't have brought it up, turned bright red, and proceeded to apologize profusely. Of course, Frank thought that I, as his superior, would be upset with his blatant disregard of our Sergeant's direct order. So he also began apologizing to me. Meanwhile, poor Kira was completely at sea, having no clue at all as to what the heck was going on."

"Oh, yes, I see ..." Mrs. D nodded her head. "Kira's feelings were hurt, being the only one in the room who knew absolutely nothing about any of this. It must have been particularly galling to her that Alex knew so much about it while there she sat, completely in the dark. After all, if Frank could justify breaking his word in order to tell Alex, ostensibly because he'd never dream of excluding her from anything important, then why on earth wouldn't you tell her? Especially when it's *your* system, to begin with."

"Yes. That's pretty much it, in a nutshell. But the thing that was most upsetting to me is that she couldn't – or wouldn't – see anyone else's side in the matter, not even for a moment. All she could think of, and I really do hate to come right out and say this so bluntly, but all she could think of was herself."

"Will –"

"My apologies, Mrs. D, but please bear with me, for just a moment. This isn't the first time I've noticed that about her. It's just the first time you're hearing anything about it, because I forgot to mention it to you the night we had our talk. You remember, the Sunday after Thanksgiving, after she'd been here for dinner?"

"Yes, I remember that conversation quite clearly."

"Well, do you also remember when I took her to see *Gasparone* for her birthday, back in September?"

She nodded. "Of course. It was quite the occasion, as I recall."

"Yes, it certainly was. The show was actually most enjoyable, and afterwards we went out to a wonderful little place for a drink. Well, we got to talking about one thing and another, and were really having ourselves quite the time. After awhile, naturally, it was getting to be pretty late. When I mentioned it, however, she said she wanted to stay – keep the party going, if you will. I told her that although I'd surely love to, I was on the early shift that week, and would therefore have to be getting up at three-forty-five the next morning. And all that on top of having yet to walk her home, then make my way back to Brooklyn. She responded with what I thought was a joking comment, which implied I care more about my job than I do about her. Well, I just laughed it off in the moment, but she did seem to cool a bit towards me. Which was all the more noticeable because, up till that point of the evening, she'd been far more flirtatious than she'd ever been before; almost startlingly so, to be perfectly frank. This may sound queer, but in all this time since, a faint but distinct dissatisfaction with the tenor of that conversation has always been somewhere in the back of my mind. I've never said anything to her about it, although now that I'm giving it some thought, perhaps I should have been just a little more honest with her."

"Well, Will, you're not wrong there; honesty *is* the best policy, whenever it does no harm. But I really don't think the scenario you just described sounds like anything too serious."

"In and of itself, I would tend to agree with you, it's probably not. But if it's part of a consistent pattern of behaviour, marking a clear lack of empathy, then ... Well, anyway, back to to-night. I mean, I told her the fact that Frank hadn't kept *his* word had nothing at all to do with me. Not only that, but I couldn't have had any way of knowing that he had told Alex and was, frankly, blind-sided when she brought the subject up. I just don't understand why Kira can't, or won't, see that."

Mrs. D held his gaze but said nothing, so Will continued on.

"I walked her home, of course, but the whole way there she would barely even talk to me. I tried again to get her to look at it rationally, but I might just as well have saved my breath; it was an exercise in futility. Her mind was made up – I was the villain, and that was that."

"Will, Will, Will." Mrs. D shook her head to and fro several times, then looked at him with what he could only describe as great focus. "So, let me see if I've got this straight. Frank chose to dishonor his word, which, of course, had nothing whatsoever to do with you – especially given that you chose to honor yours. As a matter of fact, you feel that you handled the whole situation with integrity, overall. And not to put too fine a point on it, but Kira has some nerve being mad at you because you did. Is that about right?"

"Yes. That's it! That's it, exactly. You have such keen insight, Mrs. D. For some reason, I couldn't seem to get my hands around everything, to sort out how I was really feeling about the whole thing. I don't know how you do it, really I don't, but somehow you always help me to see things so much more clearly." He gave her a grateful smile.

"That's very kind of you to say, Will, and I do appreciate hearing it – but now I must ask you to listen very closely. If it is your intention to one day have a successful long-term relationship – and this is regardless of whether it's with Kira, or anyone else – then you must accept that there will be times when you are going to have to apologize and let something go. Even if, and sometimes especially if, you know that you are in the right. I think that's one of the true secrets of a long, healthy marriage, like the one my Walter and I had."

Will was silent.

"The point I'm making here, Will, is that no one is perfect. And while it's so very easy to see the mote in your neighbor's eye, it is, at the same time, dang near next to impossible to see the beam in your own. Sometimes I think that's just the way the good Lord made us, so we have to work a little at getting along with one another, and thereby earn all the joy that that brings us. So. The question you need to be asking yourself is this: are you going to choose to be righteous about being right, even if it means being alone?"

"My goodness, Mrs. D, what a concept!" Will sat back hard in his chair, giving his head a few good shakes, trying to take it all in. He had to admit, he felt a little bit dazed.

"Well . . . one thing's for sure – you have certainly given me a lot to think about, and not for the first time either, as I'm sure you must know." Mrs. D responded to his compliment with a warm smile and a loving pat on his hand.

"But before we close up shop for the night, I'd like to go back to my original question, if I may. What, exactly, did you mean when you said that the only really important thing is *how* a couple fights?"

"Oh, yes, that – I'm glad you remembered. Actually, it's quite simple, Will. And another Golden Rule of relationships I've learned, over the years: always keep things civil, and never 'pile on' to the issue at hand. In other words, don't ever use a fight as an opportunity to vent over silly things from the past that your partner might have said, or done – or neglected to. If you were too lazy to generate a discussion about these things back when they occurred, even though you really were bothered by them, you've got no business bringing them up during the current set-to, just to use as more ammunition. It isn't only that that's not a fair way to fight, it's also precisely how things can escalate and go terribly awry, spiraling all out of control. That's when we can end up saying things we don't really mean, and thereby land ourselves in a world of trouble."

"Yes, I can see what you mean by that. Actually, it makes a great deal of sense, and you're right – it *is* quite simple, really. Not necessarily easy, I would imagine, but simple, none-the-less. Come to think of it, it sometimes seems as if the simplest things are the ones that wind up being the very hardest to do, as odd as that sounds." He paused here for a moment, bemused.

"Well, all I can say now is thank-you so much, Mrs. D – for listening without judging, and for sharing your wonderful words of wisdom with me. So now, if it's all the same to you, I think I will go on up to bed. I'm more than ready for a good night's sleep, I can tell you that."

"Oh, my dear, yes, of course, you must be so tired – it's been quite a long day for you, hasn't it. Not to mention an emotionally trying one. I'll say good-night, then, Will. And pleasant dreams to you!"

CHAPTER 13

MONDAY, FEBRUARY 13, 1888

Albert Washington yawned and stretched, giving his head a shake to clear out the cobwebs. He'd had a restless night's sleep, and had awoken at four-forty-five a.m. feeling just a bit nervous on this day of days – his very first as Assistant Maintenance Technician. He knew full-well that the job title they'd given him was nothing more than a fancy name for a mostly ordinary position, second-janitor, but he didn't care in the least. He was simply thrilled that he'd actually landed his first full-time job. It was something for a colored boy from the Upper East Side to be gainfully employed at the illustrious Grand Hotel, among the most exclusive hotels in all Manhattan. His proud parents had told him more than once that they still could not believe his good fortune.

At the close of his interview just the week before last, Albert knew that he had more than a fighting chance of being hired. True, he was only nineteen years old, but even with that he figured he had at least three things going for him. First, he was smart – he'd been captain of the chess team in his senior year of high-school. Second, he'd actually *finished* high-school, and with darned good grades, too. And third, without fail, Albert always interviewed well.

One of his favorite teachers at school had described him as having a calm demeanor, a natural way of being which exuded reliability and trustworthiness. He'd said that within ten minutes of meeting Albert, you just knew he could be counted on, no matter what – an attribute irresistible to any potential employer. Albert figured that went a long way towards explaining why he had never been without at least one part-time job since the ripe old age of thirteen, in the process amassing a wealth of practical experience. His teacher had also complimented him on the way he had of looking straight into someone's eyes when speaking with them, and the way he really listened, without interrupting, always making sure the speaker felt complete in his communication.

All in all, Albert felt fairly sure that these likable qualities had impressed both the Hotel Manager and the Head of Maintenance, each of whom had interviewed him at some length. So he wasn't at all surprised – pleased, yes, but not surprised – when a telegram addressed to Master Albert Washington arrived, from Mr. James Landen, congratulating him on having secured the position and requesting that he report directly to Mr. Walter Jamison first thing Monday morning, February 13th.

After eating a light breakfast, Albert left his brownstone on 61st Street, then walked the few blocks around Central Park to the train station at the corner of Sixth and 59th. He waited for the five-forty-five el, took it down to the 33rd Street exit, and walked diagonally the two remaining blocks down Broadway. He glanced at his watch. *Six-thirty. Perfect.*

Located on the northwest corner of Broadway and 31st Street, the aptly named Grand Hotel was a truly magnificent structure. Designed by the famous architect Henry Englebert and completed in 1868, it was a sophisticated example of the French Second Empire style.

The combination of several factors – the economic recovery following the end of the Civil War, the resumption of the northward migration of the City, and the burgeoning theatre district – had been sufficient to entice a number of savvy developers to build a spate of luxury hotels in this part of Manhattan known as Tin Pan Alley.

Competing with the Grand were other fine establishments such as the St. James, the Albemarle, the Victoria, and the Grand's neighbor just two blocks to the south, also designed by Englebert, the Gilsey House. Each hotel sought to exceed the others in opulence and prominence.

The Grand stood six-stories tall, with a gleaming white marble facade; it was crowned by a handsome mansard roof, characterized by steep sides and a double pitch. One of the most distinctive external features of the Grand Hotel was its chamfer, or beveled edge. Facing south-southeast and running the entire height of the hotel, it took full advantage of the unusual corner site, a sharply acute angle, which was formed by the two intersecting streets.

"Good morning, Albert," Mr. Jamison said, as an uncharacteristically tentative Albert walked into the Maintenance Head's unremarkable office. "It's good to see you again. You can put your coat in this side room, here."

"Thank-you, Mr. Jamison, and good morning to you too, sir. It's good to be here."

"Did you take the el to-day or did you walk?"

"I took the Sixth Avenue El, Mr. Jamison. It's still a bit too far to walk at the moment, but I imagine that come spring-time, I will very likely be doing just that."

"That's good, Albert. Did you have your breakfast yet?"

"Yes sir, I did. I ate breakfast before I left home."

"Well, in the future, you are always welcome to get yourself a light breakfast from the kitchen, free of cost. And the same thing goes for your lunch, as well. Just one of the benefits Mr. Landen has created to take care of his employees. Now come on with me and I'll show you where you can sign in, where your locker is, and where you can pick up your uniform." Albert followed Jamison through the main hallway. He noticed that there were already at least a dozen guests standing at the front desk waiting to check out. As near as he could tell, they were mostly businessmen, dressed in expensive suits and looking important.

"To-day you don't really have to do anything except follow me around. I want you to become familiar with the many different things that you'll be responsible for. Rather than trying to explain them all to you, Mr. Landen thought, and I agreed, that the best way to teach you would be to show you everything as I go through the day. Sort of a 'hands-on' approach, if you will."

"Yes sir, Mr. Jamison, I must concur – that makes a great deal of sense to me."

"And I'll introduce you around to some of the other fine people we have on staff here. We'll get that done to-day, too. And please, Albert – I always go by Walt. Rule Number One – we're pretty informal in these here parts. The only one who is called Mister is the Big Boss himself, James Landen. And, of course, all our guests. You will at all times address our guests by either Mister or Sir, or Miss or Ma'am, without exception. Even the children, as odd as that might seem, initially. Is that clear?"

"Crystal clear, Walt."

As they made their way through the hotel, Albert couldn't help but marvel at the meticulously sculpted wood molding up high between the ceiling and walls and framing the guest-room doors, to say nothing of the richly finished, burnished hardwood floors. He felt a great happiness and a deep sense of gratitude, having been given the opportunity to work in such a beautiful place. It was even more exquisite than he had imagined.

To-day was the first day of May Morrow's new job.

At seven a.m., the energetic twenty-year-old caught the Ninth Avenue El at 50th Street, three short blocks from her boardinghouse on West 48th, near Tenth Avenue. She traveled three miles to the second-to-last stop, Battery Place Station, then continued east, on foot, the remaining quarter-mile to Garrigues Chemicals, a wholesale chemical company located on Front Street. Even though the train ride took about thirty-five minutes, she didn't mind it at all, especially now that day-light was coming earlier and she could actually enjoy a good book during her trip.

While it was true that her starting salary was barely competitive, May had chosen to hire on, anyway. Mr. Garrigues had assured her that as his telegraph operator, a vital function these days for any organization relying on sales, she would be looking at "frequent" raises if she did well – which she knew she would. So, ever-confident, she had gladly accepted the position. Besides, she had formed the opinion that Mr. Garrigues was a man of his word, though she would have been hard-pressed to explain exactly how she'd arrived at such a conclusion.

Not at all naive, however, Miss Morrow was well-aware that a hundred-thousand workers had been let go in the past year, nationwide, due to the current state of the economy. She knew if she hadn't accepted Garrigues' offer, any of hundreds of other applicants surely would have, in a trice.

She loved the physical space in which she was to work. It was open and airy, with a large window which let in plenty of light, especially in the morning. Looking southeast, straight ahead from her second-floor vantage point directly above the building's main entrance, she enjoyed a fantastic vista, which included the East River on over to Brooklyn. And, if she looked to the left, she had a fabulous view of the Brooklyn Bridge as well, just a half-mile off to the east.

May loved life, plain and simple.

Her friends playfully teased her that she always perceived the glass as being not only half-full, but also just on the verge of *being* filled. And she would laugh right along with them, knowing that what they said was perfectly true. She was the quintessential eternal optimist, and that optimism and élan exuded from her charismatic personality.

Her relationship with her parents was a very healthy one. She knew they fully supported the decision she had made, immediately upon graduating high-school in Albany, to pick up and move the one-hundred-and-forty miles downstate to New York City. Her reasoning had been simple: it was there that she would find the greatest opportunities. Her parents, she had recently discovered, had shared a long-standing joke, since she'd been about fourteen, that May was really a baby robin. It was their parental duty to gently nudge her out of the nest the moment she was ready to fly, but not a minute sooner or later. They firmly believed there was an optimal time for cutting young ones loose, so as to distill in them the sense of responsibility which would be so desperately needed to survive in these difficult times. The fourth of five children, May knew that this strategy had not failed her parents yet. So by the time she graduated, it was a *fait accompli* that May would become a productive, hard-working member of society.

Her mother and father had done their job well. May was wise beyond her years, and possessed a commensurate level of overall maturity. To the outside observer, though, it was puzzling, even odd, that she'd never had a serious gentleman friend. It was not that she wasn't attracted to the opposite sex, for she certainly was. And she was good-looking enough to attract nearly any one of them, without even factoring in her ebullient and infectious personality. No, the reason, which she'd more-than-once confided to her girl-friends, was that the boys her own age were too immature, for the most part, while the men who were mature enough were simply too old for her. She felt she was at an awkward, in-between age, but it didn't faze her in the least. With patience being confidence's cousin, she was fully prepared to wait the few years it would likely take for the boys her age to become men. Meanwhile, her girl-friends had told her that the combination of her unique qualities, augmented by a certain aloofness, made her simply irresistible to most of the young men who were fortunate enough to make her acquaintance.

By now, Will and Kira had more-or-less made up. Will had really taken to heart what Mrs. D had said a couple of weeks ago, about no one being perfect. Kira apparently still didn't see that she had behaved at all inappropriately, so there was no hint of any apology forthcoming from her. But gradually, over the two-weeks-plus since the dinner debacle, Will noticed that she'd warmed back up to him, to the point now that it seemed as if nothing untoward had ever happened between the two of them.

   Will did not hold any of this against her. He rationalized the over-all situation by coming to a straight-forward conclusion: as Kira was the most important thing in his life, if she felt that he wasn't acting that way, well, she was probably right. His logical plan of action then was just as straight-forward. And quite simple, really. He would just have to try harder to make sure she knew how important she was to him. To that end, he had already picked out a special gift for her to celebrate Valentine's Day to-morrow – a lovely cameo brooch she'd once pointed out to him in a shop window on one of their promenades. He couldn't wait to see the look on her face when she opened the beautifully wrapped box, itself accompanied by a gorgeous bouquet of a dozen long-stemmed American Beauty roses.

CHAPTER 14

Frank and Alex were engaged in a spirited discussion about the pros and cons of again inviting Will and Kira over for dinner. Frank knew that Alex wanted to simply invite them, but he thought that might not be such a good idea. He wasn't really sure where the two of them actually stood at the moment, as Will had barely spoken a word to him about Kira in recent days.

"Now, don't you go making up a lot of nonsense over something as insignificant as that," Alex said. "I saw Kira just the other day, and she was in an excellent mood. When I asked her about Will, she said they were doing just fine."

"I suppose that's all well and good, but I still don't know ..."

"Well, you don't have to, because I do. I want you to ask Will if he and Kira would like to come over this Saturday. We can't let the disaster of the last time be a reason to avoid inviting them over again. When you fall off the horse, you have to get right back up in the saddle. You'll see. I'm sure he – they – will accept."

Frank and Alex had long ago agreed on a satisfactory working arrangement regarding who would have the last word in various arenas: for all things private and domestic, it would be Alex, while Frank's purview, logically, would be all things public and professional. Granted, this particular situation was a bit of a cross-over, given that Will was both friend and Superior Officer. But Frank could not refute Alex's logic when she pointed out that it doesn't get much more domestic than dinner at home with friends. Ultimately, then, he had little trouble acquiescing to his fairer half.

"Oh, alright then, hon . . . I guess you've been right about them so far. I'll extend the invitation to-day when I get to work, first thing. I know he's on the early shift this week, but I'm sure I'll run into him before he leaves."

Frank was not looking forward to this mission, as neither he nor Will had exchanged a word about that awful night in all this time. Left to his own devices, which he felt were probably pretty much the same as most any man he knew, he'd much rather let sleeping dogs lie.

Frank arrived early for his shift, and managed to catch Will as he was wrapping things up for the day. "Greetings, Will . . . how are things going with 'you-know-what?,'" he said, as he approached his desk. He couldn't have known that that was the phrase Will and Mrs. D used to describe his system.

"Good, good. Thank-you for asking. But I must confess, Frank," Will said quietly, getting up to close his office door, "I've recently gotten a bit frustrated. I have this improvement I really want to make to my system, but I need at least one more storm to try it out on. And we haven't had a decent one since early December."

"What if we don't get another one before April?" Last week, Long had briefed the senior staff on his decision to keep Will's system a secret till at least April second, taking the opportunity to reiterate his mandate of silence on the subject.

"Well, as I already explained to Sergeant Long, the system's in pretty decent shape as it stands to-day. It's just that I really want it to be as good as it can possibly be when it's unveiled outside this Office."

"With no offense intended, I have to say that it sounds to me like you're being something of a perfectionist."

Will responded with a brief chuckle. "No offense taken, Frank – and no argument given, either."

Frank smiled at his friend before continuing. "Seriously, though, won't the process be ongoing forever, as you continue to make it better and better over time?"

"Well, put that way, I suppose there's no arguing with that, either. Point well-taken."

"You know, come to think of it, Will, it really has been pretty much clear sailing since mid-January," Frank went on, reluctant to broach the subject of the dinner invitation. "I wonder if it's possible that it could be because the climate is getting warmer, overall. As I recall, it does seem like we've had less snow in recent years. I've been following the work of John Tyndall, lately. He discovered some years back that gases like water vapor and coal gas can block the heat which radiates from the earth, thus trapping it in our atmosphere and warming the climate as a result."

"Yes, I've been following his work as well, and it's all very interesting. Whether his ideas have merit, or not, it will be a good topic for discussion at some future point. As far as right now goes, though, something's telling me that winter will be going out with quite a bang this year. Yes, indeed."

"'Something's' telling you? Are you saying that you were able to determine that by using your forecasting system?"

"Well, no, it doesn't really work like that. My system can only make predictions as far out as a few days, six or seven at the most. The 'something' I'm talking about is more of a – let's just say, a feeling. An intuition."

Satisfied with Will's response, but still in no hurry to bring up the idea of dinner, Frank moved the conversation in a different direction. "Say, Will – I've just now remembered something I've been meaning to ask you about. How have you been getting the observations from Headquarters you've needed to keep working on the development of your system all this time?" His question reflected their increasing comfort level in privately discussing Will's system, Sergeant Long's commandment not-withstanding.

"Oh, that's been fairly simple from the start. Do you remember me telling you about the fellow I trained for Abbe? The one who took over for me after my transfer?"

"Yes, I do recall your mentioning him. Glynn Gardner, wasn't it?"

"Yes, that's right. Good memory. Well, anyway, he makes me a copy of the morning obs and drops it in the Interoffice communication pouch every day, so that I'll have it the next morning. And whenever it looks like I might have a storm to work with, I simply ask him to include the previous day's afternoon and evening obs, as well."

"Oh, I see."

Except he didn't, not really. He couldn't help wondering why Gardner would take such a big risk, when it would be so easy, not to mention potentially serious, for him to be caught. Better to save that inquiry for another time, he thought; Will was beginning to look anxious to leave. As Frank had finally run out of conversations to delay the inevitable, he figured he'd better just get on to the main question, before Will made his departure.

"Listen, Will, I don't want to hold you up or anything, but before you go, there's something Alex and I were wondering. Would you and Kira be interested in having dinner at our place again, maybe this Saturday? Alex has promised, on her honor, that this time there'll be no more slip-ups."

Will laughed out loud. "That's really funny, Frank. Alex is quite the little wag, isn't she. But it's true enough that we never really did get around to talking about that night. Well, suffice to say that there are absolutely no hard feelings over here."

Frank found Will's choice of words interesting. It sounded as if he were speaking just for himself, but of course he could have been speaking for Kira, also.

"Well, I must admit, I sure am glad to hear you say that. Even though it's pretty much what I've known, all along." Frank paused for a moment before continuing tentatively, "So . . . how does Kira feel? I mean, is she angry with Alex and me?"

"What? Angry with you two? No, of course not. Now, me – well, that's another story."

"She's angry with you?"

"Actually, no, not anymore. She was for awhile there, but we're just fine, now."

"Gosh, Will. Once again, I'm so very sorry for being the cause of all that unpleasantness."

"Frank, there's really nothing for you to be sorry about. In the final analysis, it has nothing to do with you. It wasn't even what happened at your place, *per se;* it's more about what happened after that."

Frank shot Will a quizzical look.

"I explained to her that Long had ordered us not to discuss this with anyone. But since you told Alex, she thought that I should have told her. She just could not get over it."

Frank felt his face flush. "Will, I never should have –"

"Frank. If you think about it, and trust me, I have, that's really not the point here. In fact, truth be told, if it were the other way around, if it were me that was married to Alex, I'm pretty sure I would have done the same thing. The point here is that Kira and I, we're *not* married. And she couldn't see why that should make any difference." Frank nodded thoughtfully, but remained quiet.

"For me," Will went on, "the real issue was that even though logic dictated I couldn't possibly have known that you had told Alex, till her little 'slip-up' of course, that meant absolutely nothing to her. She insisted on blaming me anyway for not telling her. I told her not only did that make no sense at all, but I also felt she was being childish and immature about the whole thing."

Frank took in a sharp breath. Not sure what to say, he took what he thought would be the safest path. "So, how do you feel now?"

"How do I feel now . . . that's a very good question. We haven't talked about it much since it happened, which to me would be the common-sense thing to do. But then again, nothing about any of this makes much sense to me in the first place. Mrs. D, whose opinion I hold in the highest esteem, basically advised me to take it in stride, and I really have been trying to do so. I even went all-out on Valentine's Day, showering her with presents and attention, in an effort to show her how much she means to me. But something still seems to be off, somehow. I can't explain it, I wish I could. It just feels as if – for me, anyway – something has changed." Frank felt for his friend, who paused here for a few moments, shaking his head ruefully.

"I tell you, Frank, I sure wish I had more experience with women. You know, something that could give me a point of reference about any of this. It's all just so darned confusing – confounding, really." Will paused again, seemingly lost in thought. Then he slapped both palms on his desk and gave his head another shake. "Well, one thing I do know is that I'm not going to act on anything right now. I've just got to wait and see how things unfold between us. I mustn't do anything rash."

"That sounds like good judgement to me, Will – and, for what it's worth, would be what I would advise, as well."

"Thank-you for that. It's good to hear that I'm probably on the right track here."

"So, then – what do you think? Do you want to come over on Saturday?"

Frank was relieved when Will beamed at him. "Sure, Frank, absolutely. Thank-you for the invitation, and please be sure to thank Alex for me, too, if you would. I'll try to reach Kira by telephone now, before I go, and ask her. If the date works for her, I'm sure she'll say yes. Same time?"

"Yes, seven o'clock."

The operator was able to make the connection easily, and Will's call to Kira was brief. She said she'd love to join him for dinner at Frank and Alex's, and they agreed to meet there at seven on Saturday.

In that moment, Will couldn't help but think about Mark Twain's "elephant in the room."

CHAPTER 15

SATURDAY, FEBRUARY 25, 1888

Sergeant Long answered the telephone as Will was making his way towards the hall leading to the break-room. The Sergeant stopped him in mid-stride, motioning him over and indicating that the call was for him. "It's Kira," he said, as he handed him the receiver.

Will was surprised that she'd be calling. He took the earpiece from his boss and waited a beat before beginning to speak, giving him a chance to leave the area. "Hello, Kira," he then began, somewhat tentatively, his tone concerned. "How are you? Is everything alright?"

"Oh, Will, no, not at all," came the rejoinder, her voice a distant fog. "I'm afraid I'm calling to tell you just the opposite – I'm feeling as sick as sick can be. I know I must sound terrible, please forgive me. Obviously, I'll have to cancel for to-night's dinner with Alex and Frank. Which would make me feel even worse, if that were possible. I mean, I know how much we were all really looking forward to it. But what else can I do? I hate to say it, but I think it's very likely I have come down with that nasty flu I've been hearing so much about lately."

"Oh, no, Kira. I am so sorry to hear that. Gosh, that's simply awful. Are you able to describe your symptoms for me?"

After Kira had run through her long list of ailments, Will found that he agreed with her self-diagnosis. It probably *was* the flu. The nasty virus had certainly been making the rounds lately, especially in the Manhattan area.

"Listen to me, sweetheart. I don't want you to give another thought to having to cancel for to-night. There will be plenty of opportunities for the four of us to socialize in the future, so there's absolutely no harm done there. Alright, then. Now that that's settled, would you like me to come over this evening and do my best Florence Nightingale impersonation for you? The masculine version, of course.

"And, as part of the treatment, I'll bring along a bowl or two of Mrs. D's famous chicken soup. I'm sure she'll be happy to whip up a batch when she hears you're ailing. As odd as this might sound, when I was so sick a few months back, I'm quite sure it helped to cure me."

"Oh, Will, would you really? How terribly sweet of you. Of course I'd love it if you came to nurse me back to health. But only if you're sure it would be no trouble for you."

"Trouble? What trouble could it possibly be? We were going to be having dinner together anyway, at Frank and Alex's. I'll just redirect my feet to walk a bit further up-town, and they'll take me straight to your place. Couldn't be simpler. And the good news is that I should be able to get there not too much later than our original date at seven; I'd already gotten permission from Sergeant Long to leave at four o'clock, just like the last time."

"Well, alright then, I gratefully accept your generous offer. Is Frank still in the Office?"

"Yes, he's still here. I'll go let him know immediately, although I'm not sure how he'll manage to get the word to Alex."

"Oh, I know they're pretty friendly with one of their neighbors who has a telephone. I'm sure Frank will give them a call and ask that they give her the message."

"Well, that makes me feel a whole lot better, for Alex's sake. I really should get going now, Kira. There are a few things I need to finish up here before I can leave. And as soon as we hang up I'll relay the request to Mrs. D the same way, by telephoning our neighbor, so she can start brewing up some of her magical elixir."

Mrs. D added the finishing touches to her simmering soup and turned down the flame. Already the warm kitchen was filled with its delicious aroma.

"Thank-you so much for doing this for Kira," Will said. "I know how grateful she'll be, especially if it works for her like it did me, back in December."

"Oh, you're more than welcome, Will. Honestly, it's my pleasure, I assure you. And, as a matter of fact, the timing could not have been better. I was actually beginning to feel just a bit under the weather myself, and this provided precisely the motivation I needed to whip up a batch of my secret remedy. I'm afraid I must confess that I would have been simply too lazy to bother, had it been only for me."

"Well, thank-you, again. But I'm surely sorry to hear you're not feeling up to par. Hopefully you'll be much better in no time. I know that magic soup of yours will fix you right up. I'm living proof of it! Now I think I'll head on up to have a quick wash-up and change. When do you think it will be ready for delivery?"

"Ideally, it should continue to simmer for a few more hours, but I can have it ready to go by about, say, six-fifteen. So take your time upstairs. And when you do come back down, maybe we can fit in a quick chat about how things are going with Kira. It feels like it's been awhile."

"You know, it feels the same way to me, too, which makes that an excellent idea, Mrs. D." Will bounded up the stairs, taking two or three at a time.

At five-thirty, Will returned to the kitchen smartly dressed in his chestnut corduroy trousers, new dress shirt, and calf-length Chesterfield coat.

"My, my, don't you look nice, Will." Mrs. D held him at arm's length and turned him slightly to and fro, eyeing him appraisingly.

"Why, thank-you, Mrs. D." Will bobbed his head with a grin as he doffed an imaginary cap. "I just thought I'd dress up a little, it being Saturday night and whatnot. I mean I am out to lift Kira's spirits, after all. I know that she'll appreciate the effort."

"You know, I believe she will, at that. Now, do sit down here with me for a few minutes and fill me in. What's been going on with the two of you? As far as I can recall, the last I heard you say is that things were 'fine,' or some such description."

Were someone else to inquire in this fashion, other than Frank, of course, Will would probably have felt the question a bit too personal, maybe even impertinent. That certainly was not the case with Mrs. D, though. In his entire life, Will had never met anyone with whom he found it easier to talk, on any subject. And that included his own mother – especially if the conversation, like the one at hand, had anything at all to do with women.

So the two dear friends, far more like mother and son than landlady and tenant, sat together at the kitchen table as Will caught Mrs. D up on the status of his relationship. He thanked her again for the wonderful advice she'd given him, and told her he'd taken to heart her remark about no one being perfect, really going out of his way to give Kira the benefit of the doubt. And because things were relatively good with them at the moment, he chose to downplay his experience of her "hot and cold" mood swings. But Mrs. D, as usual, saw right through him. Tongue-in-cheek, she compared Kira's behaviour to that of the eponymous character in the wildly popular Stevenson novel, "The Strange Case of Dr. Jekyll and Mr. Hyde." Albeit to a much milder degree, of course.

Charmed by her witticism, Will gave Mrs. D an appreciative smile and the two of them enjoyed a good chuckle together. In his heart of hearts, though, he couldn't help but feel that, once again, she'd hit the proverbial nail squarely on its head.

PART II

The Approaching Storm

From the War Department's Signal Service

Washington City, Sunday, March 11, 1888 – 7 A.M.

Indications for 24 hours, commencing at 3 P.M., Sunday, March 11, 1888.

Fresh to brisk easterly winds, with rain, will prevail to-night, followed on Monday by colder brisk westerly winds and fair weather throughout the Atlantic states; colder fresh westerly winds, with fair weather, over the lakes regions, the Ohio and Mississippi valleys; diminishing northerly winds, with slightly colder, fair weather, in the Gulf states; light to fresh variable winds, with higher temperature, in Kansas, Nebraska, and Colorado.

SIGNALS. – Cautionary southeast signals are displayed on the Atlantic coast from Norfolk section to Wood's Holl section.

RIVERS. – The rivers will rise slightly.

CHAPTER 16

THURSDAY MORNING, MARCH 8, 1888

Will was assigned to the early shift again this week, as he had been for the past few months. His eagerness to begin plotting the surface map from Tuesday's observations had brought him into the Office well in advance of his scheduled starting time. The map would have been finished by now, but Sergeant Long had kept him occupied most of yesterday on a "special assignment," a first since Will's seminar two months ago.

As far as Will was concerned, the number of Canadian reporting stations was meager, at best. None-the-less, there was enough significant information in the observations he'd just finished plotting to grab his attention. Some frigid air, unusually cold for this late in the season, appeared to be moving southward from our "neighbor to the north," poised to enter the northern-tier states. Given the overall synoptic situation, he wondered whether this might be the first inkling of what he'd been feeling for awhile now, that the piper would surely come a-callin' to collect. If this was confirmation that one last winter storm was on the horizon, from the looks of the indicators it could be a bad one. For the sake of his forecasting system, he certainly hoped that would be the case. He figured he'd have the chance to apply it to-morrow, which should be within three or four days of the event. If yesterday's morning obs showed what he was expecting, he'd soon be asking Glynn to start including the intermediate ones.

As Will had explained to Frank not long ago, he had made a key improvement to his forecasting system by including all three sets of daily obs from the reporting stations, rather than just the morning ones, whenever he suspected a storm might be on its way. The reporting times were standardized at seven a.m., three p.m., and ten p.m. Each individual observation was received by Headquarters, via telegraph, and compiled less than twenty-five minutes later. This compilation was then provided to the forecaster on duty, or his assistant, who would draw up the surface map to be used for the final step of the process: the forecaster's indication.

Will had been careful to keep Greely and Abbe in the dark about his forecasting system, all the while laying the groundwork to ensure he'd be able to continue working on it after he'd left his detail at Headquarters. Knowing that Abbe would want him to train his records-compilation project replacement, Glynn Gardner, Will had taken special pains to cultivate a warm friendship with the young man. As a result, Glynn was more than willing to make and send him a copy of each day's morning obs. And whenever Will thought an east-coast storm might be brewing, he had him send along the afternoon and evening observations, as well. Of course, early on, Will had needed to give Glynn a reason for wanting these data, so he'd simply told him he was doing research for a forecasting system, promising to tell him more as things progressed. By the time last December's storm rolled around, Will had pretty much brought Glynn up-to-date on his system.

Glynn Gardner had never felt put-upon by being tasked with providing Will his own set of morning obs. To his mind, it really didn't amount to that much extra work, as he had to record and compile each set of telegraphed obs for the forecasters, anyway. Once that was complete, it would take him, roughly, another twenty minutes to make a copy for Will.

Glynn knew he'd been considered amongst the best telegraphers at Fort Myer, which had no doubt led to his being offered the choice assignment at Headquarters. As the person now responsible for

Abbe's records-compilation project, he had unrestricted access to all of the incoming observations, so he felt there was very little chance he would be caught making a copy for Will. He would simply slip that copy into the Interoffice pouch each day, transported to New York via the reliable Railway Mail.

Glynn was once stopped and questioned by Greely, but he replied innocently that he was just sending some records to Will Roebling, per his request. Apparently that answer was satisfactory, as the Major General declined to interrogate him further. And even if all else had failed and their clandestine operation been discovered, Will had sworn to Glynn that he would find a way to cover for him, somehow. Glynn trusted Will's promise that if anyone's head were ever to roll over this, he'd see to it that it would be his, and his alone.

Will knew he could have gone directly to Abbe or Greely with the request for the observations, but not wanting to "rock the boat" or go through the red tape he figured would be involved, he thought it would just be easier to go straight to the source. Besides, he'd made sure that neither of them knew anything at all about his research, and decided it would be best to keep it that way, at least for the time being. Will had sensed the Professor was less than keen about losing him to New York in the first place, and he surely didn't want to risk doing anything which might put the kibosh on his transfer. Like Sergeant Long, he too had definitely seen stranger things happen in the U.S. Army.

One thing Will had never been able to figure out, though, was why, in all this time since the seminar, Sergeant Long hadn't asked him how he'd been getting the obs each day. Clearly, he knew the surface maps were an integral part of his forecasting system. Heck, on most days, Will drew them up in his office in plain sight of the Sergeant. He was prepared to explain everything, had Long ever made any inquiry; inexplicably, he never did.

At ten-thirty, like clockwork, Will received Wednesday's shipment from Glynn in the Interoffice mail. Before starting in on his map, Will scanned the obs, paying particular attention to those from the several Canadian stations. His face lit up suddenly.

Oh, my gosh – I think we're in business!

Will knew that Glynn always worked the early shift, enabling him to deliver the compilation of the previous evening's ten o'clock obs to the forecaster on duty at the earliest possible juncture. After the forecaster had drawn up the surface map and made his indication for the nation, Glynn would then telegraph it to the other Offices and official outlets by the mandated seven a.m. deadline.

Will waited patiently as the operator made the connection to Headquarters, then again for the time it took Glynn to make his way to the telephone.

"Glynn, hello," he then began, making a conscious effort to control the level of excitement in his voice. "I just received yesterday morning's obs. And thank-you, again. I've only had the chance to give them a quick once-over, but that was enough for me to know that I'd like you to please include the intermediates, from here on out. I think there's a very good possibility that a winter storm is brewing for the Northeast, maybe even a significant one, probably arriving sometime early next week. This is exactly what the doctor ordered in terms of what I need to test out my system. And, as always, I promise to keep you posted on what I find."

Will was confident the recent Fort Myer graduate would one day become an accomplished forecaster in his own right, and welcomed any opportunity to assist in his training and development.

"Aye-aye, my good friend," Glynn replied, "consider it done – the intermediates are yours for the asking. But now let me ask, doesn't it strike you as being just a bit late in the season for a significant winter storm? I mean, the crocuses and daffodils are already in bloom down here. Not to mention that it's been at least sixty degrees every day, for pretty much the last two weeks."

"I know, it does seem odd. And we've had the same exact situation up here in New York, by the way. But just take a look at those temps in Canada. The bitter air is clearly on the move south. Of course, that would not be at all unusual if this were January, or even early February. But nearly mid-way through March? And I'll tell you what raises a huge red flag for me: the temperature contrast between this frigid air to the north and the unseasonably warm, humid air across the Gulf states. Only time will tell, of course, whether it ends up translating into a storm, but I have every reason to believe that that's *precisely* what's going to happen."

CHAPTER 17

THURSDAY AFTERNOON, MARCH 8, 1888

Kevin Patrick McCormack had all but been given the biggest order of his life, courtesy of his Number One customer. The euphoria he'd felt since completing the telephone call which had started the ball rolling, two days ago now, still permeated his every waking moment. Apparently, at least according to his office-mates, he was guilty of going about his daily business with a child-like grin plastered across his face.

Kevin, or Pat as he preferred to be called, knew better than to count his chickens before they'd hatched, but he also knew that in this case all he had to do to seal the deal was arrive at his customer's office in Philadelphia by two o'clock Monday afternoon to complete and sign some contractual paperwork. Wild horses couldn't keep him from being there – and with bells on, too, for that matter.

Pat was an up-and-coming salesman for a large, indoor plumbing supply company headquartered in his home-town of Boston. Since September, his sole product line was the revolutionary new, one-piece ceramic toilet, among the company's hottest-selling wares, and by far its most profitable. A main selling point of this sleekly designed apparatus was its patented flush-out siphon, which had only recently been commercialized following its demonstration a few years prior by its inventor, the renowned British sanitary specialist Thomas Twyford.

All in all, things were looking mighty good for McCormack, and his gratitude knew no bounds. His income, comprised solely of direct-sales commissions, had been steadily increasing since he'd joined the company last July. In to-day's economy, that was not bad at all, especially for a young man of just twenty-four. Pat was a natural-born, highly skilled salesman, which was why the company had given him an exclusive on this very popular line in the first place. While he always made it a point to stay current on the latest scientific discoveries, even tinkering with a few inventions of his own, he knew, without a doubt, that his forte was in sales. Pat felt fortunate, indeed, to have landed a position in a company whose commission structure gave him exactly what he wanted – the opportunity to "write his own ticket" in terms of earning a comfortable living for his family.

Pamela, Pat's wife of three years, though ordinarily amongst the most supportive of spouses, had been quite vocal in her displeasure when she'd heard the news about this upcoming trip. And she'd felt every right to be so – her sister was getting married this Sunday. True, she knew that Pat's biggest customer was certainly important, and business was business, there was no denying that. But, really, did he have to leave to go there *this* Sunday? After all, this was the biggest day of Clary's life. Her wedding to Arthur had been planned for more than eleven months now, longer than he'd even had this job.

Pat had apologized profusely to Pam, bringing her flowers and other tokens and trinkets and promising to make it up to her if she'd only try to see things from his perspective, as the household breadwinner. In sales, he told her, one has to set their appointments at the customer's convenience, and not the other way around. And remarkably, in this case, the commission from this one single transaction would be a full one-third of his entire earnings for all of last year. Not to mention the bump in overall sales he'd likely realize in the Philadelphia area, solely from the word-of-mouth advertising which would be generated by a deal this large.

More inconvenienced than angry, and knowing that her husband would never deliberately do anything to cause her the slightest harm, she eventually saw his point and, finally, forgave him. At least he'd be at the church for the nuptials themselves, which was really the most important part of the day, after all.

Pat's plan was to slip out of the reception early and hail a horsecar to take him directly to Park Square Terminal, in down-town Boston. From there, he would catch the six o'clock train. After changing in Providence, he would get into Grand Central Terminal shortly before midnight. He'd then walk the fourteen short blocks to his favorite hotel, the Grand. He had already been designated as one of their "preferred guests," owing to the dozen or so times over the past several months he'd stayed there while traveling to, or through, New York City. He figured he'd be able to get at least seven solid hours of sleep before hurrying back to Grand Central to catch the nine o'clock to Philadelphia on Monday morning. Even though this timetable was admittedly a bit tight, he had little concern. These were the same trains he had taken the two previous times he'd been to see his Pennsylvania customer. Indeed, if history were any teacher, he knew he'd arrive for their appointment with plenty of time to spare.

CHAPTER 18

FRIDAY, EARLY MORNING, MARCH 9, 1888

It was barely four-thirty when Will arrived at the Office. At this hour, the streets were shrouded in an eerie silence which had an odd effect on him, both calming and energizing – for which he was especially grateful this morning. He figured that, at best, he'd only gotten about four-and-a-half-hours sleep.

After getting home around three yesterday afternoon, he immediately drew up his Wednesday morning surface map. He then talked a bit with Mrs. D, happily took a quick jog around the neighborhood in the nearly sixty-degree weather, and returned home to one of her fabulous chicken dinners. At six-thirty, he excused himself to up go to his room to resume work on his forecasting system. He did not finish tinkering with it till nearly ten, well past the eight-thirty bedtime he usually imposed upon himself while on the early shift. And on top of all that, despite being dead-tired, when he finally did manage to get his body settled in beneath the covers, he discovered he was much too excited to fall asleep right away. Laying there, staring up at the ceiling, his mind whirled with wondering what the next few days might have in store. His imagination ran wild, conjuring up all sorts of unprecedented outcomes.

Knowing that Glynn normally gets to Headquarters at five sharp, Will had planned to place the telephone call to him about a minute or two after that. But in a moment of magnanimity, he'd decided to allow him till five-fifteen, so that he might have the chance to get his coffee and settle in for the day. That, he reasoned, was the very least he could do for the poor, unsuspecting Mr. Gardner. The young man was about to be inundated by a spate of ridiculous requests, the likes of which he'd almost certainly never received before. And even though Will knew Glynn to be tolerant of how over-bearing he could be when really excited about his research, it did not take a genius to see that to-day's demands could leave his normally easy-going colleague feeling quite irritated.

Will had figured out the entire plan on his way into the Office, making judicious use of his commute-time contemplation. First, Glynn would have to telegraph him last evening's obs immediately, or read them to him while they were still on the telephone call. Next, he'd have to do the same for the seven's, as soon as he compiled them this morning. (Will decided he could wait till the ten-thirty Interoffice delivery for yesterday's morning and afternoon obs.) And in order to telegraph or telephone in the three o'clock's from this afternoon, which Will would need the instant they became available, he knew that Glynn would either have to stay late at the Office a minimum of two-and-a-half hours, or leave at his normal time and then turn right around and come back – never a pleasant prospect for any working man.

Next, he'd have to transmit this evening's obs the minute he arrived back at the Office to-morrow, plus the obs for the morning and afternoon as soon possible, which meant he'd end up having to stay late another day. After hearing all this, if Glynn still hadn't terminated their connection abruptly in understandable disgust, the topper would be learning that he'd have to repeat the whole process again, on Sunday. Even though all Signal Service Offices were officially closed from midnight till five p.m. in honor of the Sabbath, the observations from the vast network of reporting stations continued to be transmitted during this time.

"Glynn, buddy, hello. I've been up practically all night," Will began excitedly, after getting him on the line.

"You mean because of the storm?"

"Yes, of course I mean because of the storm. Now it's still early in the game, mind you, but I'm fairly certain there's going to be one, and maybe even a dangerously intense one, at that."

Glynn's tone immediately became concerned. "Gosh, Will, that sounds like it could be pretty serious. Is there anything else I can do to help you?"

"Well, Glynn, I'm very glad you asked. Because now that you mention it, there *is* something you can do. A whole lot of 'something's,' actually." In Will's guilty, over-active imagination, he could just picture Glynn's face, eyes rolling Heaven-ward, lips mouthing the words, "Oh, Brother." Never-the-less, he took a deep breath and plunged in.

When he'd finished reciting the litany of outrageous requests, Will went silent, letting their significance sink in for a few moments. He could hear the clock ticking as he waited, holding his breath in anticipation.

After a pause, which had seemed like an eternity, Glynn finally responded. "Wow, Will. You don't ask for much, do you. Okay, my friend. Here is what I will do. And just let me say, right here and now, that it's a darn good thing Camille didn't make any plans for us this week-end, or I wouldn't be able to make any of this work." Will was heartened by Glynn's manner: resolute, but not unkind.

"After we hang up, I will go organize yesterday evening's obs and then call you right back with them. And I will *telegraph* you this evening's and to-morrow evening's obs by five-thirty a.m. to-morrow and Sunday; I sure hope you still remember your Morse code."

"I do, actually. Well, for the most part, anyway. I'll do some brushing up in the meantime, as well, you can count on it. And your plan sounds good, so far."

"Okay. Then, I will *telephone* you with the morning and afternoon obs each day, as soon as I get them. That way, you'll have all three sets of obs for to-day, to-morrow, and Sunday. Will that give you what you need?"

"Absolutely, Glynn. And thank-you, thank-you, *thank-you!* I can not tell you what this means to me. And please, rest assured – I know what it is I'm asking of you, and I shall find a way to make it up to you, somehow. I really will."

"It's alright, Will, really, it is," Glynn responded. "I mean, yes, it *is* asking a lot, you're right about that. But I imagine, when it's all said and done, over the course of the next three or four days you'll have logged at least twice as many hours as I have."

"In the annals of human history, my good friend, truer words were never spoken!"

As promised, Glynn telephoned back almost immediately. Within the hour, Will had finished poring over yesterday evening's observations and was ready to begin drawing up his surface map. He knew Glynn would be calling again in a few hours with this morning's obs. He also knew he might never get the time to fully analyze yesterday's morning and afternoon obs after they arrived in the mail. By the time he finished with to-day's morning obs, Glynn would be calling with the afternoon ones, and they, of course, would have priority.

He couldn't be certain till he plotted yesterday evening's obs and received this morning's from Glynn, but it was looking more and more likely that the anomalously bitter-cold air mass he'd been tracking, as it moved inexorably southward from Canada, would be interacting violently with the massive amount of warm, moist air sitting over the eastern United States, extending well out into the Atlantic. As part of his on-going research, over the past several days he had been in touch with some of the pilot-ship captains who routinely provided useful information to the Signal Service. They all reported that the water temperatures in the Gulf stream were running unusually high for this time of year. And all of this, his forecasting system virtually screamed, could only result in a very intense winter storm for the Northeast – most probably an out-and-out blizzard.

"Oh, my Lord, yes," he whispered into the stillness of his office, sitting all the way back in his chair and shaking his head slowly in amazement. "It looks for all the world like the piper has finally come a-callin' after all ... and I fear the payment he'll be demanding is going to be mighty, mighty steep."

CHAPTER 19

At eight-thirty sharp, Glynn's telephone call came through. "I have to admit, I'm still amazed by this latest marvel of modern technology," Will muttered, aloud, "absolutely unbelievable. Makes you wonder what in the world they will come up with next?"

He then launched into a quarter-hour of furious scribbling, transcribing the morning observations from each of the one-hundred-and-seventy Signal Service reporting stations in North America, as rapidly as Glynn could dictate them.

After thanking Glynn profusely once again, and hanging up the receiver, Will went to his office and spent the next forty-five minutes examining the data and constructing this morning's surface map. When he was finished, he sat for a long moment staring at it in stunned silence. He simply could not believe his eyes.

"Oh . . . *s-h-i-i-t!*," he finally mumbled to himself, under his breath.

And so it begins . . . Ten-twenty-eight-millibar high centered in west-central Canada. Minus twenty-two degrees in northern Montana. Sub-zero air penetrating into the Dakotas. High ridging south-southeast into northern Kansas. Inverted trough extending north from extreme southeastern Nebraska through western Minnesota. Bitter air to the west,

seasonally cold air to the east. Ten-thirty-five-millibar high centered just north of Lake Erie. Gulf wide-open. Very strong return flow around the Lake Erie high.

It was plain to Will that the sub-zero air was destined to continue moving south in the coming days, and that was very bad news, indeed. He was astonished by how little the air mass had modified, given that the vernal equinox was less than two weeks away. He knew that this cold – almost certainly a record for so late in the season – would surely be astounding and, unfortunately, have cataclysmic effects. Like it or not, he concluded, the northern Atlantic states were in for something of a reckoning.

The research project that Will had conducted several years ago, under the tutelage of Professor Loomis, suddenly flashed in his mind's eye. It seemed odd to him now that when they'd spoken on the telephone in December, the subject had somehow never come up.

To satisfy one of the requirements of Loomis's Theoretical Meteorology course, Will researched and wrote a treatise on explosive east-coast secondary cyclogenesis. After reviewing his work, the Professor told Will that it was on a level commensurate with a Master's thesis, maybe even a Ph.D. dissertation. Unfortunately, as it would be several years before Yale (or any other university, for that matter) would offer meteorology as a major, Will was forced to choose another specialization and elected to graduate with a degree in Civil Engineering.

Secondary cyclogenesis occurs when the primary low-pressure system (or "low") weakens, and another storm, the "secondary" low, develops to its east or southeast, eventually taking over the circulation. It was generally known by most forecasters that lows, primary or otherwise, will eventually "occlude," a process in which the warm, moisture-laden air is "overrun" by the cold air. This warm, moist air – the source of the low's energy – gets lifted higher and higher into the atmosphere during this occlusion process, ultimately cutting off the storm's energy source altogether. Such is the normal cycle of decay which eventually befalls all non-tropical cyclones, sooner or later.

Will had hypothesized that there was another source of energy, high up in the atmosphere at about that magical eighteen-thousand-foot-level, which had a strong influence on whether the weakening low would "jump" to a region of more favorable conditions, generally further east where the occlusion process had not yet manifested. In this way, a new low could form. He had since observed that this secondary storm formation had, in fact, played an important role in some of the big storms of the Northeast, and had designed his forecasting system accordingly.

In the case of this current storm, however, there was no indication of any secondary formation. Instead, his system indicated the storm would form in the northeastern Gulf of Mexico, cut northeastward across the Carolinas, and emerge out over the Atlantic somewhere around Norfolk, Virginia. From there, it would slowly inch its way bodily up the coast just offshore, and then stall for a day, or more, somewhere off the coast of New Jersey, before occluding. With so much cold air available to entrain into the storm along that track, and with the abnormally warm sea-surface temperatures, Will suspected that the entire Northeast could be looking at a blizzard unprecedented in modern times.

Thus far, Will had been very careful not to alert his Office associates to his conjecture about any coming storm. After all, Long had decreed that there be absolutely no discussion of Will's forecasting system, making it clear that he intended to keep it under wraps till at least April, when New York would begin making its own forecasts.

But now he was definitely beginning to reconsider his position. Perhaps he *should* inform the Sergeant. If he were right about what was coming (and he was pretty sure he was), there would be enormous hardship – maybe even hundreds of fatalities – which could be prevented. If by speaking up he could lessen this catastrophe, even in a small way, didn't he have some sort of responsibility to do so?

At the moment, Will really did not know what to think or, indeed, which way to turn.

One person with whom Will did wish to discuss this was Professor Loomis. He thought he might have the opportunity to speak with him on the telephone later in the afternoon, before going home. Long had mentioned that he'd be leaving the Office early to-day.

Will knew that Headquarters would have no way of foreseeing the extraordinary combination of events which would be unfolding in short order. He knew that when these disparate air masses met, the resulting cyclogenesis would be explosive. Most importantly, this violent reaction would be occurring over the warm ocean waters far offshore, in an area impossible to observe. And the timing, too, could hardly have been worse. The convergence would take place late on the Sabbath, when Headquarters was not only closed for most of the day, but staffed by its most junior crew, to boot.

Will saw the clear hand-writing on the wall: the Signal Service would, quite simply, be caught with its proverbial pants down.

For the past week, Will had been assigned the early shift and Frank the late one, leaving little opportunity for their paths to cross. For the next several days, however, Will knew they'd both be working the early shift.

Will was so engaged in the process of completing his surface map, he was oblivious when Frank entered his office and approached his desk, just in time to hear him utter the latest "holy shit" under his breath.

"What is it, Will? What's the matter?"

TIMOTHY R. MINNICH

"Frank!" Will jumped back in his chair a little as he looked up, somewhat startled. "Oh, nothing, it's nothing," he said, recovering quickly. "I just got so engrossed in plotting this here surface map, is all."

Will paused awkwardly before going on, doing his best to rein in his excitement and speak in a casual tone. "I'm working with this morning's obs – you know, the ones that Glynn sends me."

"Yes, I can see that. But from what I recall you telling me, he sends them in the Interoffice. So, since these are to-day's obs, that means he must have just telephoned or telegraphed them to you. Which means they are for something far more urgent than your general research."

Will remained silent.

"You know what I think?"

"No, Frank, what do you think?" Will knew his irritation was showing, but the last thing he needed right now was to be subjected to the third-degree. By Frank, or anyone else for that matter.

Frank continued, undaunted. "Well, I think there's probably a really big storm brewing, which would make a certain amount of sense given your behaviour of late. You've been acting awfully strange to-day, Will. Last week too, come to think of it; as near as I could tell, that is. I barely managed to catch a glimpse of you a few times, and that was just as you were leaving for the day."

Now completely dumbfounded, Will once again made no reply.

"So, then, what's the story, pal o' mine? I mean, unless there's some reason you feel you can't tell me what's got you in such a state . . ." He left that statement hanging in the air, apparently hoping that Will would take the bait.

"Frank, go close the damn door and come back here and sit down. It's rather ironic that you're saying all this. You'll see why in a minute."

Frank closed the door and sat down. "I'm listening."

"First, before I go any further, you must promise me that what you are about to hear will be kept in the strictest confidence, at least for the time being. I need to hear you tell me that you'll do that."

"Of course, Will, I promise. On my word of honor, I promise. Do you really think I would say anything to anyone after what we all went through at the 'Last Supper?'"

"Okay, that's good." Will ignored Frank's cleverly irreverent play on words. "I hear your promise and I trust you. I'm taking you at your word. Now I'll get right to the point. I think that Sunday night, early Monday morning the latest, New York City and the surrounding area is going to be hit – and hit hard – by a blizzard of epic proportions."

"What in the world? A *blizzard?* The damned crocuses are practically blooming, and it's been sixty degrees the last couple of days. A blizzard? Come on, now, Will, are you sure?"

Will chose his words carefully. "At this point, I would rate it at about an eighty-five-percent chance. Maybe ninety."

Frank let out a long, low whistle, shaking his head slowly, as if to help him take it all in. "Have you told Long yet?"

"Well now, you see, that's the ironic part. On the one hand, I do feel I have a responsibility to tell him. To notify the public, really. I mean, Frank, this thing's going to be so big I think people are going to die."

"Am I hearing you correctly? Did you just say *die?*"

"Frank, listen to me. If my forecasting system works as well as I think it does, and there's plenty of evidence suggesting it does, then there's nothing else to conclude. Conditions will be so horrific, so overwhelming, that people *will* die!"

"Will. If you're sure, or nearly so – and eighty-five or ninety percent certainly qualifies as nearly sure in my book – then you *have* to tell the Sergeant."

Will nodded briefly, then continued. "But on the other hand, as you well know, Long is adamant about not wanting Headquarters to learn about my system before April. And since we're not making our own forecasts, officially, till then, what on earth could Long possibly do with this information? That's assuming, of course, that he even believes any of it in the first place. For all I know, he might not. I mean, let me tell you, this is a once-in-a-lifetime – hell, maybe even several lifetimes – cataclysmic event we're looking at here."

Will stopped dead, stunned for a moment by the mental image he'd just conjured. Then, returning his attention to Frank, he went on, shaking his head and shrugging helplessly. "Believe me, Frank, I can honestly say that I finally know the true meaning of the word 'conundrum,' because I'm certainly caught fast in one right now. And it's a real hum-dinger."

Frank was silent for a long moment, nodding thoughtfully before responding. "Yes, I see exactly what you mean. But you do still have at least some time, don't you? What I mean is, you don't need to make a decision right here and now, on the spot. Because, after all, who knows? Maybe things will change over the next day or two."

"Yes, I suppose that's always a possibility. I mean, let's face it – this *is* the weather we're talking about here." Will's attempt to add a wry twist to his words only ended up making hin sound far from convinced, and his lame stab at humor fell flat. In the meantime, Frank had risen and was moving towards the office door.

"But Frank," Will called out to him as he was leaving, "again, please don't say anything to anyone yet, not even to Alex. At least till to-morrow, which will give me some much-needed time to think this whole thing through. I promise we'll talk about it again then, at some length."

"My friend, my lips are sealed, so don't you give it a second thought. I'm on the early shift again to-morrow, so I'm sure we'll have plenty of opportunity to catch up with each other. And I won't mention it again, under any circumstances, till we do."

"Thanks, Frank, I really do appreciate that."

How oddly disconcerting, Will thought as Frank closed the door behind him. *Just who is the superior here, anyway?*

CHAPTER 20

FRIDAY, EARLY AFTERNOON, MARCH 9, 1888

Kira stood utterly still in her foyer, breath caught in her throat as she stared at the telegram clutched in her hand. A portrait of wide-eyed anticipation, she remained motionless for nearly a full minute before getting up the courage to open the small, brown envelope with slightly trembling fingers.

She hadn't managed to get much sleep at all last night. Her nerves had just about reached the breaking point, waiting to hear whether she was still in the running for the part. Her first audition for the play, actually more a comic operetta, had been on Wednesday. The role she was up for was a juicy one, with several singing lines in each of no fewer than three appearances. She knew she'd performed quite well in that initial tryout, and had walked away feeling as if the part had truly been made for her.

The director, by all appearances an honest and decent man, had been most encouraging to her as well, taking her aside to let her know, privately, that only a very few would make the cut for the final audition. And that if she were among those chosen, she'd be notified promptly by telegram. In the long, up-hill battle of seemingly endless failed auditions, Kira could not remember ever having been more excited about any potential role. She really thought that this could be the one, finally, to mark the true beginning of what she'd been yearning for, all these years: a stellar career on the Broadway stage.

Within minutes of opening the deceptively bland envelope, Kira had grabbed her hat and coat and run out the door, making a bee-line for Alex's apartment.

"I'm so glad you're home," she said, somewhat out of breath, as her friend opened the door. "I couldn't wait another minute – I just had to rush right over and share this with you."

"Why, hello Kira, what a nice surprise! Come in, please. You had to rush over here to share what with me?"

Face beaming uncontrollably with a smile stretched ear to ear, she handed Alex the telegram.

Kira Smith. Congratulations. Your final audition is scheduled for Monday, March 12th at 7:45 a.m. at the Bijou Opera House, 1239 Broadway, between 30th and 31st Streets. Get a good night's sleep and please be prompt. Yours truly, Director William Sampson.

"Merciful *Heavens*, this is absolutely fantastic! Oh, I'm so very, very glad for you, Kira dearest! Well, this certainly calls for an honest-to-goodness celebration if anything ever did," Alex said, reaching up to the cabinet, high above the sink, for the bottle of "top-shelf" whisky Kira knew they kept for only the most special of special occasions. "I don't think Frank will mind at all if we treat ourselves to a little toast with some of the 'good stuff.'" Kira's grin widened, if that were possible, as she nodded vigorously in agreement.

Kira held the last lingering note of the final song she would be singing as her character in the play. At the conclusion of her heartfelt recital, Alex leapt to her feet to give her friend a standing ovation, cheering enthusiastically.

"Bravo, Kira, bravo! Those are absolutely wonderful, and you sang them all beautifully. And I couldn't agree with you more – this part really was meant for you to play. But we could go on and on forever about the audition, so I do hope you'll forgive me if I change the subject now, if only so we can catch up a little. I mean, we've only seen each other, what, maybe twice since that disastrous dinner? So. How are things with you and Will? And are you completely over that flu? You look just fine to me."

"Oh, yes, absolutely. As awful as I was feeling that night – and again, I'm so sorry to have ruined our dinner plans – it was pretty much gone by the next day, remarkably, so I was really lucky in that regard. Will elected to play nursemaid and brought me over some sort of specially made chicken soup, something he called 'Mrs. D's magic elixir.' I guess that did the trick, somehow or other."

"Gee, that was mighty sweet of him."

"Yes, I suppose."

"You suppose?" Alex was struck instantly by her friend's singular lack of enthusiasm.

"Well ... I guess the truth is, Will and I just don't seem to be getting along all that well. At least not at the moment, anyway."

"Oh? And just what the heck does that mean, 'not getting along all that well?'"

"See, that's just it – I don't know, exactly. For some reason, it's been hard for me to put my finger on. It's just that he seems, well, a bit distant, like his mind is preoccupied with something terribly important. And it surely isn't me, I can tell you that with certainty. I've asked him about it several times, and he's said there's nothing wrong. Somehow, though, I just can't quite believe it."

"Whoa there, girl. Are you *sure* this isn't all some flight of fancy, or maybe just a product of your over-active imagination? The Will that I know absolutely adores you."

"I know he certainly used to, that much is true. But the way he's been acting lately, I'm just not so sure that's still the case anymore. And, truth be told, I've found a way to turn a negative into a positive. His being distant has given me the chance to really focus much more on my career. I can't explain it, and this may come out wrong, but ... I sort of find it motivating to *not* think about him. I mean, if I'm able to put him out of my mind, I can actually focus much better on my performance, especially when it counts the most. I really do think that's one of the reasons I got this final audition."

Alex could not believe what she was hearing. *Oh, no – here we go again.*

"Well, Kira, you two *must* have a conversation about this, and fast. Plain and simple. You need to come right out and tell him how you're feeling, and then just ask him what's been going on. But, and this is a very big and challenging 'but,' it is absolutely essential that you frame the conversation in a very particular way. He has to know that he is completely free to say whatever is on his mind, without being concerned that he might hurt you by saying something you might not wish to hear."

Kira gave Alex an uncertain look, but said nothing.

"Do you understand everything I just said? It simply can't be any other way. If you two can't talk to each other openly and freely, then you have nothing. No, wait, let me rephrase that: no matter what you might think you have now, if you cannot communicate with each other you will end up resentful, and worse. Trust me, I know."

That last bit appeared to really catch Kira's attention. "You know? What are you saying, Alex? I thought everything was really good between you and Frank."

"Oh, it is, it is. Now. But it's only because we took on doing the hard work to make it that way. We went through, let's just say, a rough patch a few months back. And maybe that's why he ended up telling me more about Will's forecasting system than he should have." Alex felt a certain measure of relief in confiding all this to her best friend.

"Kira, there were a few days there when we were really having it out with each other, and I know now that he was looking for some way, any way, really, to reconnect with me."

"Alex, dear, I'm so sorry, I had no idea . . ."

"Well, actually, hearing that does my heart good because, at the time, I didn't want you, or anyone else for that matter, to know about it. No one can really know what goes on inside a marriage but the couple themselves, which is why it's always best not to judge.

"Anyway, Kira, my point is this – listen to what I am telling you. I speak with the voice of hard-won experience. The two of you are so great together, I just don't want to see you doing anything, or neglecting to do something, that will gum up the works. Will really *is* quite special, and men like him come along very few and far between, believe me. I know that you're sharp enough to have realized that by now."

"Well, I certainly can't argue with you there. No, indeed. And I really want to thank you, Alex, your concern is very much appreciated. You surely do look out for me, don't you?"

"Come on now, what else would you expect? I mean, isn't that what friends are for?" They embraced, smiling.

After a few moments, Alex asked, "Well, then, what did Will have to say about your getting this final audition? He must have been ecstatic for you."

Kira grinned sheepishly. "Oh, gee ... um ... I guess I haven't actually told him yet. I mean, I only got the telegram, what, less than an hour ago, and then I rushed right over here."

Alex favored her friend with an exaggerated roll of her eyes and a slight shaking of her head, laying it on just a bit thick for effect. "Oh, my Lord, don't you see? This is exactly what it is that I'm talking about, so mark my words. Will needs to be the *first* one you think of when there's something to share that's as important as this."

Kira gave her friend another quick hug, then stood back and brought her right hand to her forehead. "Aye-aye, my Captain – I hear and I shall obey." Alex couldn't help but laugh aloud at such antics and, within seconds, the two of them had dissolved into a delightful fit of the giggles.

CHAPTER 21

The telephone rang at four-thirty. Will knew it was Glynn, calling right on time as usual. "Okay Will, do you have paper and pencil ready?"

"I'm ready when you are."

For the next fifteen minutes, Will wrote down the observations which had been telegraphed to Washington from all the reporting stations. He copied them onto a basic template he'd designed, similar to the one he'd used for Abbe's project while at Headquarters, with a row for each station and several columns in which he'd record all the data in the precise order that Glynn read it. That way, the time and effort they'd need to expend on each call could be kept to a manageable minimum.

"Well, that does it for now, Will," Glynn said when he had finished reading off the data. "And remember, I will be telegraphing to-night's ten o'clock's to you first thing to-morrow morning."

"That's great, Glynn. And thank-you."

"You're welcome, my friend ... oh, and Will?"

"Yes?"

"Are you ready to let me know yet what your system is showing?"

Will hesitated for several moments. Though not at all prepared to answer that question in any detail at this juncture, he was, at the same time, mindful that only yesterday he'd made the promise to Glynn to him in the loop.

A thousand thoughts cascaded through Will's mind. How could he tell Glynn what he thought was going to happen? He was pretty certain the storm's reach would extend as far south as Washington, though its impact on that area would likely be less severe. At the same time, how could he not tell him? Where would he be right now without Glynn's generous, even selfless, assistance? As far as he knew, Glynn was an honorable man, but could he really be trusted not to say anything to Abbe or Greely? And could he possibly be unaware that Headquarters was going to relinquish its forecasting authority to the Regional Offices less than a month from now? How could he tell Glynn what he hadn't even told Long yet?

Will sifted furiously through the morass of conflicting possibilities, desperately seeking some sort of solution. Coming up empty, he realized he now faced a conundrum even bigger than the one about telling (or not telling) Long. Just when he'd reached the point where he feared his head might explode, he suddenly heard Frank's voice from their conversation earlier, offering up that excellent advice about taking advantage of the time he still had to take a step back and just see how things might unfold.

"Will? Are you still there? Will?" Will could hear Glynn toggling the receiver hook, obviously thinking the connection had somehow been broken.

"Oh, yes, Glynn, sorry, I'm still here. I just got distracted for a moment, that's all. Okay, let's see now . . . Well, we've certainly got plenty of time before the arrival of the storm. That's assuming, of course, that I'm right in my prediction about there being one in the first place. How about this. I'll take to-night to reassess where things currently stand, and then I will fill you in on everything when we talk again to-morrow morning. I promise."

"That'll be fine, Will. And I do appreciate it."

"But Glynn, in the meantime, please do not say anything to anyone about this."

"Will, what in the world are you talking about? I *can't* say anything to anybody. Have you forgotten? I have no authorization to be sending you all these obs to begin with."

Of course, that's right. How in tarnation could something like that have slipped my mind?

"You're right, Glynn – please forgive me. The more overloaded my brain gets, the less it seems to work properly. Okay then, we'll sign off for now and speak again in the morning. And thank-you again for all your help thus far."

"You're very welcome, I'm sure. And I want you to know that I'm happy to help in whatever way I can, truly. I'll talk to you to-morrow then. Good-night, Will."

At Headquarters, Glynn packed up his things and prepared to leave for home. He thought that Will had certainly been acting very strangely on the call, and wondered whether it was because he was still excited about a coming "superstorm," or now embarrassed because there probably wasn't going to be one, after all. Realizing that he would just have to wait for Will's update to-morrow morning, Glynn decided to hold off on saying anything to Camille till then.

And yet, it's always better to be safe than sorry, isn't it. Perhaps I'll stop off on my way home and stock up on some wood and coal and other essentials, just in case. Couldn't hurt.

True to his word, Sergeant Long had left the Office early for the day. Will knew that this was his opportunity to reach out to Professor Loomis via the telephone, and he placed the call shortly after the Sergeant's departure.

"Professor Loomis speaking."

"Professor? Elias? This is Will. Roebling."

"Hello, Will! How funny that you should telephone me in this precise moment. I was just this very minute sitting here thinking about you. The world works in strange ways, indeed. Anyway, how is the work on your forecasting system coming along?"

"Well, as fate would have it, that's exactly what I wanted to talk to you about. Do you have a few minutes you can spare to speak with me right now?"

"Yes, as a matter fact I do."

"That's wonderful. But before I go any further, you must promise me that you will not tell anyone what I am about to say."

"Not *tell* anyone? Who, pray tell, is this 'anyone' to whom you refer and what, exactly, is it I must promise not to tell them?"

"I'm sorry, Professor, I know I'm being cryptic. Let me explain the whole story, if you will, and I think you'll understand what I mean."

Will knew full-well that what he was about to do was in direct violation of an order from his Superior Officer which, in the Army, was very serious indeed. It was one thing to have innocently shared what he already had with Mrs. D (and perhaps even Glynn); it was quite another, entirely, to deliberately divulge information which had been specifically restricted by Sergeant Long, to anyone – in this case Professor Loomis. Still, Will felt beholden to the Professor for everything the man had done to help him with his career. Therefore he also felt compelled to sound a warning by sharing what he knew about the threat of an impending "superstorm."

He started the conversation by recapping what he'd told him back in mid-December. He hadn't planned on it, but he found himself telling the Professor about Headquarters' decision to have New York and the other Regional Offices start making their own indications. He told him about the seminar he'd delivered in January and how, since then, Sergeant Long had given him free rein to work on refining his system.

Even though Loomis made a comment at that point, saying that was generous of the Sergeant, Will could sense he was growing impatient with the conversation. He knew that he needed to speed things up. He hadn't even gotten to the main point of the coming storm yet. His segue into the details of how his system was predicting an approaching storm, possibly a monster, was rather clumsy and disjointed, and he felt the Professor was coming close to ending the call. Not having had enough opportunity to lay the groundwork as he'd intended, Will muddled through the rest of the conversation as best he could, all the while attempting to relay the urgency of the situation. Clearly, though, judging by the questions he was asking, Loomis did not believe a snowstorm was on its way, let alone a life-threatening blizzard.

Finally, Will thought he should just cut his losses and get off the telephone. He had far better things he could be doing with his time. He knew it would be a colossal waste of precious energy trying to convince Loomis – if he chose not to believe, which was certainly his prerogative, well, so be it. Out of a deep sense of loyalty, Will had taken a personal and professional risk in sharing this information with the Professor. To say he was disappointed by his reaction was an understatement. But at least Loomis was cordial when they made their good-byes before hanging up, so he supposed he should be grateful for small favors.

Will returned to his office and sat in his chair, staring blankly at the wall. He was disturbed by the outcome of the call; he certainly hadn't seen that coming. A moment or two later, he decided it was time to shake it off and get back to the work at hand.

Alright then, the hell with him. He'll certainly see soon enough now, won't he. Although the snow won't start till later up in New Haven, it looks like they'll end up having it even worse than New York City. And one thing's for sure: when all is said and done, he certainly won't be able to say I didn't warn him.

CHAPTER 22

FRIDAY EVENING, MARCH 9, 1888

The sun was just about to set as Will stepped onto the sidewalk outside the Equitable Building. He stopped for a moment to take in the beautifully nuanced shift in light unique to the gloaming, one of his favorite times of the day. He then set off for Brooklyn at his usual brisk pace.

The first thing he intended to do after arriving home was spend an hour or so brushing up on his telegrapher skills. He was slightly taken aback by the brief wave of nostalgia he experienced just thinking about it, and allowed himself a quick smile. He thought that it would be just like old times again, back when he was at the Fort.

Will was surprised to notice he'd broken a light sweat after being on the road only a short time. The overcoat he wore was a thin one, but with the temperature still hovering near sixty and his rapid rate of locomotion, it made for a warm walk.

As he entered the Bridge's pedestrian path-way, he looked around with great interest at the throngs of people, generally men, but also the occasional woman, eagerly returning home as they neared the end of a long, hard week of labor. With but one, often abbreviated, day left to complete the work-week, they were no doubt deep in thought reviewing the plans they'd made with their spouses and families for Saturday night and the Sabbath. How happy they all seemed, thoroughly enjoying what they could only have concluded was a serendipitously early start to spring. Indeed, one newspaper had actually gone so far as to proclaim that – Hallelujah! – winter was already over.

And the fact that it was staying lighter so much longer now certainly added to this notion, and to the general euphoria which seemed to hang palpably in the air.

Although Will was enjoying this brief respite from all of the stress and tension in which he felt mired, its calming effect was short-lived. His pleasant daydream was brutally interrupted by a sudden onslaught of images of the coming storm, the enormous and terrible impact it would have on virtually everyone caught in its path. By Monday morning, tens – maybe hundreds – of thousands would find themselves in a position of extraordinary hardship, and many of those would be waging a desperate battle for sheer survival. And as he had implied earlier to Frank, too many of them would find themselves on the losing end of that proposition.

Will felt a connection, a camaraderie, with his fellow commuters as he neared the apex of the main span high above the East River, the mid-way point marking the boundary between Manhattan and Brooklyn. The hardy pedestrians. All those riding in the carts, wagons, omnibuses, and horsecars. And, of course, patrons of the el. How utterly ordinary, orderly, and carefree their pilgrimage to and from Manhattan seemed to be, looking at them in this moment. And within a very few days, he thought, how completely chaotic it was destined to become. Based on what he knew would be the power of this storm to devastate an urban populace, Will believed the death toll in New York City alone, sadly, would likely top two hundred.

He suddenly flashed back to when he was five or six, and had that same surreal feeling of actually knowing what was about to happen with the weather while not another soul around him had even the slightest idea. Except this time the circumstances were profoundly different. This time the stakes were much, much higher.

Will had never believed in psychics, or seers, as they were commonly called. He felt that they were merely a sophisticated form of confidence artist, exploiting those with either a persistent sadness, usually from the loss of a loved one, or a general unwillingness to be responsible for what they, themselves, had created, looking to lay blame elsewhere. As someone firmly grounded in science, he'd always maintained that these so-called "seers" had no true powers or special abilities.

Now, though, he felt he could understand (albeit not necessarily agree with) what many had claimed for years to be true: there really were people with the ability to see certain things before they happen. In fact, with this new awareness, he even dared admit that he might belong in this group, as this innate ability described exactly what he had experienced when he was much younger. As to why he had never acknowledged it before, he thought one possibility was that these clairvoyant episodes had occurred when he was but a mere child, and had never really happened since – at least not that he could recall. But then his logical mind took over. Of course, his "knowingness" had nothing whatsoever to do with any psychic abilities. It was simply the application of good old-fashioned science, and that was all.

Or was it? Damn! One more thing to file away for future consideration.

After brushing up on his telegrapher skills, Will's plan for the rest of the evening was to plot this afternoon's surface map, then apply his forecasting system to hone in on the blizzard's start-time.

He knew two things: first, the storm would begin, innocuously enough, as a mild, gentle rain sometime around noon on Sunday. Second, at some point late Sunday night or early Monday morning, that rain, ever-increasing in intensity, would abruptly turn into a fierce, howling, wind-driven blinding snow, with rapidly plummeting temperatures. What he did not know was when, precisely, the transition would occur. And this timing was absolutely critical.

If the change-over were to occur early on Sunday night, for example, say eight or nine p.m., that would probably bode well for the majority of the workforce. By the time they awoke on Monday morning, sometime in the pre-dawn, any question about what to do would already be moot. They would have no option but to remain safely indoors.

On the other hand, if the change-over were twelve hours later, by the time the snow began in earnest most would be well into their shift at work, and would find themselves trapped there. This scenario, Will reasoned, would be worse, as helpless wives and children would be stranded at home, ill-prepared to fend for themselves.

Unfortunately, there was a third scenario which, he reluctantly concluded, would be both the worst and the likeliest of all. If the change-over were to occur sometime early Monday morning, with no advance warning from the Signal Service about the storm's severity, people would simply bundle themselves up and brave the elements to get to their jobs. After all, it would be the first day back after the Sunday break. For most, the need to show up for work on time was an absolute imperative – especially in light of how difficult it was to find a decent-paying job in these hard times.

Undoubtedly, most people would rationalize that the startling and wholly unexpected "mini-blizzard," while impressive and supremely inconvenient in the moment, would almost certainly be abating soon, and there would be no question as to what they would do.

Which would leave them totally at the mercy of Mother Nature gone berserk.

Wilma moved the bubbling seafood pan to the cooler side of the stove-top to bring its contents down to a simmer, and filled the large spaghetti pot with water. She lugged the heavy pot over to the hot portion of the stove-top, then sat down to rest a bit and await Will's arrival as the water began its slow march to the boiling point. She was eager to surprise him with this new dish she'd discovered a few months back while leafing through one of the older volumes of her Godey's Lady's Book magazines – a seafood pasta dish which sounded, from the recipe, like it would be delicious. She had been meaning to make it for them ever since.

Recently they had entered into a most agreeable arrangement in which Will would join her for dinner each night, unless he notified her otherwise. The two of them had gone back and forth for quite awhile before she finally agreed to accept a nominal remuneration for these meals, in the form of a small increase in his rent. She didn't really need the extra money, and certainly didn't want to charge him, but he'd insisted – and that was that.

"Will, dear, I'm so glad you're home. I've prepared a special surprise for our dinner. It's something new, and I'm really excited for you to try it out with me," she called out from the kitchen, as soon as she heard him come through the front door, then stop to take his shoes off in the vestibule. "It'll be ready soon, and I have a feeling that you're really going to enjoy it."

She could hear Will bounding up the stairs two at a time, as he did most days, calling out as he went, "Oh, Mrs. D, you're simply the best! I'll be down in a jiffy."

Will hadn't been able to give much thought to anything but his surface maps and the storm till now, when it suddenly dawned on him that he really needed to take advantage of this opportunity to relax and enjoy a satisfying and hearty meal. Even though it was early, only six-thirty, he was ravenously hungry. Perhaps it had something to do with the unmistakable and irresistible aroma of seafood simmering on the stove, replete with garlic and other flavorings. He couldn't quite distinguish the type of seafood, but that hardly mattered given that he liked it all; it was by far his favorite entree.

After finishing the first course, a beautifully dressed, crisp garden salad, Mrs. D prepared the plates for the main dish – first the spaghetti, then the seafood with the delicate sauce on top, all sprinkled with freshly grated Romano cheese.

"Oh my, Mrs. D, this looks and smells incredible. You've really outdone yourself here."

"Well, let me suggest you taste it first, dear, before making such a declaration. But I must say, it certainly does seem as if it turned out rather well. I do hope you'll like it."

Will dug into his generous serving with gusto, then sat back after the first few bites, pausing to ruminate. Maybe it was the stress of the storm with all its attendant complications, or the enormous amount of energy he'd been forced to expend in recent days, or a general sleep deprivation. Or maybe it was some combination of all three. Regardless, whatever the underlying factors might be, one thing he knew for sure: Mrs. D's seafood pasta dish tasted better than anything he could ever remember having eaten before – better, even, than anything he could have imagined. For the time being, his work could wait. There was nothing else to do now but enjoy this remarkable meal and the delightful company of its caring creator.

"Well? What do you think?" She looked at him expectantly, eyes opened wide and lower lip slightly tucked under her front teeth.

In that moment she reminded Will of nothing so much as a sweet little school girl, proud of her accomplishment and eager for teacher's approval. Suddenly, he was struck by a bittersweet glimpse of the wonderful, rare relationship that she must have had with her Walter.

He shared as much with her, after telling her just how amazingly scrumptious her dish tasted – out-doing anything he could ever have anticipated.

"Your insight about me and my Walter is right on target, Will," she said somewhat wistfully, staring past him in a brief moment of apparent reverie. "We surely were blessed in each other, I can tell you that, for each and every one of our joy-filled twenty-four years together." She paused for just another few seconds, then continued brightly, "Now – as far as this dinner goes, I'm so happy that you're enjoying it as much as I am. And I'm thinking it's something we should plan on having for special occasions, from here on out."

Without knowing exactly why, Will felt this to be the right time and place to bring up the subject of his current dilemma, his extraordinary conundrum. Of course, it was no coincidence that he just happened to be sitting with his Number One confidant, whose wisdom he had come to rely on in any sort of sticky situation. So while the two of them savored their meal, Will slowly opened a discussion with Mrs. D about everything he was currently dealing with. She was rapt with attention. He went into more detail about his forecasting system, explaining as much as he thought her capable of understanding. He told her all about how he'd been fine-tuning, verifying, his system since his transfer from Washington. He reminded her about his seminar and Sergeant Long's subsequent decree not to discuss his forecasting system with anyone. He told her about his conversations with Glynn and Frank and all about the Signal Service's game-changing "about-face" in protocol, ceding full responsibility for making their own forecasts to the newly appointed Regional Offices, come April.

But everything he related up to this point was to provide the background, the context, for the most important thing he needed to tell her: that a blizzard unlike anything she'd ever experienced in her lifetime would almost surely be bearing down on all of them – hard – in less than two-and-a-half days. And, of course, that he had no idea what he would tell Glynn to-morrow. Or Frank, for that matter, to follow up on their conversation earlier. Or Sergeant Long. He was especially stumped by how to approach the Sergeant with all this. By now he had gone over the situation so many times in his mind, it was as if he were delivering a rehearsed speech, clearly communicating his conundrum.

Wilma listened intently to everything Will was saying. When he was done, you could have heard a pin drop as she sat in stunned silence for a long moment. She hadn't a clue how to even begin to formulate a coherent response to any of it.

On top of her deep concern for Will, given the enormity of what he was up against at work, thoughts flashed through her mind about their own situation here at home. *Good Heavens – what provisions do we need to stock up on? Do we have enough wood and food? What about Blanche and Charley – what should I tell them? Oh, dear God – Charley's a harbor pilot; weekends mean everything to them, especially in to-day's economy. I can't see him not going out at the break of dawn, to-morrow or Sunday. Will he be safe? Could he possibly die? Oh, my poor Blanche!* Her thoughts raced on and on, chaotically.

After nearly a minute, she began, deliberately, "I really don't know what to say about all of this, Will. You've got me at a complete loss here. You're absolutely sure this is what's going to happen?"

"Unfortunately, yes, Mrs. D. Pretty much."

"Well, we do have some time anyway, which, when you think about it, is a whole lot more than most people will have, poor souls. Two-and-a-half days, as you say."

"Yes, we do have a little time, which is a very good thing. And actually, that's what Frank said as well. Unhappily, though, that doesn't get me one whit closer to knowing what in the heck I should do about any of this."

"No, Will, I reckon it doesn't at that," she replied, shaking her head sadly.

It was nearly eight-thirty by the time Will made it back up to his room, where it took him less than a half-hour to get up to snuff on his telegrapher skills. He had just finished plotting his three o'clock surface map, and was already deeply engaged in the mental exercise of narrowing down the blizzard's start-time, when he heard a light, familiar rapping on his door.

"Come on in, Mrs. D, please."

"Will, I do hope you'll forgive me for bothering you while you're working, but I think I just might have come up with the solution to your conundrum."

"Praise the Lord! And do tell. Oh, but before you do, just to be clear, there is nothing you could do that could possibly be a bother to me."

"Well, thank-you, that's very kind of you to say, my dear. Alright, then. Obviously, I've been giving this a lot of thought, and what I've come up with is that you, we, are looking at this whole situation incorrectly. You are taking all of the responsibility for what might happen because of this storm and placing it squarely on your own shoulders – and only your shoulders. And it doesn't need to be viewed from that perspective. Actually, it shouldn't be viewed that way at all. Because nothing could be further from the truth."

"That sounds like a very interesting line of thought. Please, do go on."

"I'll be happy to. Well, as far as I can see, what it all boils down to is simply this: tell Frank, tell Long, tell Glynn, tell Kira, tell *all* the people you care about – and then just let it all go. Let the chips fall where they may, as the saying goes. You see, that way *they* will then be the ones to decide for themselves what to do, or not do, about the storm. Your conscience will be clear, having done everything you can do, simply by sharing with them the invaluable gift of your foresight."

"You know, Mrs. D, I think you might really be onto something there. It's just sort of common sense, isn't it, when you think about it. I mean, what in the world am I doing, walking around as if this burden were mine alone to carry?"

Oh, my good God – I've been so wrapped-up in all the complications surrounding the political intrigue at the Office, I never even gave one single thought to warning Kira! How is that even possible?

"Yes, that's exactly what I'm saying, Will. You see, the answer popped into my head just a few moments ago, when I was reviewing my thoughts from our conversation earlier. I asked myself, 'What on earth should I tell Mrs. Potts?' Then it came to me, and quite decisively. Since I know of something that would likely endanger her and her husband, well, I'm very clear: I have a responsibility, an *obligation* really, to tell her. And I will. I will tell her, them, as soon as possible, which, unless they've already gone to bed and don't hear me knocking, will be as soon as we're done here.

"Now, and this is the important part, what they choose to *do* with that information is not only completely up to them, it is, more to the point, totally out of my hands. I will walk away at that juncture, without getting drawn into convincing them or defending anything I've said. That's the critical part, Will, and also the hardest – telling your truth, without feeling the need to convince someone else to believe it, or defending your position about it, in any way."

She paused for a moment, as if wanting to let what she'd said sink in just a bit before continuing on.

"When it comes right down to it, that's really all I can do. That's all anyone can do. And that's what one should do."

"Well, whaddya know. I'll be damned! Oh, please forgive me." Will quickly caught himself; he had long ago made a commitment to never insult Mrs. D by using profane language in front of her.

She chuckled lightly. "Relax, my dear. I'd say that's perfectly understandable under these particular circumstances."

"Thank-you for that. And yes, I'd say so, too." He smiled warmly at her.

"You know something, Mrs. D? The more I think about everything you've just said, the more I see that it is absolutely correct. Which, of course, is only what I would have expected, coming from you." He gave her arm a quick tap for emphasis, his face lit up by a grateful grin. "Anyway, I do believe I'll now be sleeping much better to-night, thanks to you."

Important mental note to myself – I must call Kira the very first thing to-morrow morning. I still can't believe it's slipped my mind till now.

"Yes, well, you're very welcome, Will. And please see that you do. Sleep well to-night, that is. I have a feeling you're going to be needing as much rest as you can possibly get over the next few days, just to be able to keep your strength up. I'll say good-night, then, my dear."

"And good-night to you, too, Mrs. D. I think I'll finish up soon and turn in for the night. And I know I'm repeating myself, but thank-you so much."

"You're welcome, my dear boy, you know that. I'm always happy to help out in any way that I can." Mrs. D closed his door behind her as she left, then headed down the stairs.

Back in the kitchen, sitting alone at the table, Mrs. D posed the thought, aloud, "Well, now that that's all settled, I very much wonder just how in the hell *I'm* ever going to manage to get any sleep to-night. And I can't even bear to think about poor Blanche and Charley. What a horrid mess! I'd better get over there quickly, before I lose my nerve."

Will heard Mrs. D's soft footfalls coming up the stairs at about ten o'clock. He figured he could wait till to-morrow to find out how she'd fared on her mission to warn their neighbors. At around ten-fifteen, he finally finished calculating his best estimate of when the blizzard would be starting, after which he quickly washed up for the night and climbed into bed. By ten-thirty he was fast asleep.

CHAPTER 23

SATURDAY, EARLY MORNING, MARCH 10, 1888

The day promised to be sunny and unusually warm yet again, this first Saturday since the last of Sergeant Long's weekly seminar series. A light wind was blowing from the south as Will sat at his desk in the tower of the Equitable Life Building at the corner of Broadway and Cedar Street. He was waiting patiently for day-light to break, at which point he would be able to scan the sky for cirrus clouds.

On his commute in, Will had formulated a plan for sharing his knowledge of the coming storm with all the people in his life. Expanding on Mrs. D's common-sense advice, he now knew not only precisely what he would be saying, but to whom and when, as well.

It was strange to think of how a seemingly unresolvable conundrum had evaporated so easily, simply by virtue of changing one's way of looking at it. For that is precisely what Mrs. D had helped Will to do – completely alter his perspective.

Another important mental note: when all of this is finally over, I must remember to buy the dear lady a gift of chocolates.

At first glance, the surface map he'd plotted last night with yesterday afternoon's obs showed nothing to indicate that a severe storm would soon be affecting the area. Of course, that was why the official indication had no mention of it, whatsoever.

There had been a few cirrus clouds late Friday, and Will needed to see how the direction and speed of those wispy tell-tale precursors had changed. Yesterday they'd been moving from the west-south-west, or from a direction of 235 degrees, at an estimated forty-miles-per-hour. He was able to ascertain all this by using the cloud-motion system he'd established last year, within the first few days of his arrival at the New York Office. Using a compass from a fixed-location on the observation deck, he had painstakingly ground-truthed landmarks for the eight cardinal and intermediate directions, from which he could accurately observe the clouds' direction of motion. Application of a simple trigonometric formula based on an assumed cloud height of 18,000 feet allowed him to estimate their speed.

To-day, he expected to see that the motion of the cirrus clouds had backed about 50 or 60 degrees to a direction from the south, or from 235 to about 180 degrees. He anticipated that incorporating this information into his forecasting system would result in further confirmation of the impending blizzard.

As the sun's first rays came across the horizon, however, he was quite surprised to discover that the motion of these delicate forerunners of the storm, brilliantly illuminated overhead and to the east, had backed much further. They were now moving from the southeast, or about 140 degrees, and their speed had nearly doubled.

While Will had been engaged in observing the cirrus clouds, Glynn had been busy telegraphing Friday's set of evening obs. After returning from the observation deck, Will quickly transcribed the telegraphs and had last night's surface map plotted by six-thirty. He hadn't had the time last evening to do a complete comparison of yesterday's morning and afternoon maps, but he certainly had plenty of time now and would be able to fully compare all three. After a bit, he was able to conclude that conditions were evolving pretty much as his forecasting system had predicted.

Relatively tepid ten-thirty-five-millibar high centered north of Lake Erie now moves southeast to upstate New York, a bit weaker. Frigid high over west-central Canada now centered just over the Canadian border where Montana and North Dakota meet. Expected. Central pressure stronger. Now up to ten-thirty-two. Surprising. Ridging all the way south into the Texas panhandle. Hmm. Inverted trough a bit further east, now cutting through central Minnesota. Weak low now discernable in north-central Iowa. Junction between the inverted trough to the north and the strong Arctic front on the move south and east. Gulf still wide-open for business. As expected.

Will knew that things would really be coming to a head now, with less than forty-eight hours remaining before the onset of the blizzard. He had spent a good part of last evening fine-tuning his prediction of the start-time, and estimated that the change-over in Manhattan would likely be somewhere around four or five a.m. Which was, of course, just as he'd feared – the worst-case scenario.

It would be at least another thirty minutes before Glynn would be calling with this morning's obs, so Will knew he had a little time to begin implementing the first part of his communication plan. He found Frank and requested that he join him in his office, making sure he closed the door behind them.

Frank had given Will a wide berth so far this morning, apparently relying upon his assurance that he'd share what he could, when he could, about the impending storm. As they settled into their chairs, facing each other across the desk, Will could read the apprehension in his friend's face.

"Okay, Frank, this is it, as promised. I'm now going to tell you everything I believe will be happening, including how the events will most likely unfold. I'm also going to tell you precisely what it is I'm going to say to Long. And to Glynn Gardner in Headquarters. And to Kira. You can do whatever you want with this information, within certain limitations, but you'll end up seeing – hell, you probably already do – that you, yourself, will then have this, this, let's call it this 'burden of responsibility' to bear. And trust me, it isn't to be taken lightly – indeed, it comes with a cost.

"I'll be giving Long all the details of what I believe is going to happen over the next few days. It's not a pretty picture, but you already know that. Now, since he is the Commanding Officer of a strictly enforced hierarchy, I am going to ask that you not mention anything at all to the rest of the staff here, as that will be his responsibility to deal with as he sees fit. Are you with me so far?"

"Yes, certainly."

"To reiterate, for absolute clarity, what I mean is, do you understand that deciding whether or not to inform anyone else on staff here will be entirely up to him – not me, and not you?"

"Yes, Will, I do understand exactly what it is you're saying. And for what it's worth, I'm in complete agreement with you."

"Excellent, and good to know. Thank-you. Now, the decision to tell Headquarters, or not, will also be his, and his alone. Here I have to tell you that I certainly don't envy him that decision, not one single bit. If you thought that *I* had a conundrum to deal with . . ."

Frank nodded thoughtfully.

"Personally," Will continued, "if I were him, I would tell them everything. I'd also tell the staff here, too, for that matter. But I'm not him, and again, being that this is the Army, it's simply not my call to make."

It was evident to Will, from the look of deep concern on Frank's face, that he understood everything he'd said, but he needed to be sure, so he spelled it out again. "Again, just to be clear, if it were up to me, I'd tell Headquarters everything. I mean about my research, my forecasting system, the storm – the whole caboodle. Somehow, though, I don't think the Sergeant is going to do that. And if I'm right, and he doesn't, that will make things much more difficult for me, certainly. Unfortunately, that's just how it has to be."

"Yes, Will, you've made yourself quite clear. I understand completely."

"That's good, Frank, and thank-you again – particularly for putting up with my slight obsessiveness on the subject." He gave his friend a wry, self-deprecating grin. "Now, about Glynn. I don't believe the two of you have ever met, have you?"

"No, we haven't, actually. But Will?" Frank, clearly disturbed, interrupted Will's train of thought. "What *is* going to be happening here, anyway? I mean, as far as you can tell, that is."

"Oh, yes, that. How could I have forgotten? Well, Frank, the outlook is still pretty grim, much the same as what I told you yesterday. It was yesterday when we talked, wasn't it? To be honest, I can't even quite remember. The days are all something of a jumbled blur to me at the moment."

"Yes, Will, it was yesterday when last we spoke."

"Right. Well, essentially, nothing much has changed since then. Still expecting temps near zero, winds of . . . what did I say yesterday?"

"Fifty or sixty in the City, and more like seventy or eighty out at sea," Frank recalled, immediately.

"Right, right. Well, if anything, I now think those predictions might even be slightly on the conservative side!"

"Oh, shit."

"A sentiment with which I concur whole-heartedly, my friend. Oh, and the start-time, the change-over from rain to snow? Looks like it'll be happening at the worst possible time: four or five a.m. Too late to deter people from leaving for work, and too early to ensure that they arrive there safely. I hate having to say this, Frank, I really do – but I absolutely fear the worst."

Frank sat perfectly still in stunned silence. Will joined him for a moment, in a display of camaraderie, before continuing on.

"Anyway, getting back to what I wanted to tell you about Glynn. I know you have no way of knowing how much he has risked by providing me with all of the obs to support my research, especially lately, as we've been closing in on this event. He wants to know what's going to happen, and logically so. This beast will be hitting him in Washington City as well, just not nearly as hard as it will us, up here – though harder than I had originally thought it would, truth be told. So, when I talk to him in a little while, I will be explaining everything to him, too."

"I see ..." Frank's tone was cautious; it was evident that he wasn't sure exactly what Will was attempting to communicate.

"The reason I'm telling you this is because Glynn will then be taking on the same responsibility that you just did, Frank. Which brings me to Kira and, by extension, Alex."

Frank's right palm flew up, seemingly involuntarily; he looked for all the world as if he were taking a court-room oath. "Will, I swear – I haven't said a word to Alex."

"That's good, Frank," Will said, smiling, amused by his reaction. "Because now it will be easier for you to have this discussion with her. And as far as Kira goes, rest assured – I will try to reach her by telephone to-day and fill her in on everything. Hopefully, that should be well before you get home to have the conversation with Alex." Will's grin widened.

Frank returned Will's amused smile, all the while trying desperately to conceal the horror that had just swept over him. Alex had told him all about Kira's incredible excitement over being called back for a final audition, which was scheduled for early Monday morning. Judging from what Will had just said, it was pretty clear that, as of yet, he knew nothing about any of that.

Dear Lord, I need to get out of here, and fast – before Will puts it together that I already knew about Kira's final audition. And I'm afraid "conundrum" will be far too paltry a word to describe the Hell he's in store for, once he finally does learn the date and time she's committed to being there.

It was seven-forty and the telephone call was for Will. As his conversation with Frank had lasted quite a bit longer than he'd anticipated, he was now going to have to reverse the sequence of the second and third parts of his plan. He had to get the seven's from Glynn on this call and, as promised, bring him up to speed on the storm. His conversation with Long, therefore, while certainly critical, would simply have to wait a bit.

Will pressed the bell of the receiver to his left ear, leaving his right hand free to write. He spoke clearly into the mouthpiece. "Hello, good buddy, I'm ready when you are. And when we've finished, I will make good on my promise to tell you everything I know."

"Thank-you, Will, I really do appreciate that. Okay, here goes." Glynn quickly read off the morning's observations, after which Will explained, in great detail, all he knew about the advancing storm.

The next few minutes were devoted to a discussion of all the nuances – philosophical, moral, ethical, professional – relating to responsibility in the matter. Will made sure Glynn recognized that the decision to tell Headquarters belonged to Sergeant Long, and *only* to him. If he opted not to do so, then that was that. But it was imperative that he, Glynn, not divulge anything to anyone at his Office. After all, Will cautioned severely, this was still the U.S. Army and the chain of command *must* be followed. There simply could be no excuse for violating protocol which, to him, was very cut-and-dried in this matter. A slip-up might very easily be devastating. Heads could roll.

Glynn reassured Will that he thoroughly understood the extraordinarily delicate nature of the situation, and promised to do his utmost to keep all information about the storm securely under his hat, for as long as necessary.

After hanging the telephone earpiece back on its hook, Will began the work of plotting the morning's seven o'clock obs. In short order he had completed the surface map, noting that it continued to evolve very much in the fashion his forecasting system had predicted it would.

Little change to the position or intensity of the high in the Northeast. Nearly stationary. Arctic high pressing southward through western Montana, still centered north of the border. Minus twenty degrees in North Dakota and Montana. If anything, the high's even stronger than last night. Central pressure now about ten-thirty-four. Ridging down all the way to Dallas. Weak open-wave low in Iowa moves northeast to southern Wisconsin. Inverted trough north through central Wisconsin extending through western Lake Superior. Cold front from the Wisconsin low south-southwest to Dallas and then northwest through El Paso. Increasing pressure gradient east of cold front and inverted trough to eastern Pennsylvania. Strong Gulf influx of moisture continuing. One-point-four-two inches of rain in Shreveport in the past nine hours – that's the first indication of a new storm center possibly forming.

CHAPTER 24

SATURDAY, MID-MORNING, MARCH 10, 1888

Will made his way through the communal area of the Office, intent on reaching Sergeant Long, his furrowed brow a clear indication of his deep preoccupation. He had spent the better part of the past quarter-hour lost in imagining variations of their difficult, but ineluctable, conversation. Just as he was walking past the telephone, its shrill ring startled him out of his reverie. Automatically reaching out to pick up the earpiece, he was struck by a premonition that the person on the other end of the line was Kira. Truth be told, she was the absolute last person, in this particular moment, with whom he wished to speak. Without knowing exactly why, Will was determined to have his "blizzard conversation" with Long before the one he'd have with Kira. Perhaps he was hoping that Long might see his way clear to legitimizing all of Will's further conversations about the storm, by granting him license to speak to others about it.

"Will, is that you answering the call? How fortuitous. It's me, Kira, calling."

"Why, hello, Kira, what a pleasant surprise. It's good to hear from you. How are you faring to-day?" He was fairly sure his friendly tone belied his actual state of frustrated inconvenience.

"I'm good, Will. Actually, very good indeed."

He thought he detected an unusual note of excitement in her voice as she hurried on. "And I want to say, right off, that I know it's been quite awhile since we last spoke, and I'm very sorry about that. You see, there's just been so much going on, and I have –"

"No, no, Kira, please. Forgive me for interrupting, but I feel I must stop you right there. If anything, I should be the one apologizing to you, of that I am certain. The truth is, I've been absolutely swamped around here, of late." It took some effort for Will to keep a straight face. Though technically accurate, his communication could only be characterized as a gross understatement of the current situation. But all of that would have to wait for the conversation they'd be having later, of course.

"Well, alright then, Will, have it your way," she responded, her voice lilting pleasantly. "And I accept your apology, gladly. But now that we have all that out of the way, please listen closely, as I've got some simply marvelous news to share with you. I know that you'll be very happy to hear that yours truly has landed ... get ready ... drum-roll, please ... a *final audition* – ta-da! It's for a fabulous acting part in a play – a comic operetta, to be precise. I have solo singing lines in three separate appearances! This could be really big for me, Will, I just know it. It's the type of role a performer can really get noticed in."

"Oh, Kira, that's absolutely wonderful. Congratulations, my dear! But hold on there just a minute. You say this is a *final* audition? When did you have the first one?" His query held a note of urgency.

For a brief instant, Will felt himself beginning to panic, as he searched his memory banks furiously. His preoccupation with all things storm-related had been so great lately, it wasn't at all difficult to imagine that she'd mentioned something as important as an audition and he'd forgotten all about it. But then he recalled how much time had elapsed since they'd last spoken, and he relaxed immediately. By now, he had become familiar enough with the whole process to know that final auditions generally followed closely on the heels of initial ones.

"Oh, that one was just a few days ago. This past Tuesday, to be exact. And I'm awfully sorry I didn't tell you about it beforehand, Will. I suppose I'd kind of made up my mind, going in, that I'd wait and see whether I'd get the final audition before saying anything. I guess I don't have to tell you about theatre people and their silly superstitions, do I. But that's all water under the bridge now, anyway. Because Hallelujah! I got it!

"You know, Will, they don't go around offering final auditions to just anybody, that I can promise you. I mean, I can't even remember the last time I had one, myself, before now. And I surely don't want to put the kibosh on it by what I'm about to say, but, well, I've been feeling mighty good about this one. Will, I really think I'm going to get this amazing part!"

"Oh, Kira, that's so good to hear. I'm so very, very happy for you! If there's anyone who deserves a break like this, well, it's you – you've worked so long and so hard for it." The smile which stretched from ear-to-ear lit up Will's whole face, and for that one split second he forgot about anything remotely connected to the storm, probably for the first time in nearly a week.

"Thank-you, Will, thank-you ever so much. That's so sweet of you to say, and so very nice to hear . . . it really means a lot to me, I want you to know that." She paused for a moment, then went on, giggling delightedly, "I just hope you won't think me too terribly immodest when I say that I can't disagree with a single word you just said." The endearing trill of her laughter was followed by a long, contented sigh. Will found himself reveling in her good spirits. Truly, he could not have been happier for her.

"Now, let's see, what else . . . Oh, yes, it says here that I have to be at the Bijou Opera House at, where is it again, ah! here it is – 'at seven-forty-five Monday morning.' I just read that straight off the telegram. Oh, Will, I wish I had the words to describe how incredible it was to receive such a wonderful telegram! Now the Bijou's on Broadway, between 30th and 31st Streets. That's not where my first audition was, but it is where the play is going to run. And Will? I have this great idea. If you could manage to get a couple of hours off on Monday morning, we could meet after the audition for a late breakfast, or an early lunch, somewhere in between your Office and the theatre. How does that sound to you? What do you say? Oh, Will, it's all just so . . . so terribly exciting!"

Will stopped breathing in that moment, struck dumb by what he'd just heard. All the light drained instantly from his face, which had become a twisted mask of shock and confusion. Never, not in his wildest imagining, would he ever have thought that God could be so cruel.

Fuck! What a nightmare – this simply cannot be happening!

CHAPTER 25

SATURDAY, LATE MORNING, MARCH 10, 1888

Will was beside himself, racking his brain to try and remember what he had said to Kira in the latter part of their conversation. He knew that everything seemed fine when they'd hung up, but that was about all he could recall. It filled him with horror to learn that her coveted and dearly won final audition was timed to coincide so perfectly with the onslaught of the devastating blizzard. In that instant, it had simply been too much for him to handle. He knew he hadn't mentioned anything about the storm to her, having been at a complete loss for words.

After taking the time he needed to calm down, he decided that what he really wanted in the moment was a friend, someone with whom he could discuss this perfect – and perfectly appalling – example of the irresistible-force paradox.

"Frank! Could you come in here for just a minute, please?"

His carefully constructed plan, which only two hours ago had seemed so intelligently thought-out, so reasonable and plausible, had just officially gone to Hell in a handbasket. And all in less than thirty seconds.

"Frank. You're never going to believe what I'm about to tell you – I know it shocked the hell out of me. I just now got off a telephone call with Kira, and she told me about a final audition she has for a play. It's something she's wanted so desperately for so long, and it's scheduled for the first thing Monday morning! *A final audition! Early Monday morning! Sweet Jesus!* I called you in here because I need someone I can commiserate with. My God, Frank, what on earth am I going to do?" Will stared helplessly at his friend, his face a perfect portrait of torment.

Though outwardly calm, Frank's insides were roiling; this was the moment that he'd been dreading. Things had now gone from bad to worse – much, much worse. He prayed that Will wouldn't think to ask him if he'd known anything about the audition. That little bit of added drama was about the last thing either of them needed in the midst of all this madness.

"Is it safe to presume, then, that you didn't give her any information about the storm?"

"Yes. I mean, no – not yet, anyway. You see, it was my intention to tell Long first, and I just happened to be on my way in to see him when the telephone rang. Naturally, I answered it. Kira was on the line, calling with the good news about the audition on Monday. She was so happy and excited she could barely contain herself."

Frank knew he had to tread very carefully. The last thing he wanted was to be trussed up in the middle of this insane situation – yet here he was, for good or ill. So he took a deep breath and forged ahead, giving his friend the best advice he could come up with in the moment.

"Alright, alright, Will, one step at a time. And the first step is this: you just need to go see her to-night and calmly tell her everything you know. Of course, she'll probably still be determined to go to the audition, storm warning be damned. And who can blame her, really? But at the very least, you can tell her what she's going to be up against, maybe help her to be prepared, at least somewhat. After that, well, it will be her decision to make, won't it?"

Will was silent for so long that Frank took the opportunity to change the subject, hoping his transition would not perceived as too abrupt or rude. "So, am I correct in assuming that you will be coming in to the Office sometime to-morrow?"

"Yes, you are. I'll be here, bright and early," Will replied, taciturnly. "Glynn will be telegraphing me this evening's obs about five a.m."

"Of course. Well, maybe I'll stop by around ten or so for any, you know, last-minute updates."

"Sure, Frank, sure. Whatever you want. You just name it."

Frank was taken aback. "Will! You don't mean to say you really mind, do you?"

"No, no, I'm sorry," Will said, shaking his head forlornly. "I guess I'm just really feeling the pressure, right about now. Please forgive the sarcasm in my response. That's not at all how I actually feel, I assure you."

"No apology necessary, my friend. I understand completely."

"Thank-you for that. And thank-you, too, for listening about Kira."

"Sure, buddy. Anytime, you know that." Frank smiled ruefully. "I only wish there were something more I could do, some way I could be of real assistance. I can only imagine how terrible this whole situation must be for you."

"Thanks, Frank. Really, I do appreciate the support." Will hung his head for just a moment, then raised it back up and slapped both palms decisively on his desk. "Well, regardless of how helpless I feel right about now, I guess I can't afford to waste any time wringing my hands in lamentation, can I? Not when I'm seriously overdue in having that conversation with Long."

"Gotcha, partner. You can bet I'll be on tenterhooks, waiting to hear how that communication turns out. So for now, I'll bid you adieu." With that, Frank snapped Will a mock salute, and turned and left the office.

"Excuse me, Sergeant. May I come in and speak with you for a minute?"

"Why sure, Will, come on in. Actually, your timing is rather seren-dipitous. I was, just this minute as a matter of fact, coming over to see you."

"Oh, really, sir? What about?"

"Well, I wanted to let you know about several rather interest-ing discussions I've had with General Greely, over the past couple of days. It seems that the order for each Region to start making its own 'forecasts' – oh, by the way, that's what they're going to be officially called now, it came from much higher up than he. I take it that meant Congress, although I can't be sure. Then again, I don't really give a crap, if you'll pardon the vulgarity. As I'm sure you must know, I'm just not that much of a political animal."

Will hoped his outward expression had remained neutral, because inside he was snorting wildly at such hypocrisy – a sentiment he was certain would be shared by everyone else who works in the Office. He peered closely at the Sergeant's face, but saw no recognition as Long forged ahead.

"Anyway, Will, apparently the General has been on the receiv-ing end of some pretty nasty criticism aimed at our Office by that low-down, dirt-dealing bastard, Abbe. That pompous, arrogant son-of-a-bitch went so far as to imply that we don't have, well . . . let us just say, 'what it takes,' when it comes to making good forecasts. Which makes absolutely no sense at all, given that he knows you are here, and everyone knows that he's always thought mighty highly of your skills.

"No matter how hard I try, I honestly can not figure it out. I don't know whether Abbe's just feeling jealous, or maybe he's reeling from some imagined loss of power or control. Whatever the motivation, he's clearly up-in-arms about something, and has been inciting the General against us. That good-for-nothing bootlicker."

A startled Will was reeling at Long's remonstration. Till this very moment, he hadn't the slightest inkling that the Sergeant harbored any antipathy at all towards Abbe, much less this full-blown enmity he seemed to have no compunction about expressing – and to a subordinate, no less. But as he couldn't quite make out what he was getting at, Will figured his safest bet would be a generically supportive response.

"I'm very sorry to hear that, sir. That's really rather unfortunate."

"Yes, I couldn't agree more. And it's deucedly unfair, for that matter; no one likes being stabbed in the back."

"Well, I suppose I'm telling you all this by way of explaining the decision I've finally reached. If there were any chance at all of my enlightening Headquarters about your forecasting system – before April, that is – well, now they can all just go suck eggs, as far as I'm concerned. Greely and I do go back a long and notably significant way, that's true enough. Even so, I must say I was rather offended by some of the remarks, made by Abbe, of course, which the General saw fit to pass on to me."

"Yes, I can see how you would really be incensed by that." Will kept his tone dispassionate to belie his incipient undercurrent of panic. After all, how much could one man be expected to take? And could God possibly have any more horrifying, unworkable coincidences in store for him on this catastrophic day?

"Anyway, Will, I realize that none of this actually affects you directly, other than, naturally, it is your forecasting system we're talking about here. I just thought it was something you should know."

For one brief moment, Will thought he might be coming close to losing his mind. What was left of it, anyway.

Well, shit, shit, and more shit – isn't that just hunkey dorey. How kind of you to keep me informed about something which "doesn't affect me directly." I can't wait to hear what you'll have to say now, my dear Sergeant, about warning Headquarters about the monster blizzard!

"Alright then. I believe that's quite enough time spent on all that ridiculous flapdoodle. Say, Will, now that I'm through spouting off, what was it you wanted to talk to me about?"

Will knew he was dangerously close to a complete loss of control. Thankfully, he managed to rein himself in just enough to give the Sergeant a coherent reply.

"Oh, yes, that. Uh, nothing much, really. Well, I guess that's not quite true, sir. Um, it's just that, at this point, I'd like a little more time to think about what I want to say. Will you be here, in the Office I mean, for the rest of the afternoon?"

"Yes, I will, as far as I know now, although I will be going out to lunch in about an hour. Say, I've got an idea – why don't the two of us have luncheon together? We can go downstairs to that fancy French restaurant that's so conveniently situated just off the lobby, and we can talk while we enjoy a rather good meal. That will give us a good chance to catch up on some things. And, what the heck, I'll even foot the bill." Long favored Will with his heartiest grin, punctuated by a few robust pats to the back of his shoulder.

"Why, sure, Sergeant, that sounds just great. Thank-you, sir, for the generous invitation."

Somehow, Will managed to match Long's genial conviviality with a broad smile of his own. All the while, however, he was thinking that this was one confab likely to be seared in both their memories for a long, long time to come.

CHAPTER 26

SATURDAY, EARLY AFTERNOON, MARCH 10, 1888

Will advised his luncheon companion that he'd be relying on him to recommend something from the menu. He, himself, did not understand a single word of French. Sergeant Long responded with a smile, saying that would be just fine. He couldn't read the language either, but he did have a general idea about some of the more palatable items being offered. Besides, he informed Will, the waiter, though obviously French, has an excellent command of the English language, and would be only too happy to answer whatever questions they might have.

Even though he was currently overwhelmed by the madness and confusion swirling around the great "blizzard-to-be," Will still had the presence of mind to be able to fully appreciate the upscale restaurant's main dining room. Its rich, white mahogany finishing provided the perfect complement to the walls, which were colorfully done up in a beautiful mosaic tile. Eagerly soaking up the sumptuous atmosphere, he confided to his boss that he'd been wanting to eat here for some time now. In addition to the prices being well above his pay grade, however, he'd always felt it was just a tad too upper-class for someone like him. While Long nodded in tacit understanding, he apparently held a very different view for himself, as he offered that this was his fourth or fifth time dining there.

It didn't take long for the Sergeant to settle on the *huitres a la poulette,* a rich oyster and pastry appetizer, followed by *filet de boeuf, jardiniere,* a beef filet garnished with an array of colorful julienne vegetables. Will ordered *consommé en tasse,* a savory, flavorful broth elegantly served in a delicate porcelain tea cup, and the *filet de boeuf, jardiniere* for his entree, as well. For dessert, they decided to share the *glaces assorties,* an assortment of ices and sherbets in various mouth-watering flavors.

"So, Will, what exciting plans do you have for your day off, to-morrow?" They were just finishing up their first course.

"My day off?"

"Why, yes," the Sergeant responded, eyebrows raised. "To-morrow *is* Sunday, in case you hadn't noticed. And after this afternoon, you're not scheduled to come in again till Monday morning. Pretty much like it's been since you started here, almost a year ago, now." Long raised his napkin to his lips as he peered at Will intently, furrowing his brow. "Are you feeling quite alright, my boy?"

"Uh, yes, boss, sure. I feel just fine." Will took a deep breath and held it for nearly a count of five as he steeled himself for what he knew had to come next. It was now or never.

"Well, um … actually, again, that's not exactly the truth, sir, if you'll forgive me. In point of fact, I'm facing down a distinctly remarkable dilemma. And I'm sorry to have to say that it involves you, directly, sir."

"Me?" Long's eyebrows shot up quizzically as he moved on to his filet, which had just arrived. "What dilemma could you possibly have that would involve me – directly or otherwise?"

After taking another deep breath, Will launched into his explanation. He shared all the reasons he was convinced that a major storm was brewing. He detailed how he'd been fine-tuning his forecasting system with the obs that Glynn, from Headquarters, had been forwarding him all along, once-a-day. And that he'd been receiving three sets of observations daily, over the past few days, to more effectively track the storm's progress. He told him that while Glynn knew everything about the storm, he was sworn to secrecy concerning the rest of the staff there, especially Greely. He told him about Frank knowing, and that he, too, had promised – and could be counted on – not to breathe a word. He even told him about Kira, Alex, Mrs. D, and

Mr. and Mrs. Potts. In a rare moment of self-serving convenience, he elected not to mention his recent and rather inauspicious telephone conversation with Professor Loomis.

A mesmerized Long listened intently without uttering a single word while Will talked for nearly twenty minutes non-stop. It was as if the flood gates had opened. The Sergeant was not a stupid man. He knew instantly that Will had just succeeded in very neatly placing the ball squarely in his court. Touché.

Just then, as if right on cue, the waiter arrived with the *glaces assorties.*

Long had to admit to himself that in addition to how outrageous all of it sounded, he did find a certain degree of humor in the situation. And even though it was coming at him from straight out-of-the-blue, he'd always had a keen ear for the truth: if Will was saying this blizzard was going to happen, he had very little reason to doubt that it would.

Which left him, of course, wondering just what in Sam Hill there was that he could do about it.

The Sergeant placed both his palms flat on the table and took a long, deliberate breath before beginning to speak. "Well, Will, I'm obviously going to have to give all this a great deal of thought, at least for the next little while. There is one thing I can tell you for certain, though. The assertion you made earlier, that your dilemma involves me, directly, was dead-on accurate, after all. In fact, I'd say it involves me right up to my eyeballs and beyond."

Though silent, Will nodded his assent.

"Come on now; finish up your dessert so we can get ourselves back up to the Office, on the double. I definitely need some time alone to ponder all the variables before deciding what I'm going to do."

The Sergeant immediately summoned their waiter and took care of the bill with great dispatch, after which they moved with alacrity towards the elevator. As they hurried on their way, Long, a pace or two ahead of his subordinate, shook his head slightly, in wonderment, as he mumbled to himself under his breath, "Yessiree, Bob – isn't this just a fine kettle of fish."

CHAPTER 27

Will glanced up at the clock. It was nearly time for Glynn's call with the afternoon obs. He and Long had been back from lunch for a good two hours now, and he'd yet to hear a peep out of the usually loquacious Sergeant. In fact, Long had sequestered himself in his office immediately upon their return, ensuring his complete privacy by closing the Venetian blinds in the window connecting his office with the common area. As this was a relatively rare occurrence, several of the other staff had reacted by giving Will odd, questioning looks. The noncommittal shrugs he gave in response effectively discouraged any further inquiry.

It was evident to Will that Long was giving serious thought to the unprecedented set of circumstances which left him with a conundrum of epic proportion. In all likelihood, the Sergeant was every bit as stymied by all of this as he had been, probably even more so. Will believed that his boss would probably gain more with Headquarters in the long run if he were to level with Greely, right now, about Will's forecasting system. Not to mention all the people who could be helped, were an indication issued giving warning of the storm.

Still, Will could not suppress a faint, sardonic smile, recalling the Sergeant's ludicrous reference to himself as "not much of a political animal."

Not much, no, Sergeant. But wait – didn't I just hear a stuffed bird laugh?

Just then the telephone rang. It was Glynn, right on schedule, as usual.

"Okay, Will, here are the afternoon obs." Glynn read off the data with the confident meter of a skilled dancer leading a long-time partner.

"Thank-you, buddy," Will said after he'd recorded the last observation. "I trust you'll telegraph this evening's obs to me to-morrow morning?"

"Yes, Will, you'll have the obs by five. Then I'll call you with the morning ones – and yes, the afternoon's, too."

"That's terrific, Glynn. And thank-you, again."

"Really, it's hardly a problem for me at this point. I think I've actually grown accustomed to our crazy schedule. But I do have a couple of quick questions for you – about the storm, I mean." Will could hear him lowering his voice, making sure no one on his end would be able to overhear their conversation.

Obviously intent on leaving Will no room for equivocation, Glynn hastened to continue. "What do you envision, here in Washington City? I mean, when will the snow start, and how long will it last? How much will fall? How strong will the winds be? No one here at HQ, Will, and I mean absolutely no one, has any clue, whatsoever, that it's going to snow anywhere along the east coast on Monday. I even happened to overhear an exchange between Abbe and the shift lead-forecaster – the word 'snow' was never mentioned, not even once."

Will suddenly felt as if the walls were closing in on him. Not only was each and every conversation taking longer to complete than he'd planned, or even had time for, really, but it seemed that every such intercourse inevitably led to a follow-up one. And, of course, he had yet to sound the alarm to Kira.

"Glynn, I'll be happy to answer all your questions, really, I will. But first, I should probably tell you about my conversation with Sergeant Long, earlier this afternoon. As you can imagine, he was fairly unnerved by the idea of an impending "superstorm." Then he told me he needed some time to decide what, if anything, he was going to tell Greely. After that, he completely isolated himself in his office, where he's been for, oh, about the last two hours or so – presumably stuck in figuring out what he's going to do. Based on some confidences he's shared with me quite recently, though, I don't believe he's going to be telling Greely much of anything."

"Oh. I see," Glynn responded slowly, clearly disappointed.

"And you should also know that I told Long everything – and I do mean everything, Glynn. I told him all about the storm, all about our arrangement to get me the obs each day, and, most importantly, that you know all about my forecasting system, including the details of this storm, but that you are absolutely, and reliably, sworn to secrecy."

"Okay," Glynn said quietly, apparently beginning to appreciate fully how much pressure Will was operating under. "But let me ask you something – why wouldn't he want to tell Greely? I mean, isn't warning the public about what's going to happen with the weather, well, the Signal Service's main mission these days? Especially in a case like this, where the threat is so severe."

"On the face of it, your logic is inescapable, and I couldn't agree more. But, and this is one more thing you'll have to keep to yourself as well, while I've always known about Long's close relationship with Greely, I've only just learned that he can't stand Abbe. Absolutely abhors the man. So back in January, when I gave a presentation on my forecasting system to the staff here, he decided he would not be sharing it with Headquarters immediately. He thought it would be much better for our Office if we were to surprise them, come April, with our unparalleled success in making forecasts for the entire New York Region."

"Wait a minute, Will. What do you mean, 'our success in making forecasts for the entire New York Region?' What the heck is all that about?"

Will rested his head against the wall adjacent to the telephone installation. Then he took a deep, calming breath, exhaling slowly to give himself time to reorganize his thoughts. Really, though, he supposed Glynn's ignorance shouldn't have come as that much of a surprise. By now, he certainly knew that anything is possible in the Army.

"Oh. Well, I'm actually making reference to the confidential memorandum Long received from Greely, sometime back in November. It informed him that our Office was to be one of a number of newly designated Regional Offices which would be responsible for preparing their own forecasts, beginning this April. Apparently this came down from Congress, or somewhere high up. I'm very sorry to be springing this on you, Glynn. I had no idea that you hadn't heard the latest scuttlebutt."

"Oh, that's alright. Of course you couldn't have known. But no, I hadn't. Although, now that you mention it, that certainly does explain a number of mighty peculiar things I've noticed around here lately. Anyway, Will, please tell me more about the storm at hand. After all, HQ is my problem, not yours."

Will allowed himself the briefest moment of exultation at the thought of a problem which wasn't his, even if only to the first order. He then proceeded to oblige Glynn by detailing the effect the storm would have on Washington City. "It's going to begin quite a bit sooner down by you than it will up here. I believe that heavy rain will turn quickly to a heavy, blinding snow – around, say, seven or eight Sunday evening. And –"

"That soon?" Glynn interrupted. "I thought you said the change-over would be more like sometime Monday morning."

"Well, yes, it will be – up here in New York. But you will go over much sooner than that."

"Damn. Well, that changes everything for me." He then went on to say something about the plans that Camille had made for the two of them for Sunday evening.

Will, having finally come to the end of his patience with all of these time-consuming tangents, knew he had to extricate himself from this conversation, and fast. He felt stretched in so many different directions he likened it to being a twenty-pound piece of taffy caught in a pull – the latest Atlantic City boardwalk fad, according to what

Mrs. D had recently heard from Mr. and Mrs. Potts. So he resorted to a tactic he had never employed before, and was not happy about using it now: he told his friend an outright lie.

"Glynn, I'm very sorry to have to interrupt you, but Sergeant Long is calling for me and I must run. We can talk more when you call with the obs mid-morning to-morrow."

"Sure, Will, it's okay, I understand. But I just want to add one more thing, really quickly. I've been studying HQ's maps myself, the last day or so. For what it's worth, with a little imagination I think I can see how things can evolve just as you have predicted. But don't worry, as I've already told you, I absolutely promise I won't say anything, to anyone, in the Office. And, of course, I'll telegraph this evening's obs to you first thing to-morrow morning, and then call you as soon as the sevens come in. We'll talk again, then."

"Okay, thanks again, Glynn. Good-bye."

"Wait! Are you still there?"

"Yes?"

"Instead of telegraphing you this evening's obs, I'll call you with them, when I get in at five. That will give me the chance to speak with you that much sooner."

"That'll be fine, Glynn. Good-bye. And, as always, thank-you."

Will breathed a sigh of relief as he hung the receiver back on its hook. He stared for a moment at this modern miracle of communication as the thought ran through his mind that this was one of those times when a good stiff drink would surely come in handy. Maybe more than one, at that.

CHAPTER 28

It was five-thirty, and Will had just finished plotting the three p.m. surface map when Sergeant Long strode purposefully into his office, pulled the door shut behind him, and noisily took a seat in one of the visitor chairs. He stared intently across the desk at Will for a few moments, fingers steepled and forehead creased, then sat back with a sigh and rested his hands on the chair's arms.

"Alright then, Will. It has taken me a little while, but I have finally come to a decision."

Will was careful to present his superior officer with a composed, neutral face, even though internally he was kicking the man for taking so damn long. By this point, he had grown quite anxious to get the word out to Kira, and the clock was ticking.

"First off, I will start by saying that I believe you are a very special meteorologist, and a gifted forecaster. I think the system you've developed is, well, extraordinary, not to put too fine a point on it. I believe that you will be the one who puts the New York Regional Office on the map, if you'll pardon the pun. As for your prediction of this blizzard . . . well, if a gun were put to my head, I would say you're right. In other words, Will, I have a lot of faith in you. But the truth is, even with all that, I can't be absolutely certain. Nobody can. Only God really knows. And last I looked, He wasn't telling."

Ordinarily, Will would have acknowledged the Sergeant's humor here, but he was unwilling to do that now. He was having trouble keeping his impatience at bay, and just wished Long would just hurry up and get to the point already.

"Well, what it all boils down to is this. I've decided I'm not going to share anything you've told me about the storm with Greely. As a matter of fact, even if there were a way I could be absolutely sure of it, I probably still wouldn't tell him."

"I understand, sir." Will, of course, could not have disagreed more with this decision, but this was still the Army, and he was smart enough to avoid saying anything of the kind. All he wanted now was for Long to go away, so he could finally call Kira. Unfortunately, the Sergeant had more to say.

"Now, as for Mr. Gardner, I have to say I find it most unfortunate that you have told him about the storm."

Will started to speak up in his own defense, but Long quickly raised his right palm, effectively heading him off at the pass.

"Hold up there, Will, please. Just hear me out on this. I said it was unfortunate, and that's true. What I did not say was that I blamed you for telling him; actually, I don't. In fact, if I were in your position, I'm quite certain I'd have done the same thing, myself. Having said that, though, I just want to ensure that he does not slip up and say anything to Greely, or Abbe, or anyone else down there. Because if he does, well, I'll be the one whose head will be on the chopping block. Do you understand what I'm saying?"

"Yes, sir, I do."

"Alright, then, let's talk about that for a minute. How can you be so sure that he'll keep mum and not share with anyone at Headquarters what you've told him about this storm?"

Will had never before experienced the Sergeant communicating with such focused purpose. His eyes fairly burned with the intensity of it. Suddenly all thoughts of Kira slid straight to the back of his mind, yet again, where they would remain till he and Long were finished.

"Well, as I mentioned at lunch, he's always been somewhat afraid that he would get caught breaking protocol by providing me with the obs every day without a direct order from a superior officer. He feels he'd likely be in a world of trouble if that were to happen. At the very least he would probably receive a strong reprimand, and it's entirely possible he'd lose his plum assignment at Headquarters. And if the brass down there should happen to learn anything about my forecasting system through back-door channels, he would almost assuredly have to confess to being the one who sent me the obs. Consequently, he surely has a vested interest in remaining silent. To echo your vernacular, he'd like to keep his own head off the chopping block."

Long peered thoughtfully at Will for several moments, but said nothing, so Will continued. "Now, I know he was hoping that you would tell General Greely about the storm, which would naturally lead to a legitimate discussion about my system. But even though that would make his life so much easier, he understands completely if you don't. In fact, he told me as much, just this morning, after I told him I was fairly confident you would be electing *not* to tell General Greely."

"I see." Long paused again. "And when do you expect to be talking with him again?"

"First thing to-morrow morning. He'll be calling me then, with this evening's obs."

"You're coming into the Office on your day off?"

"Yes, I am."

"And he's going in to Headquarters on his day off?"

"That's right."

"Holy shit. Now I think you're both deranged. Well, since I need to come in for a few hours to-morrow morning myself to catch up on some paper-work, I guess I'll see you then. As for right now? I'm heading home, and glad of it."

"Okay, boss. I guess it has been something of a long day, hasn't it. I'll bid you good-night, then." The Sergeant seemed to hang back for a moment, and Will had the strangest feeling that he might be looking for some sort of apology, given his afternoon of protracted consternation which was a result of their earlier discussion. Knowing that he had nothing to apologize for, Will resisted the temptation to do so, politically prudent though it might be. He smiled pleasantly at the Sergeant till, after a beat or two, the man finally gathered himself to leave.

Will heaved a huge sigh of relief, once he knew he was alone. He then made his way as quickly as he could to the telephone where, at long last, he placed the call to Kira.

"Damn!" he exploded, jamming the earpiece back onto its hook after the operator had informed him his party had not answered. "I guess she's not at home. I'll just have to try her again later, before I leave for the day." Always on the lookout for the silver lining in any situation, he was happy that he now had some time to devote to the three p.m. map.

High in the Northeast moves east to the Gulf of Maine. Ten-thirty-three-millibar Arctic high in the upper plains now centered in South Dakota. Southern Wisconsin open-wave low moves northeast to the western shore of Lake Michigan. Noticeably stronger. Closed circulation. Inverted trough along the western shore of Lake Michigan up through Lake Superior. Cold front from the southern Wisconsin low all the way to Brownsville. Rain continues along the Gulf with massive moisture influx, but still no sign of cyclonic circulation in the Southeast. Hmm . . .

The key to Will's forecast of a monster blizzard rested in the development of a new surface low-pressure system on the Gulf coast, either in Alabama or along the Florida panhandle, which he'd expected would be happening right about now. From there, the storm would deepen explosively, first moving northeast out over the open Atlantic, then crawling more northward right up along the coastline – just offshore.

As he now stared at the three p.m. map, Will had to admit to being flummoxed. For the first time since his system had heralded the storm's arrival, a shadow of doubt began to creep across his mind. There was nothing at all on this map to indicate that the new low had actually begun to form yet. He continued to look at his map for a long moment, a vaguely disquieting feeling in the pit of his stomach. Then he shook it off and returned to the other tasks he wished to complete before leaving for home.

At about six-fifteen, Will knew that he'd had enough. He decided it was high-time that he, too, call it a day, and so he packed up quickly and started out for home. He'd practically made it all the way to the Bridge before realizing that he had forgotten to try again to reach Kira before leaving the Office. At that moment, any passers-by would have been treated to the odd tableau of an intense-looking young man giving his forehead several animated, resounding smacks. He simply could not believe that he'd done it again.

Damn! Well, Mrs. Potts is usually at home this time of evening, so I can probably borrow the use of her telephone.

As Will was crossing the Bridge, he noticed that the pedestrian traffic was made up of fewer businessmen than he was accustomed to seeing. More families and couples seemed to be out and about, enjoying the unusually mild weather of this mid-March Saturday evening. It got him to wondering: given a choice in the matter, would he really prefer to be wrong about the storm?

Of course I would . . . how could I not? If the storm materializes as I've predicted, virtually everyone in the Northeast will be severely impacted. And that includes more than one million people in New York City alone! Hundreds could die, and countless more sustain permanent – perhaps crippling – injury. It makes the mind reel.

But what can I do? What can anyone do? The weather has always done what it will. What God wills, actually. Man proposes, and God disposes. A-men.

CHAPTER 29

SATURDAY, MID-EVENING, MARCH 10, 1888

Will was a wreck by the time he made the turn onto Sands. He couldn't seem to shake the disquieting feeling that this forecasting system of his might not be as great as he'd thought.

No matter how hard he tried, he just could not come up with an explanation for why that new low hadn't developed yet. And if it didn't show up on this evening's map, then his near-certain prediction of a blizzard was in serious jeopardy.

"Will? Will, dear – is that you?"

"Yes, Mrs. D, it's just me, home from the salt mines. And, I might add, if you'll forgive me, after one *hell* of a day."

"Oh, my poor dear. Well, I'm glad you're finally home. Maybe now you can relax, at least for little bit, anyway. I have dinner all ready for us, so do hurry back down."

"Ahh – words to soothe my troubled soul! Not to mention my empty belly. Don't you worry, I'll be there in just about two seconds."

Will suddenly remembered – again – that he had yet to reach Kira. He was beginning to think there was something really wrong with his brain, that he kept forgetting like this. And then, irrationally, he felt a stab of anger at her for not being at home earlier to take his call.

Will glared at his reflection in the looking glass, then spoke to himself sternly. "You must reach Kira, you dunderhead. To-night."

A moment later he was on his way downstairs.

"So," Wilma began, as they were sitting down to dinner, "while I am surely anxious to hear whatever you want to tell me about your "day from Hell," first things first. What's the latest on the blizzard? I haven't been able to concentrate on a single thing all day other than this coming storm. Do you still anticipate that it's going to be a whopper?"

"A whopper, eh? That's actually a very good way of putting it, Mrs. D. Yes, I still believe that it will be. However, in the interest of full disclosure, I'd have to say that at this particular moment, I'm not quite as sure about it as I was before."

"Oh, really? Well, that's good to hear."

Will went on to explain that he'd been counting on the storm, the blizzard-to-be, having already formed on the Gulf coast by this afternoon. And that so far, it had not. He told her that whatever this evening's surface map showed would be critical. "If there is still no circulation down there by that time, then it's likely that the blizzard will not be materializing here."

"But that's good!" she repeated. "We need a blizzard around here like we need a plague of locusts." For the first time since Will had broached the subject of the storm, she felt a glimmer of hope that just maybe they could escape unaffected.

"Well, I couldn't agree with you more. But even given what I just said, at this moment I would still rate the storm at a seventy-percent probability."

"Oh, I see. Then you're still fairly sure it is going to happen."

"Yes, I suppose I am. Although just not as much as I was earlier to-day, before I spent some time studying this afternoon's weather map. Till then, I would have put the odds at about ninety percent."

"I see. Well, let's just hope the downward trend continues."

"Oh, I almost forgot – yet again. I know this sounds ludicrous, but I still haven't managed to reach Kira to warn her about what's coming."

"What? You mean to say that at this point she knows nothing at all about it?"

"Yes, that's right. And, unfortunately, it's much worse than her just not knowing. She called me at the Office this morning to tell me that she's terribly excited, and extremely hopeful, about a final audition she's landed for a great part in an upcoming play. As you well know, she's worked long and hard for an opportunity just such as this and, sadly, they come few and far between. Anyway, you'll never believe when it's scheduled for: seven-forty-five on Monday morning. *Monday morning!* Damn it!"

"Will. Will. Calm yourself, dear. After all, it's still only Saturday."

"Why, yes, that's true. But I know, from first-hand experience, just how quickly time speeds up as a big event draws near. And this is a big event, if ever I've seen one. I can't really explain it, but somehow an entire day will seemingly pass by in a matter of hours.

"Anyway, I tried calling her back earlier this evening from the Office, but she must have been out, because she didn't answer. I really need to reach her to-night, if at all possible. Do you think Mrs. Potts would mind letting me use her telephone?"

"No, of course not, Will. She'd be only too happy to help you out. Why don't we finish eating first, and then we can go over together. The last thing I heard from her was that Mr. Potts wasn't lucky enough to get a ship to-day, so he is definitely going back out again, early to-morrow morning, your blizzard prediction be damned. I'm sure they'll be very glad to hear that the odds of the storm occurring have dropped, even if just by twenty percent."

"Oh, alright then," he answered, sounding just a bit testy. "I guess another hour or so isn't really going to make much of a difference anyway, at this point."

"Will, is something wrong? You don't seem quite yourself. Is it because of the terrible day you had?"

Will hung his head for a moment, then looked up at her wearily. "Oh, Mrs. D. I am so very sorry. I certainly don't mean to be taking it out on you, of all people. It's just that I've been completely drained by all the lunacy I've had to contend with, over the past few days. And my boss, locked into his weird and self-serving politics, has not made things any easier, I can tell you that. Earlier to-day, he informed me that he decided he won't be telling Headquarters anything at all about the storm. Which means, of course, that the general public will have no warning, whatsoever. Can you imagine that?"

"Oh Will, no. You must have felt just horrible hearing him say that."

"Yes, as a matter of fact, I did. Actually, I still do. In my mind's eye, I keep getting these terrible intermittent flashes of bodies lying in the streets, half-buried in the snow, their faces frozen in a rictus of death. Then I can't help thinking about how a word of warning might have made all the difference, maybe even kept those poor souls safe at home with their loved ones. Who will now be tasked with burying a beloved family member." He shook his head hard, as if trying to dispel such images of horror and desolation. He then gazed at her for a long moment, as she watched the expression of deep sorrow on his face metamorphose into one of fierce determination.

"Mrs. D, whatever you do, please double- and triple-check all the supplies you stocked up on to-day, and go out first thing to-morrow to purchase anything else you can think of that we might need to get us through at least the next week. Even though it's the Sabbath, I'm sure that you'll be able to find some places open, at least during the early part of the afternoon. There won't be any maddeningly long lines to deal with, either, because you'll be the only one out there with any idea about what's going to happen." Pausing here briefly, he reached into his overcoat pocket and removed his billfold. "And," he then continued, "I absolutely insist on contributing something to the cause." He pulled out a crisp five-dollar bill and laid it on the table near her place-setting. Her eyes went wide.

"Yes, no. I mean, yes, I will certainly make it a point to go out to-morrow and get any extra provisions we might need, but no, I can't accept this from you." She pushed the bill back towards him.

Will's hand came down over hers, arresting the forward motion she was making. "Yes, of course you can, as much as it might grieve you at first. This is a very unusual situation we're facing, you cannot deny that. And to paraphrase Hippocrates, and maybe even Shakespeare, 'desperate times call for desperate measures.'

"I tell you what. If you like, just use this money to reimburse yourself for some of your, let us say, 'special' provisions. You know, of the liquid variety." Will gave her a sly wink. "I'm sure we'll be making quite a dent in your secret supply over the next few days, wouldn't you agree? Which you'll then have to replenish, naturally, once you have the opportunity." He reached over and gave her hand a few quick pats.

In that moment, Wilma realized that any continued protest on her part would only fall on deaf ears. "Alright, then, Will," she finally acquiesced, graciously, "I will do just as you ask. And thank-you, very much."

"I'm sure I'm the one who should be thanking you, my dear."

Wilma sat back in her chair and clapped both palms on the table. "Well, my boy, now that we've got all that settled, here's a novel idea. Let's eat! Then we'll get right on over to see Mrs. Potts, so you can tell her, in person, what you've just told me. And you can place your call to Kira. After all that, we'll skedaddle right back here and break open that good bottle of whiskey I've been saving for a rainy day. Or maybe, in this case, I should say a snowy one! Anyway, we'll enjoy a few drinks together, which will finally give you a chance to relax, probably for the very first time to-day. Best of all, you'll still be able to get to bed by nine o'clock, the latest. Which, even though you'll be going in early to-morrow, will get you a good night's sleep. We both know how important that is, especially now. And last, but not least, to-morrow morning, before I go out for those extra provisions, I will stop by Mrs. Potts' and telephone you at the Office for an update. Whew! That sure was a mouthful-and-a-half, wasn't it? Well, what do you say?"

"What do I say? What could anybody say to that, Mrs. D? You've certainly left no stone unturned, as far as I can tell, anyway. Now, let's eat!"

Wilma had correctly anticipated Blanche's reaction. By her own admission, she did, indeed, glean a ray of hope from hearing that the odds of the storm had lowered, even if not dramatically. In general, all things considered, Wilma felt she was being surprisingly calm.

Of course, Blanche had no problem at all with Will using her telephone to try to reach Kira. She and Wilma went into the parlour and closed the doors, giving Will a bit of privacy out in the hallway where the machine was located. While Will was waiting for the operator to make the connection, Wilma took the opportunity to tell Blanche about her plan to come over to-morrow morning and call him at the Office. That way, they could get any last-minute news on the storm's progress or, hopefully, lack thereof. Blanche agreed immediately, telling Wilma how grateful she'd be to get the very latest update.

Will was greatly relieved to hear the operator's nasal intonation, "Go ahead, please. Your party is on the line."

"Kira? Hello – it's me, Will, calling."

"Will! I'm so glad to hear from you. Surprised, but glad. Where in the world are you calling me from? Please do not tell me that you're still at work. Not at this hour."

"No, no, I'm not. Actually, Kira, I'm at Mrs. D's neighbor's house. You remember, Mrs. Potts?"

"Why yes, of course, but . . . Will, tell me – is there something wrong?"

"Well, yes, Kira, as a matter of fact, there is. Something is terribly wrong, actually."

Later, those words were about the only part of the conversation that Will was able to recall clearly. The rest of it had gone that badly.

CHAPTER 30

SUNDAY, EARLY MORNING, MARCH 11, 1888

It was three-thirty and, of course, still pitch-black outside. Even at this ungodly hour, Will had awoken before the alarm went off. All things considered, he'd slept soundly, and for that he was deeply grateful. His first waking thought, however, a painful one, was about Kira and their disastrous telephone conversation the night before. He knew he had to do everything in his power to reach some sort of resolution with her, and quickly. First and foremost though, he had to get into the Office and determine whether the storm had actually taken shape yet in the Southeast. He figured that if it hadn't, there would most likely be no blizzard arriving in New York City after all. And if there were no blizzard, well, obviously, everything else would be moot.

He dressed quickly and put the coffee pot on the stove. Smartly resisting the temptation to save a little time by leaving the house without eating any breakfast, he prepared himself some eggs, bacon, and toast. Mrs. D was still sleeping, as she usually was whenever he got up this early, which of late was more often than not. As always, he took care to move about the kitchen quietly so as not to disturb her.

He could tell there was no actual precipitation yet, but the humidity had increased dramatically through the night all the same, so he knew the rain would not be too far off. It was surprisingly chilly though, especially given the unusually warm weather of the past several days. A quick look at the thermometer outside the kitchen window told him it was thirty-four degrees. He reckoned he'd better wear his warm coat to-day.

Will got to the Office a little after four-forty. Glynn would be calling at about five with last evening's obs. In his head, he could actually hear the faint sound of a drum-roll beginning to build. After all, those obs are the ones which will make or break this blizzard of his.

He couldn't resist having a good chuckle at such hubris – "this blizzard of his." But then he really got to thinking hard about it. Up till now, he'd thought the choice would have been obvious: if he had his druthers, of course he would prefer that the storm not happen.

Why, then, he thought, was he sitting here on tenterhooks, hoping that last evening's map would show the storm having already formed over the Southeast? Will gave his head a few hard shakes, knowing he had to get a hold of himself. If anyone knew this, he did – when it came to the weather, what will be, will be. His only job was to make the best prediction he possibly could, given all the tools at his disposal.

It was barely four-forty-five when the ring of the telephone gave Will a bit of a start.

"Will here." Of course, it was Glynn. Who else would it be at this hour?

"Okay, good buddy, get ready for the obs."

"In just a minute, Glynn, if you don't mind. What's going on down there, right now?"

"Oh, yes, sorry, I meant to tell you. It's raining pretty good now, but the wind is still light, from the southeast. Looks like 130 or 140 degrees. Temperature forty."

"Thanks. No rain up here as of yet. Wind is light, 110 degrees. But the temp's down to about thirty-four."

"That's quite a precipitous drop. Pretty amazing. So, are you set?"

"Go ahead, let 'er rip."

Even before Glynn had finished, Will was able to ascertain that the storm was indeed forming, albeit a bit later than the start-time his system had originally predicted. The positioning seemed to be pretty much dead-on but, of course, he couldn't really be sure till he plotted the surface map and drew the isobars.

"Well, Will, that's it for now. Would you give me an update when I call back with the sevens?"

"Of course, Glynn, I'll be happy to."

"Good-bye, Will –"

"Wait!" Will had suddenly flashed back to his conversation with Long yesterday afternoon, in particular the comment he'd made about his head being the one on the chopping block. "You haven't let on to anybody at Headquarters that you know about this storm, have you?"

"Will. I thought I had made myself pretty clear yesterday when I promised you that I wouldn't. And I am someone who keeps his promises."

"I'm so sorry, Glynn; I never meant to imply otherwise. It's just that Sergeant Long grilled me mightily about it yesterday, after we spoke. At least I think it was after we spoke. Damn it all to Hell! I have to tell you, my brain is so layered with minutiae – mostly political claptrap – I can't keep track of when anything happens, anymore. Lord knows, I can barely keep track of the days."

"Now I will be telling Camille, mind you," Glynn responded. Will was glad his friend had moved so quickly past his muddled apology. "You didn't say anything about not telling her, just HQ. But I'll make sure she understands fully the . . . how shall I put this . . . the 'sordid politics' of confidentiality, as far as anyone in the Office is concerned, while she takes care of finalizing all the preparations for the storm on the home-front."

"That's fine, Glynn, that's all fine. Look. Let's just forget I even brought it up, shall we?"

"It's okay, chum, I really do understand. You go take care of business now. We'll talk again around seven-thirty. Good-bye."

Let's see. High in the Northeast recedes to eastern Canada. Arctic high yesterday in South Dakota now drops to Kansas. Ten-thirty-seven milli-bars, that's up about four. Yes, there's another high beginning to press down from southern Canada, north of Montana. A trough or cold front extends west from a weak low centered over northwestern North Dakota separating the two highs. Upper Midwest low moves east-northeast from the western shore of Lake Michigan to near Alpena. Interesting. No weakening. Still about ten-oh-seven millibars. Cold front clearing New Orleans, extending south well into the Gulf. Still massive Gulf moisture influx. And yes! Yes! There it is! Can't draw a closed isobar just yet, but the storm is clearly getting organized. Looks like the center is forming right where Florida, Alabama, and Georgia meet. Very heavy rain. Oh, my God . . . over four inches in Pensacola in just the past seven hours! This morning's analysis should seal the deal. About two more hours.

Will sat at his desk feeling strangely exhilarated. He had to admit, it was difficult to imagine a more complex or convoluted situation than his current one. Still and all, he was now able to acknowledge that when it came right down to it, being accurate in his prediction was more important than he'd thought.

He knew it was crucial that he speak with Kira, and just as soon as he possibly could. He figured it could wait till after the sevens, though. She'd probably still be asleep at this hour, anyway, and he had abso-lutely no interest in rousting her from her slumber to continue their difficult discussion.

At that moment, Will heard the unmistakable sounds of Sergeant Long's arrival. There was something about the Sergeant's physical presence and bluster which seemed to fill whatever space he entered. It was clear he was making a bee-line for Will's office, charging past the two newly hired, entry-level technicians who, for some odd reason, had shown up at the Office to-day. Truth be told, Will couldn't figure out what the dickens they were doing there, when they could just as easily have been at home, sleeping. All Signal Service Offices were officially closed at this hour on the Sabbath.

As he walked into Will's office, the Sergeant pulled the door closed behind him, ensuring they would not be overheard. "Looks like the rain is about to begin shortly," he said to Will. "It's really raw out there."

"Yes, it's already into Washington City. I figure about eight or nine for here."

The Sergeant looked searchingly at Will for a long moment, almost as if he were hoping to hear some good news which might ease his heavy burden. Will sat silently, returning his gaze, leaving his boss no choice but to launch into the inevitable conversation.

"So, Will, do you have any updates for me? Any changes to report on the development of the storm?"

"Well, Boss, I do want to see this morning's obs and plot up the map before saying for sure, but so far all signs continue to point to the blizzard getting underway here in about twenty-four hours. And maybe even a bit sooner than that, actually." His earlier moment of doubt a moot point now, he saw no reason to mention anything about it to the Sergeant.

Long gestured in the general direction of Will's desk. "Is that last evening's map, there, then?"

"Yes sir, it is."

"Alright, let's have a look-see." Long spent a minute or two contemplating the map, then continued, his tone a bit puzzled. "Hmm...I'm afraid I have to say, Will, that I just don't get it. I can't for the life of me see how this is going to evolve into anything more than a harmless frontal passage. That storm in Michigan looks like it will move into eastern Canada and swing the cold front through here early Monday morning. Perhaps some heavy rain and strong winds first, maybe even a line of thunderstorms with hail – I'll give you that much – but it sure looks to me like it will be no worse than chilly and blustery for Monday. Which, when you think about it, would certainly make a great deal more sense, now, wouldn't it? I mean, this is the eleventh of March we're talking about here, for Christ's sake."

Will was momentarily unnerved. He certainly hadn't anticipated that Long would be challenging him, not at this late stage of the game. He felt himself beginning to bristle at the implication that his forecast was in error. Just as quickly, though, he managed to regain his composure, remembering that he had the power to refuse to be drawn into an argument on the subject.

Before responding, he made it a point to spend a moment or two scrutinizing the map, nodding thoughtfully. "Why, yes, Sergeant. I do see what you mean, and how it could be interpreted that way," he said, slowly. "And you know what? If I hadn't spent so much time buried in my research over the past two years, it's quite likely I'd have concluded the very same thing."

Smiling pleasantly, Will looked directly into his boss's eyes, imagining he could actually see himself bending over to pick up the gauntlet that Long had thrown. He wondered whether his carefully crafted response had done the trick.

Suddenly, the Sergeant stood erect, chest expanded outward and chin tucked slightly in, arms rigid at his sides. Will had the oddest sensation that the man had just snapped to attention, for no apparent reason.

"Well, the truth is we'll know soon enough if you're right, God help us," Long said, curtly, his words clipped. "You just make sure you're in the Office first thing to-morrow morning." And with that, he turned on his heel and marched off.

Will sat quietly at his desk for the next few moments, pondering the Sergeant's strange reaction. Evidently, Long was having some difficulty dealing with the pressure of the whole thing, and the strain was beginning to show. Well, Will thought, he'll just have to manage as best he can, like the rest of us mere mortals. Although Will could certainly empathize, he had more than enough concerns of his own that needed looking after.

Glynn called at seven-thirty-five. "Well, Will? What did your evening analysis show?" Will couldn't help but smile at the intensity of the inquiry. It was obvious that Glynn's excitement now nearly matched his own.

"Actually, Glynn, I'd have to say that not much has changed. Everything is still unfolding pretty much the way I'd expected. Rain down there will change to snow a bit earlier than I had estimated yesterday, though – maybe as soon as five or six. Also, I think I may have neglected to mention the winds. They will be very strong from the northwest, especially close to the coast. Strong enough to cause structural damage to buildings, I'm afraid . . . maybe even take off a few roofs."

"What? You must be kidding. As bad as that? Really? Down here?"

"The answer is yes, unfortunately. Every bit as bad as that, I'm afraid. I'll be able to give you another update later, when you call me with the three's. Or, if you like, you can call me back in an hour or so. That'll give me more than enough time to be finished with the seven's.

"So, what have you got for me?"

Thirty minutes later, Will had already plotted the seven o'clock obs and nearly completed the painstaking process of drawing up the isobars. He allowed himself just the slightest smile of satisfaction, preening a little over how much time he'd shaved off the entire process the past few days, simply by dint of sheer repetition.

At eight-fifteen, he rose abruptly and went to Long's office to announce that he was going downstairs for a few minutes and would be back shortly. He knew he had to get out of the confined space of the Office to clear his head, which felt like it was on the verge of exploding. The knowledge of what he could only describe as an impending disaster was a weight which pressed down on him like a shroud.

He pushed the Lobby button in the elevator and began his descent. When he got to street-level, he walked outside and took a few deep, cleansing breaths. He was just beginning to feel a bit calmer when, suddenly, he was struck hard by the thought of his unfinished business with Kira. He knew he had to get back up there, quickly, and telephone her, but first he needed another moment or two to compose himself. Sadly, he had nary a clue where he might find the magic words to convince her. He only knew it was imperative she come to understand, somehow, that she simply must postpone her audition.

A few minutes later, Will was back at his desk. Before going to the telephone to place the call to Kira, he wanted to have one more good look at his new map. What he saw made him shake his head in amazement.

If someone were in the business of providing weather indications and could look at this map now without seeing the problem, he thought wryly, that someone was definitely in the wrong business. Really, it was as simple as that.

Here we go. Stationary high in eastern Canada. Expected. Kansas Arctic high drops to Oklahoma. Ten-forty millibars, that's up three more. New Arctic high north of Montana on the move south. Trough from Lake Superior extends southwest, bisecting Minnesota. Here's where it gets good . . . upper Midwest low moves to just northeast of Lake Huron, increasing the pressure gradient ahead of the cold front. Only slight weakening. Cold front south through Pittsburgh into extreme eastern Kentucky and Tennessee. But look here. Oh, yes – yes, indeed.

There's now a well-organized low centered just northwest of Atlanta. Looks about ten-ten millibars. Cold front to the south through Apalachicola. Weak warm front extends northeast up to Hatteras. Temperatures approaching sixty in southeastern North Carolina.

Rain widespread now, along the east coast: Buffalo, Pittsburgh, Washington, Roanoke.

Will made sure that Long and the two technicians were out of earshot when he placed the telephone call to Kira. Fortunately, it took very little time for the operator to complete the connection.

"Hello, Kira? Good morning. It's me, Will, calling. I know it's a little on the early side, so I do hope I'm not disturbing you. If I am, please forgive me."

"Oh, hello, Will," she responded, her tone most assuredly guarded. Actually, you're not disturbing me at all. I was just making myself a cup of coffee, as a matter of fact. But why are you telephoning me at this hour?"

Why am I telephoning you now? Gee, I don't know, let's see... Oh, yes, now I've got it! I just thought you might be interested in knowing that if you continue with your stubborn, head-strong refusal to heed my warning, there's every probability that you'll be ending up as a goldarn frozen statistic of this monster storm. Call me crazy, but somehow or other I thought that warranted a call at this hour. Even on a Sunday.

"Well, you see, it's just that... listen, Kira... I just really need you to... to give me the benefit of the doubt here, and truly listen to what it is I'm about to tell you. I need you to try and understand just how vitally important it all is. I know that –"

"Stop right there, Will," she interrupted him, sharply. "You are not going to start in again about that stupid storm of yours, are you? You were trying to frighten the wits out of me last night, and I simply cannot, for the life of me, figure out why. Why don't you want me to go to my final audition? What on earth is wrong with you? Why don't you want me to succeed? I mean you, of all people, know full-well how hard I've worked for this, what it's taken for me to get here!"

In her tremulous voice, Will could hear the pain and confusion which had her on the verge of tears. Suddenly, he experienced a dreadful, sinking feeling in the pit of his stomach, as he saw this conversation ending no better than the last one. He forced himself to remain focused, however, as she somehow managed to go on with her protest.

"You should know, Will," she told him, her voice continuing to shake, "that I've been paying attention to the weather indications, and there is absolutely no mention of any storm, whatsoever. None. Not a single, solitary word. That's what makes all of this so frustrating, so difficult to understand. I've even talked this over with my father, and neither one of us can come up with any sort of explanation for why you are behaving this way."

Will was now beginning to remember bits and pieces of the conversation they'd had last evening. He recalled that he really had done his level-best to lay everything out for her, just as calmly as he could. Alas, it had all been for naught. She was so in love with the idea of her precious audition that she'd rejected, outright, everything he had tried so hard to impress upon her.

"Your father? What in Heaven's name does he have to do with any of this? When he and I talked on Thanksgiving, he didn't mention having had any meteorological training or expertise to speak of. Have you talked to Alex yet, Kira?"

"Well, gee whiz, Will. What a great idea that would be! Except, of course, for the fact that Alex doesn't happen to have a telephone. In case you've forgotten." Her voice fairly dripped acid.

Will was stunned. He'd never heard her talk like this before; she was almost unrecognizable. Not to mention so unreasonable, so defensive and angry. But he had to look past all that, at least in this moment. He knew he simply had to find a way to get through to her. This truly was a matter of life and death, if anything ever was.

"Listen to me, Kira, please. If you would just listen. I'm begging you here. You have to believe me when I tell you that you won't even be able to make it to your audition, to-morrow morning. And even if you do make it there, by some miracle, there will be no one at the theatre to audition for, I can promise you that. And you will never make it back home. There's even the very distinct possibility that you could freeze to death! You could end up stranded outside somewhere, and help might not make it to you in time. I know how crazy this must sound, believe me, especially to someone who's never seen the kind of weather I'm talking about here. But if you would just stop for one second and try to understand what it is that I'm trying to tell you –"

"Stop it! Stop it!" She was practically shrieking at him now. "I didn't believe you last night, and I surely don't believe you now! I *won't* believe you. Will, you know that this audition is *everything* I have ever worked for, worked so terribly hard for, my entire life. God would simply not let this happen to me. He could never be that cruel. Besides, this is New York City we're talking about – the absolute pinnacle of modern civilization. The things that you are describing simply cannot happen here, in New York City. Not in this day and age. It's *1888,* for Heaven's sake!"

In the brief silence which ensued, Will mustered up every last ounce of self-control at his command. He forced himself to retain his composure and speak as calmly as he could, knowing that anything else would only further alienate her. "Kira, sweetheart. Please, *please* just listen to me. Give me the benefit of the doubt, please. You know me. You know how level-headed I am. And you must know how much I care for you. Your well-being means everything to me. You *do* know that, don't you? There could only be one possible reason that I'm telling you all this. Just one. It's because I want to keep you safe. Can't you see that? I'm certainly not trying to –"

"Will, stop now," Kira interrupted, suddenly strangely calm. "I'm incredibly sorry about all of this, I truly am. But I'm afraid I have to insist that you refrain from calling me again. I mean, at least till after the audition, that is."

"Wait! Don't hang up! Kira, please wait – for God's sake! *No* audition could possibly be worth risking your life for! You've simply *got* to understand –"

"Good-bye, Will." Hearing the next sound which came through the line as she severed the connection, that merciless click was, for Will, tantamount to receiving a physical blow. He lost his breath for a second or two, as he stared at the now-useless receiver in stunned disbelief.

CHAPTER 31

SUNDAY, MID-MORNING, MARCH 11, 1888

Never, not in all his born days, leastwise the ones he could recall, had Will experienced a frustration remotely akin to this. Short of throwing away his entire future by contriving a plot to kidnap Kira, there was literally nothing he could do to save her from herself. Of course, he could understand how difficult it must be for her. After all, he was asking her to take at face-value his word – and his alone – about something as unprecedented and bizarre as a monster blizzard coming out of nowhere. And at the tail-end of a recently balmy winter, to boot. Especially when the Signal Service itself was putting out official indications to the contrary. But while he could see where all of that would certainly warrant a healthy skepticism, it didn't even come close to explaining her anger. Not to mention her stubborn refusal to even entertain the notion that he just might know something about some dangerous weather in the offing, official indications be damned. He'd looked at that six ways from Sunday, and found he could only see it as pure willfulness, a folly arising from her blind ambition.

He had thought of reaching out to Alex, either directly or through Frank, to appeal to her to try and talk some sense into her best friend. Then again, as of this moment, he had no idea what Alex had been told yet. Frank had said he'd be stopping in to-day for an update, so Will would at least have an opportunity to discuss it with him then. But even if Frank had told Alex everything about the storm, what's to say whether *she* would even believe him?

One thing Will could do right now, to give himself some solace, was think of the advice he knew he'd get from his wise and trusted confidant. Mrs. D would invariably tell him to leave it alone, that he had already done all he could – all anyone could, for that matter. That if he continued to press things any further with Kira, the poor girl would only be able to see his actions as those of a madman, if indeed she didn't already. That there was a simple truth at work here, as horrible and difficult to accept as it might be. He'd never be able to get her to grasp the situation clearly enough that she'd opt for safety and stay at home Monday morning.

Ultimately, Will understood that he had no choice in the matter, not if he wished to retain his sanity. As hard as it was, and as sad as it made him, he simply had to let it go. His only vestige of comfort lay in the hope that she might get up to-morrow and see the snow hurtling down in a wind-swept fury. Perhaps then she'd be willing to take a moment to reconsider the dire warning he'd tried so desperately to get her to heed.

It was nine-forty-five, and Wilma had just finished cleaning her breakfast things and tidying up the kitchen. She was now getting ready to go over to Blanche's to follow through on the plan to call Will at the Office and get the "official" update. Rain had already begun to fall, light but steady, so she donned her warm rain-coat and set out on the short walk next door. Given the mildness of the past few days, she was surprised by how raw it felt outside.

"Wilma, am I ever glad to see you!," Blanche exclaimed, opening the front door before her friend had even had the chance to knock. "Please, come on in."

As they sat down at the kitchen table, Blanche asked if she had heard anything new from Will since last evening. "Well, no, Blanche, but that's why I'm here now. Let's place that call to him, and we'll see what he has to say for himself."

"Telephone him now? He's at work to-day?" Clearly, she was perplexed. "That's odd. I thought the Signal Service Office is closed on Sundays."

"Uh, yes, you're right about that, it is dear. But perhaps you forgot? About the plan we came up with last night, I mean. Will was going to go into the Office first thing to-day to continue tracking the storm. And we said we would telephone him early from here, so we could get the latest update."

"Why yes, of course, you're right – now I recall. You must think me a dunderhead! I'm so sorry, Wilma, you must forgive me this morning. I guess what with Charley insisting on going out, and my fretting over poor Will's unfortunate situation with his sweetheart, I completely forgot just about everything we talked about last night." Blanche gave her head a few quick shakes, as if that might help her clear out the cobwebs.

"Pishposh – that's perfectly understandable," Wilma said, smiling warmly as she patted her friend's arm. "And now you've already answered the question that was at the top of my list. Regarding Charley, I mean. He did go out then, after all."

"Oh yes, he certainly did. Before dawn, as a matter of fact. I'll tell you all about that in just a moment." Wilma was stunned by the sudden look of sheer, naked anguish clouding Blanche's normally placid countenance at the thought of her husband's plight. She grieved for her friend.

"First, though, I want to talk about something I did remember from last night's conversation, and that was what Will said about the odds of the storm having decreased slightly. Everyone knows how changeable the weather can be, how difficult it is to predict with any real certainty. I have been hoping and praying that that continues to-day, and the big bad storm never even materializes, at all."

"A-men to that, my dear. I can only imagine what you must be going through right now." Wilma looked expectantly at her friend, but

Blanche seemed to want to delay the inevitable conversation about Charley, at least for a little longer.

"Oh, and Wilma! Wasn't that just awful, when Will tried his best to warn Kira about how dangerous this storm is going to be, and she refused to listen to a word of it. I felt so terribly bad for the poor dear. It must have been so frustrating for him, beyond the pale, really."

"Yes, you're so right about that. This whole situation is enormously difficult for our sweet boy. All the more so because, from everything he's told me, this relationship with her has been his very first real experience with romantic love."

"Oh, my goodness, you don't say. I had no idea! Now doesn't that just beat all? How truly sad. Heartbreaking, really, when you think about it." The two friends sat for several long moments in contemplative silence, and then Wilma heard Blanche let out a soft, extended sigh.

"Well," she finally began, "I guess before we place that call to Will for the update, I'd best fill you in on the horrific conversation Charley and I had, after you two left last evening. I reminded him about Will's system predicting the imminent arrival of a 'superstorm.' He responded that during all of his many years at sea, he'd certainly had his share of experience with storms. And some fairly big ones, at that. He even told me about several monsters that he'd never mentioned before, because he didn't want to 'worry me.' How ironic is that?

"He also claimed that this particular boat he'd be going out on, the Charles H. Marshall – I made it a point to remember the name – was especially seaworthy. He said he was leaving early to-day, and that was that. Then he added something about many large, foreign ships all arriving later to-day and to-night which, of course, always gives the pilots that much more opportunity to secure a berth. He said he'd be back early Monday. I said wasn't that just great. He'd be trying to make his way back home right at the height of the storm.

"I can tell you this, Wilma, and I'll make no bones about it. We had ourselves quite the little go-round. Maybe the worst one we've ever had, in all our many years together. He tried his best to get me to see that he really had no choice in the matter. He kept insisting that there was a good chance to make lots of money, so of course he had to go. I took the opportunity to impress upon him how little the money would mean – if he never lived to spend it. The up-shot was that he left. The selfish bastard."

"Blanche!"

"I'm terribly sorry, Wilma, really I am. And I do hope you'll forgive my shocking language. It's just that, at this moment, I'm completely under the sway of the most negative emotions, and I'm just so unaccustomed to feeling that way. To tell you the truth, it's darn near eating me alive. Right now, it's difficult to say what I feel more consumed by – anger or fear."

"I know, dear, it's simply awful." Wilma could think of little to say which would ease her friend's suffering. She felt powerless to help in any real way except, perhaps, simply to be a sympathetic ear.

"You know how much Charley loves the sea. Well, up till now, that's always been just fine by me. Oh, I know I'm not much different than other wives of seafaring husbands, when it comes to your normal, everyday fears. But I'm generally able to keep them well below the surface, and under control. Except when there are bad storms. And now, I have to tell you, I am just so awfully afraid. Terrified, really. On top of everything else, he really is getting just a bit too old for this line of work, you know, not that he'd ever admit to it. He'll be sixty next month, for God's sake! He's still in great shape, mind you, but this kind of labor takes a heavy toll on even the young men."

In the fifteen years she had known and loved her dear friend, Wilma had never seen her so upset, and her heart fairly ached for her. She reached across the table and grabbed her hand to give it a good squeeze. Then, smiling brightly, she said, "Blanche, what do you say we telephone Will right now. And who knows? Maybe all your hoping and praying has done some good after all, and he'll tell us that the storm isn't even going to happen. Wouldn't that just be too wonderful!"

"Hello, Will? Is that you answering? It's me calling, it's Mrs. D here."
Wilma was very happy to be hearing his voice, even if this newfangled instrument did tend to make a body sound tinny and far away.

"Oh, Mrs. D, I'm so glad it's you that's telephoned. You are precisely the person I need to talk to, just now. I had another conversation with Kira, by telephone of course, about an hour ago. She categorically refused to listen to a single word I said. Dammit, as hard as I try, I simply cannot fathom her stubbornness. It just seems so pig-headed to me! How on *earth* can one stupid audition be so important to her that she's willing to risk her very life for it?"

"Will, Will, you know she doesn't see it that way. She simply can't."

"I know, I know, you're right. She even said as much to me. I'm just feeling so darned hopeless and frustrated. Overwhelmingly so, really. On the other hand, though, I think you'll have cause to be proud of me. I have been consoling myself with the advice I know you would have given me. As I've already done all I possibly can, the only thing left now is to simply let it go. Easier said than done, of course. But there is no way I can 'win' this one, and I simply have to accept that. What will be, will be."

"Why, that's absolutely correct, Will. Well done, I must say. Now, let's practice what we preach, why don't we, and let that conversation go. At least for the moment, anyway. So. What does our expert prognosticator have to report this morning about any impending blizzard?"

His continued distress over Kira had already pretty much told the tale, so she knew full-well she was holding out for a long shot. Still, she had her fingers crossed. Toes and everything else cross-able, too, for that matter.

"Oh, yes, that." He proceeded to give her the dispiriting news, in all its gory detail.

Mrs. D listened intently with a sinking heart, one she did her best to hide from both Will and Blanche. After she'd thanked him for the update, he confirmed he'd be leaving the Office around five, which would get him home before six. She told him to be sure and bring his appetite, as she had a very special dinner planned for the two of them this evening. Will signed off, but not before telling her just how much he appreciated hearing that. He told her he would really be looking forward to it, as he was pretty sure it would be the high-point of his day.

CHAPTER 32

SUNDAY, LATE-MORNING, MARCH 11, 1888

By ten o'clock, the seasoned seafarers aboard the Charles H. Marshall, pilots and crew alike, knew for certain that a storm was well on its way. The sporadic rain, gusty southeasterly winds, and threatening clouds left no room for doubt. Charley Potts had already elected to share a carefully edited account of young Mr. Roebling's prediction with his fellow ship-mates, deliberately offering up a much more watered-down version than the one that Blanche, just prior to his departure, had impressed upon him with such passion and determination.

After giving the matter a great deal of thought, he had come up with several excellent reasons for choosing to down-play what she had described as Will's forecast of a "superstorm." First, he wasn't exactly sure just how much of what she'd said he could actually take at face-value. He knew his wife was prone to exaggeration if properly inspired, and could certainly see why she might have felt it duly warranted in this particular situation. In point of fact, he, himself, hadn't had the occasion to exchange a single word with Will about the storm.

Second, he felt he was appropriately skeptical of any so-called "system" which could predict a storm, regardless of how painstakingly it might have been developed. And even though what he knew of Will he liked well-enough, perhaps even more so, still, the young man did work for the Signal Service. By Charley's calculation, they were wrong far more often than right – in typical government-agency fashion, as far as he was concerned.

Third, even if Will were right, and that was a big "if" in his estimation, precious little would be gained by frightening the men needlessly at this juncture. After all, he reasoned, they certainly weren't about to turn around and head back into harbor, no matter how daunting the circumstances might be. And further, he knew the Captain to be as sharp as they come, one of the absolute best in the business. Under his able direction, they would be able to deal handily with any situation, just like they always had before.

Finally, and perhaps most important to him personally, if he were to raise a bunch of hoopla over something which turned out to be a false alarm (the most likely scenario, in his opinion), he knew he wouldn't hear the end of it. The other pilots would take great pains to make sure he'd never live down what they would undoubtedly characterize as his hysteria over "a bit of wind."

Wisely, then, Charley chose to keep his own counsel. Besides, he thought, who better to accurately judge the weather than a gaggle of harbor pilots? And he didn't hear any of them squawking about a major threat of any kind.

Still, he couldn't completely block out the tiniest niggling, disquieting thought that Blanche hadn't exaggerated Will's prediction after all and, not only that, but it might actually turn out to be correct! If so, they were in for a mighty bad one, maybe the worst they'd ever encountered. He could still see clearly Blanche's forlorn face as she pleaded her case in the kitchen last evening. She'd first tried to reason with him, then ended up begging him to reconsider his decision to go out. Eventually, she'd gotten so frustrated and angry that she'd hurled the entire contents of her nearly full glass of water squarely in his direction, dousing him pretty good. He was sure that in all their years together, he had rarely seen her so furious.

I really can't afford to think about that now though, can I. All my energies need to be focused on whatever task is at hand.

After wrapping up his telephone conversation with Mrs. D, a restless Will sat at his desk, caught in the grip of a series of conflicting emotions. God knows, he certainly could not deny that he was over-tired. Heck, he couldn't even remember the last time he'd gotten a solid seven hours of sleep. But he knew that wasn't all of it.

On the one hand, he had to admit to getting a certain satisfaction out of knowing that he had done everything possible to warn the people in his life about the impending storm – Kira, Mrs. D, Blanche and Charley, Frank and Alex, and, of course, Glynn and Sergeant Long. He knew that he and Mrs. D were fully prepared on the home-front, and would therefore be able to ride out the storm in relative comfort. He almost felt entitled to just sit back and watch, in pure enjoyment, as this remarkable spectacle unfolded before his very eyes. After all, it was the sheer majesty and awesome power of the atmosphere at its best (or worst?) which had tugged at his heart in the first place, when he was just a young child, and never let go – leading him directly to this, his life's path. And he was quite clear that he had never before witnessed a display of nature's fury as extraordinary as this storm would surely be bringing. In all likelihood, he would live out the rest of his days without ever having the opportunity to do so again. Which really was remarkable, when you stopped to think about it.

On the other hand, he felt a great discontent and a frustrating impotence. Short of some miraculous change of mind, Kira would be putting herself directly in harm's way to-morrow morning, and there was not a single thing he could do to prevent it. And then there was the redoubtable Sergeant Long. For some strange reason, Will could not shake the feeling that, in some weird and unaccountable way, his boss held him personally responsible for this storm. It followed then that Long would likely blame him for whatever consequences he might end up facing from Headquarters, in a few short weeks' time.

At that point, the Sergeant will have run out of options. He'll be forced to come clean with them about the existence of Will's forecasting system, and it will be all but impossible to elude a discussion about its (presumptive) spot-on prediction of the blizzard. Will imagined his boss was feeling none-too-pleased about that prospect.

Lastly, and perhaps most painfully, he could do nothing to warn his other co-workers of the grievous peril they, and their loved ones, would likely be facing, come Monday. For Will, this was almost unendurable. He struggled mightily to avoid being sucked into a morass of very negative "what if's."

Yet somehow, in the midst of all this insanity, Will kept finding the strength to return himself, time and again, to a calm and focused center, somewhere above the fray. Probably it was because he knew that he could ill-afford a trip down that never-ending rabbit-hole of self-absorption. Instinctively, he felt that his presence of mind – especially the ability to remain in control, even under the most extreme conditions – would be sorely needed in the days to come.

He had no way of knowing then, of course, just how right he was.

At eleven-forty-five, Will received a telephone call he hadn't been expecting. "Glynn, this is a bit of a surprise. I didn't think I'd be hearing from you again till the three's."

"Yes Will, I know, but I wanted to keep you apprised of the situation down here. I figured you'd probably want to know as soon as possible about any interesting developments." Will found it amusing that even though Glynn was almost certainly the only person at the Headquarters Office on a Sunday morning, force-of-habit had him speaking in hushed tones, as if he were still afraid of being overheard.

"Of course, that's good thinking. What is currently going on down there?"

"Well," Glynn began, clearly working hard to contain his excitement, "the barometer is falling rapidly now, about ten-twelve millibars, and the wind is picking up, now about twenty-five miles-per-hour, from about 140 or 150 degrees. Temperature forty-six. But I really called you because of the rain. It had been light and sporadic all morning, then, all of a sudden, it became heavy and convective in nature. And the sky has become quite dark – very ominous looking."

"Interesting..." Will was listening intently, soaking up every detail.

"Look, Will. I need to tell you, right up front, that what you're going to hear me say next is cause for more than a little embarrassment on my part, as I know it isn't at all scientific. Not even the least little bit, actually. So, please – allow me to beg your forgiveness for that, in advance. It's just that... I don't quite know how to put words to it... there's just this, this, *surreal* feeling all around me. I mean, when I went outside before, the birds were acting so erratically, flying around wildly, haphazardly. I actually saw four or five of them crash right into the building here, though luckily I don't think any of them were seriously hurt.

"And as if that weren't weird enough, all on its own, well, there's this stray cat – a skittish, scraggly little scrap of a thing I've seen around here several times before, hanging about but never coming too near. Well, just now when I was walking back in, it actually ran right up close behind me, as if it wanted to come into the building with me! Will, I have to tell you, this poor creature had always behaved as if it were absolutely petrified of anything remotely human. It would high-tail it anytime I made the slightest move in its direction, even with some enticing treat obviously in-hand. And now it wants to follow me inside an office building where there's nothing *but* people? I'm telling you, it's completely bizarre.

"And here's something you need to know about me: I have never been one of those out-of-whack people who believes that animals possess some sort of supernatural prescience when it comes to things like this, trust me. No, siree – my feet have always been firmly planted on the very solid ground of good old, practical science. But all this

– what I'm witnessing, right here and now? I don't expect you to understand it, because I surely don't. But you can take my word for it, if you'll have it – it's absolutely barmy!"

Naturally, there was no way Glynn could have known just how effortlessly Will understood precisely what he was describing. Will had never shared with Glynn, or anyone else, for that matter, his own omniscient experiences as a child, growing up on his parents' Wisconsin farm. Thinking back on his own keen connection with nature, particularly the barnyard animals, Will was bemused by just how close he came to qualifying as one of those people Glynn had just casually classified as "out-of-whack." Then his mind wandered for a second to his dilemma with Kira. He wondered if perhaps it might have made a difference, had he mentioned anything to her about these phenomena sometime earlier in their relationship. He supposed that if he had, it was at least possible that she might be a bit more receptive – or at a bare minimum maybe just a little less resistant – to his warning about how dangerous this storm was going to be.

"Glynn, believe me, I am more than happy to take your word for it. You can trust me when I tell you that I really do understand exactly what it is you're saying – more than you could possibly know. And I want you to know that I believe every word of it. Suffice to say that from my background, I'm quite familiar with precisely the scene you've just described. You've done a great job of explaining it, too, by the way, and I thank you for that. And I do empathize with how weird and unsettling it all must be, especially for someone like you, my friend . . . so I don't envy you that.

"But I'm afraid you'll have to forgive me just now, because I really must be running along. Please be sure to call me again though, if there is anything else you think I would want to know. I mean that, good buddy."

"Okay, Will. Thanks . . . for everything, I mean. And don't worry, if there's anything new to report from down here, I promise – you will be the first to know."

CHAPTER 33

SUNDAY, EARLY AFTERNOON, MARCH 11, 1888

Albert Washington was having himself quite the busy day at the Grand Hotel. Under ordinary circumstances, this being the second Sunday of the month, to-day would have been his one day off for the week. First thing this morning, however, Mr. Landen had sent a messenger to his home, asking if there were any way he could see his way clear to coming in after all, as Walt Jamison had been taken ill, quite suddenly. Albert had been very sorry to hear that his boss was ailing; he hoped it would turn out to be nothing too serious. He was especially concerned because he had heard that a nasty strain of the flu was making the rounds, with a number of deaths already attributed to it.

The fine, spring-like weather of recent days had apparently prompted far more tourists to venture into the City than one would ordinarily expect at this time of year. This was attested to by the fact that nearly all of the Grand's roughly four-hundred rooms were booked for the night. That alone predetermined that the pace of Albert's day would be unusually hectic, never mind the extra duties he'd necessarily be performing due to Jamison's absence.

None of which bothered Albert in the slightest. Certainly no stranger to hard work, he was delighted to have been given the chance to generate some additional income. He was always happy to earn money in whatever legitimate means were presented to him.

Fortunately for Albert, and the Grand, he'd been paying close attention to Walt's routine during the nearly one month now that he'd been working at the hotel. Not that he had been spying on his boss, or anything underhanded like that. Walt made no secret of the fact that he considered Albert to be just the talented and ambitious young man he'd been waiting for, to groom as his replacement one day. He also didn't go out of his way to hide that he was counting the days till his retirement, even though he was renowned amongst the staff as one of the hotel's most hard-working, loyal, and dedicated employees. Albert knew that the fifty-nine-year-old Jamison had been the Head of Maintenance since the Grand had first opened its doors, some twenty years earlier.

James Landen was more than pleased with Albert's performance to this point, going so far as to consider him his newest stellar employee. Of course, he gave full credit to what he called Walt Jamison's special "people skill," a sort of sixth-sense that had had him cull Albert out of the throng of applicants for the job in the first place, then give him his highest recommendation – an endorsement Landen had grown to rely on over the years. While the final hiring decision for all Hotel employees was his – and his alone – Landen had learned long ago to trust Jamison's opinion completely when it came to the very important consideration of an applicant's character. God knows, the Grand had its share of personnel problems in various departments: the Kitchen, Maid Services, and Concierge, to name just a few. Thankfully, Hotel Maintenance was not one of them.

At the moment, Landen was in his office waiting for Albert to make his way down from the third floor, where the bell-boy had caught up with him just as he was finishing a minor room repair at the behest of one of the guests. Landen heard a few tentative knocks on the door, then it opened slightly and Albert called out, "Mr. Landen? You wish to see me, sir?"

"Yes, Albert, please come in and have a seat. First of all, I asked you to stop by to thank you for coming in so willingly on your day off. And, now that you're here, I'd like to ask you whether you think you could manage to work a double shift." Landen knew that throughout the staff, he was known, and appreciated (for the most part), for never mincing his words.

"Why, yes sir, Mr. Landen. I'd be happy to."

"Excellent. Now, amongst all of the other day-to-day tasks I'm sure will be keeping you quite busy, given Walt's absence and how booked we are, there also happens to be two rather large parties scheduled for this evening – more's the pity. The only reason I say that is because, unfortunately, several other employees have had to go home sick this afternoon, the latest victims of this damned flu that seems to be flying around. I don't mind telling you, Albert, we are stretched pretty darn thin at this moment in time, sad to say. So those of us still standing will have to perform above and beyond, if you get my meaning."

Albert nodded. "I certainly do, sir."

"I thought you would. Walt's been telling me they don't come much sharper than you. Anyway, I'd like you to coordinate the set-up and take-down for the parties, just like Mr. Jamison would do himself, if he were here."

"Of course, Mr. Landen. You just tell me when and where to report, and I'll be there."

"That's great, Albert. I knew I could count on you. And I want you to know that I'll be giving you a bonus of two-hours' extra pay, in acknowledgment of the increased work-load. Also, since I know you still live with your folks, and I would not wish to cause them any concern, I will send another messenger letting them know you'll be staying on to-night."

"Why, thank-you, sir, that's so thoughtful of you. I don't quite know what to say."

"Well, I do, son. You should know that Walt and I are very pleased with the job you've done thus far and, in particular, we both appreciate your outstanding work ethic. The two of us think you have a great future, here at the Grand."

"That's so wonderful to hear. Thank-you, again, Mr. Landen."

"You are most welcome, Albert. Why don't you report back here at, say, six?"

"Yes, sir. I'll see you then, six sharp." Landen returned Albert's warm smile, as well as the quick, smart salute the young man made before turning to take his leave.

May Morrow, in a rare moment of luxurious self-indulgence, was allowing herself to sleep in to-day. When she finally did open her eyes and look at the clock, she could scarcely believe it when she read one-forty-five. She quickly calculated that she'd gotten nearly thirteen hours of uninterrupted sleep – an unprecedented event which left her feeling wonderfully refreshed and quite happy.

She had to admit, though, that her body's apparent need for such a long lay-in wasn't all that surprising. This past week at her new job had been one of the more challenging ones, thus far. To keep pace with the rapid growth of the wholesale chemical industry, the company had recently expanded its sales force by hiring on two experienced salesmen, each of whom could only be described as high-energy. According to the chatter in the lunch-room, these go-getters had netted some rather large sales for raw chemical products over the course of the week, which would account for the dramatic increase in outgoing and incoming telegraphs she'd experienced. May felt fortunate, indeed (and maybe even just a little proud, truth be told) that she'd been able to keep up – albeit only barely.

On the plus side, the hectic pace had certainly made the days fly by. May enjoyed her job and really liked the people she got to work with every day. And, true to his word, Mr. Garrigues had taken her aside Friday afternoon to tell her that, beginning next week, she would be getting a twenty-five-cent raise. Based on her average fifty-five-hour workweek, that would translate into an additional thirteen dollars and seventy-five cents per-week! May was a bit astounded by, and deeply grateful for, her boss' generosity.

During that same conversation, May had also learned they would be having a telephone system installed next week to augment their communication capabilities. She would be the company's operator for the new system. Garrigues told her that he had recently commissioned an independent survey which had concluded, somewhat to his surprise, that a full forty-five percent of their clients and suppliers already had telephone service. He had therefore come to the realization, he went on to tell May, that it was high-time to embrace this new state-of-the-art communications technology, and reap the rewards certain to be produced in sales and bottom-line revenue.

May knew that her boss was never one to procrastinate, especially when it came to making important decisions. So it came as no surprise to her when Garrigues immediately called for a special logistical meeting extremely early on Monday morning – six a.m., to be precise. The vice presidents of operations and sales, the sales team, and, of course, May, would be joining him and his secretary to discuss the installation of the new telephone system, as well as the ensuing changes in procedures and responsibilities.

By now, May had been with the company long enough to have learned that it was by paying such careful attention to detail, in every aspect of his business, that Garrigues had managed to become so successful. This success afforded him the opportunity to reward deserving employees with regular bonuses for outstanding performance – a situation rare, indeed, in the current economic climate. Predictably, this culminated in the creation of a loyal, dedicated, and hard-working staff, one more than happy to "go the extra mile" for the boss and, therefore, the company. The ever-optimistic May, quick to spot the positive in any situation, concluded correctly that being the main operator of the new telephone system could only make her services even more indispensable. And that, she reasoned, would certainly translate into additional increases in her pay, as time went on. Even though she knew how hard she'd worked to earn every last bit of it, there were times May Morrow could scarcely believe her own good fortune.

After a satisfying yawn and stretch, she got up, put on her bathrobe, picked up the newspaper one of her room-mates had thoughtfully placed outside her bedroom door, and set out for the common kitchen, downstairs, to prepare herself a hearty breakfast of ham and eggs. She smiled happily, knowing that this was one day she would not have to fight for any space on the stove, given that it was nearly two in the afternoon. Looking out the window at the dreary, steadily falling rain put only a slight damper on her good cheer, and she thought warmly of her dear Mother, imparting one of her favorite adages: "Always remember, my dear, that a cloudy day is no match for a sunny disposition."

Even though the rain would prevent her from spending the afternoon at the park as she'd intended, May easily took this little set-back in stride. After all, it was still early March – at this time of year, how many consecutive gorgeous days could one logically expect to see, anyway? She'd been grateful for the past few weeks of balmy weather. They had been an unexpected gift and, as far as she was concerned, a fine way to bring the winter to a close.

As May moved comfortably about the small kitchen, putting the finishing touches on her breakfast, she found herself dancing a step or two as she hummed the popular and catchy tune, "Oh My Darling, Clementine." Sighing softly in satisfaction, she then sat down to enjoy her meal, smiling broadly. Thirteen solid hours of sleep had certainly done her a world of good, even changing her whole perspective about to-morrow morning. In all honesty, she had not been looking forward to having to get up two hours earlier than normal, especially on a Monday, all because of that six a.m. meeting. Now, however, she was able to view this inconvenience as a nominal sacrifice she was more than willing to make, as it was all in the cause of a greater good.

CHAPTER 34

SUNDAY, MID-AFTERNOON, MARCH 11, 1888

Physically, Kira was feeling far from chipper. She had managed, however, to calm her raging emotions a bit since her last terrible conversation with Will. Alone in her suite, she'd had plenty of time to examine different scenarios which might explain his abhorrent behaviour. Unfortunately, one of them included the horrifying possibility that the once-in-a-century blizzard he'd foretold, occurring just when she'd be making her way to the all-important audition, would actually – incredibly – come to pass.

Her joyful excitement about the audition contrasted sharply with the seething wrath she still felt towards Will, and all of it had her stomach tied up in knots. Too indignant to examine the cause-and-effect relationship between her anger and her physical symptoms, she was also too proud to try and reach out to him by telephone at the Office, where she suspected he'd most likely be at the moment. Truth be told, there was a part of her which desperately wanted to hear his voice, even while she continued to be furious with him for vexing her so severely, just when she needed all the composure she could muster.

Determined to focus on what really mattered, she made herself a pot of calming herbal tea and sat down by the window to read the newspaper. She knew how important it was that she relax and take her mind off anything unpleasant, in preparation for her big day to-morrow.

After sitting quietly, reading, her attention was drawn to the soothing sound of raindrops sporadically hitting the south-facing windowpane. For several minutes, lulled into a semi-hypnotic state by the soft patter of the rain, she gazed out the window onto the thoroughfare below, West 34th Street. Her lips pulled into a soft smile of amusement, watching the antics of the pedestrians doing their level-best to avoid being hit by the droplets which fell in a left-to-right slant in the gentle breeze. The scene before her could not have been more ordinary – mostly Sunday shoppers, in groups of two or three, nosing around for early spring bargains and scurrying about while trying to stay dry.

Suddenly, she gave her head a violent shake and snorted aloud at the thought of gale-force winds howling through the streets to-morrow morning, whipping up mountains of snow. She felt her ire beginning to rise again.

He's mad, that's all there is to it. Still, I can't help but wonder . . . just what kind of idiot does he take me for, anyway?

It was three-thirty, and Will was anxiously awaiting Glynn's call with the latest update. He knew that within an hour or two, right around the time Headquarters would be reopening following its observance of the Sabbath, conditions in Washington City would be changing dramatically. In a span of minutes – literally – the mild and breezy weather, with heavy rain, would transform into a savage gale, with snow and rapidly falling temperatures. All of this would be a precursor to what New York could expect to see less than twelve hours later. With so much at stake, he could not decide which set of Glynn's next observations would be the more captivating for him: the live one from the nation's capitol or the three o'clock reports from the entire country.

Will answered the telephone on its first ring, dispensing quickly with the introductory formalities. "Alright, then," Glynn asked him immediately, "what do you want to hear first?" It was as if he'd some-how read Will's mind across the miles.

"I want to know everything you can tell me about what's going on down there right now," he answered, without hesitation. Ultimately, the logic was simple: it would take only a few minutes to absorb the current obs from Washington City, but fully twenty, or more, to receive and record them for the rest of the nation.

"Right. Washington obs it is, then. The rain is steady, not espe-cially heavy, but steady. I haven't actually checked the gauge yet, but I'd guess we've had between a half and three quarters of an inch in just the last two hours. The wind is still basically southeast since my last report, but now I'd say it's now more like 130, possibly even 120, degrees. Steady, at least thirty-five miles-per-hour. And the barom-eter is falling very rapidly now – we're already down to ten-oh-eight millibars. Temp steady at forty-five."

"Well, that all makes sense, and it's pretty much what I expected," Will said, visualizing the surface map. "The cold front should come through in about, oh, ninety minutes. The temperature will drop below freezing and the rain will change to snow, almost instantly. At the same time, and just as quickly, the wind will pick up from the northwest to fifty or sixty, with gusts to seventy or eighty. It's extremely important that you make sure you're at home and hunkered down, Glynn. It won't be pretty if you're caught outside, believe you me."

"Yes, I understand all that, Will. I've been paying close attention to everything you've been telling me. But there is something I wanted to ask you."

"What is it?"

"Well, I've been thinking, and I've decided that I'd like to stay here at the Office and keep you posted throughout the evening. That is, if you want me to."

Will would have been delighted to accept Glynn's generous offer, if not for the fact that he had already promised Mrs. D he'd be home by six for dinner.

"Glynn, I'm not sure I understand exactly what it is you're saying. You need to be at home – with Camille – don't you?"

"Yes, of course, but ... well ... I guess I have something of an embarrassing confession to make here," he responded, sounding rather sheepish. "Camille and I sort of had an argument ... well, more like a knock-down, drag-out fight, in all honesty. It was all because of the craziness about this storm. I guess what it boils down to is that she refuses to believe it's going to happen."

Will exhaled slowly into the brief silence, knowing precisely what his poor partner was going through. And just exactly how frustrating it all was, how maddening.

"Still, you can rest assured that everything will be okay at home," Glynn went on, in a rush. "We have plenty of wood and other necessary provisions – I made sure of that, myself. The apartment house we live in is solidly constructed out of brick, so she'll be safe there. And what you don't know is that we live only three-and-a-half very short blocks from HQ. I can definitely make it home to her anytime, with no problem, regardless of what might be happening outside."

"I wouldn't rely too heavily on that supposition, my friend. There's no real telling just how destructive this monster might turn out to be. At any rate, I won't be able to stay at the Office beyond five or five-fifteen, but I would certainly love to get updates from you till then."

"Can I call you after you've plotted the three's?"

"Great Caesar's ghost – you still haven't given me the three's! My God, do you know I completely forgot, and would have hung up without getting them? There's just so much going on around here, I'm afraid I'm turning into some kind of bumbling scatterbrain. I tell you what I'll do. I'll call you back after I have the three o'clock map prepared."

"Gee, thanks, Will – that'll be great! I'll be right here by the telephone, waiting for your call."

"Well, of course you're most welcome, buddy, but let's get down to brass tacks, shall we? That's really the least I can do for you, as far as I'm concerned. I mean, after all, without your willingness to keep delivering the obs to me in the first place, there wouldn't even be a three o'clock map, now, would there?"

After transcribing the obs and breaking the connection, Will found that he was suddenly feeling quite lonely. He wasn't accustomed to being all by himself in the Office and, at the moment, there was no one else he could think of to telephone.

It took him seemingly no time at all to complete his new map.

Storm really taking shape now. Center just south of Hatteras. Good. Central pressure must be down to as least ten-oh-four millibars, although the nearest station reports ten-oh-six. One cold front extends north-northwest from the storm's center through central Pennsylvania and up through extreme western New York. Another cold front extends south from the storm's center well offshore, and then curves southwest through central Florida. Amazing. No sign of a warm front anywhere. Earlier warm front dissolved. Storm and entire frontal structure still translating east. Explosive deepening imminent. Good God! Front nearly upon Washington, as I suspected. I think I'd better revise my start-time for New York City to two a.m. And there is no one in Headquarters making an indication. Heads will roll. By golly, will heads ever roll . . .

Will scrambled up the half-flight of stairs to the observation deck in order to check on the conditions outside. For the moment, the situation remained basically unchanged from the morning. The rain continued to fall steadily, but its intensity was only light to moderate. The wind was still east-southeast, at maybe twenty-five miles-per-hour. To anyone unaware of the synoptic situation now unfolding, which, of course, was practically everyone, to-day would seem perfectly ordinary for mid-March in New York: dreary, cold, and rainy. Although perhaps a bit of an aberration, given the lovely, spring-like weather the City's residents had become spoiled by the past couple of weeks.

At four o'clock, Will donned his outdoor gear and headed to the elevator. A brief, brisk walk to get the blood flowing and clear his head was exactly what he needed right about now. He had just reached the street when he remembered his promise to call Glynn. Hurrying back upstairs to the telephone, he had the operator place the call to Headquarters.

Glynn came on the line so quickly that Will wondered how the machine on his end had even had a chance to ring. He immediately reported that the conditions in Washington City were still basically the same, although the wind speed had dropped off a bit during the past four or five minutes. Will thanked him for this latest update, then reciprocated with a detailed description of how things were evolving based on the map that he'd just completed. As Will spoke, he realized just how pleasurable it was to be able to paint such a vivid picture for his friend and colleague – someone who was not only deeply interested, but trained enough to be able to appreciate it fully.

The fact of the matter was he could think of very little to do right now which would be the least bit productive, short of providing a general notification – which was impossible, of course, given Long's orders strictly forbidding any mention of the storm. Things had also now progressed past the point where his forecasting system would be of anymore use. When it came right down to it, all that Will could do at this juncture was just sit back and watch as events unfolded. His emotions were all over the map, and they ran the gamut: elation, anticipation, excitement, and trepidation, all rolling around together in varying degrees of intensity. He likened it, to some extent, to the ride he'd taken last summer on that marvelous and thrilling amusement attraction at Coney Island, the Gravity Pleasure Serpentine Railway, with all its disorienting drops, rises, and turns.

After hanging up the telephone receiver, Will again took the elevator down to the ground floor with umbrella in hand, ready to begin his constitutional. As he walked along, he was thinking about Glynn's earlier characterization of the day as surreal. Suddenly, he was struck by a vivid recollection of a prognosticative occurrence from early in his childhood. He could see, as clearly as if it were just yesterday, a summer's morn on the farm, when he was only six years old. The sky was clear that day and there was no wind; yet, at some point, he became certain – God only knows how – that a severe storm would strike in less than an hour, bringing with it some seriously damaging hail. Being too young to understand that such a premonition was anything out of the ordinary, he simply shared it matter-of-factly with his parents. Having had previous experience with this uncanny ability of his, they acted at once, grateful they'd at least been given the chance to get the horses into the barn before the storm hit, full-force.

Returning to the present, making his way along Broadway, Will couldn't help but take note of the people bustling round and about him this rainy Sunday afternoon, the eleventh of March. How ordinary they all looked. And why not? They were, of course, completely oblivious to any impending disaster. He felt his stomach clench briefly, an obvious signal of his continued distress over how monstrously unfair it all was.

As he circled back to the Office, Will found himself thinking about Mrs. D's sound advice to let go of his residual feelings of responsibility and impotence about this blizzard. Not only when it came to Kira (which was naturally the most difficult), but all things which might concern the general public, as well. He was still in the Army, after all, and therefore not to be held accountable for the fact that the Sergeant's orders basically left him bound and gagged, as far as alerting anyone else to the dangers of this storm. Consequently, the only thing left for him to do was simply accept it. Regardless of how difficult that might be.

It was four-fifty when Will stepped out of the elevator, shaking the water from his overcoat and umbrella. As he unlocked the Office door, he was again slightly startled by the jangling sound of the telephone, and raced over to grab the earpiece from its hook.

"Will, hi, it's me, Glynn. Remember what I had said to you earlier, about the atmosphere being so surreal, down here?"

"Yes, of course I do; oddly enough, I was just thinking about it only a few moments ago. Your description was both excellent and evocative. And I must say, it's beginning to feel the same way to me, too, up here."

"Yes, well, now things are ten times more intense than they were before. I mean, Will, it is absolutely *unbelievable!* Try to visualize this . . . I'm looking out the window onto G Street, where a great number of people are all standing motionless – basically stopped dead in their tracks – looking skyward, off to the west. It's no longer just the animals that are spooked; now *everyone* seems to be waiting with bated breath, expecting something huge to happen, imminently. Even though they probably haven't a clue as to what the heck that something might actually be!

"As we speak, the sky to the west looks like a roiling black mass – I tell you, I've never *seen* anything so damn scary looking!"

"Glynn, Glynn, quickly – tell me the wind direction."

"Yes! I'm glad you mentioned it. That's *another* thing. The wind has suddenly gone completely calm. I've never seen anything like it – it's absolutely amazing!"

"Okay. Just make sure you're safe, which includes getting away from the windows. I sure hope Camille is safely indoors, as well. Your current situation is mighty, mighty serious, my friend." Will paused here briefly to organize his thoughts, unintentionally heightening the dramatic effect of what he was about to say.

"What's happening down there, right now, is that all of the energy available in this rapidly deepening storm is . . . let us say . . . pooling."

"Pooling? Is that what you just said?"

"Yes, that is exactly what I said. Pooling."

"Well, what in thunder does that mean?" Glynn was obviously terrified now, his voice choking with fear and panic.

Will lowered the tone of his own voice, and spoke in a slower cadence. "That means, my dear Glynn, that all *Hell* is about to break loose down there!"

"Holy shit! Will!," Glynn practically screamed, in the next instant. "It is still totally calm right where I am, but – *oh my God!* I just saw the wind lift the entire roof clear off a building, a few blocks up the street, and –"

Without any warning, the telephone line went completely dead; the sudden silence was deafening. "Glynn? Glynn, are you there?" Will clicked the receiver hook furiously, desperately trying to reestablish a connection. "Glynn? Glynn? SHIT!"

After a few moments, the local operator came back on the line and Will requested a new connection to Headquarters, though without much hope of it going through. He waited a minute or two, then heard, in the operator's singsong voice, "I'm terribly sorry, sir, but there seems to be some difficulty with that line. Please try your call again later." He thanked her and hung up the earpiece.

Will had no way of knowing, in that moment, that he and Glynn had just shared the last words they would exchange for more than a week. Astonishingly, it would take that long to restore communications between the two great cities.

At four o'clock, the Captain of the Charles H. Marshall wrote in his ship's log that the wind was blowing a moderate gale from the southeast. An hour later he made another entry, this time describing it as a strong gale. He ordered three reefs in the mainsail to reduce its area as they headed north, towards harbor, from a position some eighteen miles southeast of the lightship – a moored vessel equipped with light beacons which aids navigation, much as the beam from a lighthouse does.

In no time, a dense fog rapidly enveloped the boat and its surroundings, and he immediately instructed the crew to direct the small vessel eastward. By moving further away from the more highly trafficked zone nearer the shore, they could minimize the possibility of a collision. He knew, from his many years of experience, that while going farther out to sea might initially seem counter-intuitive, ulti-mately, it would give them their best chance to ride out the storm. Knowing the odds they faced, the Captain silently offered up the first of many prayers for the safety of the ship and his men.

It was four-forty-five. There was nothing left for Will to do at the Office, and no longer any reason to stay by the telephone, so he packed up his things and prepared to leave for home. On one issue he was perfectly clear: he sure as hell was not about to call Kira – that ship had sailed.

As Will locked up, he wondered, briefly, just how on earth he'd ever be able to make it back in the next morning, when his shift began at five o'clock. But he let that thought go just as rapidly as it came. He would get there, alright – somehow – because he was scheduled, and that was what he had to do, no matter what. As far as being able to get back home, anytime to-morrow? Well, clearly that would be another story, entirely. He'd just have to make sure that he planned everything out as carefully and thoughtfully as he could, leaving him well-prepared for as many contingencies as his fevered imagination could conjure up.

For now, though, the thought of Mrs. D, awaiting him at home with her special dinner, made him smile. Although she hadn't let on to Will what it was she'd prepared for the two of them, he just knew it would be exceptional, if what she'd served up last Friday were any indication. He smiled again, even more brightly, as he headed out, at his customarily brisk pace, for his beloved Bridge.

CHAPTER 35

SUNDAY, EARLY EVENING, MARCH 11, 1888

Will pushed himself back from the table slowly, then let out a small, satisfied groan as he patted his pleasantly full stomach with both hands. Smacking his lips as he savored the last bite of his second piece of chocolate cake, he announced to Mrs. D that this time she had surely outdone herself. He told her that the dinner they'd just enjoyed was, hands down, the best he'd ever eaten – surpassing even last Friday's delectable feast. Smiling sweetly and obviously pleased with herself, Mrs. D told him she was glad that the recipe for the pistachio-crusted sea scallops had turned out so well. It was a new one for her – she'd gotten it from Mrs. Potts, only last week.

Will watched in consternation as all the delight drained from Mrs. D's face. Apparently, just the mention of her friend brought back a painful cognizance of her desperate situation. "Oh, Will," she sighed, after a moment, "I really am at my wit's end, right now. I simply cannot think of a single thing I can do for poor Blanche, to ease her terrible suffering. And she's such a dear friend to me, as well you know."

It took a second or two for Will to realize that she was talking about Mrs. Potts. Oddly enough, in all the time he'd been living at Mrs. D's, he had never heard their neighbor referred to by her first name.

"I take it you're talking about her despair over Mr. Potts?"

"Yes, that's it, exactly. I'm sure he's already out at sea by now; he left quite early this morning. She said he mentioned something about expecting lots of foreign ships to be coming in, all day to-day and into the night. According to him, that meant plenty of opportunity to make some good money, which is something of a rarity in his profession, apparently. He went out on, now what boat did she say? I think it was the Charles H. Marshall. Yes, that's the one. Blanche had made it a special point to remember the name of the pilot boat, of course, just in case . . . Well, I guess there's only one way to say this, isn't there: in case she never makes it back to port."

Will heard her breath catch in her throat and saw her eyes widen. It saddened him to see how pale and drawn she looked. He stared at her, helplessly, wordlessly, trapped by the feeling that there was nothing he could say which would make any real difference.

"I know Charley did his best to assure her that he'd be 'just fine,' because the boat he was going out on was 'particularly seaworthy,' as he described it, and with an excellent man in the Captain's chair, to boot. I don't think she bought into any of that though, not for a minute. No little pilot boat would stand a ghost of a chance against this monster storm, Will, would it? Not even with Vice-Admiral Robert FitzRoy at the helm . . ." She gave him the tiniest pensive smile, then her gaze wandered to the window and she stared outside for a moment.

Though quite taken by the cleverness of her topical reference, Will remained silent, looking at her sadly. He reckoned that the question she'd just posed, however creatively, was purely rhetorical, and he was glad of it – he knew that any answer he might offer would only cause her more pain.

"And as hard as she worked at convincing him to stay home with her, ultimately there was nothing she could do to stop him," she continued, returning her attention to Will. "Blanche – Mrs. Potts – is simply beside herself. She's completely convinced he's going to die. She said there's even the awful possibility, nay, the likelihood, that she's seen his face for the very last time. If the boat goes down and all hands are lost, his body will be relegated to an eternity in a watery grave."

Mrs. D sighed as she shook her head slowly, her left cheek resting against the fingers of her left hand and her downcast eyes beginning to brim. Will wished fervently that there were something, anything, he could say to assuage her suffering over her dear friend's desperate plight. He thought fleetingly of the advice she'd given him about Kira, but realized at once that the circumstances here were vastly different. Mrs. D had been forced to come to terms with the fact that, in all probability, Mrs. Potts was correct in her conviction: Charley Potts *would* most likely die to-night – and horribly. And there was nary a thing anyone could do to save him.

After a long moment, Will reached over and carefully took Mrs. D's right hand in both of his, squeezing her palm gently in silent commiseration. He understood that this was all one could do, really, in such moments – simply be there for a loved one in need.

For the second time in a relatively short span of minutes, Will listened attentively as Mrs. D recited the extensive list of all the actions she'd taken in preparation for the storm. She focused mainly on her stockpiling of provisions, detailing how she'd followed through on Will's earlier imperative to secure enough food to last the two of them for at least one week. Will couldn't help but recognize her busy chatter for what it was: an obvious attempt to focus on something other than Mrs. Potts. So he listened solicitously and asked pertinent questions, even though he already knew most of the answers. It was really quite simple, he reasoned. If this harmless little ritual helped her in some indefinable way, what power on earth could move him to deny her that?

"I must say, it certainly sounds to me like you have things well-in-hand. But just to be on the safe side – are there any last-minute items that still need attending to? You did remember to have that extra coal delivered, didn't you?" Of course, he knew full-well that she had. Besides being at the top of her list, they had discussed it briefly just last night.

"Oh, yes, yes." She nodded her head vigorously. "I took care of that yesterday. And – " Halting here for just a tick, she looked at him sheepishly. "I suppose I really should have told you about this before now, but ... well ... when the delivery man came, we got to talking, like you do, you know, and ... well, I guess the upshot is that somehow or other, I ended up telling him all about the storm. I do hope you won't be cross with me for having done so. It's just that he's such a terribly nice young man, with a sweet new wife, and if something awful were to happen to them that I might have been able to prevent, just by doing something as simple as giving him a word of warning, well – "

Suddenly, she broke down and began to cry. "Oh, Will," she managed to get out, in between sobs, "I've been through so much hardship in my life. I'd venture that everyone my age has. I don't want you to misunderstand me, though, I'm not complaining at all. In fact, it's actually much more like the opposite of a complaint, really, owing to a huge penetration I've just had, this very minute." She wiped the tears from her eyes and, after a moment or two, began to brighten.

Will reckoned he knew Mrs. D about as well as he'd ever known anyone. About as well as a person could know another person, as far as he was concerned. So it therefore came as a surprise to him that he hadn't the faintest idea what she was about to say next – and his curiosity was thoroughly piqued.

Wilma took another few moments to compose herself, blowing her nose gently and clearing her throat a time or two. Then, after a quick drink of water, she launched into her explanation.

"You see, dear boy, it's just now come to me, this very moment, that not once, before any of the hard times I've ever experienced, did I have even the slightest inkling that something bad or awful was about to happen to me. Like with my Walter, for instance. There was no warning, no advance notice. He was simply here, loving me, one minute, and then – Poof! – gone, practically the very next.

"I'm sure you're familiar with that old adage, 'ignorance is bliss.' Well, now I know what they mean by that; it really, truly is. But it's much more than just that. I now can see that none of this is even remotely about me."

Will interjected. "What do you mean by saying that, Mrs. D?"

"What I mean, Will, is that this is about *you*. My God, child! You must be some kind of . . . I don't know, super-being, or something. I mean, it has shaken me to my very core about Mrs. Potts and her Charley, leaving me feeling paralyzed and helpless. And pretty useless, too, as far as that goes. And with me all the time thinking I had such a depth of understanding about your dilemma with Kira. Why, I just naturally up and jumped right in to give you my 'sage advice,' didn't I. Like I'm so damned smart. But I'm not so smart! Who the heck am I? Just some doddering old lady who wants to pummel you with some of her 'shop-worn wisdom.'" Her darkened face glowering, she paused for a moment before concluding, bitterly, "Yes, you and anyone else who will pay the least little bit of attention, really, for that matter."

"Mrs. D.!" he cried out, sharply, sitting bolt upright. "While I'm afraid I must confess that I don't have the foggiest notion what you're going on about here, this much I do know: whatever this is, you must stop it, immediately. Stop it, right this very minute! I will not abide hearing you spoken of in such a fashion. Not even if the one doing the speaking is *you*."

Wilma shook her head sadly and gave out with a long, deep sigh, her energy expended. After a few moments, composing herself again, she nodded at him as she continued. "You're right, of course, my dear. I have gone a bit ''round the bend' just now, haven't I. I do hope you'll forgive me for that. I guess you could say that it's my way of giving in to the incredible strain that both of us have been under these past few days." She sat quietly for a moment or two, her relaxing face resuming its natural color and the spark returning to her eyes.

"Really, though, this is all I'm trying to say: I'm only now, this very minute, getting the tiniest glimpse of what you must have been going through this past week, or more. My God, Will, I simply cannot fathom how you have been able to stand it. Because I know that I surely couldn't." She looked at him wonderingly, head moving gently side-to-side.

"Ahh . . . *now* I think I understand what it is you're getting at. Thank goodness! Please, let me put your mind at ease, at once. Over the course of my entire life, as it showed up in one form or another, I've had to come to terms with having this . . . this . . . 'gift of prognosti-cation,' for lack of a better description. Although right about now, it sure as *hell* doesn't seem like any sort of gift at all, if you'll pardon my language, please. I guess the point I'm making here is that I've had this odd, unique, and sometimes frustrating ability all my life, so by now I've had plenty of time to get used to it. And as far as this storm goes? Well, I think I would have been just fine, thank-you-very-much, if only it weren't for all this craziness around Kira. I know you're aware that this is the first time I've ever cared like this about a woman. So you can easily understand why the thought of her putting herself in harm's way, when there is absolutely nothing I can do about it, is simply devastating to me."

"I know, I know, and –"

Suddenly, Will's right palm came up, and she was cut off abruptly. "Pardon me, please, Mrs. D. I would never wish to interrupt you so rudely, but now *I'm* the one who just got a major revelation." She noticed that his hand, as if under its own direction, had wandered down till it rested gently on his chest. His eyes had a faraway look in them. It seemed as if he were trying to focus on something in the distance.

"I can see it all now, and quite clearly, too. Kira is going to be alright. Well, at any rate, chances are good that at least she won't die. Go on, query me – how can I possibly know that?" With that, he returned his attention to her, favoring her with a warm smile.

Wilma had been watching his face closely, and was astonished to see how "light" it had suddenly become. It was as if all the tell-tale signs of the tremendous strain he'd been under had simply evapo-rated, right before her eyes. Before responding, she blinked hard a few times, in rapid succession, to make sure those same eyes weren't playing some sort of trick on her.

"Okay then, Will, I'll bite. How *do* you know that Kira is going to be alright?"

Will was surprised by the sudden and dramatic shift in his feelings. His smile widened into a brief grin, then his face took on a somber cast as he continued.

"Well, sad to say, I guess it all has to do with the terrible circumstance of our poor Mrs. Potts. You see, when I stopped concerning myself, for just an instant, with Kira's stubborn, headstrong refusal to even consider trying to reschedule to-morrow's audition, I was able to fully appreciate just how dire – truly life-threatening, really – this storm is going to be for the unfortunate Mr. Potts.

"This probably sounds horrible, I know, and I don't mean it like that at all, of course. It's just that – and I'm still formulating the words to describe this as we speak, so please, bear with me – it was only after becoming really attuned to Mrs. Potts' situation that I was able to clearly see my own. With Kira, that is.

"She, Kira, made an excellent point when she protested that 'this is Manhattan, for God's sake, the pinnacle of the civilized world.' Just that fact alone takes her chances of survival from the 'highly unlikely' category, as is certainly the case for poor Mr. Potts, to at least 'likely.' And for that, I can only be grateful."

Will paused for a moment, letting out a soft sigh. He felt a deep appreciation for the level of understanding he'd just reached, and the small sense of relief it brought him. Then a shadow fell over his features.

"But then again, on the other hand," he went on, quietly, shaking his head sadly, "I just feel so awful, so terribly hopeless, for our dear *Mrs.* Potts." He reached over and placed his hand on hers.

Apparently it was now Mrs. D's turn to be at a loss for words, so the two of them sat contemplating for a bit, in companionable silence.

"Say, I've just been struck by a terrific idea," Will said suddenly, sitting all the way back in his chair and brightening considerably. "Why not invite her over here to stay with you, starting to-night? You are certainly well-stocked with all the necessary provisions. And I would feel so much better, knowing that the two of you are in good company. After all, it is doubtful I'll be able to manage the trip back home to-morrow, once I've made it into Manhattan."

"Well, dear, that's an excellent idea, and one with which I couldn't agree more. And it just so happens that great minds really do think alike – I discussed that very notion with her, at some length, yesterday. She insists that she wants to ride it out there, mostly because for as long as her telephone keeps working, there's always the possibility that someone may call with news of Charley."

"Ah, yes, of course. That makes a good deal of sense."

"But, Will – I have to say I am a little surprised, not to mention disheartened, to hear you say that you don't think you will be able to make it back here, to-morrow."

"Well, I'm not one-hundred-percent certain that I won't be able to, and I'll surely try my very best. That you can count on. But, by the same token, we must be practical and realistic – and therefore plan for as many contingencies as we possibly can."

"You're right, of course, and I do understand. Actually, what you're saying makes perfect sense. Not that I find that at all surprising," she said with a wink, chucking him lightly with her elbow.

"Now, as far as me going to stay with her, well, I don't think I'd want to do that, either. After all, thanks to our extensive preparations, I'll be able to hunker down here quite nicely. Comfortably, even. But anyway, all that aside, I'm sure that each of us would be able to get to the other's house easily enough, if need be. I mean, we are only talking about a distance of maybe a hundred feet, here."

"Whoa there, Mrs. D. Please, whatever you do, do *not* make the mistake of underestimating this storm. As strange as this sounds, it's entirely possible that it would make little difference whether the distance you have to travel is a hundred feet or a hundred miles.

You could become hopelessly disoriented the very moment you step outside. And once hypothermia sets in, which can take far less time than you might think, all could easily be lost."

"Dear God in Heaven, Will! This is going to be much worse than anything I can picture in my wildest imagination, isn't it? And that's saying something, with an imagination like mine. Land sakes . . . I guess it's safe to say that in a case like this that old adage is right on the money – the good Lord really does move in some mighty mysterious ways." She shook her head gently before squaring back her shoulders and raising her eyebrows and right forefinger in what Will instantly recognized as a state of admonition.

"But now, my dear Mr. Roebling, I really need you to listen, and listen good, because what I'm about to say next is extremely important. With everything else you're going to be up against to-morrow, the very last thing I want is for you to be worrying yourself for even one minute about me, here at home. I'll be just fine, I can promise you that. Oh – and so will our dear Mrs. Potts. I'll make good and darned sure of it."

At that precise instant, Charley's terrible plight flashed through each of their minds, leaving them momentarily breathless. Neither said a word; they didn't have to. Each knew the other was thinking the same exact pitying thought, prompted by a deep and heartfelt sympathy. It was pretty spooky – even for Will.

Poor, poor Mrs. Potts . . .

CHAPTER 36

SUNDAY, LATE EVENING, MARCH 11, 1888

Thankfully, Albert Washington was nearing the end of his exhausting day. The last of the revelous party-goers had finally wandered off, and he had just finished cleaning up and re-setting the event room. Before being able to leave for home, though, he had to comply with Mr. Landen's request that he stop by at his office.

Albert couldn't help but be amazed at the long hours the big boss seemed to work. He idly wondered whether Landen had a family to go home to, then quickly reminded himself that was none of his darn business.

"Well now, Albert," Landen began, coming out from behind his desk and extending his arm to shake hands with the tired young man, "you'll be pleased to hear that I've gotten nothing but stellar reports about you to-day. As I mentioned in our earlier conversation, I could not be happier with your performance since you started working here."

"Thank-you again, Mr. Landen, sir. That sure means a lot to me."

"You're welcome, Albert, you're most welcome. And I tell you what, son – when we're alone, like we are now, why don't you go ahead and call me James?"

"Alright, James."

Landen was quick to notice that Albert hadn't flinched at his suggestion. He'd accepted it readily, matter-of-factly responded "alright," and that was that. Landen found this to be the quintessential example of the kind of thing that was so remarkable about his impressive new employee.

He wondered how it could be that a nineteen-year-old, fresh out of high-school, carried himself with so much poise. And a colored boy, too, for that matter, in a world where the Negro unfortunately was often so downtrodden. He had to admit that he found it amazing, and a delight to see.

"Albert, you *are* aware that you're scheduled for the first shift to-morrow, right?"

"Yes, James, I sure am." The slightly rueful grin on Albert's weary face said it all.

"Alright then. Now, I wouldn't want you getting too accustomed to this or anything," Landen continued, waggling his index finger at Albert and giving him a conspiratorial wink, "but, sometimes when Walt works a double and has to come in early the next morning, I let him stay here in one of our rooms over-night. I have to say that I think you've earned that privilege to-day, young man. Besides which, I don't know if you've happened to look outside lately, but it's raining cats and dogs out there. It's really quite nasty."

"No, I hadn't noticed the rain, actually. But it's small wonder, as I'm not sure I've ever had a busier day than the one I had to-day. So of course, staying over to-night would certainly be a great boon to me. But aren't we booked solid this evening, James?"

Landen responded with a knowing smile and brief nod of his slightly tilted head. "Well, there's booked and then there's booked, Albert, if you get my meaning. Here, you take this key for Room 620. I'm pretty sure you'll find it to your liking. Oh, and I had the messenger tell your folks not to be alarmed if they didn't see you at home to-night, that you might be staying over, here at the Hotel."

"That's so very kind of you, James. I just can't thank you enough, really, for all your consideration. Well, I guess I'll say good-night now, and then I'll be seeing you again, bright and early to-morrow morning."

Although Will had somehow managed to fall asleep by eight-thirty, an underlying restlessness woke him up around eleven-fifteen. He sat up in bed, covers pulled around him, and craned his neck to see as much as he could out the window, eagerly anticipating the change-over to snow. Unfortunately, there was not enough light for him to see too well from his east-facing, second-story vantage point over Pearl. He remained, however, genuinely disinclined to climb out from beneath the warm bedclothes just to peer out the other window onto Sands. One thing he could determine was that it was still raining, although, oddly enough, the street below seemed to have a strange sheen to it, as if it were coated with a thin layer of ice. He wondered if it might be freezing rain. It was interesting that he hadn't even considered that possibility, when it actually made perfect sense.

Judging from the persistent draught he now felt coming through the other window, he deduced the wind had backed from the south-east to a northerly direction. Even though he estimated the temperature to be just above thirty-two degrees, he still thought the rain might be freezing on some surfaces. He knew that even if the air temperature were a degree or two above that magic point, water could indeed freeze upon contact – as long as the difference between the air temperature and the dew point were several degrees or more and the wind were strong enough.

Regardless, he thought, this should not affect the change-over time for the snow. It would mean, however, that a treacherous under-coating of ice on the streets and walk-ways would be making it even more difficult, sadly, for any of the poor souls unlucky enough to be outside in this mess. And come to-morrow morning, he'd be one of them.

Had he still had some means of communicating with Glynn, he would have learned that at five o'clock, a mere fifteen minutes after their last conversation, the rain in Washington City had gone over to a blinding, accumulating snow. Of course, he had no way of knowing that Baltimore had gone over by seven, or that Philadelphia was in transition at that very moment.

Neither could he have known then that the actual change-over in Manhattan would be occurring a full two-hours earlier than his most recent projection of two a.m. (although, he would later admit to himself, the wind already blowing from the north by eleven-fifteen was certainly a sign he could have recognized). New Haven, Connecticut, home to Professor Loomis, would hang on to the rain till two-thirty, after which all Hell would break loose there, too.

With the million-and-one thoughts churning furiously through his mind, Will was most fortunate, indeed, that he was able to fall quickly back to sleep.

Kira lay abed, dealing with her own of state of restless. It was past ten-thirty, and she still hadn't quite managed to fall asleep. Determined to help move things along, she got up and made herself some warm milk – a folk remedy which almost always did the trick for her. Sipping the milk slowly, she mentally reviewed to-morrow morning's schedule for the umpteenth time.

Alright now, let's see ... the telegram said to be at the Bijou promptly at seven-forty-five, but I certainly do not want to arrive any later than seven-thirty-five, and I need to allow for time to stop and get a quick, light breakfast on the way. It's only five blocks in total, so if I leave my suite by seven I should be just fine. Yes, and I'm sure that waking up at five-fifteen will leave me more than enough time to rouse myself and complete all the necessary preparations.

Feeling a little more relaxed after finishing off the milk, she re-checked the alarm which, of course, had already been set for five-fifteen. As she settled back comfortably against the smooth satin of her pillow slips, the soothing sound of the rain, continuing its steady thrum against her windowpane, proved an additional soporific.

Within minutes, Kira had drifted off into a deep, peaceful slumber.

By ten-thirty, May Morrow had already been sound asleep for over an hour – all the more remarkable, considering how long she'd slept-in to-day.

Her plan for Monday was simple. She would wake up at ten minutes to four, move quickly through her morning wash-up and breakfast routine, walk the few blocks to the station, catch the five o'clock el, and arrive at the office in plenty of time for the big six o'clock meeting. At that time of day, it would still be too dark for her to do any reading on the el. But being well ahead of the usual commuter crowd should ensure that, for once, she'd actually get a seat the whole way there – maybe even one all to herself. For a sizable portion of the trip, at any rate. She figured that, just for this one day, it might be worth the trade-off.

Besides, I'm generally more productive and energized during the morning-time – and a little more of a good thing never hurt anyone.

"My God, it's cold," Pat McCormack bemoaned to no one in particular, as he exited the train inside Grand Central Terminal. "I could sense that the temperature was dropping as we were approaching Manhattan, but I certainly had no idea that it would be anything like *this*."

He walked apace through the spacious, only slightly warmer, interior of the station, glancing up at the over-sized clock in the main concourse to confirm his train had arrived as scheduled: eleven-forty. Along the way, he passed a man selling watches from a makeshift pavilion, a sight which had become commonplace in many train stations over the past eight years. Still, he thought it odd to see something like that at this time of night. He continued moving towards the distinctive three-story brick portal, across the exterior top of which was emblazoned, in bold white letters, *New York and New Haven Railroad.*

As he approached the out-of-doors, Pat was amazed by the roaring sound the wind was making. Suddenly, from a short distance ahead, he heard a fellow traveler who had just exited the building exclaim, "Dear *God!* It's pouring rain out here – and everything is a sheet of ice!"

Rivulets of water cascaded off the roof-tops and down the drainpipes, freezing on the sidewalks and all exposed surfaces. Not easily intimidated, Pat set out staunchly on what had now become a perilous trek down Park Avenue. He fought hard to keep his balance with every step. An icy, wind-driven mixture of torrential rain and sleet pelted down mercilessly, soaking him through almost instantly, even though the topcoat he wore was touted as being water-resistant. Overall, he was grossly ill-prepared and underdressed – exactly like everyone else leaving the station.

At the corner of 42nd Street, he crossed over to the west side of the avenue, instinctively seeking out whatever nominal protection the buildings there might afford from the fiercely howling wind blowing directly across Park.

The short, pleasant walk to the hotel that Pat had originally envisioned had turned instead into a nightmarish expedition, one in which he needed every ounce of strength and balance he could muster just to avoid being toppled to the ground. He struggled to remain as up-right as he possibly could, inching his way down the sidewalk while desperately clutching at whatever scant hand-hold presented itself along the way. The few horsecars still out at this late hour were, likewise, no match for the elements, as the terrified horses could only stamp about in place, whinnying pitifully. The poor animals appeared to be much too scared of slipping and falling to risk moving their legs forward, despite the frantic – albeit futile – efforts of their drivers to coax them onward.

It was after he'd finally made his painstaking way down Park to East 31st Street that Pat observed snow mixing in with the freezing rain and sleet. Interestingly, he noticed that the flakes were very large, despite the fierce wind. For one brief moment, he was heartened by the fact that the snow, instantly adhering to everything, had actually improved his footing somewhat. But it was a pyrrhic victory, as his route along East 31st Street now took him directly into the teeth of the savage wind. Dangerously near the end of his energy reserves, he struggled mightily for the next half-hour just to be able to traverse the final three blocks to the hotel's entrance. When he finally did arrive, he was sure he'd never seen anything as beautiful as that warm, welcoming light.

Heaving a great sigh of relief, Pat pushed wearily through the revolving glass door of the Grand Hotel lobby, trudging the final short distance to the front desk to check in. Never in his experience as a traveler had he been so profoundly grateful to find himself *in*-doors, as opposed to out-.

"Great jumping Jehosaphat," he exhaled loudly at the startled clerk, shaking the water and small bits of unmelted ice from his head, arms, and shoulders. "Now just where in tarnation do you suppose all this crazy, wild weather came from? And so gosh-darned suddenly, too?"

The desk clerk could only smile brightly in welcome, nodding sympathetically. He hurried through the business of signing Pat in, and soon had him safely in his room. After hanging up his sopping clothes to dry near the radiator, and performing his cursory ablutions in the bath, Pat burrowed snugly under the smooth sheet and warm blankets. Worn out by the effort he'd just expended on his harrowing journey from the station, he would surely be getting a good night's sleep to-night – about that there was no doubt. He could only hope that to-morrow would dawn bright and sunny, leaving his sojourn through this evening's maelstrom but a distant memory.

Still and all, it would be wise to take the precaution of setting my alarm clock a bit earlier – six-thirty should do it – just in case. Who knows what will happen if this storm decides it wants to stick around for awhile.

PART III

The Blizzard – Day 1

Monday, March 12, 1888

A little past 12 o'clock on Sunday night, or Monday morning, the severe rain that had been pelting down since the moment of the opening of the church doors suddenly changed to a sleet storm that plated the sidewalks with ice. Then began the great storm that is to become for years a household word, a symbol of the worst of weathers and the limit of nature's possibilities under normal conditions.

At a quarter past 6 o'clock, when the extremely modified sunlight forced its way to earth, the scene in the two great cities that the bridge unites was remarkably beyond any winter sight remembered by the people. The streets were blocked with snowdrifts. The car tracks were hid, horse cars were not in the range of possibilities, a wind of wild velocity howled between the rows of houses, the air was burdened with soft, wet, clinging snow, only here and there was a wagon to be seen, only here and there a feeble moving man.

The wind howled, whistled, banged, roared, and moaned as it rushed along. It fell upon the house sides in fearful gusts, it strained great plate glass windows, rocked the frame houses, pressed against doors so that it was almost dangerous to open them.

It was a visible, substantial wind, so freighted was it with snow. It came in whirls, it descended in layers, it shot along in great blocks, it rose and fell and corkscrewed and zigzagged and played merry havoc with everything it could swing or batter or bang or carry away.

It was Monday morning, when a day of rest from shopping had depleted the larders in every house, and yet there were no milk carts, no butcher wagons, no basket-laden grocer boys, no bakers' carriers. In great districts, no attempt was made to deliver the morning papers. The cities were paralyzed.

-The New York Sun, Tuesday, March 13, 1888

CHAPTER 37

PRE-DAWN

A very comely Kira, curiously clad in a richly appointed, form-fitting peacock-blue gown, had just finished apologizing profusely to Will, as they lay comfortably snuggled against each other in her sumptuous bed. She'd explained that she was now quite clear he had not been trying to sabotage her audition (and career) the other night, when he'd first told her all about the blizzard. That his only concern had been, and continued to be, that she remain safe and well. She begged him to please find it in his heart to forgive her, confessing that with the able assistance of an old family friend, an esteemed member of the mental health profession, she'd managed to engage in some "rather intense soul-searching." As a result, she'd recognized that her fundamental problem, deep down, had been her own misguided sense of unworthiness which, in turn, drove her to push him away, however unconsciously. Ultimately, and happily, she had come to a wonderful realization. She now firmly believed with all her heart – not to mention mind, body, and soul – that he truly did love her, every bit as much as she loved him.

Will gazed, awestruck, at her beautiful face. He simply could not get over the amazing lightness in her bearing. It was as if a five-hundred-pound weight had suddenly, and quite miraculously, been lifted from her shoulders. For the first time, she now appeared to him, unequivocally, as the strong, confident, remarkable woman he'd always known she was at the core of her being.

Playfully running her slender graceful fingers through his hair, she brought her lips close to his ear and, in a breathy voice, whispered softly, yet unmistakably: "And now, my dear Mr. Roebling, it gives me great pleasure to inform you that the time has finally come for you to have your way with your future bride-to-be." She gave him a shy, yet sly, smile, glancing up at him sideways through fluttering lashes, playing the perfect coquette. Will was reminded fleetingly of the feeling he'd had all the way back in September, when she was being so flirtatious with him while they waited for the curtain to go up on *Gasparone*. Yet this was profoundly different, of course – their courtship was six months further along, and they were now deeply in love and about to be married.

Will, exultant, could scarcely believe his great good fortune. Of course he had been keenly anticipating the consummation of their relationship, but was now nearly overwhelmed to discover that Kira felt *exactly* the same way.

And just look at the way that gown hugs every delicious curve of her ripe, womanly body!

Will felt ecstatic, sure that he was the luckiest of men. He was quite certain that, in all his life, he had never known a happier moment. Giving out a long, blissful sigh of contentment as he closed his eyes, he then leaned in to kiss her delectable mouth.

Suddenly, and with a great shock, he was jolted by the familiar, insistent, and always unwelcome clanging of an alarm clock. As inherently unpleasant as it was to be so rudely awakened from a deep sleep at the ungodly hour of three-thirty a.m., that was *nothing* compared to the utter wretchedness which swept over him as he watched his delightfully vivid, boldly erotic dream evaporate precipitously. In a matter of mere seconds, the poor young man came crashing down from the warmest heights of Heaven to a cold, dark, and harsh reality.

"Oh, no, no, no, no," he moaned pitiably, grasping his head with both hands and rocking side-to-side, then smacking his forehead into his palms in a staccato finish, "damn, damn, *damn!*"

Standing before the partially snow-plastered, north-facing window which looked out onto Sands, Will could not believe his eyes.

Sweet Jesus, how can this be? It's a total white-out!

Quickly pulling on his pants and bounding down the stairs, he turned on the porch light to get a better view. "My God, the snow has to be six inches deep out there already," he whispered out loud, incredulously. "It must have changed over much sooner than I'd thought. And the *wind!* I can't see any further than ten yards, if that."

Well, alright then, William Augustus Roebling, this is it! And you'd better get yourself a move on, too – and fast. It's certainly not going to get any easier to slog your way through this mess, what with the wind howling on mercilessly and the snow getting deeper and deeper with each passing minute.

While Will was awakening to a world gone white, Charley Potts and the rest of the pilots, already well past scared, were now in the icy grip of an escalating terror. The strong easterly wind which had been pummeling them so ferociously the past several hours had suddenly gone completely calm, leaving in its wake an eerie stillness. Unfortunately, the drop in wind had produced no lessening of the huge waves crashing into them from the southeast. The barrage continued relentlessly, threatening to engulf the little craft at any moment.

At three-fifty-five, with the Charles H. Marshall positioned about twelve nautical miles east-southeast of the Sandy Hook lightship, the wind suddenly erupted from the northwest with such astounding force that the boat went over on her beam ends, further panicking the already terrified men. Fortunately, she righted herself again almost immediately. Two hours later she was still afloat, God love her, but the accumulation of ice on her masts and sails – indeed, coating just about every square inch of her surface – was so great that she resembled nothing so much as a small iceberg.

Charley, the crew, and the rest of the pilots had long since resolved to pay the strictest attention to each and every one of the Captain's orders. Desperate to feel at least some small sense of control, they followed them precisely, hoping to avert a disaster – at least for as long as they possibly could. Overall, to a man, they had tremendous faith in their Captain, knowing of his vast experience with many storms during his nearly forty years on the high seas. But neither he nor any of the other poor souls tragically trapped out on the open, angry waters this day had ever experienced anything remotely resembling what was occurring now. Of the hundreds of other vessels now stranded off the coast, dozens had already capsized and sunk. And the savage storm had only just begun.

As terrified as he was, fearing for his life at every second, Charley Potts found it surprising that his thoughts and concerns were far more for Blanche and what she must be going through right now. He felt profound remorse for having summarily discounted practically everything she'd said to him about the storm before he left. He was deeply saddened to know that she must be suffering terribly at this very moment, an absolute nervous wreck. And even if, by some miracle, he did manage to survive this ordeal, how many days would it be before he could make his way back home to her, and relieve her anguish? And, of course, what if he didn't survive? Which was looking more and more likely, as the storm raged on implacably. The answer to that was simple, and devastating: Blanche would not only lose her husband, she would also be robbed of whatever modicum of comfort she might have gleaned from the closure of a proper burial.

And what about their children? Even though they'd been grown for some time now, with families of their own, how would they feel when they heard about their father's horrible death, the victim of a monster storm out at sea? Especially when they learned he could have avoided such a sorry fate just by listening to their mother, who would undoubtedly be retelling the sad story for many years to come.

Charley was struck hard by the irony of it all. The most important thing in his life had always been the ability to provide for his family. Yet here he was about to die precisely because he'd dismissed the passionate warning sounded by his devoted and despondent wife. He had a sudden vision of her tear-stained face as she pleaded with him, and could still feel the shock of the cold water she'd hurled at him in abject frustration.

Oh, Blanche, my poor, darling Blanche. I am so very sorry, my dear, and can only hope that someday you'll find it in your heart to forgive me, and will remember me with fondness.

May Morrow, moving about as quietly as she could to avoid disturbing her room-mates, was beginning to wonder whether it mightn't have been a good idea to allow herself more time to get ready this morning. Her normally easy and efficient routine was a bit out-of-kilter somehow, what with the need to be in so early. So focused was she on the task at hand, she paid little heed to the strange, keening sound which seemed to be reverberating just outside the boardinghouse. It never even occurred to her to check on the weather conditions till just moments before she was ready to leave, when her thoughts invariably turned to whether she'd need to break out her warm fleece-lined winter overcoat one more time. Yesterday, as always, she'd taken note of the indications in the newspaper which said that Monday would be fair, but breezy and chilly after Sunday's rain.

She leaned over the coal stove to peer out the window, and was at once startled and confounded. For some unknown reason, her view appeared to be totally obstructed. The light inside the kitchen was so pale, and the darkness outside so complete, that she was unable to discern the opaque mass of snow, originally wet but now frozen solid, which had plastered itself to the lower panes.

At first, completely flummoxed, she could think of no plausible explanation for her inability to see out the window. Finally, she figured that it must have something to do with the fact that it was still only four-forty a.m., therefore still pitch-black outside. Also, of course, she was quite unaccustomed to being up at this time of day. Even though the odd noise generated by the wind was now beginning to make more of an impression upon her, she could never have imagined in her wildest dreams that, in that moment, the world as she knew it had been completely altered by the sudden and totally unexpected arrival of a freak storm. One which had already developed into a ferocious blizzard.

All in all, she found the situation odd, to say the least. But then she figured maybe she was being given a sign that she should wear her warm overcoat after all, probably for the last time this season. Besides, it was her nicest coat, and she surely didn't want to seem under-dressed when she arrived for the meeting. Appearances were so important these days, especially in the professional world.

Up in Room 620, luxuriously ensconced in what he was sure had to be the most comfortable bed he'd ever slept in, an awakening Albert Washington knew instantly, not even half-way through his first yawn and stretch, that something very strange was happening outside. It was only five o'clock – still pre-dawn – but an eerie light filtered through the curtains, none-the-less. And he heard a loud, continuous whistling sound, similar to the one which might be made by a very strong wind. Quickly, albeit reluctantly, he got out of bed and rushed over to the windows. Pulling back the draperies, he let out an involuntary gasp.

He simply could not believe his eyes!

Even though the visibility was so poor he could barely manage to see down to the street, the scattered diffuse light from below reflected off the mantle of white, affording him a brief glimpse of a scene limning the utter chaos which had already gripped the stirring City. From his lofty vantage point on the highest floor of the Grand Hotel, looking east-southeast onto Broadway between 31st and 32nd Streets, he was able to discern several horsecars and private carts and wagons hopelessly stuck in the deep snow. Frantic drivers lashed futilely at their poor beasts of burden in a desperate, though ultimately unsuccessful, attempt to free their vehicles.

When the wind gusted, all Albert could see was a mesmerizing mass of riotous snowflakes. In between the gusts, however, he managed to make out a number of damaged telegraph poles. Some were leaning sharply to the left, while others were lying flat on the ground or hanging in mid-air, partially suspended from a tangle of black wires standing out in bold relief against the backdrop of pristine white. Mouth agape, he continued to stare out the window for several long moments, transfixed by this stunning display of Nature's devastating fury.

Then suddenly, almost as if he'd just been goosed by some unseen hand, Albert turned quickly on his heel and covered the distance from the window to the washstand in only a few strides. He knew his shift didn't actually begin till seven, so technically he had lots of time on his hands. But on a day such as this, he could scarcely begin to imagine what would be in store for him once he'd reported for duty. Something told him he'd better get downstairs just as fast as he possibly could. It was highly likely that most of the hotel staff would be unable to make it in at all to-day, what with the flu and now this monster of a blizzard.

It wasn't hard to figure that his services would be sorely needed, and right quick at that.

After washing up and dressing swiftly, Albert headed down to the kitchen to fortify himself with some good hot coffee and a quick bite of breakfast. By six o'clock he was knocking on the door to James Landen's office. Not surprisingly, Mr. Landen had yet to arrive.

Kira Smith was, of course, unaware of the starring role she had played this morning in Will's compelling and graphic dream. By stark contrast, Will was the furthest thing from her mind as she reached over to shut off her alarm clock. She felt grateful for the restful quality of the sleep she'd gotten, especially given how excited she was. Overcome with anticipation, really. Calculating quickly, she figured she'd been sleeping, uninterrupted, for more than six hours – which really was not too bad, considering the circumstances. She smiled contentedly as she stretched, then quickly got out of bed to begin her momentous day.

Feeling a decided chill in her suite, she turned up the steam heat, saying a silent "thank-you" again for the generosity of her father. His subsidy of her high rent afforded her such greatly appreciated amenities, and she knew just how lucky she was that it did. She then moved rapidly into the bathroom to draw herself a hot bath. Whenever she could, she enjoyed taking a relaxing bath first thing upon rising, mentally going over a checklist of the day's planned activities as she soaked. To-day, however, she needed to be particularly cognizant of her tight schedule, and had therefore allotted only fifteen minutes for this early morning indulgence.

Ordinarily, Kira would fix herself something for breakfast before going out in the morning. But her program to-day included a quick stop at her favorite delicatessen, which was conveniently located along the way to the Bijou, right on Broadway. There she intended to get a freshly brewed cup of coffee and a hot, buttered English muffin, topped with honey, a particular favorite of hers. So all she needed to do now, once she got out of her bath, was dress herself up exquisitely, focus on any last-minute preparations for her final audition, and leave at seven sharp – just as planned.

Kira smiled as she lowered herself into the steaming, scented water. Life really was good, after all. Then her eyes lit up like two glowing emeralds as her smile widened. Somehow, call it faith or what you will, she just knew she was going to get this part.

As Will stepped out onto the front porch, at a minute or two past four, the northwesterly gale was blowing so hard it took nearly all of his strength to pull the door closed tightly behind him. He gingerly eased his way down the north-facing porch steps, taking great pains to avoid being swept off his feet.

It was one thing for him to know, intellectually, that the blizzard had taken shape precisely as his forecasting system had predicted it would. It was quite another though to actually be experiencing its ramifications, first-hand. He realized immediately that the mere fifteen extra minutes he'd budgeted for his trek to work this morning was laughable, at best. There was simply no way he'd be getting to the Office to-day by five o'clock.

Then again, it was a fairly safe bet that no one else would be there at five, either. And as there wasn't any task he could think of that urgently required attending to shortly thereafter, what difference could it possibly make, anyway? Other than the Army being the Army, of course.

He allowed himself a wry smile.

That smile was long gone by the time he'd made his laborious way down to the street, however. In fact, Will was beginning to think that getting himself to the Office to-day at all might not be in the cards anymore – his commitment to duty be damned.

As prepared as he'd felt he was, knowing in advance the magnitude of this storm, Will was still astounded by the life-threatening conditions now confronting him. The cold was already unheard of for the twelfth of March in New York – twenty-six degrees, according to the kitchen window thermometer he'd checked just moments ago. And he knew, by this time to-morrow, the temperature would drop at least another twenty degrees, far more typical of the Arctic than the streets of Brooklyn. As for the snow, there appeared to be somewhere in the neighborhood of eight inches piled up already, but any confirmation of that rough estimate was rendered impossible by the fierce wind.

Interestingly, there were large swaths of ground completely barren of snow, especially along the south side of the east-west-running street, where the relentless wind displaced the flakes as quickly as they fell. On the north side, however, right up to the fronts of the south-facing houses, the snow was already amassing in enormous drifts which were growing right before Will's eyes. The nearly quarter-inch-layer of ice coating the streets and sidewalks only made conditions that much more treacherous. Especially dangerous were those areas where the snow had been completely blown away, along with whatever bit of traction it might have provided.

Having made the left onto Sands at the end of his walk-way, Will had only three short blocks to go before reaching the Bridge entrance. Of one thing he was certain: had he not walked this same path six-days-a-week for the past year, he'd never have been able to navigate it in this moment. All familiar landmarks were obscured by the blinding snow, which, to his surprise, still appeared to be mixed occasionally with ice pellets or sleet. An excellent judge of distance, Will surmised that when the wind blew its hardest, which he estimated was roughly fifty-five or sixty miles-per-hour, the visibility was reduced to a mere ten or fifteen feet!

As he made his way, haltingly, along Sands, Will noted that he traveled alone, which was certainly not unusual for this time of day. Experience, however, told him that that would no longer be the case by the time he reached the Bridge. Given the horrific conditions he was fighting his way through now, he shuddered to think of the extreme hardship he would face on his way across the main span, where man and beast alike would be unprotected from the elements. He had a sudden, despairing vision of the horrors which must be overtaking the growing throngs of shocked and bewildered pedestrians in the City. Some of them would soon be fighting for their very lives, attempting to negotiate the now unrecognizable maze of crisscrossing canyons currently comprising the frozen island of Manhattan. His heart went out to them.

Will was indeed grateful that Mrs. D had thought to insist, in the note she'd left for him this morning, that he take on his journey to-day at least a half-pound of the dried beef she'd bought as part of their emergency supplies. She'd been especially concerned about his having something nutritious to eat, once she'd learned there was a good chance he would not be able to make it back to their well-stocked pantry. Will knew that in a situation as onerous as this, a ready and convenient source of energy and sustenance would surely prove indispensable.

At five o'clock, the mournful howling of the wind woke Wilma Duncan from a restless sleep. She was not at all surprised that she'd slept so poorly, as thoughts of Blanche and Charley continued to weigh on her heavily. Too timid to venture a look out her bedroom window, she put on her robe, went downstairs into the kitchen, and made herself her regular morning cup of coffee. She knew Will was already gone, his breakfast dishes washed and stacked neatly in the drying rack.

Finally, fortified by several deep swallows of her hot, percolated brew, she summoned the courage to peek outside. Although still quite dark out there, she could see in an instant that Will had indeed been correct – not that she'd ever had any real doubt. She had, of course, been keeping her fingers crossed for some kind of miraculous reprieve, but that was all water under the bridge now.

The blinding snow created a strange aura, disturbing and surreal. Despite having lived in this house for nearly forty years, she was sure that she'd never before experienced anything quite like this. Thanks to Will, of course, she'd been given the opportunity to fully prepare for this storm, and was certainly better equipped than almost anyone else in terms of necessary supplies. It was therefore dismaying, even a little embarrassing, to discover that she was still left with a feeling of anxiety and fear.

She decided she'd wait till it got light out, then weigh her options relative to making a trip next door. She really wanted to check up on Blanche, but hadn't quite figured out yet whether she ought dare hazard it.

Before any of that, though – breakfast. And a hearty one, to be sure, on this day of days.

CHAPTER 38

6:30 AM

Will raised up his eyes and lifted his arms high, almost as if in supplication. Grinning ferociously, he gave his head a great shake as he let loose with a few wild "whoo-hoo's." After what had seemed an interminable passage through the very corridors of Hell itself, the sweet relief he felt, staring up at what he could make out of the familiar outline of the Equitable Building, was nothing short of indescribable. His three-mile commute, a trip which ordinarily took him anywhere from forty-five to fifty-five minutes, depending on whether he was in a hurry, had just taken him – *could this be right?* – nearly two-and-a-half hours! After laboring breathlessly up the seven flights of stairs, he dug the Office keys out of his ice-caked trousers and opened the door to the Signal Service tower. He knew he was fortunate indeed, at least for the moment anyway, that the building's electrical power was still up and running. For obvious reasons though, he'd known better than to even consider taking the elevator.

As expected, the Office was completely empty. Will knew he was not only the first to arrive, but quite possibly the last, given the horrific travel conditions. He moved quickly through the common area and into his own office, thrilled at long last to be able to sit down and rest. After carefully removing the frozen outer-layers of his clothing, he hung them near the radiator to dry. As far as he could tell, he hadn't suffered any frost-bite, although he couldn't be sure of that just yet. Of one thing he was sure, however – his prolonged battle with the elements had left him enormously fatigued in spite of his youth and superior physical fitness.

"And to think," Will mused aloud, grinning wryly and shaking his head, "it's still only six-thirty in the morning!"

He walked over to the telephone, picked up the earpiece and gave the handcrank a few turns, but harbored little hope the service had somehow magically survived the onslaught of the devastating wind.

No response from the switchboard. Well, no surprise there. And from what I saw on my way in, I expect it will be quite a long while before normal operations will resume.

During his odyssey, one of the more fearsome sights he'd borne witness to was the great number of telephone and telegraph wires which had blown down and were now whipping around wildly in the savage wind. Many poles had been felled as well, creating that much more mayhem for those souls unfortunate enough to be caught out on the streets. He wondered how much longer it would be before the electrical power stopped working as well, adding further insult to injury.

Will walked back to his desk and sat down heavily. The euphoria brought on by reaching the safety of the Office had now dissipated, leaving him present to the stark reality of his harrowing passage across the Brooklyn Bridge. End-to-end, he knew the distance was only about one-and-one-eighth miles, but to-day it had felt, for all the world, like a hundred-mile stretch through forbidding terrain. Gone had been the friendly nods and "hello's" he'd normally exchange with his fellow pedestrian commuters. Everyone had been caught up in their own personal life-and-death struggle, desperately trying to remain on their feet in the face of the thick layer of ice the earlier freezing rain had deposited over every square inch of the Bridge, including the now-useless hand-railing separating the pedestrian lane from that of the horse-drawn vehicles. Their singular goal was to survive the howling gale which buffeted them all mightily, one-hundred-and-thirty-five feet above the dark, churning waters of the East River. Will estimated that the gusts had frequently exceeded sixty-five or seventy miles-per-hour. And as impossible as it was to imagine, he knew the wind was only going to get stronger as the storm progressed.

He recalled how the terrified travelers, himself included, blinded by the snow and sand-blasted by the rock-hard pellets of sleet, had huddled together instinctively in small groups of ten or twelve. The violent wind whistling wildly through the hundreds of suspension cables had created a piercing, eerie cacophony which had nearly driven him half-mad. Whenever the wind slackened enough that the group was able to stand almost erect, they would inch forward, *en masse,* till being forced to hunker down again. Will could still feel his and his desperate companions' intense focus on the monumental task at hand – maintaining a tight grip on one another while waiting for the brief lulls which enabled them to resume their painfully slow progression towards the relative refuge afforded by the *terra firma* on the other side of the river.

And he knew that if he lived to be a hundred, he would never forget the horrifying experience of seeing that poor, doomed wretch, who'd obviously lost his grip and his footing at the worst possible moment, being wrested from the safety of the group ahead of his by a vicious gust of wind, then blown clear off the Bridge into the freezing water below. There was only a split-second in which the man's frantic, fading scream could be clearly heard before being drowned out by the continuous roar of the wind, but Will knew that awful sound would forever remain etched clearly in his mind.

Notably, there had not been a single patrolman to be found anywhere. The entire police force, like all the other members of the City's benighted population, had undoubtedly been taken completely by surprise. Just as in the wild and woolly days which preceded development of the great centers of civilization, it truly had been "every man for himself."

Pat McCormack reached over and shut off the jangling alarm clock, instantly sensing there was something very strange afoot. The room was still quite dark, even though he knew the sun should have been up by now. But that was only a part of how distorted everything seemed to be, in the moment. He couldn't quite put words to it, but he perceived that what little light there was, managing to filter feebly through the slight opening between the closed drapes, had a strange, indescribable hue. He also heard a faint but constant high-pitched sound, reminiscent of a hurricane he had lived through as a young child. Finally, he thought he heard a peal of thunder, which made no sense at all given how cold it had been last night.

Suddenly and vividly, he recalled his ghastly trek from the train station. He threw back the covers, then hurried over to the window to pull open the drapes.

"My God!," he gasped, thunderstruck, clapping himself on the chest as he took an involuntary step backwards.

The view from his window overlooking Broadway was altogether shocking – there was snow *everywhere*. He was aware, of course, that his room was on the fourth floor. In fact, he had requested and stayed in Room 411 during his past several visits to the Grand, one of the many perks of his status as a "preferred guest." Looking out on the monstrous drifts below now, though, he felt oddly disoriented. Hand on the Bible, he would have sworn he couldn't *possibly* be located any higher up than the third floor. Never, in all his days, had he ever seen, or even heard of, such an accumulation of snow in such a short period of time.

Looking onto 31st Street, he had the thought that the scene there would have been comical, indeed, if only it weren't such a potentially deadly situation. He could make out only a very small portion of the street (the visibility was that bad), but he was still able to see that all traffic – horse-drawn and pedestrian – was at a virtual standstill. He saw one horse actually lying on the ground, unable or unwilling to navigate though the deep, swirling snow.

"How in God's name am I ever going to get back to Grand Central Station?," he asked himself aloud. "For that matter, even if I could figure out a way to get there, how on earth will they ever manage to get the trains running in this ridiculous mess?"

Pat immediately thought of telephoning his customer in Philadelphia to ask for a one- or two-day postponement of their appointment. He certainly wasn't about to risk life and limb in what would almost assuredly end up being a vain attempt to get there. Thankfully, he had every confidence his customer would not be put out by his request to reschedule.

He knew how fortunate he was to be so blessed, and had great empathy for all the people who would be faced with the prospect of losing their jobs should they fail to show up for work to-day. In the current economy, with such a large number of workers vying for so few jobs, he knew that many of those lucky enough to have secured a position would feel compelled to get to their places of employment. And sadly, many of those might, in the process, sustain serious injury – or even lose their lives. Pat shook his head slowly, disheartened at the thought. He returned to the bed and sat quietly for a moment, hands clasped and eyes closed, offering up a quick prayer of gratitude for the familiar creature comforts surrounding him in what he'd come to think of as "his" room at the Grand Hotel.

Then he sprang into action.

In very short order, he shaved, dressed, and made his way downstairs to the hotel operator to place his telephone call. When he reached the front desk, however, he was dismayed (though not really all that surprised) to learn that there was no telephone or telegraph service available, as the ferocious wind had taken down any number of wires and poles. The clerk apologized politely for the inconvenience, adding that they were very fortunate to still have electrical power, given the devastation outside.

Of course, there was no way Pat could have known, in that moment, that overall conditions in the City of Brotherly Love were only slightly better – leaving Pat's customer with concerns far more pressing than their appointment that afternoon.

The important meeting was to have begun some thirty minutes ago now. The el in which May Morrow rode had taken nearly an hour just to get to the 14th Street Station. This was less than half the distance of her normal commute, which usually took only thirty-five minutes, start-to-finish. Even though the progress they were making was painfully slow, she was grateful the train kept moving at all. She had no idea if the el she'd boarded had originally been the five o'clock but, then again, what did it matter?

After the forty-five arduous minutes it had taken her to traverse a mere four blocks, she had finally arrived at the 50th Street Station at about five-thirty. Sharing her experience with a few of the other brave souls there – some of whom, she learned, had been waiting for over an hour – she was thankful to see the train pulling into the station, and counted herself lucky to be among those who found room on it. Although the temperature inside the car wasn't much of an improvement over the icy cold outside, at least she and her fellow passengers were protected from the biting wind. Praising Heaven that she had on her warmest coat, along with a hat, scarf, and mittens, May felt she'd be able to ride out the train trip handily, and was reasonably certain she'd succeed in facing down the elements once she'd arrived at her stop. Whenever that might be.

She gazed out the window in utter disbelief at the terrible conditions below on Ninth Avenue. Her heart went out to several horses she saw down there which, apparently having broken free from their cars, were clearly spooked and wandering about aimlessly. There was so much blowing snow that she was frequently unable to see anything other than a swirling, hypnotizing sea of white. Whenever she could make out the buildings on the west side of the street, she saw drifts growing rapidly in front of them which looked to be four feet deep already, maybe even more. She saw no sign of the storm letting up. In fact, impossible as it seemed, May thought the blizzard might even be intensifying.

Only now did the thought cross her mind that perhaps the decision to hazard the commute to work, under these brutal conditions, had not been such a wise one after all. Surely Mr. Garrigues, knowing she travels such a long distance, would have shown forbearance had she been unable to make it there. But she quickly rejected that notion, remembering again the critical nature of this meeting. Indeed, how unseemly would it be if the "low-man on the totem pole," particularly one upon whom such important new responsibilities were being bestowed, couldn't even make it into the office for a meeting as consequential as this one? *Especially* when that "man" is a woman!

She shook her head at the thought, managing a weak smile.

It sure is perturbing, isn't it, how we women have to go so far above and beyond to prove ourselves in this man's world. No. As difficult as this has been already, and as challenging as it will no doubt continue to be, I definitely made the right call to come in to-day. About that, I am positive. And while I'll certainly be well over an hour late to the meeting, you know what "they" say – "better late than never!"

CHAPTER 39

8:00 AM

By now, blizzard conditions had paralyzed much of the northeastern United States as the already powerful Atlantic cyclone continued to intensify. Seamen on ships off the middle Atlantic and southern New England coasts noted rapid pressure falls, sudden wind shifts to the northwest accompanied by tremendous increases in speed, precipitous drops in temperature, and a change-over from heavy rain to heavy snow. Rain gradually spread across southern and southeastern New England. As the cyclone intensified and moved slowly northward towards the southern New England coast, however, much colder air behind the front extending to northwest of the low center continued to move eastward across Long Island, western Connecticut, Massachusetts, and Vermont, instantly turning the rain to heavy, blinding snow.

An hour earlier, official reports from both New York City and Philadelphia had already recorded an astounding ten inches of wind-whipped snow on the ground, with winds averaging nearly fifty miles-per-hour. In Atlantic City, New Jersey, gusts as high as eighty were reported!

A key element of Will's forecasting system, something he'd featured in his January seminar, was the inherent connection between the weather conditions on the ground and those high above the earth's surface. From his recent cirrus cloud observations, he knew that a powerful injection of energy at a height of roughly eighteen-thousand feet was well on its way to "closing off," or isolating, the current cyclone all the way up to twenty- or even thirty-thousand feet. The storm's circulation extended that high into the atmosphere. The fast-flowing current of air miles above the earth's surface[6] would typically keep storms moving along, ensuring their effects would not be prolonged across any one area. In this particular case, however, Will knew this closing-off process meant the normal upper-air current had been displaced, far to the south. As a result, the blizzard had stalled off the coast of southern New England, and might even loop around, protracting its already catastrophic impact upon the devastated region.

As for New York City, at least up till this point, it was clear to Will that his forecasting system had worked remarkably well. Of course, with all means of communicating with the outside world suspended, he had no way of gauging just how well it was performing thus far across the rest of the Northeast. Over the next week or so, as the official reports became available, he was hoping to be pleasantly surprised.

Included in Will's prediction of this storm was its unusual orientation, where all of the weather typically associated with a cyclone's wind direction was "backed," or shifted counterclockwise, about ninety degrees. This was confirmed by the rapidly falling barometer, along with very strong winds from the northwest. The heavy precipitation which would normally occur with a northeasterly wind was now happening, instead, on a northwesterly wind.

---

6 This fast-flowing current of air would, five decades hence, be christened the "jet stream."

Will strongly suspected that in places like Virginia and northern Maryland, including Washington City, the storm had already subsided and the skies were bright blue. Clearing skies after a winter storm would ordinarily be accompanied by strong northwesterly winds. With this atypical orientation, however, the winds there would be blowing from the southwest. He also thought that the heavy snow would persist for some time, unabated, across a large region: eastern Pennsylvania, most of New Jersey, the New York City area, most of Long Island, eastern New York State, western Connecticut and Massachusetts, and most of Vermont.

He was confident the tempest would continue to intensify for at least another eighteen to twenty-four hours. The last set of nationwide observations he'd been able to get from Glynn yesterday afternoon confirmed that rather than being a mature cyclone, the storm was still an open frontal wave – albeit quite a strong one. That meant there was ample opportunity for it to continue gathering energy before the inevitable weakening, or occlusion, would begin.

As with any cyclone, he knew that the attendant cold front would eventually catch up with and overtake the warm front at the surface, thus cutting off, or occluding, the storm's energy source – the Atlantic Ocean. As the occlusion process continued, the warm moist air would be displaced higher and higher into the atmosphere till it would no longer be available. At that point the storm, having run out of "fuel," would begin to dissipate. However, because of its unusual intensity, Will knew this monster would be slow to fully disintegrate, and the strong winds and residual snow would probably last another full day, maybe even longer.

Tears flowed freely from Kira's eyes as she stood stock-still, in utter shock and disbelief, on the frozen sidewalk in front of the Bijou Opera

House. She'd arrived at the theatre five minutes earlier, only to be horrified at finding the entryway locked up tight, with nary a soul in sight. She'd pounded desperately on the doors for a few minutes, but there had been no response.

Dear God, could it possibly be that he arrived at seven-forty-five, and seeing that I hadn't yet, he just up and left? I thought he was supposed to be a gentleman! Wouldn't you think he'd wait for at least a lousy ten minutes? Damn! Could anyone really be that *big of an ass? Damn! Damn! Damn!*

As angry as Kira felt towards Director Sampson at that moment, it paled in comparison to the wrath she'd been consumed by, just an hour earlier, upon opening the outside door of her suite. Jolted by the monstrous havoc with which Mother Nature greeted her so inhospitably, she'd suddenly become enraged. Rather than feeling any sense of gratitude or shame towards Will – for roundly abusing him when he'd tried his best to warn her about the storm – Kira was so completely wrapped-up in her own world, and the enormous impediment now confronting her at the worst possible moment, that she'd wasted no time in actually *blaming* him for this catastrophe.

She now stood shivering pitifully in the theatre's front doorway alcove, the howling wind plastering the swirling snow into the salt-water of her tears, creating a sub-freezing slush on her already angry-red cheeks. While the alcove did afford a modicum of shelter from the elements (being on the west, or leeward, side of the street), she was none-the-less exposed, yet quite oblivious, to the very real threat of incurring an excruciatingly painful – even dangerous – case of frost-bite. To make matters worse, the fierce northwesterly gales were depositing ever-increasing masses of snow into a drift growing rapidly in front of her very eyes. It would not be too much longer before she'd literally run the risk of being trapped in place. If that were to happen, freezing to death would become a very real possibility – if not a certainty.

The fifty-five minutes she'd struggled to travel just the five blocks, and all without any coffee or breakfast, had already taken a heavy toll on Kira. Her white-hot anger and the adrenaline coursing through her veins, however, prevented her from realizing just how perilous her situation really was. Obviously not in her right mind, it was only now starting to dawn on her that perhaps Sampson's absence had nothing whatever to do with any dearth of character on his part. Nor was it likely an insult personally directed at her. In all probability, he had been delayed by the storm, just as she had.

Against all reason, she made up her mind to wait for him. It never occurred to her, not even for a second, that he might not be coming at all.

Surely he'll be arriving sometime soon. I mean, after all, this audition is the most important one of my life – and even I was a few minutes late!

The frying pan and breakfast dishes were washed and put away. Wilma now began to work up the courage she needed to brave the elements on her walk over to Blanche's house, even though it was only a hundred feet or so by her reckoning. After much deliberation, she'd ultimately concluded that she must go. She simply had to see how her friend was faring, and offer whatever solace and moral support she could. Despite the fact she could barely see twenty feet out the kitchen window, she felt she'd be alright so long as she bundled up tightly in her warmest things. Unfortunately, Will's warning last evening was relegated to the back of her mind.

The force of the blowing wind created a continuous, loud whistling sound, reminding her of the handful of cacophonous hurricanes she'd survived while living in this house. Checking the kitchen window thermometer, she was a bit alarmed to note that the temperature had now fallen to twenty degrees, a full five-degree drop from just three hours earlier.

Wilma figured it was simply too daunting to try leaving her house by the front door. Although she could see that the wind was keeping the front porch largely snow-free, at least for the moment, she could also discern the presence of a thick layer of ice on the steps, which clearly posed an unacceptable risk to her safety – especially in the face of the powerful northwesterly gale. She therefore chose to exit though the back porch, walk down the single step, turn right, and follow the familiar foot-path worn by years of travel through the row of enormous pines separating the two houses. From there it should be relatively easy to wend her way back to the entryway at the rear of Blanche's house.

She was confident that Blanche would be up by now. But even if she weren't, or if she couldn't hear the knocking over the roar of the wind, Wilma still had no cause for concern. She knew the secret location of the spare key Blanche always kept hidden on the back porch. All in all, she was satisfied that she'd worked out a solid plan of action to accomplish the short – albeit treacherous – trek.

Bundled to the nostrils in coat, hat, scarf, gloves, and heavy boots, Wilma stepped outside. She noticed right away that the wind pattern had exposed a patch of bare ground but, looking beyond, she could see a large drift, already quite deep, extending from the corner of her house all the way across the path. The thought immediately registered that if she wanted to make it back to her own hearth to-day, she'd best not stay at Blanche's for too long a visit.

The fierce wind and bitter cold all but took her breath away as she approached the apex of the drift. Even though she'd been outside just a scant few minutes, she had already expended an alarming amount of energy, and had only covered a very short distance.

Maybe this wasn't such a good idea, after all. I'm surely not as young as I used to be, am I. And, heck – let's be honest here – that really is quite the understatement!

Immersed in a sea of white, Wilma's disorientation was complete. She could make out no landmarks, whatsoever. Though ordinarily as familiar with Blanche's yard as she was with her own, she now looked around wildly, desperately seeking some assurance that she was still on the foot-path. Fear and panic gripped her suddenly, like a vise. She was sure that she should have reached the row of pines by now. All at once she heard Will's voice echoing through her head, begging her not to make the potentially tragic mistake of underestimating the sheer magnitude of this storm's destructive power.

In a matter of mere seconds, tentative confidence had been supplanted by abject terror.

She could feel her heart racing as the panic began to overwhelm her. She knew that above all, she had to calm herself, at once. The thought ran through her mind that she should have used a rope, tying one end to the porch and the other around her waist.

Will did mention that little survival trick to me, in the event I stubbornly insisted on venturing out to Blanche's. With all my careful planning, how on earth could I have neglected to remember something so vitally important? Damn!

All at once, everything around her was lit up by a brilliant green flash, the likes of which she'd never seen. She hadn't even finished formulating the question as to whether it might be lightning when an ear-splitting boom left no doubt about the answer.

My God, that was close! And beyond bizarre, to boot.

Blessedly, the wind abated for a brief moment, improving the visibility just enough to enable her to recognize the familiar row of pines and the outline of Blanche's house. Not surprisingly, she had somewhat over-estimated the distance she'd come, but she was greatly relieved to discover her bearing had remained true. A course-correction would not be required.

Winds over the ocean had now reached hurricane-force. The Captain of the Charles H. Marshall ordered his crew and the harbor pilots to take up sledge hammers, iron bars, or whatever heavy battering implements they could find. They were then tasked with beating the ice off the ropes and mast of the foresail, so that it could be lowered. Their best efforts succeeded in getting it only about half-way down, after which they had to lash it with ropes to keep it from blowing away. Repeating the process for the forestay sail, every man aboard was keenly aware that his life could come to an abrupt and violent end at any moment. By this time, the seas were running wildly in every direction, and the tempest-tossed vessel was in grave danger of being swamped.

Floating broadside to the wind, the modest little boat was drifting helplessly to the southeast. The snow and freezing rain pounded so forcefully that it was well-nigh impossible to look windward. The Captain, with no doubt the greatest understanding of what could be done about their predicament, ordered the men to take turns filling the oil bags, every half-hour. Hung out at regular intervals along each side of the vessel, these bags dripped fresh oil onto the outer-hull. The hope was that the oil would somehow modify the effects of the breaking waves, thereby reducing the likelihood of sustaining serious damage from their relentless assault. It was unclear just how much benefit, if any, the oil bags would provide in weather as wild as this. Keeping them filled under these conditions was extremely dangerous work. Still, no one dared suggest their use be discontinued.

In addition to the constant danger presented by the thundering sea, the men were well-aware of the threat posed by any large vessel passing in their vicinity. With the near-total lack of visibility, such a ship could come crashing through their small boat at virtually any moment, and the sheer violence of the wind and waves would render any rescue attempt all but impossible.

Charley Potts no longer thought of his dear Blanche – or anything else, for that matter. Save for responding to the occasional new order from the Captain, he, the crew, and his fellow pilots had adopted a singular, mindless focus. They worked instinctively, in silent unison, in much the same way that ordinary ants organize themselves to cooperate in building and maintaining their colonies. Each man had reached the inescapable conclusion that his very life might well depend upon how long they could continue to function effectively as a team. Each, therefore, applied every attention to the task at hand and performed his duties with the utmost efficiency.

This was survival in its rawest, purest form. Simply put, there was no room for any wasted energy – mental or physical.

Sergeant Francis Long finally arrived at the Office. He was not at all pleased, though only somewhat surprised, to find Will there all by his lonesome. Thus far, none of the other full Monday morning contingent of six had managed to make it in.

"My God, Will, the damage out there – it's absolutely mind-boggling!" Long stomped his feet and clapped his arms, dislodging piles of snow and ice onto the floor. "Well, my boy, what can I say? You certainly were right about all of this. Yes, indeed, were you ever."

Will just looked at him, shook his head slowly, and shrugged. "I only wish to God that I weren't."

Long understood that Will, not only as his subordinate but also as a gentleman, wouldn't dream of saying anything which might remind the Sergeant that he'd been "told so."

"You know," Long opined, "if I had truly believed you in the first place, and known it was going to be this bad, I probably would have handled things quite differently. I would almost certainly have informed Headquarters. Of course, then again, it's anybody's guess as to whether or not they would have believed me, now, isn't it."

A few awkward moments passed in silence before the Sergeant continued.

"Right . . . well, then . . . Would you say that all this is turning out pretty much in the fashion your system predicted?"

"Actually, sir, yes I would. Just about precisely, in point-of-fact."

Long shook his head in amazement. "Well, I'll be damned. If that don't beat all – and then some! And just how much longer do you reckon this madness is likely to go on?"

"Well, boss, while we both know that anything is possible, this much is certain – though I am sorry to have to say it: it's going to get worse before it gets better. I believe the wind will increase even more, there will probably be thunder-snow with cloud-to-ground strikes, the temperature will bottom-out somewhere in the single digits, and the snow will continue till sometime to-morrow. As near as I can tell right now, the storm is nearly stationary, centered east of Cape May and south of, say, Montauk Point. It won't be occluding for awhile yet, so it has plenty of time to continue to deepen."

Suddenly, as if Mother Nature herself wished to emphasize Will's graphic synopsis of the situation by adding an appropriate exclamation point of her own, a bright green flash lit up the entire room. Within two seconds, the air around them was rent by a loud crashing boom.

"Holy Mother of God," the two awe-struck men whispered, in unison.

CHAPTER 40

9:00 AM

Blanche moved busily about the kitchen, apologizing yet again as she prepared a second cup of piping hot tea for her still half-frozen friend. Sometime earlier in the week, she'd had to remove the spare key from its hiding spot under the planter on the back porch to replace one that Charley had lost. In the midst of all the upset surrounding the storm and his leaving, it had simply never occurred to her to tell Wilma.

"Oh, stuff and nonsense, my dear," Wilma remonstrated, between sips, to a still-contrite Blanche. "You know it's all my own fault. There was no earthly reason for you to tell me about the key, especially with everything else you had to contend with. I mean, how could you possibly have known I'd be coming over here to-day? And to the back door, no less. Now, I want you to stop all this worrying and fussing about it. I've thawed out quite a bit already, and I really am beginning to feel much better now, thanks to the reviving power of your delicious tea." She reached over to give Blanche's hand a pat.

"Well, I certainly am glad to hear you say that." Blanche gave her best friend's hand a squeeze and smiled warmly at her, but was not at all convinced that she was telling the whole truth. When she'd first come in, her face had been an alarming red from exposure to the elements; there was now a slightly ashen tinge to it. And she kept rubbing her hands together, as if she were trying to coax the circulation back into them.

"But I suppose I really must confess," Wilma went on as she sat back, seeming subdued, "it was getting pretty scary, being trapped out there like that. Thank God you were able to hear me knocking on that window."

When Wilma had finally reached Blanche's back porch, her elation had quickly turned into horror upon discovering the door locked and the key missing. With no way of knowing where in the house her friend might be, and recognizing that she, herself, would not be long for this world if she failed to get inside – and quickly – she had simply begun pounding on the door as hard as she could. After a full five minutes of this, an all but worn-out Wilma realized she had no choice but to make her way around to the west-facing side of the house, rap on the kitchen window, and pray that Blanche was close enough to be able to hear it.

What she had not counted on, however, was the nearly six-foot drift which now ran along that side of the house, and through which she'd have to plough if she wanted any hope at all of getting Blanche's attention. Still, that idea seemed far better than attempting to get all the way around to the front of the house where, for all she knew, her knocking could prove every bit as futile.

It had taken Wilma nearly fifteen minutes of burrowing to reach the window and start tapping. Fortunately, she'd been able to get Blanche to hear her over the howling wind. Wilma could see the look of shock on Blanche's face as it registered that her friend was outside and in trouble, waving both arms frantically in the direction of the back-yard. Then she saw Blanche hurrying to unlock the back door.

As she turned from the window, Wilma had been quite dismayed to discover that her return-trip to the back porch would require double-duty: the wind had wasted no time in completely filling in the trail she had blazed through the drift mere minutes before. By the time she'd made it all the way back to the rear of the house, she was beyond exhausted and almost frozen through. There were no words to describe her relief as Blanche practically carried her from the porch into the warm kitchen.

"Well, Blanche," she said, brightening a bit, sipping her tea, "seeing as how I'm quite recovered now, let's talk about what brought me over here in the first place, shall we? But before that, may I please telephone Will at the Office? I sure would like to get the latest update on the storm, and I know he'd be happy to hear that the two of us are doing alright."

"Oh, no, my dear, I'm afraid that won't be possible at all. The telephone stopped working sometime early this morning. And given how terrible conditions are right now, I fear that service isn't likely to be restored till sometime well after the storm has passed."

"Now, isn't that just a durn shame. But not at all surprising, really. I guess it's only to be expected during weather as bad as this," Wilma waxed philosophical, sighing with a shrug. She thought, fleetingly, of reminding Blanche that the telephone service had been the primary reason she'd elected to remain in her own home, but quickly realized that would only cause her friend further upset. Even the slimmest hope of the service being restored sooner, by some miracle, was better than no hope at all.

Frank Gorman, fearfully red in the face and panting hard from exertion, was the third to arrive at the Signal Service tower. Despite the distance between his 13th Street apartment and the Equitable Building being a relatively short two miles (for the most part straight down Broadway), his trek to-day had taken him nearly three hours to complete.

"I'm very sorry to be getting here so late," he said at once, directing his apology equally to Will and the Sergeant, as the three of them stood in Will's office. "Our neighbors ran into some rather serious trouble, and had to ask Alex and me for our help. You see, the wind had blown their stable door wide-open, and their two horses – God only knows why – had run out into the storm and gotten stranded somewhere in the back-yard. We had to help them corral the poor beasts and get them back inside, or who knows what might have happened to them. We were successful, fortunately, but it took the four of us nearly an hour to get it accomplished."

"That's quite alright, Mr. Gorman," Sergeant Long responded, giving Frank a hearty clap on the back, "and very well-done, too, I might add, as one with more than his fair share of respect and admiration for the fine and noble equine. Truth be told, I'm just pleased you were able to make it in at all. As you can plainly see, we're only three of six, thus far. Oh, and before I forget, I want to take this opportunity to clear the air here – although I'm sure it hardly matters all that much anymore. Will has informed me that you have known all along about his forecasting system's prediction of this storm, and have been reliably and faithfully discreet in any and all discussion of the matter – for which I wish to offer you my sincere thanks."

Frank breathed a small sigh of relief. On top of everything else, he had not been looking forward to treading on eggshells around his friend (and superior) and the big boss, all on account of that very delicate subject. "That's mighty kind of you to say, sir. And you are, of course, most welcome."

A short, somewhat awkward pause ensued, as the men seated themselves around the desk. "So, Frank," Will inquired, "tell us – what is it like out there on the streets right now? How long did it take you to get here?"

"It's an unmitigated disaster, plain and simple. Everywhere you look, you see evidence of how totally unprepared just about everybody was. Scores of poor unfortunates appear to be suffering from the frostbite, and many are stumbling around completely disoriented because the visibility is so terrible. The snow is getting really deep, with some of the drifts already five- and six-feet high. And in spots where the snow has been blown away, the treacherous layer of ice on the sidewalks and pavement is making it impossible to even remain up-right, what with the wind pounding away so mercilessly.

"I saw two telegraph poles snap off right in front of my very eyes, and was fortunate indeed that neither struck me. There are downed wires all over the place, even some live electrical ones that are arcing and sparking. Horse-drawn carts and wagons are stuck everywhere, hopelessly mired in the snow. I saw one horse on the ground, help-lessly entangled in some of the wires.

"I passed by several windows that were blown out, with flying glass all around. Every ten or fifteen minutes or so, there is a huge bolt of lightning, mostly a strange green color. Have you ever heard of anything so weird? And all of it cloud-to-ground. I tell you, it's an absolute catastrophe – it's like the end of the world out there!

"Oh, and to answer your second question. Even at my laziest pace, it rarely takes me more than forty minutes to get here, but to-day's nightmare journey took me darn close to three hours."

Sergeant Long, apparently feeling that he'd heard enough, got to his feet. "Well, gentlemen, I must see whether I can establish any type of communication at all with the other Offices, and then I'm going to check on the instruments." He turned and left Will's office.

"I wish you good luck with that," Will muttered under his breath after the Sergeant departed. He was fairly certain that, barring divine intervention, Long would be unsuccessful with any attempt at outside communication.

With Long gone, Will took the opportunity to ask Frank how Alex was doing.

"Well, as luck would have it, she didn't find it all that difficult to believe in your prediction, so she was able to get herself prepared, mentally and physically. But I know this whole situation has caused quite a falling-out between her and Kira."

"Really? You don't say."

"Yes, and I don't mind telling you, it's an absolute shame, given how close they've always been. Kira stopped by our place yesterday afternoon, and I overheard Alex trying to talk some sense into her, saying something about at least keeping an open mind. I definitely did not want to be part of that conversation, so I made myself as scarce as I possibly could."

"Well, I can certainly understand that."

"Oh, but I did happen to overhear Alex chiding her when Kira said – talking quite loudly at that point, so it was hard to miss – that she thought you were *deliberately* trying to sabotage her chances for the part because, for some unfathomable reason, you don't want her to succeed."

"Now, isn't that just too rich! She said the same thing to me, as well." Will shook his head sadly, incredulous. "I still can't believe any of this is really happening, Frank. It's all just so damned ridiculous!"

"Of course it is, Will. And that's exactly what Alex told her, too. Then Kira turned on *her,* raising her voice even more, and asking something about why she was defending you instead of her. She left shortly after that. I have to tell you, Alex was pretty upset over the whole thing. She still is. Not only is she terribly worried about Kira's physical safety should the poor girl be caught out in the storm, but she also said she was beginning to fear for her mental stability, as well. She actually came right out and said that she was afraid her best friend might have, and I'm quoting her here, 'lost a few of her marbles.'"

"Well, my dear Miss Morrow, I certainly must commend you, and heartily so, on your obvious dedication to the company. You are the only one, thus far – other than yours truly, of course – who has managed to make it in this morning for our momentous six o'clock meeting."

May acknowledged his compliment with a slight bow of her head and a quick, mock curtsey. "Well, I do thank you most sincerely for that profusion, Mr. Garrigues, kind sir," she said. Then she arched an eyebrow at him and chuckled wryly as she went on. "Even if it is a shade past nine." Garrigues, delighted to discover that his exemplary new employee was also quite the little wag, responded with a hearty chuckle of his own.

She had finally arrived at the office at about eight-thirty, nearly frozen and covered in snow and ice particles. Garrigues had immediately installed her in front of the still-paltry fire he had started in the wood stove just moments earlier, allowing her some time to defrost before peppering her with the obvious questions. After May had been warming up for about fifteen minutes or so, he thought it apropos to inform her that the installation of a steam-heating system would be his very next effort at modernization. Smiling and nodding vigorously in a show of agreement, she told him she thought that would be an absolutely splendid idea.

Most of the rest of the morning was taken up by an exchange of "war stories." May recounted, in graphic detail, how she and several other commuters had managed to escape their immobilized, elevated train-car, about a hundred yards shy of the Rector Street Station, by gingerly climbing down a jerry-built contraption that several good Samaritans had assembled from two small ladders and some rope. After being stranded for nearly an hour in the freezing, draughty wooden car, no doubt sandwiched in between other trains similarly trapped, she had realized there was little hope of their being rescued anytime soon. When the opportunity presented itself, therefore, she had screwed her courage to the sticking point and followed three or four men down the make-shift exit to take her chances braving the elements below.

She told Garrigues that once she'd reached the sidewalk, she'd felt fortunate indeed that the raging wind was directly at her back, propelling her forward, as she traveled on-foot the remaining half-mile to the office. Along the way, she'd had to be especially vigilant to avoid those areas where there were downed electrical wires, some of them hissing and writhing like angry snakes. May had been particularly appalled by the sight of a terrified cab horse snared by wires encircling its neck. Tragically, before the poor beast could be released, he was dead.

Garrigues listened wide-eyed with rapt attention, his admiration for the plucky young woman obvious. "My dear, there is simply nothing else to say. You are one very strong, and most courageous, young lady." He then responded in kind, sharing the experience of his own harrowing commute from home, starting on West 42nd Street at five o'clock and ending more than three hours later with his arrival at work, just about twenty-five minutes before May got there.

Of all the trials and tribulations he recounted, May was most affected by his description of the "raining sparrows," although she did her best to hide just how much it upset her. Garrigues told her he'd discovered that the overhead el tracks provided at least some small sheltering effect, so whenever possible he had elected to walk beneath them. Upon doing so, though, he noticed that his head and shoulders were being repeatedly plunked by things small and hard, seemingly falling from the sky. It had taken him awhile to realize that he was being struck by the icy bodies of tiny sparrows, frozen solid and as hard as rocks. The poor creatures had obviously sought refuge amidst the nooks and crannies of the el girders, before succumbing to the bitter cold and being blown off by the fierce winds. This, of course, only added to the already vast array of airborne projectiles punishing the hapless pedestrians.

May was fascinated and amazed by her boss's tale. She congratulated him for his true grit, as well as his determination to make it in, against all odds. The two of them then decided to celebrate their success by placing a friendly wager as to whether they'd be joined by any of their other co-workers on this unwonted day.

"There, there now, Miss, you can trust me. This will help you, I promise. You're about the tenth person to-day whose ears I've had to rub with snow. Looks to me like you've definitely got yourself a good case of the frost-bite going. I'll bet you can't feel a thing right about now, can you?"

The patrolman was fast becoming gravely concerned, as his questions were not eliciting any hint of a normal response from the poor young woman he had happened upon, just moments before, in front of the Bijou theatre. On top of the frost-bite, he suspected she was suffering from a dangerous case of hypothermia. He knew he had to get her somewhere warm – and very soon – or the consequences would be dire.

"Whatever be ye doin' out here, anyway? And all by yer little lonesome too, in all this atrocious weather?"

He began to shepherd her along the street, in the direction of his sister's apartment on West 29th, near Seventh Avenue. He'd just now come from there, after stopping by to check up on her and to warm himself up a bit, as well. He hoped she wouldn't mind too awfully taking this poor lass in, at least till she could thaw out a little and maybe regain some of her senses. He could tell by the way the young lady was dressed and manicured that she was no trollop or hussy. So he knew he needn't fear for his sister's safety, or reputation.

Continuing in his attempt to establish any form of communication with her, he said, "I'm not sure why you were standing out there, dear, but it's pretty obvious to me that no one is going to be showing up at the Opera House to-day." Suddenly, she turned her frighteningly red face to look up at him, then opened her mouth as if to offer some sort of response. None was forthcoming, however, and she fainted dead away, her eyes rolling backward and her legs going completely limp.

The kindly patrolman, fast on his feet, quickly caught her up in his arms, before she could hit the icy sidewalk and do any further damage to her storm-battered body. Wasting not a moment, he lifted her up high and draped her over his shoulder, securing her coat and scarf around her head and body to protect her, as best he could, from the wind and snow. Then he trudged onward to complete the one-fifth-mile journey, doing his best not to jostle his comatose passenger. Unfortunately, their path now took them directly into the teeth of the wind.

As he forged his way through the ever-deepening snow-drifts, he kept up a steady stream of patter, his mouth positioned not far from her ear. In addition to hoping his words might register with her, somehow, maybe even aid in reviving her a bit, he knew his warm breath on her ear could only help with the frost-bite. About half-way to his sister's, he was gratified to hear her mumble something faintly in response to his ongoing prattle.

Thus far to-day, only twelve guests – all enterprising businessmen – had checked out of the Grand Hotel. And all before six a.m. Of course, James Landen had finally figured out a way to make it in, to the obvious delight of young Mr. Washington. Landen understood completely. With Walt Jamison still out with the flu, Albert would necessarily be taking his orders from someone else. And how much better, for a neophyte like Albert, if they came directly from the head-man himself – who knew and liked him – rather than any of the myriad mid-level-management minions who'd otherwise be vying for control of the hotel on this exceedingly challenging day.

"So, Albert. Needless to say, I'm very glad you decided to stay over with us last night, as you can well imagine. I hope you enjoyed a good night's sleep, as this promises to be one hell of a day."

"I did, James, thank-you. And unfortunately, as far as what we're in for to-day, I'd say you couldn't be more right.

"Yes, well, this is one time *I* can say, with all honesty, that I wish I weren't. Fewer than half the shift has made it in so far this morning and, as you well know, we were already terribly short-staffed from last night. The Reservations department and the Kitchen staff are decimated. We have skeleton crews, at best, operating in both areas. I have a plan of action already in place for the Kitchen but, for obvious reasons, Reservations will be more problematic."

Albert nodded his understanding.

"And so that's the assignment I wish to discuss with you, my good young man. I'd like you to work in concert with what's left of our Reservations team. You've met John Romano and Hazel Carson before, haven't you?"

Albert nodded again. "Yes, I have. As I recall, they both seemed very nice."

Landen smiled. "Yes, you're right about that, they are indeed." His smile widened as he looked at the bright, eager expression on Albert's face, and he made a mental note to congratulate Walt again for such a fine acquisition to the staff. Then he rubbed his hands together briefly, and placed both palms flat on his desk.

"Alright then, Albert, here's what I've come up with so far. At the moment, we have twelve vacancies over and above the six rooms reserved for staff, which includes 620. We also have at least twenty people in the lobby already, looking for rooms, and it's barely nine o'clock. John and Hazel are under strict orders to collect one night's deposit from them, after they've been informed that they'll be sharing their assigned room with an appropriate, and respectable, co-tenant. You see, Albert, I don't wish to send away any paying customers to-day – 'walk-in' or otherwise – but I would guess we're going to have to be dealing with a few hundred of them. Maybe even more than that.

"So here's where you come in. I want you to put your organiza-tional- and people-skills to good use, by way of implementing an *ad hoc* emergency system I've come up with. Are you okay with that?"

"You bet I am, James."

"Good, good. That's what I thought. I want you to know that I realize what I'll be asking of you is a great deal, but I really do believe, judging by everything I've seen up till now, that you're just the person for the job, and will be able to fulfill it handily."

"You can count on me, sir – I won't let you down. And I want to take this opportunity to thank you, not only for choosing me for this particular assignment, which sounds like a mighty interesting challenge, but also for the overall faith in me that you've expressed."

"Well, Albert, I must say that you've earned it, and that you are most sincerely welcome," Landen said warmly, reaching over to give Albert's shoulder a few robust pats. He then delved into the details of how Albert would be making the room assignments. He didn't want any solo guests put into one of the vacant rooms; those were to be held in abeyance for families or large groups. He was to start by taking inventory of the walk-ins, then go room-to-room, beginning with the less pricey upper-floors, and match them appropriately with the currently registered guests. Those already occupying the rooms would be required to share – no exceptions – regardless of whether they had previously made a reservation for an additional night or nights. (As the majority of the rooms were unreserved at this point, this was likely to be a minor issue, at best.) Albert was to inform the guests that this process might be repeated, if the need arose. He was also to collect to-night's room charge at that time, if they did intend to stay over – again, no exceptions. Unless, of course, they happened to find themselves without sufficient funds on their person. In that case, they should see Landen directly, to make arrangements for their future payment. If, per-chance, their intention was to leave the hotel to-day, they would have to do so immediately – not at the eleven a.m. checkout-time to which they would normally have been entitled.

Landen went on to say that customary room rates would apply. There would be no discounts offered as an accommodation for the inconvenience of room-sharing. On the other hand, he would not be charging an inflated rate, or any other type of premium, just because of the blizzard. He knew that many of his competitors would be doing precisely that, having no compunction at all about taking unjust advantage of helpless people caught up in such a desperate situation. "Business is business," he told Albert, "but fair is fair." The young man nodded in agreement.

Once he'd explained everything to Albert, Landen asked him if he had any questions. After a few moments of obvious consideration, he replied that the only thing he was still unclear about was his authority to force otherwise paying guests out of the hotel, should they disagree with the terms being set forth. Landen told him to respond to any recalcitrance on the part of a guest by saying the following: "In this dire, life-threatening emergency, the Grand's 'official policy' is to offer shelter to as many as possible, and the Management has asked me to convey this specially designed plan to achieve that end. If you are unwilling to cooperate with this plan, you will find yourself facing forcible eviction immediately." If, after hearing that, they still insisted on being difficult, Landen said to let him know at once, and he would drop everything to step in and personally handle the situation, forthwith.

The two men shook hands to seal their agreement, and Albert set off at a clip to begin his new assignment – one which Landen was sure would be keeping the young man on his toes, non-stop, for at least the foreseeable future. And although Landen couldn't help but yearn a little for those days when he enjoyed a youthful vigor like Albert's, he didn't envy him one bit the task now set before him. When all was said and done, its accomplishment would no doubt make yesterday's frenetic pace seem like a stroll in the park.

CHAPTER 41

9:50 AM

Patrolman O'Malley's florid face was creased by a frown of concern. He had to admit he was less than pleased with Kira's progress. Truth be told, he was becoming increasingly alarmed by how little she seemed to be making. It had been a full fifteen minutes since he'd deposited her in the armchair by Mabel's wood-stove, drawn up as close as considerations of safety would permit. Yet she still appeared listless, and mostly unresponsive. One thing she had managed to do, in a squeaking rasp of a voice, was tell him her name and, in clipped, partial sentences, what had brought her to the Bijou in the midst of this ungodly nightmare of a storm.

He strongly suspected she was in desperate need of the kind of care she would be able to receive only in a hospital. Unfortunately, at this point, getting her there would be much easier said than done. Bellevue, the only facility in all Manhattan which offered emergency services, could ordinarily be accessed easily by horsecar, but it would be quite a long while before there would be any available to transport her. And at nearly a mile across town, carrying her there seemed all but impossible.

Fortunately, Mabel appeared to be just fine with looking after her new, albeit uninvited, house-guest. "Jon, dear," she began, smiling sweetly, "why don't you go back out on your beat and leave Kira here under my care? You can check up on her in a couple of hours, when I'm quite sure you'll be making your way back here to warm yourself up – maybe even with a nip or two of the good stuff."

Jon smiled back at her, a little sheepishly. "You must know that I never wanted to burden you with all this, Mabel, it's just that she's –"

"Now, you just hush yourself, brother of mine. Not only is she no burden but, well, seeing as how I'm all by my lonesome here, I could use the company, really. That dreadful moaning sound the wind insists on making really does give a body the shivers. Anyway, while you're out keeping the streets safe for Democracy, I'll see if I can't coax her into drinking some warm whiskey and getting some sleep. Right about now, I think a long nap would do her a world of good, don't you?"

Jon nodded in agreement, but was still hesitant about leaving his sister with such an onerous responsibility. He peered at her intently for a long moment, considering. Then he saw Mabel's eyes roll backward as she shook her head, laughing.

"Alright, then, you kind-hearted prince among men. Listen up. Even *you* have to admit that you really have done all you can for her, at least for the moment anyway. And not only that, but you still have a job to do out there, don't you. So, there it is. And now, off you go." She made shooing motions at him with her hands and arms.

"Well, okay then, Mabes," he responded, finally satisfied, "if you say so, I'll go. And thanks." He reached over and pulled her in for a quick bear hug, then held her at arm's length and eyed her appraisingly. "You know, dear sister, when it comes right down to it, you really are quite wonderful." He waited just a beat before continuing, wryly, his right hand pressed to his breast. "And I want you to know that I mean that with all my heart – no matter what anybody says." Mabel responded with a throaty chuckle and a playful punch on his left arm. He knew she appreciated both his playful teasing and his sincere gratitude. They walked to the door arm-in-arm, then exchanged kisses on each other's cheeks as he prepared to depart.

"I'll be back in a couple of hours, then," he said, looking at her fondly as he pulled on his gloves and adjusted his scarf and hat. "And," he continued, with a warm, engaging grin and a merry twinkle in his eye, "I promise I'll do my level-best to avoid bringing you back any other 'blizzard refugees.'" She gave him a merry grin of her own and a few pats on the back.

With that, he stepped out the door and back onto the streets he was sworn to protect. He knew he was fortunate that his hardy constitution would enable him to resume walking his beat. The conditions he faced out there continued to be far-and-away the most challenging he could ever recall having experienced.

Aboard the Charles H. Marshall, conditions remained materially unchanged. By now the boat appeared a complete wreck, encased almost entirely in ice. The men continued taking their turns filling the oil bags every half-hour. At this point, the exclusive mode of travel on deck was crawling on all fours, secured by a rope knotted firmly around the waist as a precaution against being washed or blown overboard.

Charley knew that some of the men (and he included himself in that number) were trusting in Providence to pull them through safely. Outwardly, not one of them displayed the least bit of fear. What lay deep within each man's heart, however, could be known only to himself and the Good Lord above.

Certainly the day-time hours were better than the night, but that was about the only positive thing that could be said regarding their situation – save, of course, that they were all still breathing. They remained in constant motion as much as possible, rubbing their hands, faces, and ears, doing everything they could to improve their circulation and reduce the chance of developing a debilitating case of frost-bite.

Frank looked steadily at Will, taking the time to choose his words carefully. The two of them were still alone in Will's office, engaged in their conversation about Alex and Kira.

After a long pause, Frank finally continued. "Well, Will, I hope you'll excuse my hesitation. It's just that what I'm about to tell you now is something I promised Alex I wouldn't. But while I remain conflicted about that, it's easy to see how terribly troubled you are by all this, and – as your best friend – I feel I can no longer keep my counsel. You must swear to me, though, that you won't let on that I've told you. In all probability, I'll end up confessing it to her myself, but that will be for me to decide – if and when I feel the time is right."

"Of course, Frank, I understand completely. And thank you for your confidence in me. I promise that I won't breathe a word of it to anyone. Not even Mrs. D, who I share just about everything with."

Satisfied with Will's response, Frank then nodded and took a deep breath. "Okay, Will. After Kira had stormed out of our house the other night, Alex came to me, deeply troubled about her friend's state of mind. She said that Kira told her she was having second thoughts about her relationship with you, even saying she thought it possible that you were, and I'm quoting Alex here, 'a little bit crazy, what with all this insane talk about some ridiculous killer storm.' Apparently, their conversation had rapidly deteriorated from that point.

"She went on to tell me that not only was she concerned Kira might be losing her marbles, she was also very much afraid that unless the girl came to her senses soon, she would end up, and again I will quote her, 'throwing away arguably the best thing that had ever happened to her.' Of course, I agreed.

"Our discussion went on into the night. After much back-and-forth, Alex arrived at what we both thought could be the most viable explanation for Kira's bizarre behavior. If, for some inexplicable reason, she is harboring some deep-rooted feelings of inadequacy and unworthiness, this could be causing her to act in ways which would sabotage her own happiness."

Frank looked at Will, trying to gauge his reaction to all of this so far. As there was not much he could discern in that moment, he continued. "Alex also said that if you and Kira *did* stop keeping company, she was confident that with her God-given assets it would take no time at all to attract any number of 'replacements,' perhaps some unsavory ones. Sadly, it would be consistent with this strange sense of being undeserving that she would make the terrible mistake of marrying someone who would not treat her well, leading to a miserable future."

As Frank finished, he was shaken by the pained expression which suddenly appeared on Will's face, and his heart went out to him. It was plain to see that this disturbing analysis of Kira's behavior, made by the person who knew her best in all the world, was having a profound, and deeply upsetting, effect on him.

Their conversation over for the moment, Frank got up to leave. Just then, Sergeant Long re-entered Will's office. Even knowing it would have taken nothing short of a miracle, Will couldn't help himself, asking, "Any luck with the attempt at communications?"

Long shook his head, frowning. "Not a bit, I'm afraid. As sorry as I am to have to report it, the fact is we are completely dead in the water." He exhaled loudly before continuing. "And just to make things even more interesting, it would appear that the anemometer has now frozen solid. It's not registering any information at all."

The wind-recording instrument, attached to a sliding iron pipe, was held in place by a screw on the top of a very long pole – twenty-five feet high and only four inches across – affixed to the tower.

The Sergeant's frown deepened into a grimace. "Which means, unfortunately, that I'm going to have to climb up there and fix it."

Will's jaw nearly hit the floor. "You're going to have to do what!? Are you crazy? I beg your pardon, sir, but with all due respect, have you completely lost your mind?" Protocol thrown to the wind in that moment, Will stared openly at the Sergeant in utter disbelief.

Frank had paused in the doorway, apparently having heard this last exchange and waiting to see if he might be of some contribution.

"Look, Will," Long responded easily, thankfully showing no offense in the least, "you know all about my adventures in the Arctic under Greely, so you know that I know a thing or two about dealing with the cold. You also know that I owe the man for this job I happen to enjoy – and you know he will want to have these records. And while I'm certainly not 'crazy,' as you so eloquently put it," he continued with a grin, "I suppose it could be said that I am a bit remorseful . . . concerning my decision not to tell him about your system and its prediction of this storm, that is." He paused a moment, sighing heavily. "So you see, if there is any way I can begin to make up for that, I've got to do it – it's as simple as that. And right now, what that translates into is me climbing all the way up that there pole and fixing that damned anemometer."

Will recalled learning that in 1881, Long had volunteered as a cook for an Arctic expedition under the command of none other than General Adolphus W. Greely. As it turned out, the party had become stranded for three excruciating years before finally being rescued, during which time hunger and the constant cold had taken a terrible toll on the men. When help had arrived at long-last, Francis Long, half-frozen through but with a gun still firmly in-hand, had been discovered – barely alive – several miles from the camp, searching for food for the others. In all, twenty of the original party of twenty-six had perished. Greely and Long were two of the six who had somehow, against all odds, survived.

"I understand everything you've said, boss. I do. I am still asking you to reconsider – please. I know the records are important, vital even, especially with an outlier event like this one. But I just can't believe they are worth risking your life for. If that pole snaps, you're a goner. And sir – that too is as simple as that."

The Sergeant leveled a determined look at his subordinate. "I appreciate your concern for my well-being, Will. I truly do. But there's no denying that I have just a bit more experience under my belt than you do, and along the way I've accomplished a number of things that were far more challenging than this. I agree with you that it's dangerous work, but you'll just have to trust me when I say that I know I can do it."

Finally realizing that talking him out of it was a lost cause, Will nodded in reply. Though still concerned about how risky the venture was, he went on to express his support. "I'd surely like to be able to help you, sir, but I'm afraid there's very little I can do."

The Sergeant gave Will a wry smile. "Well, you're certainly right about that, Mr. Roebling, there is little you can do . . . other than prepare me a nice hot toddy, which will help me thaw out once I make it back down. You will find the 'special' ingredients for that marvelous and restorative concoction in the upper right-hand drawer of my desk."

Moments later, Sergeant Long began his slow shimmy up the frozen pole in the near-hurricane-force winds and paralyzing cold. Will positioned himself directly underneath the Sergeant's ascending body, hoping that in the event his boss fell, he would be able to catch him or, at the very least, break his fall somewhat. Given the disparity in their size, he couldn't help wondering what else he might break in the process.

When Long finally made it to the top, he held on to the pole for dear life with one hand, while adjusting the instrument and replacing some wiring with the other. Will knew he was reaching deep into the reserves of energy and courage that he had managed to harness during his miraculous survival in the Arctic. After what seemed an eternity, Long finished making the repair and began his sliding descent. By the time he'd reached the bottom, so much ice had accumulated on his hat, scarf, moustache, cheeks, and eyelids that he looked, for all the world, like a giant snowman.

As they made their way back inside, they were greeted by a standing ovation of enthusiastic cheering and applause offered up by Frank and the recently hired technician, who'd wandered in sometime during the past half-hour. Will joined in whole-heartedly. Long nodded and smiled weakly at them all in acknowledgment.

"Alright, Will," he then croaked, barely audibly, "I'd say it's high time you went and fixed me that toddy!"

Still shaking off the effects of her earlier efforts to help save their neighbors' horses, Alex Gorman sat in her kitchen, relaxing over a cup of hot coffee. She was at once deeply grateful for the comfort and security of this warm and cozy room, and terribly concerned about the well-being of Kira, Will, and Frank. Most particularly, she was worried about Kira.

Despite their blow-up yesterday, Kira was still Alex's best friend, whom she loved dearly. Spending that hour outside earlier in the extreme elements had been more than enough to impress upon Alex just what Kira would be up against if she foolishly ventured out into the storm. Alex shook her head sadly. Kira's stubborn, immature obstinance regarding Will, combined with her damned blind ambition, would almost certainly end up costing the poor girl dearly to-day. She couldn't decide who she felt worse for in this moment: Kira or Will.

By now Frank should have arrived at work, but of course she would have no way of knowing for certain that he had. Given how strong, sensible, and well-prepared he was though, she had every reason to trust that he got there safely – just as she had every reason to believe that Kira had rashly placed herself in terrible danger.

A solemn Alex gazed wonderingly out the window at the incredible, awe-inspiring display of nature's fury, resigned to the fact that, as much as it pained her, there was absolutely nothing she could do in this moment for either her best friend or her beloved husband.

CHAPTER 42

11:30 AM

Wilma had now been at Blanche's for more than two-and-a-half hours – far longer than she'd originally intended to stay. But it had taken her that long to recuperate from her traumatic trek through the storm. Although she now felt almost completely recovered, she realized her return-trip would take her through snow which had gotten quite a bit deeper in the interim, and this caused her some considerable angst. Never-the-less, she remained steadfast in her determination to get back to the familiar surroundings of her own home.

This time, though, she decided she would go out through Blanche's front door, turn right and walk along Sands, then turn right again – up the walk-way to her own front porch and door. She believed the street route could provide better landmarks, and felt that attempting to go through the back-yards again would simply be too dangerous. Besides, she thought, by now that drift in back would almost certainly be much too deep to plough through.

Wilma didn't waste any time in deluding herself. She knew that without the tempering effects of the trees, going by the front route would expose her to the full-fury of the gale-force wind. From what she could see out the kitchen window, it appeared to be blowing even stronger now, if that were possible, promising to make the journey home that much more punishing.

Refusing to make the same mistake twice, she was careful to remember Will's direction about the guide rope, and had Blanche tie her securely with a two-hundred-foot length of strong, light-weight cord they had found on the shelf above Charley's work-bench. Wilma could take solace, therefore, in knowing that even if she did become disoriented, she had only to follow the rope back and it would lead her to the safety of Blanche's house. And assuming she made it to her own front porch, she could tie it off there for reuse by either of them in any subsequent trips.

Before Wilma left, she and Blanche embraced for a long and poignant moment. When they finally broke apart, Wilma told her friend how impressed she was with the fortitude she was showing in the face of the situation with her Charley. She then went on to offer the reassurance that she herself would be just fine on her own till Will's return, as her wood and food supply would hold out for at least a week. Blanche responded in kind, doing her best to put Wilma's mind at ease about her own choice to remain at home alone, and thanking her profusely for risking so much just to come over and provide her with some moral support.

Earlier, Wilma had made it clear that her original invitation still stood, and that Blanche was welcome to come back with her when she went home and stay as long as she liked. Blanche thanked her and expressed her deep gratitude but, as Wilma had expected, she said she still preferred staying in her own home for the remote possibility that her telephone service would somehow be restored and she might have some news – any news – about Charley.

Wilma told her friend that she completely understood, as she was holding on rather fiercely to the hope that Will would be coming home very soon – even though the chance was mighty slim, at best.

With one last hug and a kiss on the cheek they made their final good-byes, promising to check in on each other via the tie-line on Sands Street, just as soon as the worst of this disastrous, blasted blizzard had taken its leave.

May had already been informed by Mr. Garrigues that he intended to head back home to his wife and family on the West Side. He'd told her he was quite confident that he would be able to make it, especially with the oases of taverns and bars along the way offering temporary shelter – not to mention the opportunity to "fortify" his strength and courage. Truth be told, he'd confessed, a part of him was actually looking forward (just a bit) to the adventure of the whole thing.

"Well, Miss Morrow," he began, as he prepared to make his departure, "there is an ample supply of wood here, enough to last for at least several days, so you certainly shouldn't be cold. And there's an adequate variety of staple foods in the cabinets, too. Nothing fancy, I'll grant you, but nourishing none-the-less, so you won't go hungry, either. Above all, I want you to please make yourself at home, and feel free to help yourself to whatever you might need to do so."

"Thank-you, sir, that's very kind of you. And don't worry, I'm sure I'll be putting your provisions to some very good use."

"I'm glad to hear that. I guess the best thing you can do then is just stay here and relax, making yourself as comfortable as possible while staying safe. I will be back as soon as practicable – whenever this storm abates, that is."

Whenever this storm abates . . . I wonder why that simple phrase has such an ominous sound to it?

"Thank-you, again, Mr. Garrigues. You are most considerate, and I could not be more grateful."

After giving May some last-minute instruction on the operation of the stove, Garrigues said his final good-bye, closed the door behind him, and embarked on his return-trip home.

Sergeant Long, already happily at work on his second hot toddy, appeared to have recovered nicely from his harrowing ordeal scaling the anemometer pole. His obvious, and certainly understandable, sleepiness not-withstanding, Will thought he seemed to have suffered no lasting ill-effects at all.

"Oh, my stars and garters, I sure am powerful tired all of a sudden," Long announced, stifling a yawn. "Can you imagine that. Well, I guess when it comes right down to it, I'm just not as young as I used to be. Of course, then again, who is? Anyway, I think right about now would be a good time to go take myself a brief siesta." With that, Long retired to his office and closed the door.

Now that his attention was no longer focused on his boss, Will began to have an antsy feeling which he could only associate with an incipient case of cabin fever. After all, he'd been cooped up in the Office since six-thirty with no communication from the outside world, beyond what Frank and the Sergeant had had to offer when they came in. And that was hours ago, now. He thought that if he had to be so cut-off from everyone and everything, he'd much rather be at home with Mrs. D.

Hmm . . . interesting. The thought of somehow being isolated with Kira had never even crossed my mind.

If he'd really had his druthers, though, Will would much rather have been out in the storm, perhaps being of service to someone. Anyone. Either way, he knew he had to leave the Office – and soon, just to keep his sanity.

I guess I should probably head on home and check up on Mrs. D. She must be quite worried by now, the dear thing, no matter how brave a face she put on for me last night. And, of course, there's poor Mrs. Potts, and everything she's up against. Perhaps I can be of some help there, too. At the very least, I have to try.

Frank had left the Office just moments ago. There was very little that could be accomplished there right now as all communications were down, so Will had given him permission to go on home to be with Alex. He told Frank not to concern himself with whatever Long's reaction might be. Will would take full responsibility for having sent him home early. He was fairly certain that the Sergeant would not raise any objection to it, anyway.

Besides, Will thought, the new technician will still be here, and he can tend to anything the boss might need when he wakes up. After writing a brief note of explanation to Long, Will donned his warm, dry outer-garments, made his farewell to the technician, and left the Office, just minutes behind Frank.

CHAPTER 43

1:15 PM

O h, now isn't this just great – the damned Bridge is closed! I guess I shouldn't be all that surprised, though.

"Well, I've made it this far," Will said out loud to no one in particular (not that anyone could possibly hear him over the roar of the wind, anyway), "maybe I'll just head on up to Kira's and make sure she's okay."

Actually, Will was torn. Frank's earlier words were still freshly seared into his consciousness. Chasing Kira down right now, under normal circumstances, would have been the absolute last thing he'd want to be doing. But there was nothing normal about this situation, and something was telling him at this particular moment that going to her suite was, in fact, the right thing to do.

He could not seem to shake the disturbing feeling that she was in substantial danger, at this very moment, despite the earlier penetration he had shared with Mrs. D. How could he possibly live with himself if her life really were in jeopardy and he'd done nothing to try to help her? Besides, he thought, what else could he be doing anyway, right now? He certainly wasn't going to stand here and freeze to death, which meant that he had to go somewhere and do something. Going to check up on her was as good a plan as any, with the added advantage of making him feel like he was doing something useful.

Will traipsed back though the ever-deepening snow towards Broadway, figuring he could follow this major artery north all the way up to West 34th. He knew that Manhattan, itself, was oriented more northeast-southwest than true north-south, and that Broadway actually ran more northeasterly than north, at least along the lower portion of the island. Thankfully, this would place the northwesterly gales at a right angle to his path, more or less, for most of the trip – leaving him only a single block to traverse while facing directly into the wind.

Even though it was still very early in the afternoon, Will was amazed at how dark it was. The day-time sky did not yield much more light than it would have had it been late evening.

Jon remained quite concerned about Kira's condition. She had awoken an hour ago, but was clearly a long way from being recovered. As her attempts to communicate were quite labored, and what little she did manage to get out made almost no sense at all. Although Mabel said she was fine with Kira staying at her place indefinitely, Jon continued to believe that the severely traumatized young woman should be under professional care – and the quicker the better. Unfortunately, as neither of them knew of any doctors who lived locally, a house-call was obviously out of the question.

The conditions outside made it next to impossible to get around, incredibly challenging for even the most physically fit, like O'Malley himself. One of New York's Finest – the apt and popular phrase coined fourteen years earlier by then-Mayor William Havemeyer – Patrolman Jonathan O'Malley had probably saved the lives of a dozen people to-day since bringing Kira to Mabel's this morning. Included in that number were several children who had been sent out in the early dawn, mostly to buy milk and food for their younger siblings at home, by parents who sadly had seriously under-estimated the horror which awaited them on the streets.

Just moments before returning to Mabel's, while walking his beat on Seventh Avenue, Jon had discovered, quite by accident, an under-dressed elderly man, frozen-solid and almost completely buried in a snow-drift. Fortunately, a passing pedestrian had stopped to offer his assistance. Together, Jon and this good Samaritan had managed to carry the body to the basement of a nearby building, later designated as one of several make-shift morgues created to handle the scores of casualties which would be incurred across the City over the next couple of days.

The good news, however, if any could be called thus under such exigent circumstances, was that the number of people on the streets was slowly dwindling, as many had apparently either gotten to their destination somehow or, more likely, managed to seek temporary shelter elsewhere.

In most cases, that "elsewhere" was one of the plethora of bars and pubs which, on this atrocious day, were, not surprisingly, doing a booming business – so long as they didn't run out of liquor. A few of the less-scrupulous saloon-keepers were charging a premium for their highly coveted wares. Most, however, had actually reduced their prices. Some were even holding impromptu contests of various types of skill, including acumen in the recall of minutiae, and the winners could drink for free – benevolent gestures greatly appreciated by the hordes of storm-beleaguered customers. The kindly patrolman could personally attest to all of this, having stopped in at several such jam-packed "watering holes" for warmth and libations while out walking his beat.

Travel conditions not-withstanding, Jon was giving serious consideration to the idea of bundling Kira up and carrying her, over his shoulder, to Bellevue, in much the same manner as he'd originally transported her to Mabel's after rescuing her from in front of the Bijou. A thoughtful man, he had spent a good deal of time deliberating over the matter while on patrol, and had come up with what he believed were three good reasons which made this a feasible plan.

In the first place, the emergency-room was not at all likely to be crowded, as no doubt only a scant few would be able to get there, at least till the ferocity of the storm had subsided to some degree.

Secondly, he reasoned that all the doctors, interns, and nurses from last night's shift would, most likely, still be at the hospital. After all, where else could they have gone? If he could just manage to get Kira there, he felt certain she would be able to get the medical attention she needed, without which she might be in serious trouble.

Finally, even though the hospital was nearly a mile away, it was, none-the-less, a direct path down 29th Street across Manhattan to First Avenue. And this, he figured, would be the key to his plan's success: he would have the wind at his back the entire trip. If Jon's struggles on his beat to-day had taught him anything about getting around during this blizzard, it was that it's infinitely easier to navigate with the wind at one's back. Also, if he were fortunate enough to encounter long stretches along 29th where the snow had not piled up too high – a distinct possibility, he thought – the constant force of the wind might actually help him in moving along.

He told Mabel he'd wait another fifteen minutes to see whether Kira showed any real signs of improvement. If not, he'd probably be taking her to Bellevue.

→ ❋ ←

By now, Wilma had been home for over an hour, after taking a full thirty minutes to travel the short distance from Blanche's. Having made the unfortunate discovery that conditions were so bad that walking upright was no longer a viable option, she had quickly resorted to crawling on all fours. That way, she could not only avoid being toppled over, but might minimize the relentless, merciless lashing of the delicate skin of her face by shards of ice crystals, cruelly transformed from the softer snow by the fierce wind.

The short segment of Sands Street that Wilma had to navigate was devoid of deep snow, at least on its south side where her house and Blanche's were located. The wind had blown most of the snow away, depositing it in the now-mountainous drifts piled up against whatever large objects and structures were in its path, exposing a treacherous undercoating of ice – which, in and of itself, would have made walking extremely difficult, even under tranquil conditions.

With nothing to hold onto and virtually no traction under-foot (or under-hand), Wilma expended most of her energy simply avoiding being swept off the street. Still, unlike what she had experienced during her earlier trip, she was confident she would arrive safely. She even allowed herself a smile or two, imagining just how ridiculous she must look, scuttling along on her hands and knees in the snow like some kind of overgrown crab.

After finally making it back to her own kitchen, Wilma Duncan quickly stoked the fire which had all but gone out. She then decided that a short hot toddy, a warm snack, and a well-deserved nap sounded like just what any competent doctor would order for her, right about now.

Somehow, May had managed to make it all the way up to Broadway and Canal since leaving the warm confines of her workplace, just fifteen minutes earlier. Even though she had promised Garrigues that she would stay put, she'd begun having second-thoughts not long after he left. Less than two hours later, she'd already found herself bored to tears and completely incapable of facing the prospect of being cooped up alone for what might, ultimately, turn out to be days. The thought of being separated from her friends and room-mates at the boardinghouse, not to mention all of the amenities to which she'd grown accustomed, soon became insupportable. As challenging as she knew it would be, she had set out on a course for home. At least she'd had the forethought to leave her boss a note, figuring he'd most certainly be returning to the office before she would.

May knew she'd be taking a great risk by going back out into the storm, and was less than thrilled to be doing so. But she had a deep-rooted faith that, somehow, she'd be alright, so long as she left when she did and avoided traveling after darkness set in. In fact, she had actually gotten a strong "nudge" telling her she should go – that some great experience or huge opportunity awaited her out there. Although what that could possibly be she couldn't begin to imagine, much less articulate. But in her vast experience (all twenty years of it), she had learned to trust these feelings when they came to her. So after packing some staples from the office pantry and stuffing her clothes with newspaper and other insulating materials she'd found lying around, she had bravely ventured out of the secure haven of Garrigues Chemicals.

So far, on her trip up Broadway, she had crossed the street several times, seeking out whatever small advantage in locomotion she could find. With the northwesterly gales whipping straight down the cross-streets, she found that the protection afforded her by walking along the more-sheltered western sidewalk was nearly equally offset by the significant increase in the number and depth of snow-drifts she was forced to plough her way through. In the end, she decided it was a toss-up as to which was the lesser of the two evils.

Her plan was to walk up Broadway to 42nd Street, then the four blocks over to Tenth Avenue, and finally up Tenth to her boarding-house, just around the corner on West 48th. This, she reasoned, had to be the safest route, as it should certainly be the most populated, which would become vitally important should she happen to require any assistance. It would also offer her the greatest opportunity to seek temporary shelter along the way; she knew there was a bar or pub on virtually every corner.

James Landen's faith in his newest employee turned out to be well-founded. As luck would have it, Albert was a natural-born manager. He executed all aspects of the hotel's emergency plan flawlessly and without assistance, save for having had to call Landen in around nine-thirty to evict a guest who stubbornly refused to comply with one of the edicts. The occupant in question had been planning to leave, but refused to do so in advance of the eleven o'clock checkout-time – which was, the guest had vociferously remonstrated, "posted right there on the door!"

With assistance from John and Hazel, Albert had managed to find accommodations for a total of one-hundred-and-forty-one paying walk-ins – all but twelve of them in rooms already occupied by pre-existing guests who had opted to extend their stay. There were still seven empty rooms available in addition to the six reserved for employees. Landed was particularly impressed by Albert's clever development of a master guest list by room, which included confirmation that each previously registered guest had paid for their extra night. With the increased complexity of strangers sharing rooms, Albert had known that the hotel's existing reservations system would be inadequate to keep track of all the guests.

In the throes of this dire emergency, the Grand, like every other hotel in Manhattan, was stretched to its limit, and beyond. James Landen could only imagine how much more difficult things would have been on this daunting day without the superb performance of young Mr. Washington, and was grateful beyond measure.

CHAPTER 44

3:00 PM

The cyclone had now moved to a position just south of Rhode Island. A ship east of Long Island reported a pressure of nine-eighty-four millibars, and Block Island, about thirteen miles south of the Rhode Island coastline, recorded nine-eighty-seven millibars (a drop of seventeen millibars in the past eight hours).

Snow had already ended by mid-morning across southern New Jersey, Philadelphia, and all but the northeastern-most portion of Pennsylvania, with skies having cleared by early afternoon. But with the forward-motion of the cyclone now slowing to a crawl, it would be many hours before the clearing line could advance further north and east. Instead, blizzard conditions, raging on from central New Jersey into New York City and Long Island, had increased in coverage over New England, and now encompassed nearly all of Connecticut and most of Massachusetts.

In New York City, at least sixteen inches of snow were officially on the ground, with two feet the norm in outlying areas. Because of the high winds (averaging around fifty miles-per-hour), accurate measurements were nearly impossible to make, with some drifts actually surpassing twenty feet.

The north-south-oriented front which had stalled over central New England was very pronounced, with twenty-degree temperature differences common over short distances separated by this air mass divider. Colder air was now beginning to filter slowly eastward into eastern Connecticut where rain was changing to sleet and snow.

Inland sections of Massachusetts, Rhode Island, and New Hampshire were also receiving heavy snow, even though they were in the oceanic air mass to the east of the stationary front. Southeastern coastal New England, however, remained under the influence of warm maritime air; temperatures were rising slowly towards forty degrees with strong easterly winds and occasional heavy rain.

Once he'd arrived at Bellevue, Patrolman O'Malley did not have long to wait. The triage nurse, a Miss Nancy Petersen, had rushed over to tend to Kira immediately after he'd carried her through the emergency-room doors about a half-hour ago, staggering just a bit from sheer exhaustion. Shortly thereafter, she was admitted to the hospital for hypothermia and frost-bite.

Nurse Petersen confirmed his earlier hypothesis – the emergency room had practically been a ghost-town the entire day, with only eleven patients having shown up since she came on duty at midnight. She said that ordinarily, early on a Monday afternoon, there might be as many as forty or fifty patients waiting to be seen. To-day, with the one-horse ambulances and other customary forms of transportation unable to navigate the streets, there was pretty much no way for the sick or injured to get there.

When O'Malley gave Miss Petersen a thumb-nail sketch of what had happened to Kira, she told him the poor girl was indeed lucky he'd found her when he did. Even so, she opined, it was entirely possible Kira had suffered "some sort of permanent injury," quickly adding that a formal assessment would be forthcoming from the intern who was treating her now. She stressed that Kira was in very good hands, Dr. Clarence Sanders being one of Bellevue's finest interns. She also offered that, based on her experience, they would most likely be keeping her for at least a few days for observation and treatment.

The patrolman could sense that Nurse Petersen was in no real hurry to break off their conversation. He assumed this was partially because there were no waiting patients in need of her ministrations. And O'Malley was definitely in no hurry at all to go back out and tackle Armageddon again. He hadn't even fully defrosted yet from his most recent travail. Accordingly, he launched into a much more elaborate account of how he'd happened to come upon Kira standing outside the Bijou Opera House, apparently waiting for someone who clearly was not going to be showing up. He talked about rubbing snow on her ears, carrying her to his sister's, the nap and warm whiskey she'd had, and his ultimate decision to brave the elements in order to bring her in to the hospital.

Electing not to short-change the attentive nurse on any of the more dramatic elements of the story, he then detailed his construction of a sled from a washboard, several planks, some rope, and other sundries. Thankfully, he'd been blessed by the inspiration to create this make-shift conveyance at the very last minute, just as he was making preparations to carry her over his shoulder all the way down 29th Street.

Although aware that his recital was now beginning to border on braggadocio, he found it impossible to stop, not with the spell-bound nurse hanging on his every word and asking all the right questions at just the appropriate places. So he continued on, not quite able to determine at this point whether her interest were strictly professional or if, maybe, there weren't something more to it. He couldn't deny she was quite cute, maybe even a knock-out. All the more impressive, he thought, given that the first time he laid eyes on her was at the end of a fifteen-hour shift.

Jonathan then explained the process he'd gone through in deciding to carry Kira in, prior to coming up with the idea to construct the sled. Taking just a bit of story-telling license, he said that because 29th Street would be a straight-shot to the hospital with the wind at his back, he'd thought it would likely be a "relatively easy jaunt."

He also mentioned that the street's slight downhill pitch, once east of around Broadway, had proved helpful. While true, this was not something he'd known about in advance. But surely there was no need to disclose that much information, was there?

Eventually, after milking as much narrative out of the story as he possibly could, and recovering enough of his physical strength to resume his patrol, it became pretty obvious to all and sundry that the time had finally come for him to take his leave.

"Well, Nurse Petersen –"

She immediately cut him off with her raised palm. "Please, Officer, do call me Nancy."

"Oh, alright then – well, Nancy, I must say, this has been quite an unexpected pleasure. I've certainly enjoyed meeting you to-day. Frankly, I can't remember the last time I relished having a conversation as much as I did this one."

"Thank-you, that's very kind of you to say. And likewise, I'm sure, Patrolman O'Malley." She lowered her eyes and performed a brief mock-curtsey to accentuate her response.

"Jon. Please," he said, smiling broadly, charmed by her histrionics.

"Well, alright then – Jon it is. Say, Jon, here's an idea: why don't you plan on stopping by again, to-morrow, maybe sometime in the late afternoon? I'm scheduled for second shift, so, one way or another, I'll be here."

Almost as an after-thought, she hastily added, "By then, you see, I should be able to give you a comprehensive update on our patient's progress and prognosis."

They both knew he had no compelling reason to follow up on Kira's condition. Bringing her in, while indisputably heroic, had been just a part of doing his job, as far as he was concerned. This, then, confirmed things for him – she really was interested in him personally, because she obviously wanted to see him again.

Jon could not keep his delighted grin from spreading ear-to-ear. "Well, you know what, Nancy? That sounds like a marvelous idea, and I do believe I will. Stop back by to check up on the patient, that is, of course. And, who knows? If all the craziness with this storm is over by then, and you find yourself with a free moment or two, maybe the two of us can sit down to a cup of coffee, or share a small meal, or some such thing."

"Or some such thing." She leveled a direct look at him, smiling brightly.

He blushed.

"I hope you won't find this too forward of me, Jon, but – I really do like you. It's plain to see that you have a good heart, a quality I happen to find mighty attractive. And one which I find generally lacking in most men to-day, by the way.

"So, I hope I'll see you sometime to-morrow. And if you can't make it then, I mean because of the storm, I'll completely understand. You just come on back whenever you can. I'll be here. You know where to find me."

What to say??

"Fair enough, Nancy . . . decidedly, fair enough."

Truth be told, O'Malley was a bit taken aback to be spoken to so forthrightly by this delightfully bold young woman, an unprecedented experience for him. He was, none-the-less, more excited and intrigued than anything else. Other than exchanging good-byes, there was nothing more for him to say, so he turned and left the hospital to do further battle with Mother Nature – still the angriest and most violent he'd ever known Her to be.

The raging blizzard aside, to-morrow could not come fast enough for Patrolman Jonathan O'Malley.

"Now where do you suppose she could be?," Will wondered. If Kira had gone out this morning after all, which he knew she'd had every intention of doing, it was most unlikely that she'd be at home now.

The entry-way to her three-story apartment building was currently completely inaccessible, as were the entrances to all the south-facing homes on West 34th Street.

The relentless wind had created a continuous unbroken drift which now extended the entire length of the complex, and it must have stood at least twenty feet high – completely eclipsing the windows on the first floor and already beginning to encroach upon those of the second. So Will was now confronted with a dilemma. Assuming he even had enough reserves of energy, should he try to dig his way through to see if she were in there? And if she weren't, then what? Come to think of it, would it even be possible to get through this drift, all by himself, without equipment of any kind?

Just then, as he peered upward through the blinding snow, he caught the blurred image of a man looking out the window of one of the second-floor units. Pin-wheeling his arms wildly, Will managed to catch the fellow's attention and, as if through force of sheer will-power, was able to coax him into opening the window, just a crack.

Ironically, the same northwesterly wind responsible for the massive obstruction of the drift also had a very positive effect: it created a space of relative calm directly outside the man's window, enabling him to hear Will's voice remarkably well.

Will shouted up, "Do you know a Miss Kira Smith in Suite 3C?"

"Yes, I believe so." At least, that is what Will thought he heard. From his position down on the street, he did not enjoy the same acoustic benefit.

"Could you please knock on her door and see if she is in? I'm afraid she might be out somewhere, lost in the storm."

"Certainly, mate. You wait right there, I'll be back in a jiffy."

The man returned to the window a few minutes later. "No, I'm sorry, guv'nor. She doesn't seem to be at home."

"Thank-you so much. If you do see her, please tell her that *Will* came by to make sure she was alright."

"Will do, Will!" From the jovial expression on the man's face, which Will could only barely make out, it was clear he was enjoying his little play on words. "Best of luck to you, now." He was still waving good-bye as Will turned to go.

Well, I guess that's that. Now what do I do? Guess that all that's left is to find me a hotel room for the night.

He turned away from the wind and ate his last piece of dried beef, giving another quick prayer of thanks for Mrs. D's thoughtfulness, before doubling back towards Broadway.

Thank Heaven I'll be walking with the wind, for the time being at least.

Will was only vaguely familiar with the hotels in this part of town. He thought his best bet would be to get back onto Broadway and head south, in the direction of the Bridge. Then, sometime before it got dark, he could check into one of the higher-class hotels he'd surely be passing along the way. In terms of finding a vacancy and something to eat, he figured he'd have much better luck with the swankier establishments than he would with those of lesser quality.

Maybe I'll try the Grand Hotel, right there on Broadway. For some reason, I've always had a hankering to stay there. It's definitely of the highest class, and I know it has somewhere around three- or four-hundred rooms. How fortuitous that I was smart enough to pack plenty of money in my satchel before I left the house this morning. I'll surely be needing it before this long day is through.

May Morrow was preparing to take her leave from Callahan's, an intimate Irish pub on the corner of Broadway and 24th in which she'd been forced to seek refuge, at least till she could warm herself up a bit and dry out her frozen, wet outer-garments. She remembered having read once that, counting both sides of the street, there was an average of six or seven bars, saloons, or liquor stores for every City block;

her experience thus far this afternoon seemed wholly to confirm that interesting statistic.

The friendly bartender, a decidedly decent older gentleman, seemed determined to see that she remained unmolested amidst a sea of crude boisterous men – all clearly inebriated. She had agreed she'd take one brandy (brandy or whiskey being the cure-all for whatever ailed one, particularly during the flu season) and a thick, freshly sliced turkey sandwich for energy, before confronting the mighty blizzard once again. The hearty sandwich was certainly an upgrade over the meager and unappetizing rations she had managed to secure before leaving Garrigues Chemicals earlier.

Having tended to several minor scrapes and cuts on her face – residual gifts from the constant pounding of the wind-driven ice and debris – May was now about ready to resume her journey. She knew she had been truly fortunate thus far, shuddering as she was briefly revisited by the ghastly images of some of the faces she'd seen on the lesser-prepared pedestrians she'd passed along the way. She remembered mostly the women whose faces had been cut, no doubt, by shards of flying glass, with tell-tale streams of blood frozen firmly in place. Because of the numbing cold, she had doubted whether these poor souls were even aware that they had been so severely sliced up, which only made her pity them all the more.

Stepping out onto the sidewalk, ears and face tightly wrapped in her freshly dried scarf, May was appalled to run smack into the body of a gentleman, in all probability an earlier guest at Callahan's, passed-out, or dead, along-side a telegraph pole and buried in snow up to his armpits. His exposed head was a bloodless pallid color, evoking a haunting image of a Marie Tussaud exhibit from her famous London wax museum. Although May had never been overseas, she knew exactly what those celebrity wax figures looked like, thanks to the museum's vivid billboard advertisement, in full color no less, clearly visible from the el on her daily trips to work.

May's first thought was that if this unfortunate fellow were not dead, he would surely be having to deal with one of the worst cases of the frost-bite imaginable. Realizing she had to do something, she did the only thing she could think of in the moment. Quickly back-tracking into the pub, she notified the kindly bartender about the poor man, then rapidly returned to the street to resume her trek before she lost her mettle.

Right about now, May was seriously doubting her sanity, having made the decision to abandon the warm, safe confines of her office haven and embark on this ludicrous odyssey. Running into that frozen man, seeing him up-close and personal, had made an unshakably disconsolate impression on her. Gone in a flash was her original optimism that she'd be able to make it all the way back home to-day. She'd even begun to question – something she never, *ever* did – the strong "nudge" she'd gotten, even though it had seemed so unambiguous at the time. But let's face it, she thought wryly, however else her adventure thus far might be described, it could hardly be characterized as some "great experience" or "huge opportunity."

Sunset was still several hours away, but the day's meager light had already begun to fade noticeably, save for those moments which were illuminated by a nearby lightning strike – an added and terrifying cause of concern for everyone still out on the streets. She told herself it was high-time to begin looking for a hotel, any safe haven in which she could spend the night. Although she had nearly three dollars left, ordinarily more than enough for a relatively decent room, she knew that these circumstances were anything but ordinary. Any room, assuming she'd even be lucky enough to find one, would almost certainly end up costing her a pretty penny. She couldn't be bothered worrying about money now, though, not in this life-or-death situation. Her only priority had to be finding a secure shelter in which she could ride out the storm.

For the very first time since her ordeal had begun to-day – well before dawn, now seemingly a lifetime ago – May Morrow found herself, most uncharacteristically, anxious and afraid.

CHAPTER 45

4:00 PM

Truly breathtaking to behold, the towering monolith of white stretched across the entire east-facing facade of the Grand Hotel, extending all the way up to the third-floor windows. Impossibly it had to be, by his quick estimation, more than forty feet high!

Will stood for a moment in awestruck silence, resembling nothing so much as a supplicant standing before one of the great altars of Christendom. His emotions were roiling, his heart at once grateful and despairing. He was moved beyond words by the gift of bearing witness to such a majestic spectacle, and sunk to great depths by the crushing disappointment of possibly having just lost his last best hope of finding shelter for the night. In the next instant, knowing that standing still would result in certain death, Will forced his feet to keep moving further down Broadway.

As he neared the corner at 31st Street, however, his despondency transformed quickly into elation upon discovering that the hotel's southeast-facing main entrance, located at the base of the beveled edge of the two acutely angled adjoining lengths of the building, was – miracle of miracles – entirely free of snow! The building's odd geometry, in conjunction with the relentless wind, which had now backed around from its earlier north-northwest direction to a west-north-westerly one, had worked in the clear favor of the Grand's fortunate guests – a fraternity Will was desperately hoping to be able to join in the next few minutes.

With sweet sanctuary now safely in sight, Will found it much easier to dispel the terrifying image of the disoriented, stumbling pedestrian he'd happened upon three blocks earlier, at the intersection of 34th, Sixth, and Broadway. The poor man's face was a mask of horror – completely encased in ice, eyelids frozen half-open. Despite the exigency of his own situation, Will had reached out instinctively to grab hold of him, intending to effect a rescue by guiding him into a nearby saloon. Just as he'd nearly gotten his hands on him, however, the wretched fellow had suddenly toppled over, face-down, into a large snow-drift. With the snow blowing so hard and the drift being so deep, Will was unable to locate him for several precious minutes. After frantically digging down more than a foot, his hands freezing inside soaked gloves caked with ice, he finally found the unfortunate man and pulled out his practically unconscious body. With the help of another good-hearted passerby, Will managed to drag the barely breathing bloke into the saloon where the other patrons immediately leapt to his aid. Will was struck, and not for the first time to-day, by how the storm was bringing out the best in so many.

At that point, Will had been sorely tempted to stay put for a spell, and take the opportunity to dry out his wet gloves and warm himself up with a hot toddy. His memory of the two he'd made earlier for Sergeant Long was still fresh in his mind, even though that now seemed like days ago. But as he stood in the doorway of the bar, pulled strongly by the inviting warmth within, a vague yet insistent presentiment had come over him, saying in no uncertain terms that – for some reason – he had to keep moving. He couldn't come close to putting his finger on what that reason might be, but felt it compelling, none-the-less, and so he'd forged ahead continuing his trudge down Broadway.

Just as Will was about to push through the revolving glass doors and enter the blessedly safe haven of the Grand Hotel, a figure, appearing to be that of a young woman, materialized at his side, seemingly out of thin air. As bad off as Will knew his own condition to be in that moment, the poor girl was obviously in much worse shape. Even though she was bundled up admirably, it was evident that she was on the verge of collapse. Her appearance evoked the image of a statue crudely carved from ice. Then again, he could only imagine how he must have appeared to her, or to anyone else, for that matter. At the precise moment they emerged together from the revolving doors, her legs suddenly gave way like jelly, and he quickly wrapped a steadying arm around her, lest she do herself any further damage by hitting the lobby's hard marble floor in a dead faint.

Albert, who by now had his routine down pat, immediately approached Will and the girl to welcome them to the Grand. Naturally assuming they were a couple, he then asked Will if he and his missus needed a room for the night – or had they just stopped in to warm themselves up a bit, like so many others had throughout the day. Will could only manage to mumble, indistinctly, "room."

Mr. Washington inclined his head politely, going on to say that the room rate is four dollars per person and that payment would be required up-front. Will nodded his assent. Albert then said something about the "emergency policy" the hotel had adopted because of the storm, resulting in the possibility that they might have to share the room with other guests, a situation he would explain more fully, momentarily. After asking that they please make themselves as comfortable as possible in the lobby which, thankfully, had a roaring fire going in the massive stone fireplace, he said he'd be back to get them in just a moment.

Will half-carried, half-walked the piteous girl over to the sofa nearest the hearth. To Will, it felt heavenly to sit in front of the delicious warmth emanating from the fire. In fact, in no time at all, he needed to shed his outer-layers. Glancing over at his new-found friend, he saw that she was fast asleep. So he removed her coat, insulating stuffings of newspaper and various plastic packing paraphernalia *(clever girl!)*, scarf, hat, gloves, and boots, and spread them out with his own garments and accessories on the hearthstone where they would quickly dry.

The serving girl from the lounge adjacent to the lobby came over and asked Will if he'd like something to drink. This time he acquiesced, gratefully, ordering himself – what else? – a hot toddy. While he was enjoying his much-needed and well-deserved libation, giving serious thought to what on earth he was going to do about the girl, Albert reappeared at his side.

"Alright then, sir, I thank you for your patience. It was necessary that I check the registry concerning room availability. I'm very pleased to tell you that you and the missus are, indeed, most fortunate." He briefly explained the hotel's current practice of "doubling up," and that, except for a few families and couples, forced-sharing between strangers was the rule right now in all but eight rooms of the entire hotel. Of these, six still had single occupants, while two, each with a pair of twin beds, were still vacant, having been held till now for families or groups that might happen to come along. As it was getting rather late in the day, and therefore much less likely they'd be seeing anymore families or groups, he'd decided he could let them have one of the two vacant rooms.

Will immediately expressed his heart-felt gratitude to Albert, having grasped the whole of the situation in an instant and coming to the only logical conclusion he could. On the one hand, he could confess his lack of connection to Mystery Girl, which would put him in a room with a complete stranger and leave her to the same fate. Under that scenario, he would have no idea what harm might befall her, as she was currently sound asleep and would probably remain so for a good long stretch. And while he was sure that an establishment as beyond reproach as the Grand would do its level-best to protect her, even they could not guarantee that some unsavory character might not figure out a way to take advantage of the situation.

On the other hand, he could go along with Albert's presumption that they were a couple, in which case he would be able to carry her to their room and make sure she was safely installed (and unmolested) in her own bed.

Though the circumstance was complex, in the end it was a simple decision, really. Will paid the eight dollars and, in exchange, received two keys for Room 419. Albert then said that some items on the menu were unavailable due to the storm, but assured him there would be a reasonable selection for dinner this evening, should they desire room service. Will thanked him again and gave the helpful young man a generous gratuity of six bits.

Although grateful for the warmth and comfort she enjoyed in her well-provisioned home, Wilma could none-the-less already begin to feel the stirring of cabin fever. The unremitting roar of the wind in combination with the ever-deepening drifts of snow gradually encasing the house left her feeling claustrophobic, entombed.

By now, the rising snow had completely covered over the south- and east-facing downstairs windows and would soon reach the ones on the second floor. Looking out an upstairs window above the kitchen (facing west, in the direction of Blanche's), she could see an enormous drift running the length of the pine trees – the same row of ordinarily familiar pines in which she had gotten so terribly disoriented earlier in the day. She knew their height to be about sixty feet, and when the wind slackened briefly, she could see the drift had climbed half-way to the tops of the trees – which meant that it was, amazingly, a full thirty-feet deep!

It was then that Wilma surrendered all hope of Will making it home anytime soon. Most uncharacteristically, she found herself, for the second time to-day, profoundly fearful – but this time it was for *his* survival. And she couldn't help but wonder if Blanche were really doing alright at home by herself which, of course, got her to thinking about poor Charley again.

Oh, Lord o' mercy – that poor, poor man. I'm truly afraid that he and his ship-mates, God bless them every one, don't stand a ghost of a chance of getting out of this thing alive.

CHAPTER 46

5:30 PM

Will had finished carefully tucking Mystery Girl into her bed half-an-hour earlier. He noted that her dress was surprisingly dry, no doubt due to some combination of her "insulating ingenuity" and her brief stint in front of the roaring fire in the lounge. After observing her for a long moment to ensure she was suffering no ill-effect from her exposure to the cold, he decided he might as well stretch out on his own bed for a bit of sorely needed rest. Strangely enough, despite the amount of energy he'd recently expended, he did not feel much like sleeping at all. Then again, he figured, it was still only early evening and he never had been too awfully fond of napping.

And besides, how in tarnation could he expect his mind to calm itself enough from the events of this cataclysmic day to be able to sleep? Especially in light of this latest turn of events, which now had him intrigued by the prospect of learning about the origins of his unexpected new companion.

He glanced over at her sleeping form, mentally taking inventory of what he knew thus far: she appeared to be neat, clean, and attractive enough, probably about his age or, perhaps, a year or two younger. Her facial bone structure was good, and she had a great figure, like Kira, though she wasn't quite as tall, maybe five-foot-five. Her smooth blond hair was well-coiffed in the modern style, with short curly bangs framing her delicate face.

Will shook his head and rolled his eyes, nearly laughing aloud at how much this clinical assessment of her reminded him of how he

interprets his weather maps. He chose to leave any further specula-
tion about the girl alone for the moment and, instead, looked forward
to discovering more about her in due course.

Still not relaxed enough to fall asleep, he swung his legs to the
floor and sat on the edge of the bed for a minute. Realizing he was
thirsty and famished, he got the urge to go down to the lounge for a
cold beer and a snack of some kind, perhaps even dinner. Will was
fairly sure his room-mate would not awaken before he returned, but
figured he should leave her a descriptive note of explanation and the
second room-key, just in case.

He found a writing pad on the night-stand and quickly composed
a thumb-nail sketch of who he was, and how she'd ended up in a bed
in this room after he'd rescued her in the lobby. He said he was a meteorologist (would she even know what that meant?), recapped the
room-availability saga, and left off with the fact that he'd be downstairs having a bite to eat in the lounge. And, in the unlikely event that
she awoke before he returned, he figured she'd probably be hungry,
so she was certainly most welcome to join him. Finally, he said she
should be able to recognize him easily as he was wearing his Signal
Service uniform, and that his name was Will Roebling. Again, just in
case . . .

Not surprisingly, the lounge was lavishly decorated, an excellent
match for the rest of the elegantly appointed hotel. It was a wood-
worker's delight, resplendent with magnificent polished oak floors,
an expensive cherry-wood bar, solid black-walnut tables, and richly
finished oak chairs. The edge of the long bar was beautifully detailed
with intricate carvings, similar to those decorating the legs and backs
of the chairs. The walls were tastefully papered with a soft floral print
in rich hues of brown and green. From the high ceiling hung several
large, ornate crystal chandeliers, filling the space with a warm and
flattering light. Spectacular hand-carved molding between the ceiling
and walls accented the beauty of the entire room, at the same time
providing the perfect complement to the molding in the hallways and
guest rooms. The windows were over-sized and exquisitely framed

by luxurious, brocade drapes held open by plush velvet tie-backs, normally affording a fine view of any activity on 31st Street.

The lounge was crowded when Will walked in, and thoughts of his mysterious room-mate faded to the back of his mind, for the time being at least, as he busied himself with finding a place to sit. Every seat at the bar was occupied, as were all the spaces around and between them. Nearly all of the eight or ten round tables were full as well. The one closest to the window, however, had only two people in residence, even though there was room for four or five. Will pulled over an empty chair and, placing it near the table, its back towards the window, politely asked the gentlemen sitting there if he might join them.

"Absolutely, good sir. Please do join us, by all means," the older one said, sociably, visibly intrigued by Will's official-looking uniform. "My name is James Landen and I am the manager of this fine establishment."

Will reached over and shook Landen's extended hand. "Very pleased to make your acquaintance, I'm sure, Mr. Landen. Will Roebling's the name – Room 419."

"Oh, please – let's make it James and Will, shall we? After all, it certainly feels to me as if this blizzard has made boon companions of us all. Oh, and allow me to introduce my good friend, Pat McCormack, also one of our guests – a preferred guest, I might add."

The two men nodded hello as they shook hands.

"Well then, Will, might I buy you a drink?," Landen went on, expansively. "And please do say yes, as Pat and I have no desire to continue drinking all by our lonesome."

"Yes, please, Will, your company is most welcome," Pat chimed in, gregariously.

Will had barely nodded his assent, smiling broadly, when Landen's surreptitious signal to their server brought the young man over. Will's order for a cold draught beer was filled in under a minute, no doubt owing in large part to his auspicious choice of table companion.

With the uniform being something of a conversation piece, it took no time at all for Will to reveal himself as a meteorologist with the Signal Service. Landen and McCormack told him that they had been discussing the blizzard – what else? – before he joined them. They were therefore delighted by his perfectly timed arrival, and appeared eager to gather his professional perspective on the storm. But first, Landen informed Will that his dinner to-night would be on the house. Very pleasantly surprised and grateful, Will ordered himself a thick New York steak, medium-rare, with a salad and baked potato.

Will must then have talked, non-stop, for about the next twenty-five minutes, somehow managing to consume his meal politely at the same time. He started out talking about the blizzard, in general, but was quick to subtly segue into his forecasting system. Without quite knowing why, he had decided, in that moment, there was no longer any point in keeping the system under wraps. He figured the logic behind this determination, beyond the anomalous existence of the blizzard itself, of course, would become clear to him at some point.

As Will was gaining momentum in describing the details of his forecasting system to his rapt table-mates, his thoughts returned briefly to an invaluable course he'd been required to take at Yale entitled simply "Seminar." Once-a-week, with no advance warning, a student was selected at random to stand up and critique a recently published technical paper assigned to the class the week prior, by Professor Loomis. While this challenging exercise in public speaking had naturally created a certain level of anxiety for Will (and his fellow class-mates at the time), he could now look back with some degree of amusement and see how perfectly that particular training had prepared him for just such a moment as this.

About half-way into his extemporaneous lecture, Will casually mentioned that Joseph Henry was his greatest childhood hero, and Landen's reaction was immediate and electric. His face lit up like a Christmas tree, and it seemed for all the world as if he were going to offer Will a free upgrade to the Presidential Suite, right then and there. Amazingly, as it turned out, Landen, a much older man than Will, had been among Professor Henry's top students at Princeton College some forty years earlier, though he ultimately chose to concentrate on business and management rather than science. But he said that he'd always maintained a keen interest in the weather, and told Will he'd never forgotten his tutelage under the brilliant Professor.

As Will was talking about Henry, he noticed out of the corner of his eye that Albert Washington had entered the lounge and was making a bee-line for Landen, obviously in need of his assistance with some urgent matter. While Landen did acknowledge the young man's arrival, his expression made it clear that he had no interest in being bothered by anything in that moment, and silently commanded him to take a seat. Will could tell that Albert was a bit surprised, even as he sat down immediately. After all, while it was plain to see that Landen was a fair bit "in his cups," who was Albert to argue with him?

Landen's earlier assertion that the blizzard had "made boon companions of us all" proved prophetic. Some of the other guests had picked up on the thread of Will's engaging discourse and, at Landen's urging, had dragged their chairs over to form a semi-circle around the hotel's impromptu speaker extraordinaire, swelling his audience to nearly two dozen. Landen had happily assumed the role of moderator, prompting Will to repeat every so often (for the benefit of new arrivals) the part about his revolutionary forecasting system and its prediction of the storm.

In truth, Will was now starting to feel slightly embarrassed by all of this unsolicited attention but, at that point, there was no way he could possibly extricate himself gracefully. The very last thing he wanted to do was repay Landen's generous hospitality by appearing to be churlish and ungrateful. So, ever the good sport, he soldiered on, making sure to glance out occasionally over the still-expanding group in an effort to make everyone feel included.

Suddenly, his eyes locked on those of none other than Mystery Girl.

She must have been standing there watching him for several minutes now. The warm inviting smile on her freshened face, as well as the sparkle in her large crystalline blue eyes, clearly signalled just how much she was enjoying his lecture.

For the space of a breath or two, Will was arrested by the beauty of that smiling face and the light which seemed to emanate from within it. He completely lost his train of thought as the rest of the room faded into the background. Somehow, though, he managed to recover himself quickly.

Only the most perspicacious of Will's listeners (which happened to include the ever-alert Landen, despite his degree of inebriation) noticed the small hitch in his delivery as he moved smoothly onto the next topic.

CHAPTER 47

7:50 PM

A famished May had thoroughly enjoyed her delicious meal of lamb chops and green beans; like Will's, it had come compliments of James Landen. She and Will had also lingered over an exquisite bottle of wine, another fine expression of the hotel manager's generosity.

The crowd around Will had long since dispersed, after almost everyone in the lounge had heard, many more than once, the captivating story of his forecasting system and how well it had worked in fore-telling this extraordinary blizzard. May, especially, had been positively intrigued. Not long after his other table-mates had departed, leaving just the two of them seated there, she and Will had regaled each other with the details of their experiences on this unforgettable day.

The conversation had then naturally segued into a discussion of each other's personal life, which they both found fascinating. Over the past hour-and-a-half, May Morrow, remarkably, had learned more about Will Roebling and his life than anyone else in the world ever had – with the possible exception of Mrs. D, of course.

Will started out by telling May all about his childhood growing up on his parents' farm in Wisconsin, mentioning his special relationship with the animals in particular, and with nature in general. He then went on to discuss: his eidetic memory; his college days and Professor Loomis; how he'd come to join the Signal Service; his life at Fort Myer (he could tell she especially liked hearing about that, as he made full use of the well-rehearsed, amusing anecdotes he'd shared with the public during his one-week, post-Christmas assignment as tour facilitator); the profound impact that Joseph Henry had had on him (even though he'd never met the man); Professor Abbe and the "special project;" some interesting background information about his forecasting system he hadn't shared with the crowd earlier; his passion for bridges (particularly the awe-inspiring Brooklyn Bridge); and (of course) his close, special, and unique relationship with Mrs. D.

He talked about his neighbors Blanche and Charley, his superior officer Sergeant Long, and his dear friends Frank and Alex. Last, but certainly not least, he told her all about his relationship with Kira. In discussing this somewhat delicate subject, Will was amazed to discover that he felt just as comfortable talking with May as he did with Mrs. D.

Will said that he credited Mrs. D's generously shared "wisdom and keen insights" for his being able to sit here now, completely at ease, and objectively discuss where things with Kira had gone so far afield. He made it clear that Mrs. D never had any interest in assigning blame, only in fostering a deeper understanding of his and Kira's relationship and forwarding his ability to be a responsible, loving partner in that relationship. It was yet another in a long list of things for which he was extremely grateful to her. In fact, Will was most forthcoming with May about just how narrow his experience with women was. This limited perspective, in his view, gave rise to what he considered to be his "complete inability to understand them at all," a less-than-flattering bit of self-awareness previously revealed only to Mrs. D and Frank. He could not believe how easy it was to talk to May about absolutely anything. And he delighted in telling her as much.

The conversation, however, had been far from one-sided. May had shared generously about her own life: her parents; her friends; life in her upstate home-town; her lack of interest in men her own age and the solid reasoning behind it; her drive and ambition; her job; and her extraordinary outlook on life. She echoed Will in expressing how remarkably easy it was to talk to him, and went on to say that while she certainly had her share of close intimate friendships, this was something she'd never before experienced.

As they were walking upstairs to their room for the night, she recapped for him what she could remember about *her* experience of their serendipitous meeting, as well as the course of events since she'd awoken in her bed earlier. She knew she'd been mighty close to collapsing out in the storm as she approached the hotel, but her memory of what happened next was admittedly "a little fuzzy." She was able to recall, however, that she received some desperately needed assistance from a "kindly, good-looking gentleman." The next thing she remembered was waking up snugly tucked into a strange bed in an unfamiliar room, then finding his note.

May said that the key to locating him amidst all the commotion in the lounge had been his having mentioned he'd be wearing a Signal Service uniform. The distinctive red, white, and gold insignia of crossed flags and flaming torch on his shirt caught her eye, and she quickly deduced it must be him. As she quietly moved closer, weaving in and out amongst the crowd of people in order to observe him without being seen, she was drawn into the orbit of his professorial recital, much like "a moth to a flame," she explained. She confessed that she'd certainly been pleased, albeit a bit taken aback, to discover that it was he, in fact, who had been commanding the attention of the considerable audience surrounding his table.

As Will and May rounded the corner at the end of the hallway, they caught sight of Pat McCormack standing in the open doorway of his room. As an acknowledged buddy of James Landen, not to mention a preferred guest, he was one of the rare few who, apparently, had yet to be assigned a room-mate. Will sensed that Pat was following their approach with great interest, a mildly quizzical look on his face.

Although Will and May had originally made eye contact when he'd spotted her in the audience sometime during the latter part of his lecture, it wasn't till the crowd had finally scattered, leaving only McCormack, Landen, Albert, and Will at the table by the window, that May had apparently gathered the courage to come over and sit down. She and Will had then just sat there, silently, staring wide-eyed at one another and grinning ear-to-ear. No introductions were forthcoming, and McCormack and Landen seemed to become ill-at-ease. It was as if they had somehow inadvertently intruded on an intensely private assignation, and they quickly excused themselves. Albert was close on their heels. Prior to leaving the table however, Landen, ever the consummate host, immediately had the hotel's special lamb chops sent over for Will's "companion," along with a bottle of his finest Cabernet Sauvignon for the two of them to share – all compliments of the house.

Will had been so caught up in the wonder of the new world opening before him that he'd never given a thought to how puzzling the circumstance must have been for his table companions. Now, however, the look on Pat's face said it all.

A convivial Pat hailed the couple as they neared their room. "Hey there, good neighbors," he called out, smiling at them from where he stood in his doorway, leaning against the jamb.

"Well, now – don't that just beat all," Will exclaimed, bowled over by the coincidence of their room proximity, especially in a hotel this size. Pat nodded vigorously in agreement.

"Say, Pat, allow me to introduce you to Mistress May Morrow. May, this is Pat McCormack, a Grand Hotel regular." May smiled warmly as she offered her hand.

"Very pleased to meet you, ma'am, I'm sure," he said, taking her hand and bowing slightly over it. Straightening and facing Will, he went on, "I must say, Will – what with all that hubbub down in the lounge before, it's a wonder to me that you remembered my name at all."

"Oh, I'm pretty good with names and such," Will responded, smiling pleasantly.

If pressed to describe his state of mind in that moment, the best Will would have been able to come up with is an odd combination of feeling euphoric and surreal. The euphoria, of course, was because of May – and perhaps a little as a result of the ego-boost provided earlier by his adoring audience (the half-bottle of wine he'd consumed didn't hurt, either). He knew the surreal feeling came largely from his exhaustion, augmented by the fact that he had never before experienced anything quite like the past couple of hours with May. He actually felt like he was floating, not walking, down the hall. What was more, he knew – he just knew – that May was feeling precisely the same way. He vaguely remembered having read poetic descriptions of this "walking-on-air" sensation in his literature courses at Yale, and was amused to find how accurately they reflected what the two of them were experiencing in this moment.

"Say, I forgot to ask you, downstairs . . . ," Pat began, interrupting Will's reverie. From Pat's curious glance in May's direction, Will wondered, briefly, if he was about to ask *the* question, then concluded that it was unlikely; a gentleman like Pat would hardly be that tactless. "When is this monster going to be ending? I really do need to be getting to Philadelphia sometime to-morrow."

"Philadelphia, you say? I'm sorry to be the bearer of bad tidings, my good man, but I'm afraid you won't be getting there anytime soon. The storm probably ended there around ten or eleven this morning, but it won't be ending here till sometime to-morrow. And God only knows how long it will take to clear the tracks. My best guess? I'd say you're looking at Thursday, at the earliest."

"Well now, isn't that just a fine kettle of fish," Pat grumbled, but without any real ill-humor. Then he paused, as if in expectation. Will had already decided he was done for the night though, and would therefore not be giving him the chance to pose anymore questions.

"Well, we'll be saying good-night then, Pat," he said brightly, with a polite nod. May joined him, smiling her farewell. He then took her hand in the most natural manner and the two continued down the hall. Four rooms further along, Will put his key into their door.

CHAPTER 48

10:00 PM

The storm center moved to a position between Block Island, Rhode Island, and Nantucket, Massachusetts. The central pressure had now fallen to approximately nine-seventy-eight millibars. The frontal zone to the north of the low remained virtually stationary and the temperature contrast across the front was spectacular: Northfield, Vermont was four-degrees above zero while Nashua, New Hampshire, to the east of the front, was registering thirty-four. Blizzard conditions persisted over much of the Northeast, and single-digit temperatures were the rule across western New England and New York.

As the storm center approached the southeastern Massachusetts coast, temperatures began to fall rapidly across eastern Connecticut and Rhode Island, where winds shifted from the east to the north, and rain changed to heavy snow. At Block Island, the temperature dropped eighteen degrees in seven hours, with northerly winds of forty-two miles-per-hour and seven inches of new snow. At Nantucket, rains ended and winds shifted to the southeast and diminished as temperatures began to fall quite rapidly. Cold air, spilling around the negatively tilted storm system which was finally occluding, was beginning to pour into southeastern New England on southerly winds. Modified by its short trajectory over the ocean, this air still produced a significant temperature fall which was to turn the rain to snow throughout the night across eastern New England.

Will and May had finally fallen asleep, but not before concluding the intimate conversation they'd begun earlier in the hotel lounge. Since settling into the privacy of their own room, they had been able to expand the discourse to include their views on topics such as religion and politics – especially religion.

Their discussion on God was probably the most intriguing. While not having ever thought of himself as religious *per se*, Will never-the-less professed to have a strong belief in God. And though May did not follow any organized religion either, Will recognized immediately that she was a very spiritual person, with a belief in God he was coming to learn was profound and unshakable.

What had sparked their discussion on this topic was Will's recounting of his ability as a child to foresee storms and other natural phenomena, and how his parents came quickly to believe in, even rely on, these "premonitions." Of course, for him, there were no premonitions – there was simply a "knowing."

The subject of premonitions got May to thinking about the difference between knowing and believing, something she had often pondered. For the moment, though, she decided to hold that discussion in reserve. She wasn't quite ready to engage with Will on that particular subject just yet. She was, however, all but certain this "magical" connection between the two of them was the huge opportunity her earlier nudge had foretold.

Instead, she took the conversation to the subject of "Divine Spirit" or the "Supreme Force." She preferred using these terms more than "God," as she believed that God, whoever or whatever It was, was generally inaccessible, and that this Supreme Force was in fact "the Word" as known in the Christian religion. She wasn't sure though how many of her beliefs had been handed down to her by her parents versus formulated on her own. She did say that she suspected they arose from some combination of the two, although, oddly enough, she couldn't readily recall any conversations she'd had with them on this specific topic.

One aspect of May's spirituality definitely not influenced by her parents was her firm belief in reincarnation. As it happened, her good friend and boardinghouse room-mate, Emma, was a member of the Theosophical Society, and they had spent countless hours discussing the works of American Transcendentalists such as Thoreau, Whitman, and Emerson, and especially the philosopher and psychologist William James. Coincidentally, her friend's father had been close to James while growing up in New York City. Much of what May learned from these talks about reincarnation rang true for her, and she had no problem reconciling this belief with her less-than-strict Christian upbringing.

She felt that people, through the choices they made, whether in this life or a previous one, were completely responsible for all the hardships which befell them. Will asked her if she thought the door swings both ways, meaning whether the same formula applied to the good things as well as the bad in people's lives. She said she believed it did, absolutely.

Most importantly though, May's belief system did not embrace the idea of fearing a judgmental or wrathful God, even though so many religions, at least in part, described relationships with their Deities in that way. Actually, she felt it was the exact opposite: God was an all-good entity which desired only good things for all people, and He, or It, embodied love, and *only* love. There simply could be no room for anything else.

It was after this back-and-forth exercise of conversing with Will that she was able to clearly articulate the essence of her spiritual belief system: Gratitude and Love, hand-in-hand, were the keys to living the spiritual, or awakened, life.

Will posited that May's keys to the awakened life, as she called it, were the basis, or foundation, of her fantastically optimistic attitude. He had to admit that he was most impressed with Miss May Morrow, especially her spiritual convictions. He clearly saw how she could be something of a mentor to him in this arena, an idea he had to confess he'd never before considered.

I must be crazy to even be thinking like this, I know. I mean, we've only just met – and yet . . . could it really be possible that I'm falling in love with this young woman?

Wilma Duncan was completely exhausted. The events of this day from Hell would have been more than challenging for a young lass still in her prime. For a woman just two weeks shy of her sixtieth birthday, they were ridiculous in the extreme. She had no illusions about the mistake she'd made on her trip over to Blanche's, and the price she'd paid for it. She also knew just how close she'd come to perishing in that blinding, freezing white-out, and how lucky she was to still be alive.

Outside, the storm raged on unabated. While she felt reassured about Blanche, and knew she would be okay, Wilma wasn't so sure about Will, even given how reliable and resourceful he was. As for Charley . . . well, she preferred not to think about how things must be for him.

Of course, there was no way she could have known that the Bridge had been closed down to all traffic. That thought had crossed her mind, however, after it had gotten dark and Will hadn't made it home yet. She prayed that if such were the case, Will had quickly found shelter someplace safe. At any rate, she suspected she would be spending a long and desolate night alone in the house.

Wilma had plenty of coal and food, so there was no question that she would be alright for some time. She knew that, ironically, she would not be getting a delivery of ice anytime soon, so she had moved the food from her icebox onto the back porch, where it was plenty cold enough to keep everything fresh.

Her electricity had been off since late morning and obviously wouldn't be returning for quite awhile, but she had more than enough candles to keep her going for many days. The ones she had lighted in the kitchen provided just enough illumination for her to read the outside thermometer: seven degrees above zero.

Even though she could still hear the roar of the wind, she noticed that it was warmer and considerably less draughty downstairs than it had been before. She thought that odd, till she realized that the snow surrounding the house was now so deep it served to block the wind, actually providing insulation against the bitter cold – much like an igloo.

She headed slowly up the stairs to her bedroom, praying she'd be able to relax herself, to calm her mind enough that she'd be able to get a sound and rejuvenating night's sleep.

CHAPTER 49

11:45 PM

A monstrous thundering wave crashed mercilessly into the helpless vessel, lifting her high out of the water and slamming her down squarely on her side. Everything below-deck shifted violently, and the pilots and crew were all sent flying leeward. Great quantities of water rushed down the forward hatch. In that god-awful moment, all hands on board truly believed that their end was indeed upon them.

Earlier in the morning, Charley Potts had maintained a singular focus which precluded any thought of Blanche. In this moment, ironically, he now could think of nothing but his dear wife. With a fervor he hadn't known he could summon, he made a passionate and determined plea to God to save him somehow from this impending doom. Should He see fit to do so, he made a solemn promise. Never again would he leave his beloved Blanche to set foot on another boat. He felt this was the least he could do for her. Little did he know, in that same instant, that no fewer than four of his fellow pilots were attempting to broker the exact same deal with the Almighty.

Whether or not it was divine Providence, none of them could ever know for certain. A great cheer erupted in the cabin, however, when the little boat suddenly righted itself again. One thing all of them did understand, implicitly: should another wave of similar magnitude strike the already severely damaged craft, they would surely be done for.

Miraculously, the Charles H. Marshall would still be afloat at morning's light. The Captain, crew, and pilots would all live to fight another day.

PART IV

The Blizzard – Day 2

Tuesday, March 13, 1888

In looking back on the events of yesterday the most amazing thing to the residents of this great city must be the ease with which the elements were able to overcome the boasted triumph of civilization, particularly in those respects which philosophers and statesmen have contended permanently marked our civilization and distinguished it from the civilization of the old world – our superior means of intercommunication. Before the fury of the great blizzard they all went down, whether propelled by steam or electricity. The elevated trains became useless; so did the telegraph wires, the telephone wires, the wires for conveying the electric lights, the wires for giving the alarms of fire. And, worse than useless, they became dangerous.

-The New York Times, Tuesday, March 13, 1888

CHAPTER 50

7:00 AM

The storm's position and central pressure had changed little since last evening. Snow was still falling over much of New England and New York, and temperatures, already low, continued to drop. Severe blizzard conditions had persisted through much of the night from New Jersey northward. At Paterson, New Jersey, the temperature was an astounding four degrees below zero, while New York City recorded just five above – the lowest temperature ever observed so late in the winter (a record which would still be standing more than a century-and-a-quarter later).

Although the storm's pressure had not risen, there were signs the cyclone was finally weakening. The pressure gradient surrounding the storm was relaxing, indicating that wind speeds were decreasing. The area of heavy snowfall had become less organized; while some locations continued to receive heavy snow, others nearby measured little. The surface low had become "cold-core," signaling that the occlusion process was now complete and the source of the storm's energy exhausted.

At Nantucket, winds remained out of the south as temperatures fell to twenty-one degrees, with occasional snow. Boston also felt the influence of colder continental air sweeping in around the cyclone center as temperatures fell over-night, despite a strong easterly flow off the ocean. In Maine, temperatures stayed in the low thirties as the colder air remained to the south.

Will awoke from a deep sleep, two all-consuming matters leaping immediately to the fore-front of his newly conscious mind: the blizzard and May Morrow (though not necessarily in that order, he thought). Looking over at May, who was still sleeping peacefully, he quietly got out of bed, collected his things, and tiptoed to the bathroom to wash up and dress. He decided to invoke his Shakespearian genius, once again, in the composition of another clever note – the gist of which was that he would be outside surveying the storm, should she awaken before he got back and wonder what had become of him.

With his head still somewhere up in the clouds from the blissful time they'd just spend together, Will carefully gathered up his outdoor apparel and left the room to make his way downstairs and order breakfast. But only a very light one. He wanted to save room for sharing a more formal, romantic breakfast with May, later on.

To be sure, he had stood at the window a goodly while, taking in as much of the scene as he could from his fourth-floor vantage point. He could see that while the snow had slackened considerably, the wind was still more than formidable. Judging from the layer of ice which had accrued on the bottom of the inside windowpane, restricting his view, especially down to the street, he confirmed it was still bitter cold outside. If anything, he expected it would be even colder to-day than it had been yesterday, much as his system had foretold.

Despite the early hour, quite a few gentlemen were already gathered in the lounge as Will sat down. Some had already started in drinking – or perhaps hadn't yet stopped from the night before. Most though were simply having a hearty breakfast before checking out, willing to brave the elements in hopes of making it into work, finally. Or at least being able to get back home. Those who were in attendance last evening during his extemporaneous address recognized him immediately, as he was still wearing his Signal Service attire.

Several of them asked for whatever update on the storm he might be able to provide.

While Will did his level-best to appease this cadre of curious admirers, chuckling inwardly over his unsolicited, new-found fame, it became increasingly difficult to concentrate on anything other than his desire to get outside and gauge the current conditions. Barely a minute after finishing his final sip of the hotel's excellent coffee and the last tasty morsel of a Berkshire muffin, he politely excused himself and made a bee-line for the lobby. There he bundled himself up tightly before going out through the beautiful revolving doors. Because of May, he knew he would always consider them to be "magical."

The sidewalk immediately outside the hotel's main entrance was still largely blown clear, as were substantial portions of east-west-running 31st Street. But the fierce winds had shifted direction ever-so-slightly over-night, which had the profound effect of rearranging – indeed, substantially increasing the height of – the now monumental snow-drift which ran along the Broadway side of the hotel. For several minutes, despite the biting wind, Will stared up in awe at the behemoth drift. He knew that nothing even remotely like it had ever been seen before in the streets of Manhattan. Nor was it likely that it ever would be again.

Yesterday afternoon it had been possible to navigate down the western side of Broadway through a narrow passage-way which had, somehow, been created between the hotel itself and the massive drift running parallel to the building. This frozen conduit carved out by nature hadn't been completely snow-free, however. The depth of the snow within it had been in constant flux. The channel would rapidly get choked with two feet of snow, or more, only to be suddenly blown nearly clean by one of the swirling, often hurricane-force gusts careening through the canyons of the City's tall buildings. The space would then fill up again with new snow, and so on, in a never-ending cycle.

To-day though, that very subtle shift in wind direction from west-northwest to due-west had caused this corridor to completely disappear. In its stead, at least along the traverse extending from the hotel apex north up Broadway, was a solid mountain of snow. As near as Will could discern from his position on the ground, this wall of white, incredibly, ran up the entire face of the eight-story building.

As amazing as that was, there would be more surprises in store when he tried crossing Broadway. He wanted to improve on his perspective of the drifts in order to get a better handle on what he and May might be up against, later on. Earlier, he'd had the idea that if she were game – and, somehow, he knew she would be – they'd first walk up-town to her boardinghouse to let her room-mates know she was safe, then tackle the long hike to Brooklyn together to make sure Mrs. D and Mrs. Potts were okay. Will could hardly wait to introduce her to Mrs. D. He just knew the two of them were simply going to love each other.

The excursion to Brooklyn, of course, depended entirely upon whether he was correct in his presumption that by the time they arrived at the Bridge, sometime around mid-afternoon, it would be open for business once again. He felt fairly confident that would be the case, as it was obvious (though only to him) that the storm's occlusion process was now complete. As a result, the wind would continue to relax its icy grip.

As Will took his first step onto a small drift running across Broadway, he was shocked to discover that the snow had, apparently, compacted and solidified during the night, at least on the surface. If he walked slowly and gingerly enough, he could actually glide across this crust for short distances without falling through. He was astonished that, in the face of such a relentless wind, a crust like this could ever have formed at all.

At first, he reasoned that the brutal wind had simply fractured the snowflakes, reducing them to ice crystals. In the presence of the extreme cold, these crystals had then packed themselves together so tightly that they created a nearly solid surface layer, a condition far more typical of the barren Arctic tundra than the civilized thoroughfares of Manhattan.

Upon further reflection though, he concluded that something did not quite ring true about this initial hypothesis, at least as the sole explanation for this phenomenon. He had experienced many blizzards in his life, especially while growing up in rural Wisconsin, and had witnessed the formation of such a crust only on the rare occasion when snowfall had turned into freezing rain at the tail-end of the storm. And that was clearly not the case here.

Putting his scientific mind to work, he began by examining some of the facts he recalled from yesterday. First, when he'd started out from home, sleet was still mixing in with the snow, which was surprising given that the temperature was already down to twenty-six degrees, and falling rapidly. Next, he remembered several moments during the afternoon when he'd had the brief thought that a crust might be forming on the snow's surface. In the excitement and exigency of the moment, though, he'd had little opportunity to pay this observation much heed.

These recollections, along with his forecasting system and the last set of obs he'd been able to get from Glynn, led him to an interesting deduction. There must have been a persistent, relatively warm layer above the surface, maybe up about a thousand feet, or so. This warm air, in turn, would have made the snowflakes much wetter than they would otherwise have been. The added moisture would eventually re-freeze in the presence of the frigid air near the ground, thus forming the crust.

He reasoned that the existence of this warm layer could have been expected, as the relatively warm maritime air was being lifted by the strong, slow-moving cold front, while the cyclone was rapidly deepening and drawing the bitter air near the surface into its circulation. As these wet flakes quickly accumulated, the formation of a nearly impregnable ice layer on top of the snow now made perfect sense to him. And once this icy crust was established, it would no longer be a surface to which further snowfall, now much drier, would bind. This, he concluded, explained why some of the drifts now reached such staggering heights, while others were so much smaller. The new, powdery snow was free to be blown into ever-increasing masses, lacking any adhesion to the snow-filled landscape, while at the same time the icy crust on the less-expansive drifts precluded their getting any larger.

The deep satisfaction that Will felt over working out this series of deductions was short-lived, however. He knew that walking on this crust with May would be hugely impractical, as any attempt to move at even a remotely reasonable pace could only result in their breaking through it. And the snow-drifts they would invariably have to traverse along the way were so numerous and deep that, far from being a mere inconvenience, they could easily pose a serious threat at virtually any turn.

Sadly, he'd just about resigned himself to having to go back up to the room and report the bad news to her when, suddenly, an idea hit him, lighting up every corner of his brain.

"Eureka! That's it! That's it!"

He turned around to face the hotel's entrance and made his way back through the revolving doors as quickly as possible, a bright grin splashed across his eager face.

Albert! I've got to find Albert!!

CHAPTER 51

8:00 AM

Will put his key into the lock and turned it as quietly as he could, then opened the door very slowly. Although it was still fairly dark inside the room, it took only a few seconds for his eyes to adjust enough to see that May slept on, quite peacefully. Not bothering to shed any of his outer-attire, he then tip-toed out backwards, closed and locked the door ever-so-softly, and headed back downstairs to find Albert. With his capable assistance, Will was hoping to be able to complete the project he had in mind before she awoke. He was very much looking forward to surprising her.

He made his way to Landen's office, finding the indefatigable manager already at his desk. "Good morning, James."

"Will, my boy, good morning. Come in, come on in. Did you two sleep okay?"

"Yes, marvelously, thank-you for asking. As a matter of fact, she's still in slumber-land as we speak. But right now I'm anxious to ask Albert something. Have you seen him yet this morning?"

"No, actually, I haven't. But I'm quite sure he'll be down momentarily."

"I'm glad to hear that. If you see him before I do, please let him know I'll be waiting for him by the fire in the lobby, warming up these here old bones," he said, jokingly.

Landen responded with an appreciative chuckle. "Fine, Will, fine, happy to do so. But before you go, uh, well, there's something I wanted to ask you. I mean, it is most certainly not my intention to be presumptuous or rude, and if I am being so, you have only to say –"

"Please, James, I am at your service. Do go on with your inquiry."

"Well, it's just that when your, your missus came over to the table last night, well, Pat and I couldn't help but wonder . . ." Landen hesitated, his voice trailing off.

"Yes?" Will, having decided by now that he wasn't going to make this easy for him, leveled a direct look at Landen, eyebrows slightly raised. At the same time, though, he was finding it very difficult to suppress the huge grin which more accurately reflected his true feelings.

"Yes . . . well, we were wondering – Pat and I, that is – whether you two were married, or what. Not that it's really any of our business on a personal level, mind you, we're quite clear that it isn't. And please don't take offense. It's just that when she came over and sat down at the close of your remarkable lecture, it was, well, frankly, just so . . . so strange, for lack of a more descriptive word.

"It seemed for all the world to Pat and me as if you had only just seen this woman in the crowd, and that the two of you were actually meeting for the very first time. And yet, at the same time, the connection between the two of you was something almost palpable. I do declare, though I've seen a lot of strange things in my time here, as I'm sure you can imagine, I can honestly say I've never experienced anything quite so befuddling as that bizarre moment."

Too kind to prolong Landen's agony any further, Will burst out laughing, nodding his head in understanding of the man's confusion. He then went on to explain all about his and May's simultaneous arrival at the hotel, saying that while he, himself, had been near exhaustion, her condition had been far worse. He described the prompt, courteous, professional service that Albert had provided, including the rather convoluted information about room availability.

Just before Will finished recounting his second conversation with Albert, Landen's facial expression changed from sheepishly bewildered to greatly relieved, and he began nodding his head rapidly. "Ah, yes, of course, now I see."

Although Will had heard him, he never broke conversational stride. He continued with a segue into how he had never before, in all his life, met any woman who intrigued and excited him the way that May does. Here he'd been thinking he was happy in his relationship with Kira (least-wise pre-blizzard, that is), but now he could see clearly that he'd just been settling – blinded by the charm of her obvious physical attributes, and lacking the confidence and experience to know how to objectively confront the situation.

He went on to say that during the course of his and May's long and astonishingly intimate, yet amazingly easy, conversations, May had basically told him that her feelings were a match for his.

When Will finally paused to take a breath, he noticed the poignant look on his listener's face. Landen took this opportunity to break in with a confession of his own. He said he was feeling "a wee bit jealous," his wife of thirty-two years having recently passed on. They'd been mighty fortunate to have lived a long, rich life together, with more than their fair share of romance.

"Oh, James, I am so sorry for your loss, truly. I didn't know," a somber Will said, haltingly. He was hoping he hadn't accidentally reopened a raw wound.

"No, no, of course you didn't – how could you have? And thank-you for your condolence. Actually, it does get just a mite easier with time, so at least there's that." He gave Will a smile, albeit a sad one.

Landen then went on to share more of his experience with his wife, who he also described as his "sweetheart." He said that he had many close friends who were couples, and they came from all different walks of life. He also said he could definitely see how truly rare it was to have these feelings – this level of knowingness about someone else. And that the great majority of people go through their entire lives without tasting such joy, so Will should, indeed, feel blessed. Especially to have found it at such a young age. Will, beginning to feel a bit embarrassed now, could only nod and smile shyly. He responded by saying that he surely did.

Landen had just finished telling Will that it makes "absolutely no difference at all" that he'd known her but a single day, when Albert popped his head into the office.

Will could not have been more pleased.

"Good morning, Mr. Landen. Hello, Mr. Roebling, a pleasure to see you this morning, sir."

"As you'll discover shortly, Albert, those are my sentiments exactly."

Albert smiled and nodded before turning his full attention back to Landen. "By Heaven, was I ever exhausted after yesterday! But I'm happy to report that I am now rested, nourished, and ready to put my nose back to the grindstone."

"That's excellent, Albert. Now, as Mr. Roebling here wants to ask you something, the two of you can talk here in my office. I have to go and take care of something right now, but I'll be back in a few minutes. Wait for me to return, and we'll go over what I would like you to be doing to-day.

"And Will, I want you to know the conversation we've just been having is one I am quite relishing. So it's my sincere hope that we can pick it up again at some later time. Good day and good luck to you, my young friend." With that, and the warmest of smiles, Landen turned and left the office.

"So, Mr. Roebling, what was it you wanted to ask me?"

"Well, Albert, when I was outside earlier this morning, I noticed that there was a crust on the snow so hard I could almost walk on it. Please note that I said 'almost.'"

"Alright . . . ," Albert responded.

"Well, right then and there, an instant before I'd resigned myself to being marooned here all day, the thought hit me. If I could just figure out a way to construct a couple of pairs of snowshoes, then my . . . my 'companion' and I would be able to get around the City, and rather easily and enjoyably at that. So, I was wondering if you might be able to rustle me up some supplies from somewhere here in the hotel. Of course, I will gladly pay for them, and something extra for your time, as well. I believe I know exactly what it is I'll be needing."

"Sure thing, Mr. Roebling, fire away. And as far as any payment for the supplies and my time, please don't give it a second thought. Let's just call it a fair trade for the 'entertainment value' of the fascinating lecture you so generously provided the hotel's patrons yesterday evening. I'm sure Mr. Landen won't mind at all. In fact, knowing him, I'm certain he'll be quite pleased."

"Why thank-you, Albert. That's very kind of you. Well, I'll need four pieces of strong thin wood to mount on each of our feet, and some leather thongs with which to secure them."

"I think I can locate exactly what you're looking for, sir. I believe the hotel has all kinds of miscellaneous supplies and incidentals over in Maintenance, thanks to our Department Head, Mr. Jamison."

"Wonderful! And Albert? Please, do call me Will, won't you?"

"Yes, Will, very good, sir. I think it might interest you to know that my kid sister, Anna, who is in the eighth-grade now, spent several weeks last year studying all about Native Americans as a part of her history curriculum. For a class project which I helped her with, she designed and built a functional pair of snowshoes – and they worked perfectly, if I do say so myself.

"I can attest therefore, from direct experience, that your idea is actually a very good one and should work just fine. However, there are a couple more things you might want to consider in terms of your design."

"I just knew you were the right man for the job, Albert – although how perfectly so, I couldn't possibly have guessed now, could I. Alright then, about those 'couple more things' – what might they be?"

"Well, first of all, cleats."

"Cleats?"

"Yes – cleats. You will need some type of cleats, or short spikes, to prevent you from sliding backwards as you're climbing up a steep drift. And if you mount them just so, on the back of each snowshoe, you'll be able to glide down the other side without being hindered by them. All you will need to do is shift your weight, ever-so-slightly, when you wish to slow-down or stop."

"Why, that's brilliant, Albert – brilliant! I certainly would never have thought of that. Thank-you, so much. And what's the second thing?"

"Yes. A walking pole, or even poles. For stability, when you go up steep surfaces or across very rough ones."

"Of course. That makes perfect sense. I can't thank you enough."

"You are most welcome, Will. It's my pleasure, I assure you. And like I said, I believe I can find all the materials you'll need in Maintenance. If you will just wait for me in the lobby, I'll clear everything with Mr. Landen and join you there shortly. I'm sure that, working together, the two of us can get this done in no time at all."

Will fairly beamed as he considered the prospect of sharing the snowshoes with May. He noticed Albert grinning as well, apparently unable to resist the infectiousness of his good humor.

CHAPTER 52

10:00 AM

Ever since awakening earlier this morning, May had been think-ing about just how blessed she truly was. She passed Will the cut-crystal cruet filled with warm maple syrup as they each prepared to dig into their own delectable short-stack of light fluffy pancakes, fresh from the kitchen, piping hot – and with an aroma straight from Heaven. There were also sausages, freshly squeezed orange juice, and of course the Grand's special gourmet coffee. They were sitting at "their" lounge table by the window overlooking 31st Street. Although they could have enjoyed their breakfast in the slightly fancier and more formal hotel restaurant as many of the other patrons were doing, May had suggested they dine in the lounge. It was, after all, the place where they had first "met."

"Well then, Master William Augustus Roebling," May began, between delicate bites, "I have to admit that I think the itinerary you've planned for us to-day is simply splendid. But I really do feel I must caution you here, lest you get too used to the idea of my being so available on a moment's notice, like this. I mean, after all, I wouldn't want you getting too spoiled, or anything like that. I'm quite certain I will have to be going back into work again come to-morrow."

Will gave her a look of mock surprise. "Ah, yes – work . . . you know, I had completely forgotten all about that minor detail. Seriously though, speaking of work, I really do have a major concern about what's going to be happening next at the Office. I surely hope Sergeant

Long doesn't find himself in some kind of hot water over this blizzard business. Me neither, for that matter."

A shadow fell over May's face, and her tone became instantly serious. "Now wait just a minute, Will. How could *you* possibly be in any trouble? You told me it was Long's decision, and his alone, to keep Headquarters in the dark about your system and the storm. And he is, after all, your immediate supervisor."

"Actually, yes, that's true, May, but . . ."

"But?" She fairly bristled with indignation.

He smiled at her. "Well . . . let's just say that you don't work for the U.S. Army, and leave it at that." She returned his smile, calming herself at once and nodding slowly in tacit understanding and commiseration.

During the next few moments of comfortable silence, she took several tentative sips of her coffee, finally raising her face as she put down her cup. "Will . . . ?" Her saucer-sized blue eyes looked directly into his, yet, at the same time, it seemed that she was somewhere else, in some far-away place.

"Yes, May?"

"I want you to know – and I feel I can tell you now – I always knew that this would happen. I didn't know when, or where, and certainly not how, or with whom, but, none-the-less, I always knew." She spoke calmly, introspectively. "There's something that I didn't share with you last night, but I want to now. Before I decided to try to make it back home yesterday, I had one of what I call my 'nudges,' or messages from Divine Spirit. A really strong one, too, which told me that not only would I be safe as long as I left right at that moment – which I did, and I was – but that some sort of great experience, or huge opportunity, would be coming my way as well. But I didn't know anything more specific than that."

Will sat very still, transfixed, his eyes focused intently on hers. May recognized in his silent communication his undivided attention.

"Looking back on it now, I'm quite sure that the feeling of excitement and anticipation I got from receiving this 'message' was what gave me the courage to brave the blizzard, ludicrous though it appeared at first blush. I mean, I can't tell you how many times on that journey I found myself questioning my own sanity, especially given the number of appalling things I was forced to bear witness to along the way. But Will, I can see it all so clearly now. It's just like what you were talking about last night as we were falling off to sleep – that what's happened to us is so far removed from anything you've ever experienced. Do you remember saying that?"

"Yes, I do."

"And do you remember me telling you about how Divine Spirit works for me?"

"Yes ..."

"Well, I'm now really clear about all of this, Will. You see, *you* are that 'great experience or huge opportunity' that Divine Spirit was nudging me towards. In retrospect, there was absolutely no rational reason for me to leave the relative comfort and security of Garrigues Chemicals to risk my very life by venturing into the madness of a storm of this magnitude. I mean, it's as if the logical portion of my mind was not functioning – or had become disconnected, or something."

She became more animated, leaning in, gesticulating with both hands. "Do you realize that it's somewhere in the neighborhood of three-and-a-half *miles* from the office to my boardinghouse?"

Will's gaze never wavered, but he remained silent.

"To any moderately sane outside observer, I'm sure I would have appeared demented, setting out like I did, all alone, at the height of such a storm – especially given what I'd already seen of it on my way in to work.

"And believe me, Will," she said, suddenly sitting straight up and back, with a self-deprecating smirk on her face, "I can assure you that the irony of this situation is not at all lost on me."

He gave her a quizzical look.

"I realize that I am sitting here going on about having lost touch with the 'rational part' of my mind with, probably, the most rational and logical person I am ever likely to meet. What I'm saying is that I now understand that I *knew* I would meet you. Admittedly, maybe not consciously – but that doesn't make any difference at all."

She could sense that he really did not know what to say. She paused briefly, then continued on after a slight sigh.

"Will, I know I am very much taking the round-about way to get to something here, and please do forgive me for that. It's just that this has all been so sudden, so unexpected, and – truth be told – more than a bit overwhelming."

Here May stopped for a long moment, her eyes on his the whole time. Finally, she shrugged and smiled, and said, "Well, I guess there really is nothing left to say except 'I love you!' I love you, and I want to spend the rest of my life with you, William Augustus Roebling."

The Cheshire cat, himself, would have been envious of the grin which stretched from one of Will's ears clear across to the other. His eyes never leaving hers for a second, he raised her delicate white hand from the table and pressed it softly to his lips, wordlessly assuring her that he felt precisely the same way.

→ ✳ ←

Wilma had been up for a couple of hours already. Although the wind still whistled loudly through the trees, she could tell that it was not blowing as strongly as it had been yesterday. Looking out the kitchen window, up at the small strip of sky visible between the house and the massive drift which began just a few feet beyond, she could also tell that the snowfall had become sporadic. She knew the great storm was finally winding down, although the outside thermometer still registered only four degrees above zero. Absolutely unheard of, in her experience, for the thirteenth of March.

She was still apprehensive about Will's safety, but kept reminding herself that he was young and strong, and – God knows – smart and resourceful. It was Charley (and therefore Blanche) for whom she had the most concern. She could continue to put Charley out of her mind no longer. Generally speaking, Wilma certainly had more than her fair share of faith. Even she had to admit though, in all honesty, that it would be nothing short of a miracle if Charley Potts had, somehow, survived the terrible night and, rather than being buried somewhere out at sea, he was making his way back home to his beloved this very minute.

Unlike so many of the doomed vessels the storm had destroyed out on the raging waters, the Charles H. Marshall had indeed managed to make it through the long, awful night. The never-ending squalls continuing to shriek through its masts though, still made it feel as if the wind would lift the little boat right out of the water at any moment.

Some five hours earlier, the Captain had decided to inspect the oil bags, at which point he'd discovered that both hawsers were gone. He had made the wise decision to keep this information from the crew, as there was nothing which could be done about it. Better that than causing them any further alarm.

At this point, though, it would have mattered little to Charley. Having survived the horrors of their dreadful ordeal thus far, he now found himself possessed of a powerful faith that God had, mercifully, granted them a miracle.

He now believed, with every fiber of his being, that the sturdy little craft and her blessed passengers had truly weathered the storm, and that it would not be too terribly long before he'd be able to see his dear Blanche once again.

Though unable to speak for the others, he could sense that some of them at least shared his optimistic belief.

CHAPTER 53

10:45 AM

As Will had anticipated, May was delighted when he surprised her with the snowshoes. She told him how impressed she was with his ingenuity in constructing them, and by Albert's cleverness in assembling the cleats and customizing the wooden walking poles. Without those poles, any viable locomotion would have been difficult if not impossible. The poles were tapered to sharp points, perfect for piercing the icy crust. A flat disc – four-inches across and one-inch thick – was affixed to each pole in order to prevent it from sinking too deeply into the snow-drifts.

Albert, had expressed his gratitude for the chance to be outdoors for a bit (even though conditions were still basically deplorable), and was now giving the appreciative couple some last-minute instruction on optimizing the use of their cleats and poles. The three of them looked up when James Landen and Pat McCormack came out to join them. Having come to send the two adventurers off, both gentlemen lamented the fact that, in all likelihood, they would not have the opportunity to see them again.

"Stuff and nonsense," Will countered, with a broad smile. "Of course we'll stop back by 'our' hotel on the way over to Brooklyn. Coming down Broadway is as good a route as any, I'd guess. And besides," he added, with a wink half-directed at May, "I reckon we'll be needing ourselves a good hot toddy and something warm from your luncheon menu, right about then."

Landen's face lit up. "Right you are!," he agreed, happily. "I'll be sure and have the chef whip up something extra-special and very nourishing, guaranteed to replenish your energy reserves. Now, off you go, the pair of you. And whatever you may encounter out there, please do be careful, won't you."

"Oh, we shall, we shall," they sang out together, as they began gliding over the icy snow.

It was a scene for the ages.

Broadway, normally perhaps the busiest thoroughfare in all of Manhattan, was completely covered by a shroud of pristine white and virtually deserted. As Will and May navigated their way along it on snowshoes, they marveled at how eerie it was to go for blocks on end during the day without encountering another soul.

The going was much easier than either of them could have imagined. The large surface area of the snowshoes, along with the integrity of the crust, kept them from falling through into the deep drifts. They soon became adept at moving rather quickly in a smooth, flowing manner which closely resembled that of cross-country skiing.

While there were long expanses of unspoiled territory, especially off to the sides of the avenue, there were also potentially dangerous pitfalls to be dealt with along the way. The most significant of these were large chunks of frozen slush, created by the struggling horsecars the day before, scattered along the street centerline.

The cars themselves also proved to be something of an impediment to navigation. A number of them had been abandoned where they stood, their owners simply unhitching the horses and returning them to the stable after realizing that their only option was to cut their losses and leave their vehicles behind. Will and May had to negotiate their way around several such cars which were being put to creative use by small groups of homeless people, or perhaps folks who'd been stranded and unable to secure a room. These "horsecar residents" were trying to stay warm by keeping up fires in the little car stoves. One such enterprising and resilient group actually appeared to be doing a bit of cooking.

Still another group had apparently elected to enliven their interim stay by consuming a rather large quantity of beer, which had been "temporarily borrowed" from a nearby abandoned beer wagon and painstakingly defrosted by the warmth of their little stove.

Will and May quickly learned to avoid these hazards, as well as others, often near-invisible. Early on though, each of them had fallen twice. Fortunately, the soft snow had broken their falls and neither had sustained any injury.

With their poles and cleats pulling them along, traveling up-hill was really no harder than walking on a flat surface. And it was only a minor inconvenience to have to zig-zag across the street every now and then in order to avoid occasional mountains of shoveled snow. These had been created by teams of entrepreneurial children and immigrants, thankful for the handsome contracts they'd been able to secure to dig out the more well-to-do business-owners.

Their plan was to follow Broadway up to 42nd Street, take 42nd northwest over to Tenth Avenue, and then, finally, Tenth up to 48th. Will said that this would be the shortest way, about one-and-four-tenths miles door-to-door.

By now the wind had abated enough to allow for periods when they could actually engage in a reasonable semblance of a conversation. One of the topics they talked about, incredibly, was the history of their sexual experience, something they'd intended to discuss the previous night, but fell off to sleep before they'd had the chance. Normally, in this day and age, it would have been downright *unthinkable* for an unmarried man and woman, after being acquainted less than twenty-four hours, to enter into a discussion of this nature. Of course, their situation was anything but "normal."

May had just confided that her virginity was still intact. She said she'd had the occasion to go out walking with any number of gentlemen, but most of her escorts had not been very mature, and nothing much worth mentioning had ever developed with any of them. Other than some moderately heavy "petting" in one or perhaps two instances, she'd never come close to having sexual relations with anyone. Having said all that, though, she did make it abundantly clear to Will that she was now quite happily looking forward to having him be "the one."

Will smiled in response, and said he was impressed with her frankness and candor in discussing a subject which, despite these modern times, was universally considered "too delicate" for young ladies. He then went on to confess that although it had been awhile since he'd technically been a "virgin," he was surely no Lothario, either. He and Kira had been keeping company for some time now and, as she had been brought up a strict Catholic, any type of physical intimacy between them before marriage was simply not in the cards. He had, however, had an intermittent courtship of sorts with a "free-spirited" young lady while attending Yale College, during the course of which they had engaged in a form of brief, unceremonious sexual congress a grand total of three times. That, he told her, was the full extent of his experience to date.

May nodded, smiling broadly. She could tell from Will's bright, avid expression that he, too, was looking forward – and most eagerly – to exploring this wondrous world which would be opening up for the two of them in the not-too-distant future.

CHAPTER 54

12:10 PM

As they approached her boardinghouse, May and Will were grati-fied to see that the entry-way appeared to be far more accessible than many they had passed along the way. They were able to make their way inside after only about fifteen minutes of digging. May could tell that Will was moved by the ecstatic welcome she received from her room-mates, all of whom expressed great relief upon finding out that she was alive and well. They said that she was the last of their close-knit group of eight to be safely accounted for.

May made the round of introductions, careful to omit any mention of Will's employ with the Signal Service and his remarkable forecasting acumen (his uniform, oddly enough, elicited no ques-tions). She knew that if the subject did arise, the two of them might never get away to continue on their journey. She gave them a some-what watered-down rendition of how they had met, leaving out the part about their whirl-wind relationship since then; mentioning it would have been superfluous, anyway. Their feelings for each other were so palpable they filled to overflowing whatever space the two of them happened to occupy at any given moment.

When May announced they had to be leaving again, a mere twen-ty-five minutes after they'd arrived, her room-mates were visibly surprised and disappointed. She apologized for the brevity of their stay, explaining that they had to make it all the way over to Brooklyn to check in on Mrs. D before it got dark. And they first had to stop back at the Grand for a much-needed hot meal and to make their final good-byes to the good folks awaiting them there.

Following an intensive round of warm hugs and good wishes, May and Will descended the outside steps, reattached their trusty snow-shoes, and retrieved their walking poles from the drift into which they'd been deeply stuck for safe-keeping. May suggested that on the return trip they might try taking Tenth all the way down to 31st, and then 31st straight across to the hotel. While acknowledging this route would be a little longer, she said it would be more of an adventure, as it would take them past places they hadn't yet seen. When Will said he thought that was a "grand" idea, smiling a little smugly at his clever play on words, May rewarded him with an exaggerated eye roll and a quick shake of her head.

It had only taken them an hour to get to May's boardinghouse from the Grand. Even with the nominal increase in distance on the return trip, Will said he thought they would probably make it back in even less time, as they would have the wind at their back for most of the way. He said that would make all the difference.

The two recently inaugurated snowshoeing virtuosos glided effortlessly along the snow's rigid crust, climbing large drifts and experiencing the exhilarating reward of speeding down the other side. By now, they knew precisely how fast they could go without losing their balance and landing upside down in a drift, legs flailing skyward.

When they went down the back-side of a snow-drift, they discovered that by shifting their weight back and laterally ever-so-slightly, they could dig in their cleats and alter their trajectory to more of a cross-drift direction. In this way, they could control their speed, extend the distance they could travel with the least amount of effort, and conserve their much-needed energy.

There was one discovery they'd both made the hard way. Each of their earlier falls had occurred while traveling over those areas where wind-whipped powder had somehow piled up on the snow's more reflective icy crust. If they did not take great care in spotting and avoiding these infrequent powdery patches, especially when moving fast, the result could be a nasty fall. At this point, with all standard forms of transportation down for the immediate future, even the slightest injury could pose a serious threat.

Meanwhile, the snow had become even more sporadic. The clouds off to the west now showed a few thin patches which, had they been more directly overhead, would have permitted a most welcome glimpse of dim, filtered sunlight. Although it was generally apparent that the storm was indeed winding down, the persistent strong winds and frigid temperatures meant the danger it posed was still far from over.

Charley knew that the stalwart Captain of the Charles H. Marshall would have been hard-pressed, in that moment, to determine which was the greatest hazard still threatening his storm-battered vessel. The little boat, greatly weighed down by the ice which continued to encrust every square inch of her surface, rode perilously low in the roiling water. The foresail had frozen so solidly it could no longer be set; in its stead, the crew had ingeniously bent and set the much smaller storm try-sail, enabling them to maintain at least some control of their craft. And the monster waves kept coming.

Despite the critical condition of the boat and the relentless onslaught of snow and wind, the men erupted in a great cheer, with one voice, when Charley gave a loud shout and pointed excitedly towards the western horizon. The sky there was brighter than it had been at anytime since they'd left port – more than forty-eight hours earlier. As excited as they were, however, they knew it would be many more grueling hours before a "coast is clear" proclamation could be made.

All that not-withstanding, Charley raised his eyes to the Heavens and mouthed the words, "Thank-you, Lord," before bowing his head and clasping his semi-frozen hands fervently in a silent moment of deep and profound gratitude.

CHAPTER 55

1:30 PM

The kitchen was now fresh out of most of the selections offered on the Grand Hotel's extensive menu, having served dinner and breakfast to more than quadruple the number of guests normally expected on an early weekday in March. Actually, it was surprising there was any food left at all, as there had been no deliveries of any type since Saturday. Of course, nothing moved on Sundays, storm or no storm.

But ever since he'd invested in a newfangled ammonia-type commercial freezer nearly a year ago, James Landen had insisted that his master chef maintain an ample supply of frozen, premium quality delicacies. These spanned a wide variety of seafood, meats, and fowl, stocked in anticipation of what he foresaw as unexpected and "special" occasions. Certainly a "post-blizzard" luncheon for his guests of honor, William Augustus Roebling and May Morrow, along with his friend and preferred guest, Kevin Patrick McCormack, and his newly dubbed "Employee of the Storm," Albert Washington, qualified as a special occasion. And one completely unexpected, at that.

For to-day's main course, Landen had proudly selected wild pheasant with sausage stuffing. This, he said, would provide plenty of needed protein for his hard-working snowshoeing travelers. Rounding out the meal was a delicious, wild-rice medley and Succotash Salad – a Grand Hotel specialty. In addition to the baby lima beans and young corn kernels, it included finely chopped onion, cherry tomatoes, a splash of lemon juice, fresh basil, feta cheese, and a sprinkling of black pepper. Unfortunately, the kitchen was completely out of dessert.

Landen did not forget the hot toddies that Will had mentioned in parting, just before he and May set out on the first leg of their journey to check in with her room-mates. The Roebling party of five was now well into their second round of these liberating libations, with Will and May in definitive – and vociferous – agreement that their delicious warmth really "hit the spot." Moreover, they both said that the sweet and satisfying drinks were a delightful and more-than-adequate substitute for any dessert. They were all having quite the time, with May regaling her enthralled audience with an account of just how she and Will had come to meet. Landen, who wanted the joyful "reunion" to never end, was thrilled beyond measure that he'd been afforded the unusual opportunity of hearing the story told from each participant's unique perspective.

Will and May could have stayed there quite happily for the remainder of the day, reveling in the camaraderie of such good company. It was with some reluctance, then, that Will announced it was absolutely imperative they get back to Brooklyn before darkness set in, as traveling at night would be far too dangerous. Besides, Will said, by now his sweet landlady must be worried sick that he hadn't made it home yet. And, he couldn't resist adding, he was really looking forward to how pleasantly surprised and delighted she would be to meet his wonderful, brand-new sweetheart!

What followed was another round of warm hugs and hearty handshakes, along with a solemn promise to meet up for a more formal reunion sometime in the not-too-distant future. After which the intrepid adventurers bundled themselves up yet again and sallied forth, "once more unto the breach" – the wild, white wilderness.

Although one-thirty would hardly qualify as late afternoon by anyone's standard, Patrolman O'Malley rationalized that he might as well stop in at the hospital to check on Kira's progress now, as he "just happened to be in the area." His joy at the prospect of once again seeing his "Nurse Nancy" had not dimmed in the slightest over the past twenty-two hours.

But as he arrived at Bellevue's emergency-room entrance, his heart sank. He could scarcely believe how crowded the waiting room had become since yesterday. New cases were coming through the door every few minutes, even though he could see that the one-horse ambulance services had yet to be restored. A quick visual survey of the patients, many of whom were still standing in line awaiting triage screening, made it clear that frost-bite or some other cold-related malady was the most common reason for seeking treatment. But there were any number of other significant complaints as well: broken bones from falling, pneumonia, severe and debilitating ear aches, and what appeared to be several fractured skulls.

Although Jonathan had certainly suspected yesterday that emergency-room visits would spike just as soon as travel became remotely possible, he hadn't anticipated this deluge. Fortunately for the already over-worked Nurse Petersen, two more nurses had managed to make it in, as had several other doctors and service personnel. Even so, it was obvious that the staff on-hand was insufficient to deal effectively with the dramatic increase in the number of patients.

Nancy's demanding work-load, however, did not keep her from bestowing upon Jon a bright welcoming smile the moment she laid eyes on him. She quickly gave him an affectionate kiss on the cheek, confirmation to Jon of her bold declaration that she was "ever-so-pleased" to be seeing him again – and so soon. Drawing on his years of experience serving on the police force, he promptly asked how he could be of assistance. She immediately put him to work securing more cots from the fourth floor. Happy to be able to help and equally pleased to be out of the bitter cold, he figured he might have the added, and delightful, benefit of stealing a few moments alone with her at some point along the way.

Jon thought Nancy "sure looked mighty fine," even better than he'd remembered. When he told her so, she smiled appreciatively, confessing she had managed to get only about four hours sleep in the past forty or so. She said that she'd been up since dawn, when her boss had rousted her from a deep sleep in the nurses' lounge.

Of course, Nancy remembered that Jon had said he'd be stopping by this afternoon, although she had expected him a bit later. She was thankful she'd had the opportunity to "freshen herself up" a couple of hours earlier, taking full advantage of the toiletries, cosmetics, and change of clothes she wisely kept in her locker for emergencies.

After working non-stop for some time, Nancy and Jon finally got a short breather. Nancy, very much against hospital regulations, quickly ushered him into the nurses' lounge for a chat and a bit of privacy. Settled comfortably on the leather divan, she first told him that, unfortunately, the patient he'd brought in yesterday, Kira Smith, was not responding too well to treatment. Dr. Sanders said he'd be keeping her for observation, at least for a few more days. Jon thanked her for the update, saying how comforting it was to know she was getting the best care possible.

Before Nancy could say anything more, Jon, who had surreptitiously confirmed they were out of sight of any prying eyes – at least for the moment – nonchalantly leaned over and kissed her squarely on the lips. While certainly surprised by this unexpected overture, the self-contained young nurse did not miss a beat. She stood up, bent over, and, grabbing both his hands, pulled him up into a very close embrace. The kiss she gave him in return left precious little doubt as to the nature of her true feelings.

They stood there, lost in each other for a very long moment, before Nancy broke away gently, saying she really needed to get back to her patients. Jon, deeply moved by Nancy's impassioned response, immediately turned a bright, beet red; his physiological reaction to her was still embarrassingly apparent. Saying nothing, but with eyes flashing wickedly, she cast him a broad smile and gave his cheek a quick peck before turning to leave the room.

It did not matter one whit to him that he was already long overdue back at the station-house, or that it would take nearly an hour's walk to get there. He simply could not leave the hospital before finding out where the delightfully adorable young Nancy lived and arranging their next rendez-vous – preferably a romantic, candle-lit dinner at a suitably posh local restaurant.

Even though Patrolman O'Malley was a sane, sensible man nearing thirty years of age, he suddenly felt just like a little kid again, one eagerly looking forward to a birthday or Christmas celebration and barely able to contain his excitement.

May God and all the Saints preserve us – isn't she just something! And to think we have this great, monstrous storm to thank for our marvelous good fortune.

CHAPTER 56

2:45 PM

T he temperature had barely budged all afternoon, briefly climbing to what would be the absurd high for the day of eleven degrees above zero. The cloud cover, which earlier had shown signs of dissipating, had thickened once more to an impenetrable whitish-gray mass. The snow had also started up again, alternating between quite light and, occasionally, moderate. None-the-less, Will and May's trip down Broadway since bidding a fond farewell to their new friends at the Grand Hotel had been a marvelous and exhilarating experience. The wind, which blew generally perpendicular to their path, had continued to slowly decrease in force, allowing them a modicum of opportunity for renewed social intercourse as they snowshoed along.

In a very easy and natural manner, they talked quite a bit about Kira. May shared Will's genuine concern for her well-being, especially after hearing of his fruitless visit to her suite yesterday, just before the "chance" encounter at the Grand which altered their lives forever. As for his and Kira's relationship, he offered, once again, that it was obviously all over between them.

"I mean, really," he said, "how can I possibly be in love with two women at once? Or, better said, now that I know how it feels to truly *be* in love, what power, on earth or in Heaven, could ever move me to settle for anything less?"

May's sparkling eyes lit up as she gave him the warmest of smiles. She casually blew him a kiss off her gloved hand, signifying her complete agreement.

Some of the kindly folks they passed along the way simply stared at them in flabbergasted awe, while others outright cheered them on as they continued their effortless glide across the icy, tundra-like surface. By this point, they were both reveling in the fact that they could now navigate the large snow-drifts as naturally as if they were native-born Aleuts.

As they were drawing near the entryway to the Bridge, May was stunned by the remarkable scene which greeted them down below, on the East River. A flurry of clamorous activity spread out before them, stretching well into the expanse normally reserved for water-craft only.

"My God, Will, do you see what I see?"

They coasted to a dead-stop. "Yes, I do, and I can honestly say I've never before seen anything quite like this."

"Why, it's fantastic – just look at all of those people!," May exclaimed, excitedly.

The river was frozen-solid, and hundreds of people were frolicking joyfully out on the ice. For May, the setting had a carnival atmosphere, juxtaposed in stark ironic contrast with the life-threatening danger of what had been, for so many, a violently destructive natural calamity. Dogs chasing sticks, kids playing ice hockey, couples ice-skating arm-in-arm, and people running and sliding in friendly competition to see who could propel themselves furthest across the smooth surface. She could even make out several horses over on the Brooklyn side of the frozen river, though how on earth they had ever managed to climb down the slippery banks with all four legs intact, she couldn't even begin to imagine.

Astonishingly, they noticed several ragged newsboys out on the ice hawking their papers. These were the first editions to carry any news of the great blizzard, although it would be days before anything resembling normal distribution would be reestablished. A kindly woman, who ran a small shop nearby, had wrapped their heads in cotton batting for warmth, giving them the oddly compelling appearance of battle-wounded soldiers.

Smiling delightedly, May looked down silently on the jubilant throng for a minute or two, utterly charmed by their creativity and exuberant playfulness. She heaved a small sigh of satisfaction, amazed at this wondrous, perfect manifestation of the power and indomitability of the human spirit.

Aglow, she turned to look at Will, but was immediately jarred by the intense expression she saw on his face; it evinced the exact antithesis of how she was feeling at the moment.

"Oh, Lord, help us – I was afraid something like this would happen," he volunteered resignedly, shaking his head slowly, side-to-side.

May's exhilaration evaporated instantly. "What are you talking about, Will? You were afraid that something like *what* would happen?"

"Well, May, I have read about this phenomenon, and it's something which occurs very rarely, maybe only about six- or seven-times-per-century. Once, I believe it was back in 'fifty-seven, there was a strikingly similar situation in this very same location during a wicked cold spell. Thousands of people had made their way out onto the ice to gambol and play, just like they're doing right now. Less than an hour later, all of the ice was simply gone. Sadly, a lot of those poor people ended up drowning that day. I don't know how many, but I do know this: as charming as it appears to be on the surface, what we're looking at, right here and now, is an extraordinarily dangerous situation."

May was stunned.

She stared at him, mouth agape, incapable of uttering a single word. Will hurried to continue, obviously aware of the fact that he had left her with many more questions than answers.

"You see, every so often, when conditions are just right, although I'm not sure precisely what those conditions are," he admitted, "very large chunks of ice in the Hudson River become dislodged and travel down-stream till they enter the New York Harbor, like a collection of miniature icebergs.

"Now bear in mind, the East River is actually not a river at all. Technically, it's a tidal strait, with Manhattan on one side and Long Island on the other. Anyway, these huge chunks of ice circle around Manhattan and move up the East River with the flood, or incoming, tide. Then, when they reach the narrowest point in the river, which is right about here where the Brooklyn Bridge is, they coalesce, or stick together. Incidentally, the river's minimal width at this particular location is a major reason it was selected as the site for the Bridge in the first place.

"Well, that certainly makes a great deal of sense . . ."

"Yes, of course. Well, when the air is extremely cold, like now, the salt-water between the ice chunks and the shoreline freezes, and you see what happens," he said, extending his arm in the direction of the people below. "The result is a solid sheet of ice, very strong and capable of supporting a lot of weight, extending clear across the river."

"Then why will it suddenly disappear? That *is* what you are saying, Will, isn't it?" May was now becoming quite agitated.

"Yes, that's it exactly. Allow me to explain. When ebb tide occurs, the resistance, or better said the forcing, which holds the ice-sheet in place, will suddenly cease to exist. The entire mass will then begin to migrate, if you will, down-stream towards the Harbor and eventually out to sea. Further, because salt-water melts much more readily than fresh-water, the ice-sheet will quickly disintegrate into the discrete chunks it started out as."

May just stared blankly at him.

"As long as the tide is still coming in," he continued, "there's no problem. But as soon as the ebb tide begins, the ice will immediately dislodge and all these people will have only a very narrow window in which to jump to shore and safety."

May's eyes flew open wide as her jaw dropped. She only now began to comprehend the full import of what he was saying. "Oh, my goodness!," she exclaimed.

"Once that happens," Will added, "I would guess that it will only take ten, maybe fifteen, minutes before this 'skating pond' they're enjoying so much is reduced to nothing more than scores of miniature icebergs, floating resolutely out to sea."

"Oh, my *God,* Will!"

"I'm not sure about the actual time of high tide to-day, but I can tell you, it's going to be pretty soon . . . maybe any minute now."

"Will," she now screamed. "Will, you . . . you have to *do* something! You must go down there and warn them. You *have* to! Even if they won't listen, you have to try. I will help you. And look over there! There are young children out on the ice! Will, those are *children* down there!"

"You're right, May, of course! Let's hurry and get down there, and we'll do what we can."

Will and May stood by the side of the frozen East River just up-stream of the Bridge, their make-shift snowshoes in hand, walking poles tucked under their arms. Several teen-aged boys and girls, standing just a few feet from the shoreline, took note of their arrival by gaily waving their hands and arms, enticing them to come play on the ice. Will immediately realized that even if he shouted at the top of his lungs, he would not be able to make himself heard over the jubilant shouts of the crowd and continuing din of the wind. His only chance at communicating his message effectively would be with those to whom he could manage to draw quite near.

Directing May to spread the word to as many as she could from the relative safety of the riverbank, Will went out a short distance onto the ice, calmly warning as many people as he could reach, while moving as rapidly as possible down-stream. He roughly followed the shoreline, always staying close enough to solid land that he could quickly get back to it the instant the ice showed the first signs of giving way. May matched his pace while on firm ground, staying abreast of him and admonishing those revelers still on the shore to remain where they were and to signal to any of their companions out on the ice to come back to shore, as well. Together, they had convinced several dozen people to move to safety, and had recruited many of them to aid in spreading the word, as much as possible, to those still in danger.

Will and May hadn't traveled more than two-hundred feet of shoreline when, all of a sudden, they and everyone else on or near the river heard a thunderous, frightening, grinding noise and felt a violent vibration. The ice-sheet had indeed become dislodged, precisely as Will had predicted it would. Except for a brave yet foolhardy few, everyone immediately set course for the nearest shore. Some were walking, but most were attempting to run, slipping and sliding across the ice in the process.

The riverbank was steep and craggy in most places along the Manhattan side. Terror spread through those confronted by a stretch of unnavigable shoreline when the mass exodus began. The difficulty of climbing onto the ice-coated incline rapidly resulted in a human log-jam, which kept spilling back onto the swiftly disintegrating ice.

Panic quickly ensued.

Many of the crowd stretched along the riverbank, May included, were reaching out to help pull the frightened people from the ice onto safe ground. Several patrolmen had made their way down to join the rescue effort as well.

Will had little difficulty in getting to shore, as he had been very close to it, by design, when the ice-sheet dislodged. But even he was in awe of how rapidly the scene had changed from a delightful romp full of unbridled joy and excitement to the sheer terror and pandemonium of a frantic fight for survival. The ice-sheet had completely disintegrated within a mere twelve minutes, save for a collection of individual "cakes" flowing gently, but inexorably, towards the sea. The surface of these mini-icebergs was generally less than five feet on a side, except for a huge one in the middle of the river which was, perhaps, about two-hundred feet across.

Miraculously, nearly everyone had made it safely to land, with at least a small measure of credit going to Will and May for their dogged determination to sound the warning to as many people as they could. By the time the last wave of stragglers made it to shore, however, many were standing waist-deep in the freezing water, and had to be rushed somewhere warm to prevent hypothermia.

Suddenly, gasps of horror rose up from the crowd as all eyes focused on eight helpless souls adrift atop three small ice-cakes, roughly fifty feet from shore. They flailed their arms wildly and screamed for help, their cries greatly muffled by the strong westerly winds. By now, a fairly large police presence had amassed along the shoreline, but there was precious little these gallant servants of the public could do in that moment. They joined the equally impotent crowd, presently at least eight-hundred strong, in following the progress of the hapless castaways down-stream.

Will and May stood for a moment on the shoreline and watched with concern as the populated ice-cakes drifted out of sight. Then, as they had no interest in joining the spectator promenade, they climbed their way back up to the road, reattached their snowshoes, and continued on towards the Bridge entrance. They now felt a renewed sense of urgency to get to Mrs. D's just as fast as they possibly could.

Will would later read in a newspaper article that a rookie patrolman, in a quick-witted and laudatory display of forethought, had swiftly alerted the local Coast Guard at the first sign of trouble. Thankfully, their expeditious launching of a small fleet of rowboats resulted in the eventual rescue of all the stranded victims.

CHAPTER 57

3:50 PM

Will was gratified to discover his presumption had been correct: the Brooklyn Bridge's pedestrian walk-way was once again open for business. Actually, walking across was the only option, as all other modes of transport were still suspended. The snow had been cleared down to the surface over most of the path, so Will and May again removed their snowshoes, then Will examined them closely for the first time since leaving their luncheon at the Grand. He was pleased to see that they had held up remarkably well, and shared as much with May.

"You know, Will," May kidded him gently, "perhaps you should look into getting a patent for these miniature marvels of transportation." Will gave her a big grin and a shrug, saying – without saying – hey, you never know; stranger things have been known to happen.

They both agreed it felt pretty durn good to be walking on solid ground again, as the hours of snowshoeing had left their ankles feeling mighty sore. It was interesting, May pointed out, that neither of them had felt any of this ankle pain during the mass frenzy down by the river. Will agreed, citing the "hyper-vigilance of such an emotionally charged situation" as the likely reason.

After flashing him a quick quizzical look, with maybe just the tiniest bit of an eye roll, May tilted her head at him and nodded, smiling. "Well stated, Mr. Roebling. Very well stated, indeed. Should you ever happen to lose your position with the Signal Service, it wouldn't surprise me at all to hear that the New York Times itself had come a knockin' at your door." Will laughed appreciatively at her good-natured ribbing.

As they neared the mid-point of the Bridge, Will was able to see that the lanes for the horse-drawn vehicles were now about half-way cleared of snow. Two shoveling crews, having started at opposite ends, were continuing their steady march towards the middle. At the rate they were progressing, he calculated it would be around midnight before the lanes would be completely clear and vehicular travel could resume. His best guess was that the el would be operational sometime in the wee hours of the morning, although he couldn't be quite so sure about that, as there were additional factors to be considered.

Because the pedestrian lane was on the north side of the Bridge, precluding any view of the river to the south, Will was unable to discern any evidence of the earlier excitement – including the lingering crowd of spectators. In his mind's eye, though, Will could still see those poor souls stranded out on the ice-floes, waving wildly in their desperation. He prayed that a rescue operation had been successfully executed.

Even though it was still very windy and bitterly cold, Will and May were able to maintain a relative level of comfort by keeping up a brisk pace. They were also fortunate to have the added advantage of the wind being squarely at their backs, helping to propel them forward. There were very few people on the Bridge, and nearly all of them were headed in the same direction they were. Will said he would be willing to bet that these were some of the same folks he had crossed the Bridge with, *en masse,* early yesterday morning. But what he could not understand was how in the world they thought they were going to be able to get back to their homes once they reached the other side, without the locomotive advantage afforded by his and May's snowshoes. He was confident that all roads in residential Brooklyn would still be snowbound and impassable, and would remain that way for quite some time. Ultimately, he reasoned that they must be desperate for some kind of reassurance about their loved ones, and were therefore willing to risk everything to find out if they were safe and well.

Bearing witness to such grim determination in the face of nearly overwhelming odds was deeply distressing to the tender-hearted young couple. They each breathed a silent prayer that their fellow travelers would be safe on the journey home.

As they approached Sands, Will could scarcely believe his eyes. He'd known before-hand that the persistent wind whipping its way across the East River would combine with the terrain in this part of Brooklyn to produce some extraordinary snow depths. But what he was looking at now was absolutely preposterous, and way beyond even his wildest imagining. Vast portions of the once-familiar landscape of his neighborhood had been transformed into a nearly unrecognizable ocean of white.

"May, look over there, quick. Do you see those twigs sticking up through the snow?," he began, barely able to contain his excitement. They were gliding down a gentle snow-drift which extended as far as the eye could see.

"Yes, I can see them..."

"Well, my sweet love, brace yourself. You are never going to believe what I'm about to tell you. What you are looking at there is the very top of a tree that is not less than sixty feet tall!"

"My God, Will, you can't be serious – that's just not possible."

"Never-the-less, it's the truth, dearest. And that, right over there, is the eave of a house. Can you see the chimney sticking up?"

"Oh, my dear God! I'm absolutely speechless."

Fortunately, there wasn't nearly that much snow in most other places they could observe from their vantage point. In fact, just as in Manhattan, there were large expanses which were nearly barren, enabling Will to easily pick out some important landmarks, particularly the cross-streets of Washington and Adams up ahead.

~ 410 ~

As they drew closer to Mrs. Potts' and Mrs. D's houses, Will could see that the snow-drifts had reached clear up to the second-floor windows on the east- and south-facing sides. The depth of the snow in the front of the houses was much less though, so the doors could be accessed with only a modicum of digging. Quite a bit more than at May's, yes – but still a good measure less than what would have been required at Kira's. They were truly blessed, indeed. It was plain to see that not everyone had been so lucky, however. Many would have to wait days, maybe even a week, before they would get dug out.

"I'd prefer we check in on Mrs. Potts first," Will said, gliding to a stop. He had already told May all about Charley's insistence on shipping out early Sunday morning, despite Blanche's desperate plea that he stay at home with her. "I sure hope she's alright."

Surprised at the reserves of energy they still possessed, Will and May began digging through the snow piled up against Mrs. Potts' front door. They had made yet another useful discovery: the snowshoes, once removed, made splendid tools for burrowing through the drift. And while it was Will who'd had the inspiration to construct them in the first place, it was May's bright idea to put them to this important secondary use. What a terrific team they made!

In seemingly no time at all, the dynamic duo had cleared the way to Mrs. Potts' door.

Blanche sat on her favorite horsehair settee in the stillness of the parlour, quietly reading through some of her most beloved Bible verses to glean whatever comfort and solace they might provide. Suddenly, she thought she detected a faint, rhythmic sound coming from somewhere near the front of the house.

Good Heavens, could that possibly be someone knocking on the front door? Who on earth would want to be outside in all that wind and snow? Surely not Wilma, again!

"Hello?," she called out, tentatively, after making her way to the front hallway. "Is there someone out there?" Her right hand flew up involuntarily to clutch at her throat. All at once, she was seized by a paralyzing fear that, on the other side of the door, some type of official was waiting to deliver devastating news about her poor Charley.

"Mrs. Potts! Mrs. Potts, it's me, your neighbor – Will Roebling!" Will shouted loudly, hoping to be heard over the wind, which was still gusting to thirty-five or forty miles-per-hour.

"Land sakes, it's Will! Oh, my, let me get the door open for you – come in, please, do come in."

"Yes, thank-you, Mrs. Potts, but only for a few minutes. We've just this minute gotten back from Manhattan, and we haven't even been over to Mrs. D's yet. I wanted to check in on you first, you see. Is everything alright with you here?"

During this short exchange, Will and May had moved quickly from the porch into the front hall and pulled the door closed behind them, stomping their feet lightly and batting their arms to dislodge the snow which had taken up residence on their outer-garments.

"Well, yes … yes, it is, thank-you, but … ," she equivocated, eyeing May queerly.

Although Blanche had never met Kira in person, she knew from Wilma's detailed description of her that the young woman standing here now, whomever she might be, was, most certainly, *not* young Mr. Roebling's Kira Smith.

"Oh! Oh, my … ," Will finally managed to stammer, "where on earth are my manners? Please, do forgive me. And allow me to introduce Miss May Morrow. May, this is our dear friend and neighbor I've been telling you about – Mrs. Blanche Potts."

After exchanging polite "how-do-you-do's," both May and Blanche promptly turned and faced Will, almost as if on cue. May gazed up at him with twinkling eyes and a comically broad grin. Blanche's face, eyes opened wide and both brows raised high, sported a perplexed expression.

Will stood mute in stunned silence, thoughts roiling through his brain.

How on earth could a fellow as smart as me not have anticipated how awkward this would be and done something to prepare for it? I suppose I could blame it on the exigent circumstances surrounding the storm...

"Well, Mrs. Potts," he began, glad to notice that her expression had softened into a smile, "here we are." He grinned at her sheepishly. "I guess it's fair to say I have some explaining to do – wouldn't you agree?"

CHAPTER 58

By now, the first of the two bottles of fine French brandy Wilma had seen fit to buy two days before the storm, mostly as a surprise for Will, was nearly half-gone. Will lifted his etched-crystal glass high and proclaimed, "A toast for our marvelous hostess – here's to the one and only Mrs. D!"

Will and May were sitting quite close to each other on the cream-colored, carved mahogany Victorian love seat, holding hands. Wilma sat directly across from them on the matching settee chair, thoroughly delighted. The air was redolent with the delicious, intoxicating aroma of their dinner simmering on the stove. It wouldn't be long now before they'd all be enjoying it together.

"You are just so amazing," May said to Mrs. D, warmly and sincerely, while shaking her head slowly, side-to-side, in mock disbelief. "While it's true that Will's been filling my head with all kinds of wonderful things about you over the past twenty-four hours, I'm afraid I have a confession to make." She hesitated, glancing quickly over at Will. "I just couldn't help but feel he was ... well ... let's just say, 'stretching the truth,' maybe just a wee bit." She held out her right hand, thumb and forefinger poised about a half-inch apart, for emphasis.

Smiling as she turned back to Mrs. D, she continued, "I mean, after all, nobody could be *that* great, was what I thought. But now that I've met you? Well, now I can honestly say that his description of you was, in a word ... inadequate. You really are absolutely amazing!"

"Oh, pishposh and poppycock, child," Mrs. D replied kindly, deflecting in a mildly self-deprecating way. "I'm sure that's just the brandy talking now."

"Brandy or no, the truth is the truth – and I'm telling you right now that this is how I truly feel," she countered, with an emphatic nod of her head and a bright smile.

"Well . . . be that as it may, I must say that I simply could not be happier for you both. That the two of you found each other in the midst of all this 'meteorological madness' – that's what *I* call amazing. It was simply meant to be."

May paused a moment to acknowledge the import of what Mrs. D had just said. She then went on to recount, in hilarious detail, the story of poor Mrs. Potts' obvious, yet unfailingly polite, befuddlement when this strange young woman had waltzed right into her front hall without so much as a "howdy-do." And how Will had then scrambled six ways from Sunday to find the right words – well, let's face it, *any* words – to adequately explain their relationship. Mrs. D was laughing so heartily along with May that the two were bent over, clutching their stomachs, near tears. Will, the consummate good sport, happily joined them in their high-spirited revelry.

When their uproarious laughter had finally subsided to some mirthful grins, May, with more accolades in store for Mrs. D and bent on "making her case," took the conversation back to the first few minutes after they had arrived. She mentioned how striking it was to observe the effortlessness with which Will had introduced the two of them. In reality, May knew that Will didn't have to say anything at all. It was obvious to her that Mrs. D, with keen perceptiveness, had instantly grasped precisely what it was that the two of them had together – all the more remarkable, given they'd just met the day before.

May glanced over at Will, who remained silent. She could see that he was quite moved to hear his beloved landlady spoken of so glowingly. Interestingly, in that moment, the cat had Mrs. D's tongue as well.

Perhaps just a tad under the brandy's influence after all, May could not keep her eyes from welling up and, leaning forward to take Mrs. D's hands, began dreamily reminiscing. "As long as I live, I shall always remember the way your face looked when you came into the foyer. We had just walked into the house, with Will calling out your name. As soon as you saw the two of us standing there you stopped, looked at him, then over at me, then back to Will. And it was crystal clear from the look on your face, even then, that he didn't have to say a thing – you just knew! Somehow, you *knew!*"

Will remained mute, apparently feeling out of his element. May thought he had a point. The conversation was definitely starting to sound like one meant more for women than mixed company.

Mrs. D then broke the short, slightly awkward silence, her own eyes beginning to brim. "May – my sweet, sweet May. You are quite right about what you observed in that moment, my dear. Our Will didn't have to say a single thing."

By now, May and Will had each delivered to the rapt Mrs. D their own unique version of the extraordinary circumstance of their meeting, and the marvelous time they'd both enjoyed as guests of the Grand. She reveled in every aspect of their stories, especially May's account of "coming to" in a strange hotel room (thankfully safe and sound), finding Will's excellent epistle, making her way downstairs (after sprucing herself up a bit, of course), and getting to the lounge just in time to catch the tail-end of his spell-binding meteorological lecture.

They told her all about the snowshoes, and about Albert Washington, James Landen, and Pat McCormack. She had another good belly-laugh thinking about how discombobulated they all had become the moment that May joined them at the table and how time had stopped for Will. They recounted every delicious detail of the fabulous luncheon which had been thrown in their honor at the Grand, a mere four hours ago, on the way back from their brief excursion to May's boardinghouse to reassure her grateful room-mates that she was safe and well.

As generally impressed with Mrs. D as May already was, what she found perhaps most remarkable was the fact that even though they'd all been together for more than an hour-and-a-half by now, the lady had made absolutely no reference to Kira, either direct or implied. This, for May, was the essence of tact and grace, and behaviour she knew she'd be wise to emulate.

"May, dear – would you care to come give me a hand in the kitchen?"

Getting up immediately, she stooped to give Will a quick kiss on the lips. "Why, surely, Mrs. D – it would be my distinct pleasure."

Once they were alone together, out of Will's ear-shot, it was Mrs. D's turn to talk, and talk she did. "May, there's something I wanted to say to you, privately. It's clear to me that you are 'the one' for Will. Of course, I know you know that. It's just so obvious that the two of you are so completely happy. You both have that 'special glow' that I've never, ever seen in him before, that glow which simply cannot be kept hidden when one is so deeply in love. For me, that's the thing that was always missing, whenever he was with Kira. Of course he mentioned Kira to you . . ."

"Oh, yes, of course. He told me everything about their relationship, from beginning to end. And he made it a special point to mention how grateful he was to you, for your wise counsel and non-judgmental support throughout."

Mrs. D smiled. "I have absolutely no intention of speaking badly about her, mind you – not now, nor ever. As far as I'm concerned, she really is a lovely and charming young lady. The only point I'm making here is that Will never had that glow, at any time, when he was with her. But how on earth could I possibly have come right out and told him I knew she wasn't 'the one' for him? Especially given how 'unseasoned' he was in the ways of romance. I'm just so thrilled that he was able to find it out all on his own . . . well, with a little help from you – and God – of course. It makes me unimaginably happy that the two of you have found each other and are both smart enough to recognize the real thing when you see it. Regardless of how 'outre' the circumstances might be."

The two women hugged each other tightly, this time both shedding a tear or two.

"Is everything alright in here? I thought I heard – oh . . ." May and Mrs. D were still embracing as Will walked into the kitchen. Suddenly embarrassed, and at a loss for words for the umpteenth time to-day, he managed to mumble, "I guess it must be a woman thing," before swiftly retreating back to the relative safety of the living room.

"Dinn-ah is served," Mrs. D called out with some pomp and fanfare, bowing slightly from the waist and extending her arm towards the dining room with great flourish. As far as her "guests" were concerned, the announcement came not a moment too soon. Will and May were positively famished, despite the ample lunch they'd both enjoyed so recently at the Grand. They hurried in to sit down at the table, eager to dig into her scrumptious breaded pork chops, mashed potatoes, hot garlic bread, and steamed carrots. Will and May agreed, most enthusiastically, that Mrs. D's lovingly prepared meal really hit the proverbial spot.

Mid-way through dinner, the conversation naturally segued back to the terrible plight of poor Blanche and Charley. It was in that moment that May received another one of her nudges – once again, a particularly strong one. After a brief hesitation, she decided to speak up. "Mrs. D," she began, somewhat tentatively, "we talked a little while ago about religion, and I told you about my . . . well, let us say, my spiritual belief system."

"Why, yes. As I recall, that was a part of our discussion I found particularly fascinating."

"Do you remember my mentioning what I refer to as the 'nudges' I sometimes receive?"

"Of course, and I remember saying that I thought they were some type of clairvoyance."

"Yes, that's right . . ." Again, May was hesitant. "Well . . . over the years, I've come to discover that it's terribly important for me to weigh things out *very carefully* whenever I have a nudge which might be about – or have an effect on – someone else. Whether or not I should say anything to them, that is. Actually, I usually end up saying nothing, having found that this is generally the best, or at any rate the safest, course of action. I make it a rule to avoid interfering, at all cost. I feel that whatever God's plan is, well, that's what it is. In other words, it's not for me to put in my two pennies' worth."

"Well . . . alright then . . ." May could see that both Mrs. D and Will were struggling to follow her train of thought, and that neither had any idea where she was headed with this particular conversation.

"Yes, well, you see . . . the few times when I did . . . speak up, that is, about a message that concerned someone else, I stopped receiving any 'nudges' at all for weeks on end. I took that as a pretty clear sign I was to mind my own beeswax. Anyway, in spite of all that, what I'm trying to say right now is, I'm pretty sure that, in this case, saying something *would* be the right thing to do. It would *not* be interfering, and could actually be mighty helpful."

Will and Mrs. D briefly exchanged puzzled glances.

"I know, I know. Please forgive the inexcusably extensive preamble. I'll hurry up now and get to the point. I just this minute received the strongest nudge about your Mr. Potts, telling me quite clearly that, against all odds, he *has* survived his ordeal at sea – albeit somewhat the worse for wear. He'll be showing up at home sometime to-morrow. Thursday, the latest."

Will and Mrs. D let out a great cheer, much to May's surprise, and relief. Whether it was a flat-out belief in her precognitive abilities, a strong desire to believe in them, or merely a recognition that there was no harm to be found, for the moment at least, in embracing such a heart-warming prediction, Will and Mrs. D were both clearly thrilled to hear about May's latest nudge.

After a brief logistical discussion, they all agreed that despite it already having gotten dark out, they should go tell Blanche immediately after dinner. Will and Mrs. D each expressed their certainty that this was the correct course of action – especially given that they knew she still held out at least some hope for the miracle of Charley's safe return.

The snowshoeing proficiency he and May had managed to attain in only a single day – granted, a highly remarkable one – gave Will a profound new level of confidence. He was sure that as long as they made their way slowly and carefully, they'd have no trouble traveling the short distance to Blanche's in the near-pitch-black. His plan was, first, for May to stay back while he escorted Mrs. D, who would use May's snowshoes and poles. Once she was safely settled in, Will would carry the snowshoes and poles back to May, and the two of them would follow together. He had no trouble convincing Mrs. D she'd be quite safe, especially with him to lean on as her guide.

Mrs. D did make the wise suggestion they hold off on drinking anymore brandy till they were all back home safe and sound, in for the night, snug and secure. Will and May emphatically agreed. Besides, they said, it was high-time they started to pace themselves. It was still on the early side of the evening, and their celebration would surely be lasting well into the night.

"Blanche?" they called out together, knocking loudly. "Blanche, it's Wilma and Will! We've come for a visit." They didn't have long to wait for the door to open.

CHAPTER 59

9:15 PM

By applying the same logistical procedure with the snowshoes, only this time in reverse, the trio made it back from Blanche's house safely and without incident. Although they had stayed much longer than originally planned, it had proven to be the right decision to go through all the trouble of getting over to Blanche's to share May's nudge with her. Hopefully, the poor woman would finally be able to get some desperately needed sleep to-night, her mind having been put at ease, at least to some degree.

Blanche had nearly fainted when Will and Wilma had knocked on her front door some ninety minutes earlier. It was one thing for Will to have arrived with May shortly before dark, both wearing the snowshoes he had fabricated to help them get around the City. It was quite another to see Will standing outside in the savage storm once again, but this time with *Wilma* in tow, also on snowshoes. And in total darkness, no less!

Wilma? Hell's bells – is that Wilma? What in Sam Hill is she doing out there? Has she lost her mind? She'll be sixty-years-old the end of this month!!

Blanche simply could not fathom how she had had the where-withal to navigate the distance separating their houses in the pitch black – with or without Will's assistance. After getting over her initial shock, though, she was able to understand how her dear friend, after a little instruction, had found that using the snowshoes turned out to be far easier than she'd originally thought.

Once Wilma was comfortably settled in, Will re-bundled himself up and, May's snowshoes and poles in hand, went back out into the night to retrieve young Ms. Morrow.

Blanche and Wilma were laughing heartily when Will had returned with May some minutes later. They took off their snowshoes and other outer-wear, joined the elders around the kitchen table, and gratefully enjoyed a much-welcomed round of piping hot tea which had been prepared for them. Just before they'd arrived, Blanche, who by now had fully returned to her reliably hospitable self, had proudly proclaimed the name she'd coined to describe the three of them: the tired traveling triumvirate. Realizing that Will and May had not been in earshot when she'd made her proclamation, and were therefore left wondering just what was so funny, Blanche was delighted to repeat her clever alliterative phrase. Will and May then happily joined in the mirth.

Blanche had laughingly commented that it truly must have been a sight to behold, watching her friend make her way on the snowshoes. Wilma reiterated that it hadn't been all that difficult, especially as she'd had the advantage of Will's more-than-capable assistance, not to mention hard-won expertise. But Blanche was not about to let go so easily of what she'd obviously perceived as an hilarious image. She proceeded to pantomime how she imagined Wilma must have looked on the snowshoes, in the dark, with the wind blowing all around her. Blanche's laughter was irresistibly contagious, especially given the circumstances, and even Wilma managed a good laugh at how comical she'd been made out to appear.

It was Wilma who had finally, and with great tact, broached the subject of the real reason for their visit. After giving Blanche a brief, general introduction to the topic at hand, she requested that May tell her the story about the powerful nudge she'd gotten yesterday morning, her subsequent decision to leave the safe confines of her office because of it – even though the timing could not have been worse, given the raging blizzard – and all that had ensued since.

May complied readily, beginning with describing her ability to "know" certain things, by way of messages, or "nudges," as she called them, which she received from Divine Spirit. She offered a few general examples, then progressed to the point where she had left the office yesterday at the height of the storm. Fascinated, Blanche interrupted her discussion along the way by asking a number of pertinent questions, which May was only too happy to answer. In fact, Blanche had become so engrossed in May's recounting of her adventure in the blizzard and her life-and-death struggle to get back home, she naturally thought that sharing it was the main reason for their visit.

But she was enlightened soon enough. Only a few brief minutes later, May expertly segued her account into the revelation she'd had about Mr. Potts earlier in the evening. Blanche, both eyes now flown wide-open, realized instantly that this was the *real* reason they had come over. The audience of three barely breathed, collectively hanging on May's every word as she spared no detail in describing the clear message she'd received only an hour ago.

Tears were streaming uncontrollably down Blanche's face by the time May had finished. She had no words to express her gratitude, or how profoundly moved she was by the fact that they had risked so much by coming over in the dark, just so May could give her this comforting bit of solace about her Charley. Instead, she expressed her thanks by giving the young woman a giant hug and a kiss on each cheek. Blanche confessed that as bad as she knew the storm must have been for him and his ship-mates, she had, somehow, never completely lost hope that he'd survive. May's "nudge," she declared, had now given her the strength she needed to continue to believe in the miracle of his return.

Safely back at Mrs. D's now, having had some time to think it through, Will concluded that he too had total confidence in May's prognostication concerning Charley. To be sure, it defied all logic and common sense, especially to a scientific mind like his. But as he, himself, had been possessed of a similar ability – albeit more during his childhood years and in a much narrower domain – accepting it became considerably easier. Besides, May's astounding experience yesterday certainly lent great credence to the existence of her amazing gift, however uncanny it might seem to be at first blush.

Mrs. D came into the kitchen where Will and May were seated and poured out a generous shot of brandy for the three of them. Apparently, the time had come to get back to their celebrating. "You know, it was actually kind of fun, using those snowshoes," she admitted. "That must have been some unique and exciting experience for you young people, cavorting all around Manhattan earlier to-day."

"Oh, that it was – it certainly was," they answered, practically in unison.

Laughing, they all raised their glasses. "To adventure!," Will called out, robustly. May and Mrs. D echoed his sentiment, and the three drank heartily.

After they had finished off their brandy, Will suddenly remembered that he and May had forgotten to tell Mrs. D about the most extraordinary event they'd experienced on the ice in the East River. "Oh, Mrs. D, I've just now been reminded. As we were making our way over to you this afternoon, something happened to us, just before we crossed the Bridge. You simply will not believe it!"

"Well now, I am intrigued. And I want to hear all about it, I truly do. But first, what say we have ourselves some dessert," she said, suddenly producing from the pantry, almost as if by magic, a beautifully frosted layer cake. "Oh, yes, and we definitely need some more of that wonderful brandy, too!"

The elegant lady was in rare form, indeed, thought Will.

Thoroughly delighted, Will looked at her in fond bemusement. "Well, well, Mrs. D, I do believe that in all the time I've known you, and that's more than a little while by now, this is the first time I've ever seen you quite so ... well ... rowdy, for lack of a better word."

"Oh, stuff and nonsense, young Will – there's plenty of life left in this old gal yet!" She raised her glass of brandy high into the air. "And, as a matter of fact, I'd like to make a little toast, myself.

"To love and happiness! And to the lucky young couple who found them both in the depths of the freezing blizzard. Now come on, Will, let's hear all about the unbelievable thing that happened to the two of you just before you crossed the Bridge."

CHAPTER 60

10:00 PM

During the day, the cyclone had drifted slowly westward across Block Island and weakened almost as rapidly as it had intensified over the previous two days. The central pressure was now nine-ninety-five millibars, up seventeen from just twenty-four hours ago. Surface pressure gradients, however, had remained strong all day west of the storm center, with a steady wind speed of forty-two miles-per-hour measured in New York City seven hours earlier. Snowfall diminished during the day across New England, although isolated pockets of heavy snow remained, with new accumulations of ten inches or more across parts of New York and western New England. Snow showers were widespread across the middle Atlantic states and the eastern Ohio Valley, although the sun's appearance earlier in the day across parts of New England was further evidence of the cyclone's decay.

The distinct thermal boundary, which had evidently played an important role in generating and maintaining heavy precipitation, remained pronounced, but began to erode under the persistent, relatively mild easterly flow to the northeast of the storm center. The temperature in Montreal rose to thirty degrees, an increase of nearly twenty since morning, and was considerably higher than cities to the south where readings were mainly in the teens. Because the rising temperatures occurred where no obvious wind-shift or propagating pressure trough was observed, it was difficult to analyze a warm front moving cyclonically around the northwest quadrant of the storm circulation. Rather, the mixing of warmer air aloft with shallow, cold surface air appeared to be responsible for raising temperatures across northern and central New England.

After working virtually non-stop for the past five hours, the pilots and crew of the Charles H. Marshall had finally succeeded in clearing the ice from her sails and spars. It was a great relief for all to know that they could finally begin making the long journey back home, after having drifted more than a hundred miles to the southeast over the past two days. The snow had ended, for the moment anyway, and the wind, while still strong, wasn't at all as savage as it had been at the height of the storm.

Though still afloat, the small vessel could no longer be described as even remotely seaworthy. Assuming they did make it back to port, it was highly questionable whether an attempted repair would prove worth-while. In reverent silence, they passed the scattered remains of several shattered boats, one of which, the *Enchantress,* had been a main competitor of theirs. The pilots and crew knew, in that moment, that they would forever hold themselves indebted to the men who had built their rugged and thus-far indestructible little craft. That indebtedness extended as well to the capable leader who had steered them so deftly through the worst storm any of them would ever experience.

Charley prayed that Blanche had not lost all hope, and that her suffering would be as mild and brief as possible. He now knew, in his heart of hearts, that he and the rest of his ship-mates would indeed be making it home safely, God bless them every one. They hadn't discussed it amongst themselves, and probably never would, but Charley felt that after the ordeal they'd all just endured, most of his fellow pilots would choose to either retire or seek some other – safer – profession. Of one thing he was absolutely certain: he would spend the rest of *his* days safely on land, close by the side of his loving wife, as often as possible. Not only did he believe that was the least he could do for her, he also felt honor-bound to fulfill on his end of the bargain he'd struck with the Almighty during his bleakest, darkest hour.

Will, May, and Mrs. D, having the time of their lives, carried right on celebrating in high style well into the evening. It was the best way they knew to cap off a momentous day, one which would surely be among the most memorable in all their shared history.

Ordinarily, none of them was prone to drinking alcohol to anything even approaching excess. In fact, spirits were generally not part of their normal routine, at all. But this night, obviously, was the furthest thing from normal. With the powerful, emotionally charged experiences of the past two days finally catching up to the three of them, they found themselves raising glass after glass, in gratitude for their great good fortune in having made it through the storm, relatively unscathed.

It was no surprise, then, that by this point the "tired traveling triumvirate" might well have been described as being "three sheets in the wind." And when it comes right down to it, they all agreed, in a relatively sober moment, why on earth shouldn't they be? Dealing with the storm was, in and of itself, extraordinarily stressful. And that was without even factoring in the enormous toll taken on their physical well-being, facing down the threat to life and limb that the blizzard imposed, especially on May. Add to that the deep concern they all continued to share over Kira's safety, the intense experience of bringing Blanche the joyous "news" about her Charley, and, wonder of wonders – the *pièce de résistance* – the newly beloved "Couple of the Blizzard," Will and May! Surely, enough excitement to last a decade

– and every bit of it happening in just the last forty-eight hours. If all that, in the main, did not justify a celebration of celebrations, well, then nothing ever would, or could.

Not surprisingly, the stories being shared grew more and more interesting and revealing as the evening wore on. And on, and on, and on . . . Clearly, none of them wanted it to end. After May had talked extensively about her parents and upbringing, going into even greater detail than she had earlier with Will, Mrs. D chimed in with some fascinating tales about her own childhood, growing up right here in Brooklyn. She shared that she had been something of a "wild child" in her younger days – rebellious, and often landing herself in trouble at school. She even confessed that at one point her parents, who had reached the end of their rope, were seriously considering sending her away to boarding-school at the tender age of fourteen if she didn't buckle down and shape up. Of course, she promptly did.

"Mrs. D!," Will exclaimed, mouth agape, eyebrows raised high, and hand pressed to his chest. Though partly genuinely surprised, he was mostly laying it on thick, for obvious effect. "I must say, I am shocked! Never in a million years would I have expected I'd hear about that kind of behaviour associated with someone as refined as *you*."

He might as well have saved his reproving breath. Obviously refusing to be cowed by Will's facetious censure, Mrs. D snorted comically, then reached further into the recesses of her memory and came out with an even more outrageous story. Whether it was true or not mattered little at that point. May laughed so hard that tears flowed down her cheeks. She later confided to Mrs. D that not only did her stomach hurt, but she was beginning to fear that she might actually wet her under-garments, when all was said and done.

The three of them simply could not have enjoyed themselves more.

After settling May in comfortably for the night in the spare bedroom, Wilma and Will made a final circuit of the first floor before climbing the stairs for the last time that evening. At the top of the landing, she gave him a big hug and a quick peck on the cheek to send him off to bed. She then retired to her own room: happy, worn-out, and even feeling just a bit sad.

Happy, beyond measure, for Will – that he had been blessed to find his true love, and at such a young age. Happy for the delightful May, too, for the same exact reason. Seriously worn out from the rigors of the extraordinary day, not the least of which was the evening of unbridled revelry she'd just enjoyed with her dear house-mates. And just a bit sad in the knowledge that the remarkable young man God had seen fit to bring to her doorstep, and who she'd grown to love so much, looking on him as the son she'd always wanted, would soon be moving on. She knew that he and May would surely be getting married – and in mighty short order, at that.

Then, just as she was kneeling down to begin her nightly prayers, a thought struck her, and she brightened a bit. With any luck at all, she realized, the happy young couple would ultimately choose to settle in Brooklyn.

After all, if there's one thing of which I can be absolutely certain, it's this: I know how much my dear, young Will loves that magnificent Bridge!

EPILOGUE

EPILOGUE

Will Roebling and May Morrow were united in holy wedlock on November 18, 1888. Frank Gorman stood up as Best Man, and May's beloved younger sister, June, served as Maid of Honor. It was the happiest of days, and an altogether splendid affair.

After returning from an idyllic honeymoon, the happy couple eagerly accepted Mrs. D's generous suggestion that they live with her temporarily, essentially rent-free, so they could begin saving up for a house of their own. It was a wonderful arrangement, as May and Mrs. D had only become closer and more dear to each other in the months since their joyous meeting. On December 4, 1889, the household was thrilled to welcome its newest resident – all seven-pounds-twelve-ounces of her – Miss Elizabeth Grace Roebling.

Mrs. D, who had never quite fully recovered, physically, following her strenuous Blizzard ordeal, was especially delighted to have the opportunity to share so intimately in her "grandchild" and name-sake's first few years (Mrs. D had been christened Wilma Elizabeth). Little Lizzie soon became the light of her life. As the years rolled on and Mrs. D's health continued its slow decline, May became her loving caretaker, till the snowy night in January 1894, when she passed away peacefully in her sleep. She had rewritten her will years before, bequeathing the house to Will and May. By the time of her passing, the young couple had managed to accumulate quite a handsome nest-egg for their happy little family.

Less than three months after the Blizzard – June 1, 1888, to be precise – Will replaced Sergeant Long as Chief Officer of the New York City Signal Service Regional Office. Officially, Long had retired. But it was never made clear whether he'd been forced out due to his unfortunate and untimely decision to keep Will's forecasting system under wraps as the Great Blizzard was bearing down on the Northeast. It seemed to almost everyone who had an opinion on the matter that that was the most likely case.

By the spring of 1894, with their beloved Mrs. D gone on to her Eternal Rest and the adorable young Lizzie growing by leaps and bounds, Will and May decided it was high-time to think about expanding the family. With that came the desire to move to the country. Around about this time, Will found he was growing just a bit bored with the Signal Service. Even though they had treated him very well over the years, he knew the time had come for a change. Perhaps he was influenced by fond memories of his professors at Yale, urging him to pursue teaching and research. Or maybe after his stint in the Army, with all the rigor of its rules and regulations, he just longed to return to the less-restrictive world of Academia. Whatever the reason, Will applied for a choice position at Princeton University (alma mater of his childhood hero, Joseph Henry): Professor and Head of its recently created Meteorology Department.

Of course Will was hired on immediately, his outstanding reputation in the field preceding him. His forecasting system had made him quite the household name by then, at least within the inner-circles of the newly burgeoning meteorological world.

His years at the Signal Service, complemented by that extraordinary evening at the Grand Hotel, had served to help Will overcome his fear of public speaking. He became a mighty good professor – much-respected, well-liked, and highly regarded for his interesting and innovative classroom style. He was also given a generous research budget, along with a small cadre of capable graduate students who, in their own right, made notable advances to his forecasting system. Will's new home at Princeton University was a happy one which lasted many years.

Meanwhile, May was thrilled with her new environs. She especially loved the charm of Princeton itself and the beauty of the surrounding countryside. In February 1895, she gave birth to their second child, a boy, August Francis (after Frank Gorman). Two more girls, Anna May and Emma Louise (after her good friend from the boardinghouse), rounded out the Roebling family over the next six years.

The Charles H. Marshall came limping back into port two days after Blizzard Monday. Miraculously, everyone aboard was still alive, although each had suffered some type of permanent cold-related affliction. Charley Potts eventually had to have several fingers and toes amputated. True to the promise he'd struck with God, he gave up his career as a harbor pilot, and he and Blanche shared fifteen very happy, land-lubbing years together. May became a particular favorite of Charley's, largely because of the special kindness she'd gone out of her way to impart to Blanche during her darkest hour.

Frank Gorman stayed on with the New York Regional Office of the Signal Service for twenty more years. Alex had her first of three children – a boy – in December 1888. (Not surprisingly, there was a record number of babies born that month.) Frank and Will remained fast friends over the years. With Alex and May forming a warm friendship as well, and the children being so close in age, a unbreakable bond was forged between the two families. In addition to spending all of the major holidays together, their visits in between were frequent and fun.

After her hospitalization, Kira Smith moved back into her parents' home in New Jersey. Although spared the agony of any amputations, she never fully recovered normal use of her feet and hands. Her career as an actress and dancer, therefore, was over before it had even really started. She remained bitter about Will, and grew apart from Alex. She never married.

Patrolman Jonathan O'Malley and Nurse Nancy Petersen enjoyed their first *bona fide* date soon after conditions in Manhattan had returned to normal. The chemistry between them was sizzling, and they were married six months to the day of their meeting on Blizzard Monday. Nancy continued in her nursing career at Bellevue for two more years before leaving to raise a family with Jon.

Because she had treated so many policemen for work-related injuries over the years, Nancy was able to make a convincing case for Jon's pursuit of a less-dangerous career, especially with young children to provide for. With initial help from a close friend, a former constable himself, Jon started out as a clerk in a Wall Street brokerage firm, eventually working his way up to becoming quite a successful stock-broker.

Kevin Patrick McCormack finally made it to Philadelphia and closed his big sale. Not long after, he was promoted to management, eventually taking over as CEO of the plumbing supply company. He remained a loyal and "preferred" customer of the Grand for many years, during which he and James Landen often reminisced fondly about their remarkable experience with Will and May during the Great Blizzard.

Walt Jamison recovered from his bout with the flu and returned to work, but retired after only six more months on the job. True to plan, Albert Washington replaced him as Head of Maintenance and enjoyed a long and fruitful career at the Grand Hotel. The capable and charismatic young man was always held in the highest esteem not only by the Management, but also his co-workers and the overwhelming majority of guests with whom he came in contact.

James Landen continued to manage the Grand in fine style, well into the next decade. Will and May kept their promise to stay in touch, spending a delightful night there on many a special occasion. Sadly, the hotel and its workers lost their greatest champion – and Will and May one of their dearest friends – in August 1897. Shortly after arriving at work early one morning, Landen succumbed to a heart attack, quite unexpectedly. He was deeply missed by all who had known him, staff and guests alike.

Glynn Gardner remained at Headquarters for a long and distinguished career with the Signal Service. Even though eventually all was fully disclosed, he never did receive a reprimand for the unauthorized assistance he'd provided Will by sending him the observations needed to develop and perfect his forecasting system. A contrite Camille apologized profusely for not believing him about the Blizzard, and for causing their epic fight – one which they would laugh about for many a year to come.

Finally, New York City itself has always considered it a great blessing to have never again seen the likes of the Great White Hurricane of '88. To this day, it continues to pray that it never will.